Cicero James

Miracle Worker

Hal Emerson

COPYRIGHT

ALSO BY HAL EMERSON:

The Exile Trilogy:
-    The Prince of Ravens (1)
-    The Prince of Exiles (2)
-    The Prince of the Veil (3)

In The Land of Aeon:
-    The Ring of Eman Vath (1)
-    The Lost Kingdom (2)
-    The Broken Peace (3)

Oberon's Children
To Die a Thousand Deaths
Bones

Table of Contents

OK, Here's the Deal

My name is Cicero James, and I died last Thursday.

I know how it sounds, and the rest of what I have to tell you is just going to make it worse. But it's true. I died, and I came back. Actually, I've died nine times in the past week. And the rest of it—why it happened, what it means, and most importantly what we're going to have to do about it—is what I need you to hear.

The others nominated me to write this. 'Nominated' is generous—they sent me to my room like a delinquent teenager and told me not to come out until I'd gotten it all down. I get it, I'm the reason all of this is happening the way it is, and I'm the one who was there for the worst of it. Thing is, even *thinking* about telling you all of what I'm about to write could get me thrown in a hole so deep I'd never see the light of another day. All of us, actually.

But you have to know what we're up against.

What *you're* up against.

I'm able to use my real name because we've put a Working on this text. The people we're mobilizing against can't read it, and if you give it to someone who means us harm, they'll just see blank pages. If you can read this, then you're one of the ones we're trying to reach. Something we managed to learn from… well, we'll get there.

What you're about to read—the events, people, places— it's all real. Most of it, though, has been covered up to keep you ignorant of it. It's hard enough for the Blissful (that's you) to remember anything about Workers (that's us) in the best of times, and this isn't the best of times. Even if I gave you a picture of me, I doubt you'd be able to pick me out of a lineup. Even if you were staring me right in the eye.

Still, we're hoping some of this sticks.

Most of the time, I seem like a regular guy. You probably pass a dozen people like me every day. That's because most of the time I *am* a regular guy. We all are. Regular, I mean. Guys and gals. Outwardly, at least. I have an apartment in San Francisco; I go to the gym and buy groceries; I worried a lot about asking out the pretty barista at my local coffee shop and when I finally got up the nerve to do it she shot me down hard. Like, really hard actually—I occasionally have nightmares about it where I'm naked and she's pointing and laughing.

But we are *also* Miracle Workers.

No one uses the "Miracle" part anymore, though—we just call ourselves Workers. We're not born, we're made. And what we do we can do because we're all half-mad. The madness is different for every Worker, but it's always there, and it lets us see cracks in reality and play with them. Widen them, shrink them, blow them right open or close them off for good. It lets us force our beliefs on the world and make them real. For us, for you—for everyone.

One of the key rules we have is the Separation: we aren't supposed to interfere in your world, or bring you into the Worker world. At least not unless you specifically seek us out through the Guild (Worker organization, don't worry about it yet) and pay us for a Working. Some of you might even have done that at some point without realizing you were doing it. Some of you probably did it and then forgot about it because people never remember what they can't believe is real. If it happened when you were a kid, there's a better chance you remember. A glimmer of a memory that you know doesn't make sense but you're convinced is real.

What's been happening has been happening in our world, but it's spreading to yours. No, not spreading—it already *has spread* to yours. And you have the right to know about it. There aren't many of us fighting back yet, but that doesn't matter. It's a fight that needs to be fought.

And we're hoping you'll fight it with us.

If you find this and read it, pass it on. We need as many people as possible. Because that's what matters, in the end— that you believe it's real, that everyone believes it's real, and that you believe we can win.

I know you have no reason to trust anything I'm saying, at least not yet. I know it's beyond anything you might be prepared to accept. But I'm going to spend the next however long this ends up being trying to change your mind.

And maybe the next time you see me, you'll really see me. Maybe the next time you see a Worker doing what we do, you'll actually *see it*. Stranger things have happened.

I'm going to start at the beginning, and I'm going to tell all of this as faithfully as possible. I'm going to try to bring you along for the ride. It's all coming out in a rush, so if I don't tell it quite right, or if I muff a word or use bad grammar or something, try not to hold it against me.

And if I don't manage to convince you… I understand. No harm, no foul, no hard feelings. This shit is insane to anyone who hasn't lived it.

But if you're in, then you're in, and here we go.

Here we fucking go.

Part One

I DON'T WANNA DO CHAPTERS,

'CAUSE THAT SEEMS TOO FORMAL.

IMMA DO 'PARTS' AND SEE HOW THAT GOES.

BEAR WITH ME.

Things started going pear-shaped last Thursday. Which is ironic, because the day started out as a long, exciting-as-watching-paint-dry kind of boring-ass Thursday until things became way more off-the-wall bonkers-interesting than I ever could have wanted.

Let's start at work.

Like I said, I have a real job. Because, you know, rent is a thing. And food. And streaming subscriptions—The Great British Bake-off isn't going to watch itself.

I was at a faux-wood desk in a mini conference room in a tech office in San Francisco trying to wrap up a presentation deck for the next morning. I got to the last slide, stopped typing, and sat back. I pressed the bridge of my nose between my fingers and rested an elbow on the desk. I yawned and shook my head, blinked several times, and then looked out the room's single small window over to my right. The sky was full of clouds that had turned pink and orange and were slowly fading to a deep blue that I think was indigo.

I remember my heart skipping a beat.

I looked at my watch. 6:30 pm.

I breathed in, and then slowly but steadily out. I was calm but shaky. Controlled energy crackled in my fingertips.

Time to go to Work.

I remember standing quickly and pushing back the uncomfortable plastic office chair—it scraped unpleasantly against the imitation wood floor—and then I swept my computer, notebook, and earbuds into the cheap company-branded backpack ('Protoline') I use for work. I turned and pushed through the room's heavy door.

A handful of people were still working in the common area—or at least diligently staring at their computer screens and making gestures that could be construed as work-related. Two Protoline software engineers were at a whiteboard muttering about something. Several others were keeping a surreptitious eye on a middle-aged man seated in an office version of a leather recliner. Like a Barcalounger type of thing. Are Barcaloungers still relevant enough for everyone to know what they are? They're a brand of uber-comfortable leather chair that leans back. And that's what he was doing—leaning back, precariously, and scrolling through his phone with long, lazy sweeps of a finger that resembled an over-stuffed bratwurst. His small eyes were glassy, and his lopsided mouth, with a small fleck of white saliva at the corner, was slightly open.

I made my way over to him.

"Heading out, Arick," I said.

Yeah, Eric with an A and a K. I… well, judge for yourself.

Arick grunted and sat up, lowering his phone and swiveling around.

"Thanks, James," he said, using just my last name. Something he does with those he considers his 'top performers'. "Finish the Flash?"

I nodded and proceeded to overwhelm him with jargon to prevent any follow-up questions. "Yep. Shared it with you a few minutes ago. Top-line trend is holding steady, so there shouldn't be too many questions. We won't know about the bottom line until end of next week, but the ratio should hold from last quarter, and it's within range of the forecast regression we ran. It's all part of the deck for tomorrow morning."

Also, I'd Worked the math to speed things up. Can't Work directly on tech, not unless you're way smarter than me and know precisely what all the little chips do, but you can Work a pencil on paper to solve just about anything if you believe in it the right way.

"You're the man, James," Arick said, turning his attention back to his phone. I caught a glimpse of the screen—some social media feed. I couldn't tell which app. They all look pretty similar these days. "See you tomorrow for the preso."

"You bet. 'Night, Arick."

Arick raised a hand in my direction without looking at me again, his attention already focused back on his phone. I'd worked this job for nearly three years, and Arick was the third manager assigned to the analytics team since I'd been there. He'd lasted the longest because he knew the least and just trusted everyone to get on with their work.

All things considered, not a bad version of a boss to have.

My non-Worker friend Roc Holliday—born Vishal Patel, an agonizingly prosaic (his words) identity he quickly jettisoned when he 'reinvented' himself after college in the model of his hero, Doc Holliday, from the movie 'Tombstone'—looked up from where he was sitting in a video conference booth. I was surprised he was still in the office. Usually Roc is out by 5 sharp, with a drink in his hand by 5:05. That day, though, he had his feet up on the table of the booth he'd commandeered and appeared to be pontificating to someone on the other end of a video call. I couldn't hear what he was saying through the thick glass wall that divided us, but he seemed to be relishing the chance to wax poetic about something or other.

He's a consultant—he partied his way through an MBA degree but still managed to pass all of the required classes to graduate. At those parties, he made friends with just about everyone who's anyone in Silicon Valley. And now he makes his way from company to company getting paid twice what I do to tell everyone what they're doing wrong.

To be fair, he's usually right.

We met a few of companies back, and he adopted me in that way that very extroverted people do when they find introverts who can be talked into things. Honestly, it didn't used to take much to talk me into things. Aside from Working, I didn't really have much going on in my life until last week hit me like a trucker trying to get through a climate change protest. And I'm a lot less introverted than the public Cicero James persona I put on.

I am, generally speaking, not that fond of people, though. And I think people assume that means I'm introverted, when actually it just means I don't like dealing with shit that's not my shit. Problems that aren't mine are boring, and I'd rather be Working anyway.

Roc caught my eye and flicked a hand at me—telling me to come over. He then focused back on the laptop in front of him.

I wanted to leave. I was dying to Work.

I detoured over to Roc.

He kicked open the door of the little phone booth conference room. It was one of the two-siders, like a train compartment, with couch-like seats on either side of a thin table set down the middle. Roc had his laptop strategically angled toward him, and a single earbud in his right ear. He's got a slight Indian accent that is very charming, and he's always dressed well and wearing some kind of cologne.

"Yeah, you could do that," he said into the earbud. "It'd be a disaster, but you could do it."

He caught my eye and made a talking motion with his hand out of sight of the camera to indicate to me that whoever was on the other side of the video call was bloviating at him.

"Look, it's your company," he said, leaning forward and clearly interrupting the talker. "I'll work with whatever constraints you want to give me. But I've done this a dozen times, and every time I've seen it done the way you're suggesting, the whole thing falls apart. I'll get paid either way, so I'm happy to build you a bridge to nowhere. But I promise you, you're going have to spend twice as much to get me or someone else to come back in, undo it all, and then redo it the way I've been suggesting for the past three weeks."

I moved into the booth and sat in the silence that followed Roc's statement as he listened to whatever the response was through his earbud. His serious business expression was funny to me, given how many times I'd seen him red-faced and sweaty singing along to Taylor Swift after a few espresso martinis.

"Sure thing, Esther, we can meet again early next week and talk more. Sagar, please make sure to send out the meeting notes once we wrap up here and get that scheduled at a time that works for everybody."

He nodded, gave a polite business wave, and then shut the laptop, plucked out his earbud, and pushed everything over to one side.

"These people are fucking masochists," he said. "I swear, they could go hire a BDSM mistress and get the same effect. They pay me—"

"An outrageous hourly rate," I said.

"Oh, absolutely," Roc said, "and then they don't listen to me. This is San Francisco, you could get someone wearing a dog collar and a leather dress, cracking a whip, to do that for you for a quarter my rate. Just hire them to stand around the office and treat you like a bad boy every time you say something, and then you go ahead and do the stupid thing anyway. Same effect but much more exciting." He flicked his hand dismissively. "People are so dumb, CJ."

I couldn't help but smile in commiseration, but my thoughts were elsewhere. I stopped my leg from bouncing under the table.

"Who cares, though, it's three-beer-Thursday!" Roc said, smiling at me, his eyes lighting up. He's one of the few people I know over thirty who still goes out drinking multiple times a week and doesn't seem to suffer any serious consequences from it. A miracle I've never been able to manage, Working be damned.

"Can't tonight," I said. I couldn't give him the real reason, so I gave my stock excuse. "Presentation tomorrow morning."

Because Friday morning is when I always schedule the presentation so that I have an excuse not to go out when I have a chance to Work.

"Cicero James up to mystery again?" he asked, eyeing me.

"No mystery," I said. "An overfull streaming queue. Have you seen The Bear yet? So good."

I shifted my glasses on my face and blinked a few times as if I were just a typical work-weary analyst ready to go home and veg out for a few hours before bed.

"You became lame a few months ago, and I'm not gonna stand for it much longer," he said, admonishing me with a strong index finger. "You're coming out this weekend. I've got plans on plans on plans."

"Great," I muttered, shaking my head and sitting back. "Last time you said that we ended up in Mexico. Which was, incidentally, about the time I ended up getting lame."

It had been a convenient excuse. Stuff had gone down in my Working life and I'd had to start taking on more solo shifts.

"Mexico is too close to San Diego for people not to end up there accidentally," Roc said, waving a hand to waft away my complaint and the memory of a desperate three-day search for his missing passport. "Saturday night. You're coming out with me."

I pretended to waffle, but internally I was intending to cave if the job went well that night. Going out with Roc was the perfect chance to let off some steam. Not to mention refill my Instruments. It's a Worker thing—I'll explain when it's important.

"What is it?" I asked.

"No chance I'm telling you before you agree," Roc said. "I tell you, you'll think of a reason not to go. You're coming. Say it."

I pretended to waffle some more but knew there was no way I was getting out of there unless I agreed with him. And I needed out—my whole body felt like a too-tightly-wound spring.

"Fine," I said. "Text me the details and I'll come."

"Yes!" Roc crowed in victory, his eyes lighting up. He reached a hand across the table and I clasped it. "Cicero James, my *man*!"

He let me go after that, and I beelined it straight for the elevator before anyone else could catch my eye or try to talk to me. I walked past a row of large potted plants, then an espresso bar, the counters of which gleamed with stainless steel appliances ready for use the next morning.

I wanted very badly to be gone—to be *out*, in my real life—but I didn't let it show. It was just another ordinary end to another ordinary Thursday. I was playing the part.

Working is strictly regulated out in the real world. I can Work as much as I want when I'm on my own at home, or in a Worker city, but I can't Work in front of or on what we call the Blissful—all you lovely people *blissfully* ignorant of what goes on behind the scenes. And for the really big stuff, the really fun stuff, you need a Guild-approved contract. The Separation is taken very seriously. And if someone were to get too interested in what I was doing, follow me, and then see me doing it… I'd be in trouble, and they'd end up with several weeks of memories removed.

Still, I was jonesing. Working is… like nothing else. Imagine the perfect caffeine high. The best scotch you've ever tasted. The love of your life loving you back. Taking the hot girl home from the bar. The Jason Momoa look-alike asking for *your* number. Winning the lottery. A breakfast burrito with tater tots when you're hungover as shit.

Working is so much better than all of that. It's injecting the universe straight into your bloodstream and lighting it on fire so sparks come out your eyeballs.

I pressed the elevator call button several more times than necessary and turned back to the office. My luckless coworkers had looked up hopefully, but Arick had settled back in his seat and was once more swiping away. They didn't want to leave until he did, despite the hour.

One of them, a young woman named Erica, caught my eye and rolled hers. I shrugged sympathetically back at her. She (like most of the others still there) was a new hire as of a few months earlier, and she was still trying to show that she was a model employee by staying until the boss left. She's tall, athletic-curvy, and has platinum-blonde hair and wide blue eyes. Mom is from Scandinavia and Dad is from England, they brought her over when she was young. She shared that in the HR-mandated 'get to know me' email new hires send out.

She's also the unspoken crush of most males—and a handful of females—in the building. And she's that kind of bantering friendly that leaves you slightly confused as to whether she's flirting with you or just being nice. And we work together, so there's zero chance I will ever attempt to find out which it is.

Where are you going? she mouthed at me.

I mimed riding a motorcycle, stuck out my tongue, and threw up a "rock on" sign.

She arched an eyebrow. I shook my head and mimed reading a book and falling asleep. She smiled, wrinkled her nose, and nodded in a "yeah, that's more what I expected" kind of way. I grinned, she grinned, we all grinned, and then she looked back down at her work.

I glanced back at the elevator indicator light—4th floor. Close. I licked my lips and shifted my weight from one foot to the other.

It wasn't like I could tell her the truth, but I was certain she'd be much more interested in me if I could.

Energy crackled in my fingertips again, and I crossed my arms and rubbed my hands over my shoulders to dissipate it, pretending I was cold, something entirely plausible given the state of modern office air conditioning practices. My ring, my band, and my watch all shifted as I moved my arms, and I felt the black tattoos around my forearms, across my back and upper arms, and circling my thighs—all discreetly covered by my conservative office attire—tense like living things until I mentally soothed them.

I *needed* to let off some steam.

Like I said, Working is carefully regulated. It used to be that we could do whatever we wanted to as long as we got away with it without being caught. Not these days, with cell phone cameras and CCTVs and drones and everything else. A more rational part of me understands that's a good thing. No Genghis Khans running around miracling themselves into world-conquering tyrants. No Mozarts leapfrogging all their competitors to write beautiful symphonies and burn out before hitting thirty. Well, actually his dad Worked on him, which is kind of even more fucked up.

The Workers Guild monitors all of that now and gives freelance Workers like me who live in the real world opportunities to really stretch our wings and fly when something bad goes down. Some of us perform official miracles for the sick and wounded; some of us work to bring back extinct species in plausible ways that'll go unnoticed by the wider world; some of us work with the police on supernatural cases; some of us are embedded in infrastructure companies to keep basic things like bridges and railroads working even when they fall into complete disrepair.

Me? I fix cracks in reality.

I don't like to brag, but all that other stuff? Nothing compared to what I do. You wanna see what you're really made of? Go fight a Terror. Go send one of the Wrathful spinning through a gateway to the Eternal. Go kick someone's mad, drug-fueled, fever-dream nightmare back into the Space Between Spaces while it tries to kill you and everyone around you.

At least… that's how I used to think about it. Now I wish I could go back and punch that part of me right in the dick.

The elevator dinged; the doors opened.

As soon as I was safely inside, I rolled up the right sleeve of my button-up shirt, revealing black letters etched into my skin. I've got nine tattoos, each with a built-in Working that I can use whenever I want. I touched the tattoo that circles my upper arm, which reads:

If I had my mouth, I would bite; if I had my liberty, I would do my liking: in the meantime let me be that I am and seek not to alter me.

I breathed out slowly and set my mind to the words. I invested them with life—I believed them to be true. I felt the changes start to happen, but I held them temporarily at bay. I rolled my sleeve back down.

The doors opened; I crossed the nearly empty lobby; I walked out onto the street.

I loosened my mental grip. With every step, I felt my psyche shifting. I was leaving behind my polite, inoffensive office persona and becoming Cicero James, Miracle Worker.

By the time I reached the end of the block, I stood with my shoulders back and my chin high. The night was chill, and darkness was falling; the sounds of city traffic filled my ears, and the wind of passing cars played with my hair.

Another several steps and my eyesight had gone blurry. As I stood on the corner, I removed the glasses I wore for the office and twisted them in my hand; they disappeared, sent back to my apartment. I glanced around—no one was looking at me. I had faded into the safe anonymity of a crowded street.

I sent back my work backpack and security badge next; they faded away as I crossed the street. By the time I reached the next corner, my drab gray peacoat had become a thick leather bomber jacket. My tan chinos had become dark jeans, and my muted Oxfords had morphed into heavy work boots.

It was cold, so I pulled my collar up and hunched my shoulders. The clouds overhead were thick and scattered with twilight colors; it had been raining on and off for the past few weeks. I made a mental note to keep my eye on them for signs of a storm.

The city of San Francisco was starting to wind down for the evening. It was a Thursday night before a regular two-day weekend, and although a few bars and clubs were open hoping to attract those of the Thirsty Thursday persuasion like Roc, most were fairly empty there in the Financial District, aside from a few spots that had die-hard regulars.

I live not too far from there, but I wasn't heading home. My destination that night was the edge of Hayes Valley, a neighborhood in the middle of the city. Or, more specifically, Alamo Square.

I reached into my pocket and pulled out an off-white sheet of paper that had been folded several times. I unfolded it and glanced down at it for the seventh or eighth time that day, digging the mental groove the words made in my mind deeper so that I could hold onto them tightly.

Terror manifestation. 63379 Steiner
Street, Hayes Valley.
Scouted **September 7th**.
Response rating **URGENT**; address no later
than midnight of **September 9th**.
10c bounty. Solo engagements accepted.

That Thursday was September 8th. The notification, which I had copied down by hand, had come across the Worker Wire that morning, no doubt just hours after the Terror had officially been witnessed on the night of the 7th. I'd seen the notification just as I was leaving my apartment and claimed the engagement. I'd been lucky—I'd missed the last half dozen solo bounties, and I don't like Working with a crew.

Other Workers aren't always… trustworthy. Comes with the territory of everyone being partially insane. And I'd taken to Working solo.

I thought about the route. Hayes Valley. Steiner Street. Close to Alamo Park and the famous Painted Ladies. I could take BART most of the way down Market and then the 22 bus up. Would take twenty minutes, maybe thirty with traffic.

Which was perfect. An easy space-time swap to make.

I ducked down an alleyway around the corner from a Blue Bottle coffee shop on Sansome. It was wide for an alleyway, but it was deserted, aside from the sounds of a half dozen tech people drinking at the bar around the corner and walking past the mouth of the alley without looking in. Too busy with work or life to notice me.

I hurried to a blank stretch of wall over a rather unsavory puddle of something at which I chose not to look too closely. I reached down and pulled up the sleeve of my leather jacket to expose my Timex watch. Except it wasn't a Timex anymore, but an unbranded black-and-silver creation of my own. The first of my three Worker Instruments.

The black leather band was worn but still holding strong; the watch dial itself was black with silver numerals. There were also three small silver sub-dials, all of which corresponded to pushers on the watch's sides. I clicked the first of those pushers, and the small hand in the corresponding sub-dial began to tick.

I stared at it, hard.

One.

The world around me slowed perceptibly: sounds suddenly took longer to reach me, and everything was distant and echo-y. More than once I've wondered if the watch makes me move faster, rather than the world move slower. I'm sure it probably does—what's more likely, that a charmed watch slows the whole world or somehow speeds up the person it's attached to?—but either way the effect is the same.

Two.

A darkness fell over the entrance to the alleyway. It didn't fade all the way to black but instead stayed a dark and ominous gray. Thundercloud gray. People could still walk in, and I could still, in theory, walk out, but the alleyway was coming unmoored from reality, and so the boundary between it and the rest of the world was starting to blur.

Three.

A tight coiling sensation violently twisted in my gut, as if a giant had punched through my back and spine, buried a hand in my guts, and begun to wrap my intestines around his fist. It's not a sensation to which you quickly become accustomed. At least not without a *lot* of vomiting.

Four.

My vision splintered. I held up the strip of paper that I had printed off at home. I stared at the address, burning it into my mind's eye. An image of Alamo Park swam before me, grayed out but still recognizable. Time slowed further, just as the little hand in the sub-dial face began to shift toward the Roman numeral "I".

Pressure built around me as if I were falling to the bottom of a very deep pool. An otherworldly weight bore down on me, forcing me out of the alleyway. I needed a place for it to send me.

"Come on," I growled.

The image in my head swung around, like a camera on the end of a long pole. Everything blurred and then came back into focus.

I was staring at a row of houses.

There.

Between two of the houses was another alleyway, similar to the one I was in. It wasn't a perfect match, but it would work.

Five.

A flash of light flared out of my watch, and, with a wrenching sensation, I was pulled out of the first alleyway and thrown into the second, halfway across the city. I just managed to get my feet beneath me to stop myself from sprawling out across the uneven ground. The world exploded in a spray of a thousand colors, like a cosmic kaleidoscope, blinding me. Everything pulsed larger and smaller and then became distorted, like I was seeing it through melting glass.

The swirling stopped, the world solidified, and I was in Hayes Valley.

I grabbed hold of a metal ring embedded in one of the walls to keep myself upright and then shook my head to clear it. It had been a while since I'd last 'ported. A wave of fatigue washed over me and then receded—not too bad because I had used the watch. I looked down at it. The main dial hands now read 7:03. I had traded the half hour it would have taken me to get there on the bus for the space to cross instantly.

I don't have time to give you all the rules—and I don't 100% know why they all are what they are—but trading time for space is an easy way to travel between two places if you know what you're doing. You don't *have* to trade time for space, but unless you really need to keep both static, it's the most straightforward way to go about it. I traded space for the luster of a diamond ring once and it damn near killed me. Turned the diamond back to coal, too. It worked, even though Marlowe (you'll meet him later) said it wouldn't, so hah fucking hah, but I wouldn't do it again if I could avoid it.

Time for space. Best way to travel.

I walked to the mouth of the alleyway and looked around. The sun had officially set, and twilight reigned. That was good. Working happens best at times of transition. Things are already changing, so why not slip in a few more while you're at it?

I started walking. I slipped a hand into my jacket pocket and felt for the metal lighter I keep there. With my other hand, I felt for my wallet. I pulled both out, then flipped open the wallet. There were several dollar bills in the billfold.

I glanced at my watch again and hit a second pusher, this one connected to the second of the three sub-dials I had installed. I paused. I sighed and looked back into my wallet, grumbling. I saw a few nickels, two dimes, and two quarters.

I did some quick mental math that was probably wrong but close enough and pulled out the dime and one of the quarters, then pocketed the wallet again. I hesitated, pulled the wallet back out, along with my cell phone, and performed the same twisting motion I had earlier; both the wallet and the cell phone disappeared, sent back to my apartment the same way I'd sent my glasses, work clothing, and backpack.

No need to leave identification lying around in case something happened.

I flicked the metal lighter open, which brought the memory of what I was looking for more clearly to mind. I sparked the light, generating a flare of chaos that would save me having to pull more energy from my body. I palmed the change and pressed the second dial on my watch.

With a flourish, I spun the change and it winked away and was replaced with a single white cylinder with a brown filter at the end. Somewhere a pack was now missing a single cigarette but did have a dime and a quarter in its place to cover the cost.

Space-time law of belief equivalency. Things that people believe to be equivalent can be swapped in space and time as long as you provide enough energy to cover the distance between them. Which isn't much when it's something small.

I lit the cigarette and pulled the smoke into my lungs. As I breathed out, the rush of the nicotine hit me and the world narrowed in and became more focused. I pulled again, and then breathed out. The metal ring I wore on the middle finger of my left hand warmed slightly, protecting my lungs. The second of my three Instruments, after the watch.

I know, people feel all kinds of ways about smoking these days. Thing is, you need a bit of chaos when you're Working. A touch of something dangerous, something anarchic.

And the reaction a lot of you are probably having to me smoking? That's exactly why it works.

I pulled the left sleeve of my jacket back and looked at the leather band (my final Instrument) around my wrist. It's etched with Celtic knots and Nordic runes—they aren't necessary, but I like the way they look. Makes me feel mystical. Which is important in Working.

The band was full of energy, which was good. I had been saving into it since my last job, and it was almost full. I'd be able to modify my body with it, changing my weight, appearance, etc..

I looked back at the creased paper with the job details on it.

Terror manifestation.

I stared at the words for a minute, really taking them in. Terrors are something of a specialty of mine, but I hadn't Worked a job concerning one in a while. The last couple of jobs I'd managed to snag had been taking on Wrathful or dispelling the Insatiable, which are more inconvenient than dangerous unless they really get out of hand.

A Terror is a being pulled from the Space Between Spaces in the form of a person's ultimate fear. Workers can manifest Terrors, of course, but the penalty for doing so is very steep—years in Worker jail and a lifetime ban from the Guild. I couldn't remember the last time it had happened. The Workers of the West—the Worker governing body that covers SF in partnership with the Worker's Guild, which is kind of like a big Worker union—cracked down on it hard a few decades back.

But you Blissful can pull in Terrors too. You can pull in a lot of things, depending on what you believe and how intensely you believe it.

I took one last drag on the cigarette, pulling it not only into my lungs but the chaos of it into my Instruments—my watch, my band, and my ring—in order to top them all off. I had used power from the watch as well as my body to 'port, so that was where the bulk of it went. I remember when even a little traveling like that would have nearly wiped me out. Back when Marlowe had just found me, an orphan working outside the Guild and violating the Separation as well as WOTW laws without even knowing I was doing it.

I need to remember to buy him a nice hat for his birthday.

Marlowe loves hats. He never wears them, but he's got a bunch.

I realized I was stalling. It's a bad habit of mine. It usually means I know something is wrong and I'm trying to distract myself into ignoring it. And, looking back, that's exactly what was happening. I knew something was off. I knew looking at the street near the house, even though there was no sign of the Terror or anything else to cause me alarm, that something was different. It looked like just an ordinary street in an ordinary, albeit dirty and recently rundown, section of the city. But *wrong*.

I don't know how I knew, but I did. And if I'd listened to that feeling, it might be someone else writing this to you now.

Maybe even *her*.

I dropped the cigarette and ground it out beneath the toe of my boot. I used the last bit of flame to energize myself, amplifying the effect of the nicotine.

And then I started toward the house.

Part Two

A Terror and a Painted Lady

I walked forward slowly but deliberately, trying to look in twelve directions at once for any signs of danger. Night was falling, and the gray-green electric streetlights lining the road and park were coming to life with flares of yellow-white light. The few people still hanging out in the park looked to be staying there for the night, retreating into deeper shadows where they were unlikely to be disturbed.

I stayed along the perimeter.

Parks aren't always safe at night in San Francisco.

The slanted street was high enough to show a view of the Bay in the distance. The slowly awakening streetlights were working together with the darkness of night to turn the city into something reminiscent of the glory of days gone by, making it possible to partially forget its current state of decay. The lights pulsed at irregular intervals; desperate-sounding music floated through the air from a few nearby bars with open doors. Powerlines above the street hummed with electricity, and I could hear as well as feel the wind of cars and buses as they drove past. People shouting about something with a desperate tone in their voices; someone panhandling on the corner as people ignored him and walked by, laughing with each other; a busker singing, but atonally, and strumming a cracked guitar with only five strings.

Altogether, it was an arhythmic city beat that fell into the cracks of my mind. An imperfect mashup of too many songs. Like an aging man trying to pretend he was still young despite his once-strong limbs loosening dangerously at the joints. The divisions of the city happened without warning—each block was different, whole neighborhoods changing from affluent to destitute one street to the next. Not like it was when I was young. It had still been patches then, but sewn together into a gorgeous quilt that made it all feel like a coherent, beautiful mess with a strong sense of self at the core. Back then it had all seemed to shine and shimmer. These days, the threads have frayed or snapped entirely and it's all drifting apart. It's all lackluster and fading.

It feels like we're all just patches these days.

Which makes it possible for dark things to crawl into the cracks of the world and hide. Hungry and toothy and watchful. Deadly and smooth. Like midnight leather wrapped around a knife handle. Semi-structured chaos. Life and death and a constant shuffle between the two.

I focused on the house.

It was a 'painted lady'—an old Victorian house of a particular style seen all over San Francisco and made culturally famous by the intro to the family sitcom Full House. This particular Lady was a pale violet currently darkened by shadows. She stood tall and narrow, about three stories high, with a below-street basement level. Her paint looked worn but it wasn't peeling, and a wide set of neatly swept and maintained wooden steps led up to her prominent front door. There were plants and some small trees along her perimeter, all recently watered and trimmed, and there was a car in the driveway. A modest Subaru.

She was not one of the famous Seven Sisters of Postcard Row, kept perfectly fresh and pert in imitation of their youth. She was further along the row, off to one side—and she wore her age proudly and well, the small cracks on her painted eaves like smile lines, and the slight sag of her once-proud stoop like sun-kissed skin. The worn places on her steps bore evidence of company coming and going over the years.

All told, to the casual eye she looked like any other house on the street, albeit a decently famous street and one of the better maintained ones in San Francisco.

But if you knew what to look for, you could see the signs.

The windows were closed, and all the shutters and blinds were drawn. The house itself looked somehow darker than those on either side of it, and my gaze slid too easily from the house on the left to the house on the right. She appeared sunken, too, as if she were at risk of somehow becoming detached from the rest of the street and falling back into the space behind her. She seemed drawn in on herself, hunched over, with the kind of spine-curving droop caused by the weight of sickness or fatigue.

When I was three houses away, the nearest streetlight sputtered and went out.

I slowed, watching both the Lady and the streetlight.

Had that been a coincidence? It was possible, but unlikely. If the Terror had picked up on my presence and was already strong enough to affect the world outside the house, it was no wonder the job had been marked as "urgent".

My pulse spiked. That made the Work even more important. There was a chance I'd have to actually roll up my sleeves for this one.

I looked around for signs of other Workers but saw none. There were a few people walking down the other side of the street, but I could tell immediately that they were Blissful—they were too calm, too happy in the presence of the house. A Worker would have felt the chill.

No, it was just me tonight.

I took another step toward the house, and four more streetlights sputtered like candle flames in high wind. They flickered with increasing violence and then, one by one, popped and went out, their filaments blown by a power surge. I clenched my jaw and breathed deeply through my nose, cold night air filling my lungs. I moved down the sidewalk, sticking to the shadows and running a hand along a low brick wall. I let the brick dust chalk up my fingertips; I stored up the feel of the decay as more heat inside me.

There was no moon in the sky, just clouds that were drawing closer and threatening an evening of mist and fog, maybe even rain. There wasn't enough breaking there yet to be of use, but I put it in the back of my mind.

Lightning is always a useful bit of chaos.

I climbed the stairs, counting as I went. All the same height. Neat and orderly. But at the top… at the top, a broken chunk of stone. Chipped paint. A smell in the air—methane, maybe. And the stench of fear sweat.

Yeah. It was definitely the right house.

I pushed up the sleeves of my leather bomber jacket, revealing thick black letters in flowing script around my forearms. I relaxed my hold on them and the tattoos flowed down onto the palms of my hands.

The right palm now read, in swirling, flickering letters

O, for a muse of fire!

The left palm, in bolder lines, read,

BLOW, WINDS, AND CRACK YOUR
CHEEKS!

Every Worker uses a channel or a conduit for big Workings. We have our Instruments—the watch, the ring, the band, or variations on those three—for storage and basic Working, and we don't even need those if we just want to Work in broad strokes. But if you want to perform real miracles—the best of the good stuff—you need something to channel your beliefs into the world. There are Academy-approved channels that are considered traditional: spectacles, gemstones, wands. I wasn't trained at the Academy. At least not primarily. So "Academy-approved" has never really been my speed. And the actual conduit doesn't matter—all that matters is that the Worker using it believes in the conduit's effectiveness.

For me, the coolest thing I ever saw growing up was a guy on a motorcycle whose entire body was covered in quote tattoos. As in text all over his body—cursive, bold, italics, caps, lower case, whole paragraphs of it on every inch of exposed skin. One bit in particular I've always remembered: a quote from Breaking Bad right across his forehead that said "I am the one who knocks". I still think he's the baddest man I've ever seen. He was also jacked, and riding behind him on the motorcycle was a gorgeous woman in leather that had curves my fourteen-year-old brain had no idea how to handle. I got my first tattoo the next day. I was under Marlowe's supervision at that point, and he freaked out when I showed him, but he and I both knew I couldn't undo it. At the parlor, they had a bunch of quotes I could choose from, and there was a whole Shakespeare section. The Muse of Fire was the first one I wanted because it was around a big ol' flame. I couldn't afford the flame, though, so I just got the quote. About a year later I got the second one, from a famous storm scene in King Lear.

As soon as I got them, the miracles I believed they held became a part of me. Now I can use them whenever I want, without needing Working aids to release the stored energy. They tax me, but not as much as if I were trying to engineer the miracles from scratch.

I've gotten more tattoos since. And I'll probably keep getting them for the rest of my life. Words have always been my thing. So that's how I store my miracles. The big ones, at least.

I held up my right hand, palm facing the sky, and let the heat in my stomach flow through me until it built to a warm glow in my palm, the black letters beginning to glow fiery orange. I held my left hand down below my waist, facing the ground. That palm grew cold, and a wind sprang up around my feet, tugging at my jean pant legs.

The cold hit a threshold and shot through my veins to my extremities, everywhere except for my right hand. I turned the heat from my right palm inward; it bubbled and hissed like molten lead in my gut, became a red-hot wire running down my right arm. The rest of my body fractured into a crystalline network of icicles. I began to sweat and shiver at the same time.

I gritted my teeth and turned both palms to face the front door.

There was a flash, and then a ripple in reality, as if everything in front of me were a pane of perfectly clear glass that I had suddenly shattered with a stone. The door's pale purple paint turned gray, and cracks began to spider around the doorknob. The air contracted, became denser and harder to pull into my lungs; the remaining streetlights grew weaker still.

The Terror had painted a facade on the house. When it had infested it, the house had begun to decay, to become more like the Terror in its formless shape where it had come from, the Space Between Spaces. I was going to have to break through that facade.

I breathed deeply and pushed more energy through my palms, using the elemental chaos of flame and wind in conjunction with the firmly structured dipoles I'd established of hot and cold. Breaking through chaos requires structure—setting up a continuum of hot and cold is a great way to do that, and harnessed flame and wind are powerful sources of energy.

The few still-lit streetlights lining the park flashed like miniature suns and then imploded with tinkling *pft!* sounds, bringing in near total darkness. But then the wind from my Working swirled around my legs, and the fire in my right palm glowed brightly, pushing back the darkness.

The wooden stoop sagged alarmingly, dropping me several inches. I hissed out a tight breath and shifted my weight, widening my stance.

I had to believe. I had to force that belief onto the world. I had to widen the crack the Terror had made so that I could follow it through. The Terror had cast its own belief on the world—I had to break through that and pull the entity out of the pocket it had made for itself.

This isn't real, I forced myself to believe. Everything here isn't fine.

My vision splintered and the doorway warped, turning crazily so that it was as if I were seeing it through a funhouse mirror. The world cracked and bent apart, and I forced my mind through the hole. The door went completely gray, and a loud echoing creak rang out, as of an ancient door being swung open on rusted hinges.

I was through.

There was a flare of furious, searing scarlet light, the sound and jarring impact of a muffled thunderclap, and then the door imploded with such force that it was ripped off its hinges and sucked into the darkness inside the house. That darkness consumed it completely, and beyond the empty frame, where the house should be, was nothingness. No light, no spark, no glimmer; not even the dim reflection of a neighbor's TV through a window. It was a black hole, so deep it seemed to threaten to suck in the entire world.

Shrieking, sickening laughter sounded from the darkness. Tendrils of shadows whipped toward me, tried to grab me.

It wanted my skin. Terrors need a body to go beyond where they manifest and walk out into the world. They need a face to wear when they commit murder and rape and feed off the darkness that lives in all souls. It wanted my body so it could tear and rend and wallow in blood.

I clenched my jaw so hard it cracked. I pulled back my right hand, then punched forward with my left. I believed that there was a storm in the palm of that hand. I believed that, in the glittering words etched into my skin, there was a storm to end all storms, a tempest of unfathomable strength and power.

I unleashed the belief, and lightning erupted from my palm.

White light exploded across my vision and thunder roared in my ears as I brought the fabled storm to life. The screams sounded again, but this time they were frightened and surprised—the Terror running, retreating into the house.

The shadows retreated with it, and I latched onto what I could see. A hallway, the beginning steps of a flight of stairs that must go up to a second floor. A slight opening to the right—a living room?

I fixed the details firmly in my mind and anchored them to reality.

The darkness retreated further, and a furious screech came from the hallway as I clawed back the house from the Terror.

I was breathing heavily, and sweat was beading on my forehead. I took a step forward, crossing the threshold. An immense weight slammed into me, trying to knock me back. The steps and the door and the entryway wavered in my mind's eye, and then correspondingly wavered in reality. I snarled and forced my belief back onto the world, forced a mental image of the real house back onto the dark void, and this time it stuck.

I took another step, still fighting against the weight. My legs were shaking, and I pulled energy from the band on my wrist to infuse them with strength. I believed myself to be heavier, stronger—and the shaking stopped.

The Terror riposted, throwing a storm of darkness back at me that snapped and whipped at my face and struck against me with gale-force winds.

A solid patch of darkness slammed into my chest.

I stumbled backward and threw my arms out to catch myself against the inside of the doorframe. I managed to stay inside the threshold of the house with a titanic effort of will. White lights winked across my vision and I coughed and wheezed as I tried to pull breath back into my lungs. I pulled energy from my silver ring, soothing the pain in my chest. I pushed forward again—one step, a second, a third—and made it into the inky black corridor.

The power of the Terror shocked me. It was stronger than any I'd encountered before.

"Shit balls Jesus goddamn fuck nuts," I growled in a constant stream of obscenities. I needed to find the actual creature, the representative belief that had drawn the Terror into reality. Whoever lived in the house had believed in something that the Terror had latched onto. A ghost story, a demon ritual—or something completely new. Whatever it was, that was what the Terror had become, and what lay at the heart of the darkness.

The shadows coalesced again, gathering strength, and shot out at me. They latched, burning, onto my arms and legs. For a searing moment, I lost control of my mind. All of my senses were overwhelmed in a rush: the smell was a gout of sulfurous flame; the sound was a slicing, dagger-sharp madman's shriek; the pain was a thousand needles in my skin.

I pulled all the strength I could from the ring on my left hand.

The laughter turned to screaming, and I screamed with it. The Terror tore at me, but helplessly. The barbs it had sunk into my flesh were burned away, though the cuts remained and began to bleed. My ring of protection cut through the shadows and sent them snapping back.

I was in a corridor. Warm yellow lights blinked back to life in the ceiling. The walls were a faded blue-gray color. There were religious trinkets on a hallway table next to the rest of the steep staircase to my left. A Catholic crucifix, candles with the Virgin Mary on them.

I paused. One of the candles was black and glowing with dark flame.

Shit.

I took another step and realized there was a boy cowering on the floor several feet in front of me, and a woman was with him—an older woman, who looked like she might be his grandmother rather than his mother. She was staring at me with wide eyes, her mouth open and frozen mid-scream.

I couldn't blame her. I'd reacted much worse the first time I'd encountered a Terror.

A deep boom, like the bass rattle of an over-amped subwoofer, shook the hallway. The trinkets on the table jumped and tumbled over, but not the black candle. The dim golden lights in the ceiling shook and blinked down at me. A background growl built until it became a wild keening, like a bestial wind, that bellowed down the tight corridor.

"Stay down!" I shouted.

The woman didn't respond—she only stared at me.

No, not me. At something behind me.

Well, fuck.

I whirled around. The Terror had assumed a form. It had become a demon, something manifested from a religious text or scripture. It had eyes like a furnace and clawed hands the length of my torso, with fingers like scimitars that dripped oily black tar. Where those drops landed, wood burned and smoke curled up into the air. Up the arms and across its deep skeletal chest, worms and spiders crawled, burrowing in and out of its scant flesh in drops of deepest scarlet that glowed with an otherworldly fluorescence.

"Gnarly skin problems, friend. Have you tried a water-based cleanser?"

The Terror opened its maw and roared at me. The sound was like the wrenching crunch of sheet metal being torn in half. The wind behind it stank with the rotten remains of decomposing corpses. Saliva flew from foot-long fangs and splashed on the floor and walls where it made the wood smoke.

Silence fell. It seemed to be waiting for my reaction.

"There's really no reason to take that tone," I said.

The Terror charged. I pivoted on my heel and flooded another tattoo with mental energy, one that I'd had etched into the skin of my upper back, from shoulder to shoulder. A Ralph Waldo Emerson quote. It says:

The best lightning rod for your protection is your own spine.

It's a little unpredictable, but it protects me in whatever way the situation requires. In that instance, my leather jacket suddenly became hard and shiny, and then it ballooned out behind me until it was two, three times its original size. The Terror charged straight into it and the jacket detached itself from me and wrapped around the shadowy beast and began to contract. The thing snarled and snapped at it with its gruesome teeth, but the Worked leather refused to tear.

I ducked down near the landing of the narrow staircase. I gathered myself, breathed in, pushed belief into the tattoos on my palms, and clapped my hands together.

The sound echoed out of all proportion in the narrow hallway. Brilliant light snapped on inside the thick leather shell that now covered the creature, and wind lifted it off the floor. The Terror bellowed again but this time in pain and anger. The smell of burning hair and skin filled the room, along with a popping sound and the heady scent of ozone.

With a loud ripping sound, one of the scimitar claws finally managed to puncture the leather and tear a line straight down the center of the shell. Light and heat burst out in a gout of flame. The woman and her grandson shrieked and fell back, shielding their faces.

"Get out of the hallway!" I shouted.

If either of them heard me, neither of them listened.

This was getting out of hand.

"All right, fine!"

I held out my hands and the leather jacket disengaged from the demon. There was long rent in it now, and instead of trying to put it back on, I tossed it to the side. My tattooed arms were fully exposed in the black t-shirt I was wearing, the letters on my palms and forearms swirling like windblown leaves.

I threw my closed left fist straight up above me, toward the ceiling and the sky outside. My right hand I pushed down open-palmed to the floor, and toward the rocky soil I knew was below.

The leather band on my left wrist began to glow, the Celtic and Norse runes turning golden, and the metal ring on my left hand shone white-hot as I summoned the energy from both, readying myself. I reached up into the sky, feeling out the atmosphere.

Still no lightning.

I'd have to make some.

Every Terror is different. You can force them back out of reality with sheer will if you catch them early enough. But this Terror had latched itself fully to life, feeding off the fear of the family that had managed to summon it. I didn't have the power on my own to dispel it with belief.

The problem with something believing itself to be a demon, though, is that it comes with all the baggage of being a demon.

Cue lightning from the heavens.

A glimmer of understanding flared in the creature's eyes, and it threw itself forward desperately, trying to reach me before I could perform the miracle.

I cried out with the effort of pulling the lightning down, grounding myself as I did with my heavy boots. The energy from my band hardened my body, and the ring protected me from the worst of the damage.

A crackling branch of white light blew through the ceiling, struck my outstretched palm, and lanced down my right arm and out my right fist at the Terror. The thing's eyes were endless pits of despair, its mouth a gaping window into hell itself. The lightning struck it in the chest and threw it up against the ceiling. Electricity flooded through me and into it, popping and crackling and singeing its flesh to a darker burnt-black.

The energy cut off, and I sagged to my knees on the floor, staring up at the thing. A black ring of smoke surrounded it, and it no longer moved. Slowly, and then with gathering speed, it began to shrink and crumble at the edges. Where it crumbled, the pieces of it became as black smoke and began to drift away, to dissipate now that it had no coherent whole around which to organize, no gravity keeping the thought of it all together.

I felt the crack in reality through which it had come begin to close. I looked over at the hallway side table and saw again the religious candles. In the center was the black candle: it was marked with a symbol that wasn't Catholic at all. It was something I had never seen before, but a sign that I knew immediately was some kind of manifestation Working. Likely it had only appeared after the boy and his grandmother had lit it.

I reached over and grabbed the candle, and when I did the symbol changed into the snarling, demonic face of the Terror I had just fought. I held the candle in my right palm, funneling energy through the Muse of Fire tattoo. The wax melted, along with the glass and the candle, and the symbol split in half. As it did it flared briefly and turned into what looked like a stylized monogram—maybe a C and an H, swirled around each other. Some kind of signature by the dick who had set a trap for some unsuspecting Blissful.

There was a rush of air, the stench of something sulfuric and rotten, and then the sense of wrongness that had settled over the house disappeared.

There was a long, resounding moment of silence, filled with me breathing very heavily and the broken roof settling. I looked around for the old woman and her grandson. They were behind me still, back toward the kitchen—which, I'd like to point out, I'd managed to keep entirely intact—and were staring at me with wide eyes and gaping mouths.

"Hey," I said, breathlessly. "Look, don't worry, pretty soon you'll convince yourself this was all a dream. I'll fix the roof before I go, and the door, too. I gotta take pictures and everything to collect my pay, so I'll set this all right before I head out. And you'll forget it all, I swear. No one ever remembers what they can't believe was real. Here, let me just check."

I took a step forward and held out my hand. They both recoiled, the grandmother grabbing the boy.

"Don't come any closer!" she cried. "Stay back!"

I sighed. "Yeah, you're probably good anyway. Just— wherever you got this candle? Don't go back there. Someone was playing with you. Were you having nightmares?"

The grandmother just stared at me, but the boy nodded.

"Yeah," I said darkly. "Someone was playing with you. We'll check it out. Maybe stay away from candles with weird symbols on them for a while, OK?"

The boy's eyes focused behind and above me. They grew wide and a tremor passed through him.

I looked up and back.

The Terror was gone. But, somehow, one of the creature's scimitar claws had broken off from its body and become lodged in the ceiling. While the body had faded away, the claw, separated from the thing itself, had retained its reality.

I'd never seen that before, and so I just stared at it dumbly as it fell from the ceiling and speared me straight through my chest.

I remember taking one big step back, trying once to breathe, and then falling sideways.

The woman and the boy were screaming. My vision blurred and went funny, distorting shapes. I slumped the rest of the way down so that I was kneeling around the scimitar-like claw impaling me. Dark arterial blood was flowing out of me and pooling on the floor. My ring was ice cold, all of its energy spent.

The world spun, and I was on the floor on my back. I looked up at the boy again, and now the grandmother was with him and she was screaming something. I couldn't hear what they were saying. I scrabbled at my shirt, trying to pull it down to touch one of the tattoos on my chest, not even sure which one I was going for, just trying for something, anything, but my fingers had gone numb and wouldn't work right.

I was very cold all over, and I was lying in a pool of warm blood.

There was a rushing sound, and then a roaring.

And then I was dead.

Part Three

COMING BACK TO LIFE SUCKS,

AND I WOULDN'T RECOMMEND IT.

NO STARS OUT OF FIVE.

Coming back that first time is… hard to describe.

I began as nothing because that was what I was and who I was and *where* I was. Then there was a light, a tiny pinprick of it that expanded instantly—instantly because there was no time and no space and no reason that the light shouldn't just suddenly be everywhere and always.

And then fire, which was pain. As if every nerve in my body had been twisted around a knife blade and was being curled like a balloon string. As if I had been dipped in acid and ice and rolled across broken glass scattered with rock salt. Every inch of me burned and screamed and quaked at the sensation, and then there was a *wrenching* that pulled me back from nothing into something and exploded me into consciousness.

I sat up and screamed. Except there was no "I" to do the screaming. There was no concept of Cicero James, no coherent whole of who I was or what I was or what I might have been. "I" was nothing more than a sensation, a feeling of *wrongness*, a feeling that *I* was somewhere *I* shouldn't be and couldn't be. And under and over it all was a profound anger at the imposition of being forced back into the world— chained back to reality after escaping to freedom somewhere beyond. Anger at the absurdity of it all—the absurdity of life being papered back over the hole that had opened and taken me down into serene nothingness, as if one could cover or fill that nothingness as easily as you could plaster over a hole in an apartment wall.

Basic senses returned first, I remember that. Sound—the echoes of the scream just pouring out of my mouth. I stopped screaming because the sound of it hurt my ears, and I flinched away from that. And then touch—I felt cold. The air on my skin was *cold*. The steel table I was lying on was *cold*. Against my skin. My... *my* skin. My *body*.

And then came joy. A blissful euphoria that rolled through me like an ocean tide, just drowning me, seeping into every pore and wrapping me in an elemental embrace. A sense of peace and rightness and order. It was light and happiness and... joy. And I wanted to shout again, but this time I also wanted to laugh or sing or... I don't know, do something— *anything*—to convey the wonderful feeling of *living*.

And then that was gone, too, and I fell back flat on the cold steel table. The falling made a crash that resounded metallically through the room.

My mind was the last thing to return, and it came haltingly. Something that had been Cicero James slowly coalesced in fits and starts once more in the core of my being. An impression of him to start with, like a bad watercolor painting but with recognizable shapes. Then lines, and details, and I remembered that once, long ago, I had been able to see. And from there I reasoned that now, here, if I opened my eyes, I might be able to see again.

So that's what I did—I opened my eyes. And I saw a bright light shining down on me, white and blue. I frowned. There was a light in the sky called the sun, and another light called the moon, but this wasn't either of those. What light was it?

And beyond—beyond that light was gray stone. No, not stone… concrete. That was the word. Con-crete.

I raised an arm to try and touch it—the light—and my arm snagged on something. I tried again, but the arm still wouldn't go, wouldn't lift the way I wanted it to. So I tried the other arm—and encountered the same problem.

This all kicked off another cascade of slowly resurrecting synapses, and I remembered that I could look at things if I shifted my head. I remembered that I could raise my head, too, which would help to look at things, and from a higher perspective. I remembered... yes. Yes, I remembered those things.

I lifted my head, and my vision swam for a minute before solidifying. I blinked, hard, and then I managed to refocus my eyes and look down.

My body was lit by the bright light in the ceiling. My torso was exposed from the navel up, but the rest of me, including my arms, were wrapped in a black bag. There were lines drawn on my chest in red pen, forming a "y" that started at the ends of my tattooed collarbone, met in the center of my chest, and then branched downward. My arms couldn't move, I realized, because they were wrapped in the voluminous black bag.

I began to breathe more sharply. I could hear the sound of it bouncing off the walls of the small room. Everything was industrial concrete and tile and stainless steel. I looked over to my left, and there was a tray of metal implements—sharp and gleaming, some with serrated edges and one with a heavy blade clearly meant to cut through bone. And beyond that was a long trough in the wall and a hose hanging down from the ceiling, coiled metal with an adjustable nozzle. The trough was clean and dry, but I could all too easily imagine it full of blood and viscera.

I was in an autopsy room.

I was in a morgue.

That realization was the final kick required to fire me officially back to consciousness. A shock raced through me that brought me fully back together, integrating me back into a coherent whole. I coughed suddenly, then hacked and wheezed and felt something come up my throat and jump into my mouth. I turned to the side and spat it out—a wad of red and yellow and white nearly the size of a golf ball landed wetly on the floor. After a moment of stunned disbelief, I coughed again, and then again, until I'd hacked up several more wads of equal size and color.

They lay on the tiled floor, and I stared at them.

Blood clots. Clots from the blade that had speared me through the chest and...

Killed me. Fucking *KILLED* me.

The realization made staying still impossible. My body rebelled against the knowledge of my death at such a deep level that there was no thought—no possible conception—of remaining still any longer.

I tried to free myself from the black bag—the body bag, a fucking BODY BAG!!—and found my limbs could only move in jerking half-motions, like a newborn colt's. I managed to free my right hand first, and then I grabbed the left side of the bag and ripped and tore at the fabric. Somehow I managed to push or pull it away, with the kind of freakish strength that comes from panic. I began to struggle with my legs: my knees worked, pumping my feet, but, overall, my lower body was uncoordinated and responding erratically.

New sounds came from somewhere. I froze, my heart thudding in my chest, pumping blood through my veins with extra vigor as if to make up for the time it had spent still and silent. I was just lucky that I hadn't lost all my blood... lost it all when...

Wait. But I *had* lost all my blood. I'd been in a fucking *puddle* of it.

I looked down, and an incongruity struck me.

The gaping wound that should have been in my chest was gone as if it had never been. There wasn't even a scar. Not a mole, not a wart, not a tiny little pimple. There was no evidence at all that I had ever been speared through the chest by a Terror's deadly claw.

Sound came again, and this time I recognized it: Footsteps, and voices. I couldn't see a door in front of me, only a wall of stainless steel storage hatches with shiny latch handles, and I realized the entrance to the room was behind me.

I tried to turn and was stopped by the heavy black bag again. I craned my neck around, leveraging my newly freed arms, and managed to clap my eyes on a closed door. A pane of clouded glass was set in the top third of the door, and there were shadows moving beyond it, shapes of people.

Fear completely overtook me. I think in the moment I thought that whoever was out there was coming to cut me open, whether I was awake or not. I don't know for sure—I was fully conscious, but I was *not* in my right mind. I was just certain in that moment that I wasn't safe, that I couldn't be seen. I didn't want anyone to find me. I had to hide—had to be out of sight.

I stopped caring about extricating myself from the body bag and, in a moment of madness, simply threw myself over the side of the table. I landed facedown on the tiled floor, my elbows and kneecaps smacking squarely against the cold, hard tile. I grunted in pain, barely suppressing a louder cry, which I just managed to hold back behind gritted teeth. My joints all throbbed in painful chorus at such ill-treatment.

I thrashed around until I was able to get my tangled feet beneath me, and then I limped in a jerking, shuffling half-run to the side of the room, to a row of metal tables I think were gurneys. They were lined up in the shadows and several of them had long sheets draped over them.

The sound of voices and footsteps crescendoed, and the metal latch door handle clicked as someone pressed it from the other side.

I threw myself back to the ground and rolled under the nearest sheet, just missing the bottom steel plate of the gurney it covered. I lay on my back, gasping for air as silently as I could, and tried to calm my pounding pulse and slow my frantic breathing.

"I'm sorry for all the hoops, but this is pretty irregular," said a female voice. "We don't usually get people checking a body the same night it comes in."

"Understandable," said a male voice.

I jerked in surprise. I knew that voice. It was John McMillin, a Guild-sanctioned enforcer. I'd done a job with him before, and I saw him pretty regularly at Worker meetings.

He was the Worker version of a cop.

"But this'll be quick," McMillin continued. "We just need to confirm the identity. We represent a third party that has been working with the SFPD to keep—"

His voice cut off, and so did all sound of movement. It appeared that he and the woman with him had frozen at the sight of the empty table.

My heart was pounding in my chest so loudly I was almost surprised they couldn't hear it.

I *had* officially died. These were the kinds of cases McMillin worked—confirming for the Guild that a dead Worker was actually dead. Because one of the most basic laws of Working is that you aren't allowed to bring anyone or anything *back* from the dead. Not even yourself.

And… somehow that was exactly what I'd done.

Or… somehow that was exactly what someone had just done *to* me.

In the moment, I wasn't sure which was the worse option. Either was bad—really bad—and my fear of being discovered turned from delusional panic to very concrete terror.

They would take me in. They would hold me. And I didn't have answers to give them. They would find me guilty. *Was* I guilty? *Had* I brought myself back from the dead without even knowing what I was doing? It was a legitimate possibility—Working can get real weird when the stakes are high and lives are on the line. If someone else had done it, where was the proof? There hadn't been anyone else there.

They would assume I'd done it. Hell, *I* would assume I'd done it.

And… I mean, *had* I done it?

I squinted hard through the small opening in the white sheets hiding me, watching them. They were still staring at the empty table that should have held a body—my body—in stunned, confused silence. By ending up trapped in the body bag, I hadn't even left that behind, so there was just a bare stainless steel gurney in the middle of the room, next to a table full of tools ready to autopsy a body that wasn't there. The clots that I had spat up were currently hidden from their view—if they found them, I wasn't certain what they would make of them.

"Are we in the wrong room?" McMillin asked. There was a subtle tone of anger in his voice, making it gruffer now. I'd heard it before.

"I—no," said the female voice. She came further forward, and I was able to see her face in a gap in the white sheets that hid me. It was indeed a woman. She was young and white-faced, her eyes wide and staring at the table as if she'd seen a ghost.

Fuck. Am I a ghost?

The pain radiating from my elbows and knees from when I'd hit the hard floor told me that if I were a ghost, we would have to rewrite several centuries' worth of lore and legend because I was a painfully solid one.

"Then where's the body?" McMillin asked.

"I don't know," the young woman said. She hurried forward and examined the table as if expecting me to have left behind a note or something, but there was, of course, nothing there. I think maybe she assumed the light was hiding me somehow, which of course was impossible, but what else was she supposed to think when confronted with the notion that a definitely dead body that she had just been about to cut open had simply disappeared?

"Photographs," said a third voice, one I hadn't heard yet. It sent a jolt through my body, and I craned my neck to try to get a look at the source, but the word had come from further back, toward the door, and I couldn't see the speaker. The voice, at least, was female.

"Wouldn't you photograph the body before beginning an autopsy?" it continued.

"Yes," the young woman said, turning back to the other voice.

"Then let's look at those," McMillin said.

"I—hadn't taken—when you came in, I put down— "

She gestured desperately at a camera with a very large flash attachment placed upside down on a small ledge by the door. The camera wasn't aligned with the hook next to the platform that must have usually held it, and I realized she was saying that she had been in the process of setting the camera up when she had heard the arrival of McMillin and the woman.

McMillin's jaw tensed, and anger crossed his face. The young woman must have seen it too because she started stammering even worse and frantically tried again to explain herself. McMillin cut her off before she got very far.

"The intake papers," he snapped. "Where are they?"

The young woman blanched again but then seemed to rally. "He wasn't pronounced dead until he was in the ambulance," she said. "He was still alive at the scene, just unconscious. The report said that they were rushing him to UCSF from Hayes Valley but he died on the way."

"Are you certain that's what it said?" the third person asked.

"I—what do you mean? Which part?"

"Died."

"I... yes," the young woman said, clearly confused. "Complete flatline, fifteen minutes before they got to the hospital. Then they transferred him. Why else would he be here?"

There was a long pause, and then the sound of footsteps walking from the door into the room. The steps were sharp and methodical, and when they came close to McMillin, a pair of low-heeled boots became visible to me. Well kept, matte black—fashionable but not unreasonably so. A professional woman's shoe, but one that wouldn't slow her down too much if quick movement were required.

I didn't dare lean forward enough to catch her face. Honestly, I wasn't brave enough right then to let out a breath louder than a mouse's fart. If they were putting the same pieces together that I was, then they knew that I was in a whole world of trouble.

I had to get out of there. I had to figure out what had happened.

The problem is, I know John McMillin. The man is about as anal as he is alcoholic (two bourbons and a scotch on a slow night, line 'em up and knock 'em back) and that was exactly what I didn't want. The man has nothing else in his life, which, you know, is sad, but also makes him way way way too thorough and (when I'm not the suspect) good at his job.

I was willing to bet he wouldn't leave until he had checked every body bag and looked under every gurney in the whole goddamn morgue. Hell, I wouldn't put it past him to stake the place out and wait for me to try to sneak past him.

So, again—I needed to leave. Yesterday.

There was only one door, and all three of them were standing between me and it. I wracked my brain for any kind of plan and came up with half a dozen really bad ones— ranging from stepping out and startling them with a naked rendition of Celine Dion's "It's All Coming Back to Me Now" to bull rushing the doorway and just hoping for the best—but nothing halfway decent. I felt my wrists and fingers for my Instruments and realized that, of course, they were gone. I wouldn't be able to use the watch to escape through space, and I wouldn't be able to use the band—if it had any juice left in it—to modify my body and make myself unnoticeable. And even if I did have them, I wasn't sure what kind of Work McMillin and the other lady might have already done on the room to keep someone like me from trying one or both of those things.

I looked around. There wasn't anything I could easily break or ruin to release a flare of chaotic energy, and I definitely didn't have time to perform any kind of order-bound ritual for a slower but steadier burn. I had my tattoos, but I didn't have one specifically for "magically escape a morgue while being pursued by enforcers" and I was really trying not to fight my way out, especially since I was cold, recently dead, and would probably have a hell of a time controlling any kind of large Working.

And even if I got out of the room, I'd have to get out of the morgue and find my clothes—and Instruments!—on the way, and who even knew where—

Focus! The room. Just find a way out of the room first.

I looked around again and my eye was drawn to the row of stainless steel hatches set in the wall opposite the door. I'd seen enough cop shows to know that those doors contained—or at least on TV shows contain—the bodies of the recently not-alive. I had also seen enough cop shows to know that people in cop shows sometimes hide in those containers.

What were the odds everyone else in the room had seen a few Blissful cop shows?

An idea came to me, and it was the only idea I'd had that didn't seem completely awful. If it worked, it would get their attention away from the door and give me a chance to sneak behind them and out to freedom. I thought about using a tattoo, but I didn't think I would need one. It was a simple Working.

I took a deep, silent breath and concentrated. I imagined myself feeling the air behind the hatch, imagined the air heating up and pushing outwards. I pushed my belief in the truth of that reality out into the world, and an even deeper chill rushed over me as energy left my body.

A loud metallic *ping* came from behind one of the hatches. To me it sounded exactly like what it was, air expanding due to a strange hot spot caused by a malfunctioning ventilation fan. To everyone else, I hope it sounded much more like an unfortunately timed shift by a dangerous felon on the lamb from justice.

I held my breath.

A second passed, and then another, and I thought that perhaps the ruse was too obvious. Perhaps they would see right through it and check the rest of the room instead. Perhaps the young woman would tell them that there were no other bodies in the morgue that night and that that one hatch always creaked and—

"Check it," the female Worker said.

"Check what?" the young woman asked. "The… you don't think that somehow he—?"

"Check it," the woman repeated.

McMillin turned on his thickly booted heel and strode over to the hatch, slowing down as he came near it and approaching cautiously. I had chosen the one lowest to the ground and furthest to the left, on the other side of the room from where I was shivering more and more violently against the icy tile floor. I swear, my teeth were threatening to tap out a Fred Astaire dance routine if I didn't find a way to start warming up.

The two women remained standing on the far side of the room; the mortician was closer to the autopsy table, while the Worker still stood just out of view, closer to the door itself.

I had to make both of them move in order to get past them undetected.

McMillin reached the hatch, knelt, and held out his hand to grab the handle. I panicked and Worked again—throwing out the first belief I could come up with, which was to tell the little hatch door that it wasn't a door at all but a wall.

I'm actually pretty good at that kind of thing. It's fairly simple, but quite effective. You just pick something close to what an object is and give it a little nudge to convince it it really is that thing. For example, doors that are shut are easy to convince that they should always be shut and that they should never open again—and therefore should consider themselves walls. *Why would you want to open, anyway?* you ask them. Opening is *dumb*. Only dummies open. Walls are where it's at. Besides, you're closed right now, so just stay closed! That's why you have a latch and a lock and all the rest of it. Just chill.

It worked just that easily. The little hatch, convinced, remained closed.

McMillin pulled on the handle… and nothing happened. He looked down, apparently thinking there was something wrong with the handle itself. He tried again but to the same effect.

He took a step back and reached down to his side. In the place where a Blissful police officer would have a gun or a nightstick or a can of mace or whatever, he had a thick black leather glove. It had rings on each finger and lines of thin metal wire coiled over and around the back of the hand in an intricate design. There was also a watch set in the wrist, chunky and metallic, and a leather strap to keep the whole thing tightly secured.

That, my friends, is what we call a Ruiner. It's a design that someone came up with for a combination ring-band-watch-conduit. Everything a Worker needs all in one little package. They come standard issue for enforcers but are otherwise tightly regulated. They have drawbacks—they aren't versatile enough for detailed Working, for example, and they suffer from the 'good at everything but great at nothing problem'— but if you need to break something with some good ol' fashioned brute force, you'd be hard pressed to beat a Ruiner.

Which meant my little tricks were about to be useless and I was royally spit-roasted.

"It's stuck," McMillin said. "Does this door stick?"

"No," the mortician said, stepping away from the table and moving toward McMillin, looking confused by the strangely punk rock glove the enforcer was strapping on. To be fair, from the Blissful standpoint, I get it, weird move. What was he gonna do to the corpse while wearing a Steampunk glove, you know? Pretty creepy.

But she was away from the door, and that's what mattered right then.

"It doesn't usually stick. And it doesn't lock like that either. It's… it shouldn't be doing that. Is something holding it shut? There's a handle on the other side too, like a little knob thing. Maybe something got caught on it. But the body wouldn't be in there—"

McMillin finished strapping on the Ruiner and held it up. The Worker woman was still too far back, and I couldn't leave the safety of the table yet. With time running out and no other options, I focused harder on convincing the little hatch it was a wall, gritting my teeth in concentration.

McMillin tried the handle one last time, again with no luck. He looked back over his shoulder at the woman by the door.

"Wait," she said. There was a pause that might have only been a second but to me felt like twelve hundred years, and then she took several steps toward McMillin, passing my little hideout table.

Hallelujah, thank the Buddha!

"Mr. James," she said.

My heart stopped dead in my chest for a good three seconds. Just shuddered and came to a halt.

And then I realized she was addressing the *hatch.*

"We are official representatives of the Workers of the West, and we need to speak with you regarding the events of last night at the house on Steiner Street. As a Guild member working a Guild contract, you and your actions are under our purview."

I ignored her completely. I mean, she was right, but fuck that, I wasn't sticking around before I even knew what had actually happened. As far as I knew, I actually *was* guilty.

And I don't have a lot of trust in due process these days.

There was an opening—just wide enough—behind the Worker woman that would allow me to reach the door. I began to shift beneath the table, doing my best not to make any noise or disturb the cloth that hid me from view. Now that they were in front of me, all I had to do was make it to the end of the gurney and then I could roll out, get to my feet, and tiptoe through the tulips right on out the door.

I paused for the briefest of moments to touch my wrists, remembering that my Instruments were still missing. I had no idea where they were. And no idea where my clothes were either.

I looked around, scanning the room quickly as I shrugged myself along the freezing tile floor. I saw nothing but autopsy equipment.

I have to leave them.

I gritted my teeth and pulled myself further along the floor, trying my best not to shake with the combination of fear, adrenaline, and cold. Jesus, the room was freezing, and the tiles felt like ice. I was amazed my breath wasn't misting out in front of me. I was also fairly certain my balls had crawled back *inside* my body.

So, let this be a lesson to you—don't roll around buck-naked on cold tile floors.

I don't know why you might need that lesson, but hey, I'm here to help.

I pulled myself to the end of the line of gurneys just as the Worker woman seemed to decide she'd had enough of waiting. "Open it," she instructed McMillin. The tall enforcer grunted and held up his Ruiner. A red light began to glow across the back of the thick leather gauntlet, as if electricity were running through the metal wires.

"What—what is—?" the mortician stammered.

The Worker woman touched her shoulder. "This is all fine," she said softly. The mortician's eyes glazed over, and her mouth fell open, almost like a very tired child who was only partially following the details of a conversation.

"It's all fine?"

"Yes," the woman said. "All fine."

That was my shot. They were all away from the door.

I rolled out from beneath the table, completely exposed, and tiptoed dramatically toward the door with all my bits flapping in the breeze. Like a perverted cartoon character sneaking away from the cartoon villain.

"Do it," I heard the woman say.

There was a loud sizzling sound, like butter on a hot pan, and I felt the tight thread in my mind that had me connected to the door abruptly sever and snap back at me.

It was the mental equivalent of being slapped with a leather belt across your bare ass. My vision doubled and I twitched violently, performing a kind of naked contemporary dance move as I lost my balance, temporarily rag-dolled, and then recovered just in time to keep myself from collapsing to the floor.

I bit my lip so hard to keep myself from crying out that I tasted blood. Through tears of pain, I slipped through the autopsy room door, my vision still swimming.

My heel caught the edge of the door and pulled it shut behind me.

BANG!

I had just enough time to recognize that I was in a long dimly lit corridor that led both left and right, and that there was a clock on the wall across from me that showed a little after 2 am.

And then everyone back inside the room started shouting.

I ducked down and away from the thick cloudy window just in time—something massive and red burst through it, smashing outward in a spray of safety glass and wire mesh.

I cursed and began to waddle down the right-hand side of the corridor toward a set of stairs. Once I was out of the way of the door and the glass, I stood and began to run in earnest, my naked legs flying.

"Stop!" McMillin shouted. "Stop now!"

"I didn't do it!" I shouted back over my shoulder. "I didn't—I swear!"

And then something caught my eye, and I pulled up.

Time seemed to slow. Through an open door, I could see my partially ruined leather jacket, the rest of my clothing, and my Instruments on a tray, waiting to be tagged and cataloged.

It didn't even cross my mind to leave them all. Instruments are like limbs to a Worker. Leaving them behind would be like cutting off a leg to escape a bear trap. You think you could do it if you really had to, but unless you *really had to*, you wouldn't just say sayonara to your left foot with the cute birthmark and the pinky toe that hasn't been the same since Cousin Charlie ran it over with his yellow Tonka truck.

I raced into the room and grabbed everything in a big bear hug, knocking over the table as I did. My band and ring had to still be severely depleted, but my watch should still have energy.

And it could get me out of the morgue.

Something shiny fell to the floor and pinged loudly as it bounced once, then twice, on the concrete and began to roll away.

My ring.

I dove for it as someone pounded down the hallway outside. I grabbed it, and a flare of warmth greeted me. Some of the energy had recovered. I slipped it on and then strapped on the band as well, and felt a brief flare of warmth there too. It wasn't much—it was hardly anything—but it might be enough.

McMillin kicked open the door, and, like a little hobbit, I touched the ring to the band and turned myself see-through. You can't be invisible—turns out that's impossible—but you can blend in really really well. You can believe you look so much like everything else in a room that you're indistinguishable. If you move, the illusion is broken. But if you stay still…

McMillin scanned the room, taking in the overturned table and the missing clothing.

He turned back to the door, then paused. His Ruiner glowed red; he clenched his fist, then raised it above his head. A pulse of red light flooded the room, and the last of the energy in my ring winked out, revealing me crouched like Gollum in a corner of the room.

We stared at each other for a moment, and then we both reacted.

I was faster, driven by adrenaline and fear and cold. I dropped the ball of my clothes, touched a quote circling my left bicep, and balled my left hand into a fist, punching the air in McMillin's direction.

The Work was completely unformed, but the quote took over for me. I had never used it on a Worker before, because Working on another Worker without their consent is very much illegal, but I had done it to Blissful while on contract, and turns out it's exactly the same.

There was a point to this story,
but it has temporarily escaped the
chronicler's mind.

Air rippled out from my fist and slammed into McMillin's temple. The Douglas Adams quote took over, and the last dozen or so seconds slipped out of the enforcer's brain as his head snapped to the side. His eyes glazed over, and he fell against the wall in the corridor outside. He hadn't even had time to protect himself with the Ruiner, which, though it glowed with a bright scarlet flash after the fact, had not been raised during my Working.

"McMillin!" the Guild woman shouted from the corridor.

That was when I realized what I had done, and that at best I'd bought myself a few seconds of freedom while condemning myself to a full trial before a Worker court for attacking another Worker. And not just any Worker—a goddamn enforcer.

Shit. Shit shit shit shit shit SHIT!

I scrabbled at the bundle of my clothing and managed to pull my watch free. I stared into its depths and pressed one of the push-crowns on the side, thinking with an obsessive, manic determination about my apartment. I wasn't in an alley or a park, so there wasn't anything to do but use up as much energy as I could and force the 'porting through.

The sub-dial ticked—once, twice—

The woman outside the room was running down the hall, I could hear her heels clicking as she came closer. She was shouting for McMillin, who was still groggily splayed out on the floor.

Three—four—

McMillin raised his head, his eyes clearing. I held tightly to my clothes and clutched my watch in a fierce, clawed grip.

Five.

The Working took over, and I was gone.

PART FOUR

HOME AGAIN HOME AGAIN, FIDDLE-DEE-DEE

I spun back out on a dimly lit street corner. Exhaustion washed over me, so intense that I staggered and fell to my knees while the world shifted in and out of focus. My hands and feet went dead and limp, and my lips were suddenly cold and numb.

For a moment, I was seriously concerned I'd overdone the Working. If you Work without an Instrument or a conduit like my tattoos, there's no upper limit to the amount of energy you can expend—at least no limit until you die, and then everything just stops. Even with an Instrument, though, if you burn through the energy in the Instrument and don't build in a safeguard to the belief you're manifesting, you can eat up so much energy you turn yourself into a vegetable. You wouldn't be dead, but I'm not sure it would be preferable.

After another few seconds, as the world steadied, it became clear that, luckily, I hadn't done that. But I clearly hadn't made it back to my apartment, either.

I was sitting on a concrete stoop on a street I didn't know. The sky above me was just starting to lighten, and I could hear traffic a few streets away.

I looked at my watch—it read 6:04 am.

The clock in the morgue had been close to 2 am. That meant I'd burned nearly four hours to make the transition, and I hadn't even made it to my apartment. I was relatively certain I was still in SF at least, but even that wasn't a guarantee.

I clutched my clothes against my naked body and huddled back against a crumbling concrete stoop as I tried to focus. My head was pounding like I had the worst hangover of my life—a common side effect of overWork. I knew it would only get worse until I could find some food and get some sleep. I hadn't tried to do a straight 'port in years. There's a reason we use parks and alleyways—they're all connected. Makes the transition much smoother and requires way less force of will.

Fun fact: it's also why scary things tend to pop out from behind trees or out of dark alleyways.

I tried to stand, and the world shifted and tilted. I quickly closed my eyes and sat back down, breathing in through my nose and out through my mouth. I felt acid come up into my throat; I forced myself to swallow it back down.

Working is about forcing belief onto the world. About shifting reality. When you spend too much energy, when you overWork, your mind starts having trouble differentiating between what's actually real and what's just possibly real. You begin to have trouble separating things that could be from things that are.

You go too far down that path, your body rebels against your mind. Makes you sick. Tries to make you stop, tries to pull you back to reality. You keep pushing, you can have a full mental break, burn yourself out. Some people have killed themselves—snuffed their own reality out like dripping water on a candle.

Like I said, all Workers are half-mad—and if you aren't careful, you can become full-mad. I've seen it happen, did a job with someone who broke in the middle of a miracle and started playing Jenga with stones from a nearby building.

It… was bad. He crushed someone with one of the stones—flattened her like a bug. It's a big part of why I don't take group jobs anymore.

Anyway. I tried to keep breathing, deeply enough to get extra oxygen into my bloodstream, and I kept my eyes firmly closed. I told myself that what I was feeling was real, which is usually my way out of the madness. It's easy to *see* things that are mere possibilities—it's much harder to *feel* them. If you can focus on your body, that's your way back to reality.

So I pushed my consciousness into my hands and feet and skin. I felt the hard ground; I felt the cold air. I felt the thick, soft leather of my jacket clutched in my arms and the scratchy denim of my jeans.

My mind slowly centered itself and began to piece back together. I took another full breath in, as much as my lungs could hold, and then pushed it fully out.

I opened my eyes and blinked furiously, resetting my vision. The world flickered, and things that couldn't be, places I wasn't, rapidly cycled in front of me. Desert palaces, solemn mountain temples, a river in a calm forest. Other cities—what I recognized as New York and London from TV shows and movies, along with a few others I couldn't place—flashed by too.

And then my vision between the blinks began to solidify. I started to see where I truly was, and to know that it *was* where I truly was. And, finally, after a dozen or so more frantic blinks, the haze began to lift and I was able to anchor myself back to reality.

I was looking across a street at a minor tent city. The central domicile was constructed from a few shopping carts used as support and barricades, and a pastiche covering of sheets and tarps of various colors and sizes, the most noticeable of which was a bright burgundy-red sort of awning over the whole thing.

And one of the denizens of the construction was staring at me.

He had a growth of several weeks' worth of beard—months, more likely—and looked like he hadn't had a chance to bathe in at least that long. He was wrapped in a thick tattered coat that looked like it might once have had a tan military print on it. His eyes were wide and surprisingly lucid, and they were locked right on me.

For a long moment, we just looked at each other. And then the man nodded in the universal sign of "I don't know what just happened, but Imma pretend I didn't see it." He then turned and ducked back under a flap of the makeshift tent and disappeared.

This interaction made me pretty certain that I was still in SF. The city's full of that these days. I glanced down around me and saw a needle in the gutter, and a small mound of human feces several paces further along.

You might be wondering why, if I'm a Miracle Worker, I don't do something about the bigger problems in the city I live in. Thing is, we aren't allowed to Work on people against their will. Terrors, manifestations of beliefs gone rogue, that's within our purview. People who seek us out and pay for a Working, we can help them, as long as we have a Work Cert from the Guild.

But how would you feel if I decided what was right for you and forced you to believe it? It would break your mind, if I could even make it stick. Because for most things to work, you have to be in it with me. For anything long term at least.

And to do something on a scale as massive as cleaning up a city? That would require a lot of belief from a lot of people.

Besides, the man who'd seen me wasn't nearly as far gone as some of the others you see these days. In fact, considering I was the one who was naked and leaning against a wall like I'd taken all the drugs, he probably thought *I* was the one to be pitied. Which, I will admit, was quite a fair assumption to make at that moment.

I started pulling my clothing back on, shaking from the cold morning air as well as the adrenaline and the continued aftershocks of overWork. In the growing light of morning, I looked at my body fully for the first time since waking in the morgue.

The wound through my chest—the one that had *killed* me—had indeed healed as if it had never existed. The dozen or so scrapes and bruises I had garnered in the process of fighting the Terror, however, had not. Several of them stood out fresh and clear in the growing light of dawn, scabbed over but still clearly new.

That was weird. But I had no answer for it.

Otherwise, though—and generally speaking—I was fine.

Which freaked me out all over again.

I pulled my pants up, buckled my belt, stuffed my feet into my boots, and stood, using the wall to help me. I took another steadying breath and walked out into the middle of the street, looked up and down it, and finally realized where I was.

I'd landed right in the middle of the Tenderloin, a couple of blocks away from Market Street.

For those not overly familiar with San Francisco, the Tenderloin is… not a neighborhood most people visit voluntarily. It's where you find the majority of the drug use and homelessness right-wing news networks exploit and left-wing news networks ignore. It's never been a great neighborhood, even when I was growing up, but these days it's… well, like I said, it's not somewhere you go voluntarily. Not unless you have nowhere else to go.

I'd needed a place to hide, a place people wouldn't come looking for me. And… well, I couldn't argue with where I'd ended up.

That's what happens when you don't take the time to properly use an Instrument and Work with full consciousness. In the case of 'porting, your unconscious takes over and you end up wherever reality best matches your needs. It's one of the first things my mentor, Marlowe, drilled into me.

Marlowe. I need to talk to Marlowe.

That was the thought that got me moving again, despite my fatigue. If anyone had answers, it would be him. At the very least, he'd know where to go to get them.

I know, you haven't met him yet. I'll intro him better soon. For now, here's a sketch: he's an old SF hippie-turned-doctor who spent his life working as a Stitcher, which is a doctor for Workers. He has a private practice now and a reputation for being—you guessed it—*miraculously* talented. Everyone who's anyone in the Worker world out west knows him, and they know him as the man to go to with strays (like me) who are too talented to be released back into the Blissful world but also too troublesome to be sent to the Academy.

He's the only Worker I think I've ever fully trusted.

I tried to shrug into my leather jacket and realized it was still in tatters from the fight with the Terror. I looked around again. No one was watching me now. It was too early in the morning for anyone to be around there. The city would wake soon, but it hadn't quite done so yet.

I buckled my watch to my wrist, adjusted my ring and band, and touched the exposed tattoo on the inside of my forearm that read:

If I had my mouth, I would bite; if I had my liberty, I would do my liking: in the meantime let me be that I am and seek not to alter me.

I breathed out slowly and let the default image of myself float to the top of my mind, then released the Work into the world.

The leather jacket rippled in my hands and turned into silver liquid. It flowed up my hands and arms, across my chest, and then over my shoulders and around my back. Once it had settled, it turned from dull silver back into leather. I pushed the Working farther down, beyond the jacket, and the silvery shine washed over my waist and torso. The rips in my jeans mended themselves, my black t-shirt sewed itself back together in the middle over where the hole should have been in my chest.

Vertigo hit me again, and cold, but not so badly as before. The effort for the Working had come primarily from the tattoo, and it was a Working I'd used enough that it was easy to lock in without much effort.

I was still scared, anxious, and exhausted, but there's a world of difference between that and being *naked*, scared, anxious, and exhausted.

I began to shamble down the street, through the detritus of dozens of human lives that no one was coming to clean up. As I went, I automatically pulled the energy of the chaos into my Instruments. I had balked at doing that for a long time— essentially feeding off the misery of everyone who had fallen through the cracks of the city. But the power to Work comes either from chaos or structure, and denying that doesn't help those living there even one bit.

Still, I hated it. I especially hated it when I had to stare it full in the face.

I, like most of San Francisco, avoid the Tenderloin whenever possible. Aside from the danger of getting mugged, it's hard to continue imagining everything is fine in life and the world when you see such evidence to the contrary.

Now that I'd been dropped into the middle of it, though, I was forced to see it again and to realize just how much worse it had gotten even since the last time I'd been there. There were tents everywhere, and people lying sprawled out on the street surrounded by evidence of drug use. Blackened glass pipes, needles, empty bottles of liquor. The smell of decay, and what was more, the knowledge that it was *human* decay, which made it so much worse.

And still the energy filled me, as I slowly left it all behind. Like everyone leaves it behind, aside from the people who can't.

I came out on Market Street, wide and broad and noisy, and crowded with buildings dozens of stories high. A MUNI bus was passing, and a scattering of people in suits and on bikes were hurrying by, even at such an early hour.

I turned back one last time to look at the path I'd taken. I noticed some graffiti on a street corner that looked like a stylized monogram. I noticed several boarded-up shop windows. There was a man near the corner stooped over, eyes glassy, rocking back and forth on his heels. I felt helpless to do anything about it, and I knew that that wasn't an experience unique to me. I remember reading books as a child, stories about ancient cities with neighborhoods that respectable citizens avoided, and thinking how awful the people who lived in those cities had to be not to do something to help those who lived like that.

And then there I was, drawing energy from it all like a vampire. Like some kind of leech attached to a dying man, draining him even as he faded away. Making excuses like everyone else.

Suddenly, I hated myself. I hated everything. And in a moment of madness, I held up my Instruments and released all of the energy that I had just gathered into them. Cold fell on me, and my vision doubled. But I locked my knees and set my back, and something deep inside me, sharp and steely, kept me standing.

I realized I was sneering in contempt, not at the people I had passed but at the invisible hands behind it all. The hands that had created it and refused to do anything about it. Because the things to do were inconvenient or hard or unpopular or all three. The invisible powers that couldn't be fought.

My concentration wavered, and my knees gave out. I managed to catch myself on a short concrete block on the corner, and I quickly lowered myself down to sit.

I needed to get home.

The weight of my predicament crashed back in on me.

Died and resurrected. Running from a Guild enforcer.

They didn't see me. I wiped McMillin's mind.

That was the one hope I had. Hope that they were still trying to confirm it was me who had been in that morgue last night. The woman who'd been there had called me by name, but had she *known* it was me? Or had they been there to confirm because they weren't sure?

It was morning now. I'd burned four hours—what if they were already coming for me? What if they were at my apartment?

Thing is, I moved about a year ago and conveniently forgot to update my Worker license, what we call a Work Cert. Doesn't affect how I get paid for a Worker job, and I'm still me, so the few times I've had to flash it, people have just checked the photo, my name, and my birthday. No one cares about the address until shit like this happens. I redirected all the important stuff, like my Blissful mail, but I never submitted the right form to the Guild to update the Work

Cert. And then a few months passed and I still hadn't done it, and nothing had happened. So I figured I just wouldn't do it until someone told me to, to see how long it would take for anyone to notice.

And so far no one had.

Which meant that if they were coming for me, there was a good chance they were going to the wrong place.

My current apartment was protected. All Worker living spaces are protected, just by the fact a Worker lives there. The stronger you feel connected to the place you live, the harder it is for anyone you don't want to get in to get in, because you believe it's safe and you believe it's your home. But they'd find it eventually. I mean, like I said, I had everything else forwarded, so Amazon knows where I live even if they don't. All they'd have to do is follow the trail of packages.

I couldn't call Marlowe where I was—I'd sent my cell phone back to my apartment before going into the Terror house—and I was way too tired to try 'porting to him. I also needed to recharge my Instruments, and the quickest way to do that was at my place too.

I'd have to risk it.

I started walking.

I'm not sure I've ever been that exhausted. I don't know how I managed to move, let alone walk as far as I did. I had to keep a hand trailing along walls and shop fronts as I went to keep myself from swaying too far to one side and dropping to the pavement in a heap.

It was still early, and most people weren't around yet. But SF is a city, and there are always *some* people around at just about any time. The people who saw me as I made it down Market all gave me a wide berth, watching me carefully from the corners of their eyes. I couldn't blame them.

My boots felt several sizes too big, and heavy as cinderblocks. I kept my head down, but not from any attempt to hide myself. I just didn't think I could fully raise it without an effort of strength you'd have to measure in herculeans.

If only it had been the weekend, I would have been able to fit in with the walk-of-shamers making their way home. But it was a Friday and—

"Shit," I said, staggering to a stop.

Work.

Blissful work.

And the weekly presentation I'd intentionally scheduled for Friday morning.

I made a guttural noise deep in my throat somewhere between anger and despair.

I love Working, but it's not a full-time job. Almost all Workers have something else they do to make real money and live in real-world cities and pay for their favorite streaming services and fancy food that impresses people on social media. If I wanted to sign up as a full-time Worker I might—*might*—be able to make a living doing it, but not in San Francisco. Not with my specialty. People who do that kind of thing usually have to move to New York or London or… I dunno, Dubai. And it comes with rules and restrictions and registration forms that make me wanna vomit and kick people.

Workers have a few hidden cities, but by and large we don't have a separate parallel society. We mostly live in the same cities you do. And we gotta show up to jobs or else our bosses fire us and we lose our apartments and we get sad.

I started stumbling along again. There was no way I was going to be able to go in today. I would have to call in sick. I'd fall asleep two seconds after sitting down at my desk. I would just have to tell Arick I needed to give the presentation another time.

What were they gonna do? People get sick. Food poisoning, the all-purpose excuse.

Besides, if the enforcers didn't know where I lived, they *did* know where I worked, forms or no forms.

I've got a LinkedIn profile.

Home was safer. Temporarily, at least.

The city began to warm up. The sky was a clear blue, a rarity on any day in San Francisco. It helped—the warmth and sunlight energized me, if only a small amount.

Coffee. Need coffee.

I didn't trust myself to stop for any, though. I felt like if I stopped moving, even temporarily, there was no chance I'd be able to start again.

I finally reached Sansome, not too far from the alleyway I'd used to 'port over to Hayes Valley the night before. There's a BART station there, technically the Montgomery Street stop, and there's an exit that pops you right up onto Sansome and Market. That's where my backdoor is.

You can go look if you want, but you won't see anything. Even other Workers aren't able to see it—it's keyed to me. I'd have to personally show it to you.

I ducked down into the BART station. I pulled up short and swore: the escalator was broken. I stumbled to the stairs.

I took the first step, managed it by leaning very heavily on the handrail. The feat was further complicated by a steady stream of Blissful pedestrians passing me on their way up. Commuters coming in early from out of town, from farther down the peninsula or from across the Bay in Oakland, Berkeley, or as far away as Walnut Creek and Fremont.

I refused to let go of the handrail and just took each step one at a time. My knees threatened to buckle on several occasions, but somehow I kept them straight enough that I didn't just tumble my way down.

I wasn't used to going that way. I hadn't in a long time. But I've always kept a backdoor handy in every place I've ever lived. Ever since I was a kid and started Working.

If you're sensing backstory, you're right. But I'm not gonna share it now. It's pretty fucked. Though that's not unique to me. You don't become a Worker—you *can't* become a Worker—without a pretty bad thing happening to you as a kid. It's what causes us to break from reality. And when we recover—if we recover—then we can Work.

I reached the bottom of the stairs and almost let out an embarrassing little moan of relief. I didn't stop to bask in my achievement, though. I carried on in my shambling zombie-like walk along the corridor at the bottom of the stairs to the Montgomery stop proper. Luckily, the loading platform was basically deserted. The most recent train had just arrived, dumped its commuters, and whisked another load off on its magical journey of dirty seats and vomit-smelling floors. I turned left into a shadowy corner and touched the nearest wall.

I looked back once, but the latent Working was already doing its job. I saw one man glance in my direction, but in the next second his eyes unfocused and slid past me. A mother and daughter, who looked like they were commuting together for a school trip or something, saw me too, and though the little girl managed to focus on me for longer—typical, kids can believe easier in weird things—she quickly found a nearby pigeon more interesting.

I breathed out and let the Working flow over me completely. I slipped sideways, as if the floor were a people mover at an airport, and the world around me darkened as if I were in a long tunnel. There was light at the end of it, and the floor pulled me forward until I popped out into it.

I materialized in a rundown but functional elevator, ascending toward the 5th floor.

I breathed a deep sigh of relief and fell back against the padded wall, not even bothered by the metal handrail that dug into my back. There was a mirror to my right. I looked over at it and was frankly shocked by the image I saw looking back at me. I had dark rings under my eyes, my hair was all over the place, and my chin and cheeks were stubbled with scruff.

I was alive, but I sure looked like I was on death's doorstep.

The elevator dinged, and the doors opened. There were no cameras in the elevator or in the corridor. There was a camera in the lobby, though, and it would show that I hadn't walked back to the apartment. I didn't know how I'd manage to get around that one, but if it came to it I'd figure something out. It wasn't illegal as a Worker to have a backdoor.

I glanced up and down the corridor. It was rundown but clean, like the elevator, and made up of industrial tan carpeting and taupe walls. It was deserted this early in the morning.

I rested my hand on the door of my apartment. The thin, worn wood warmed, and a loud click sounded from deep inside it. I pushed down on the tarnished handle and the door opened inward.

I was home.

PART FIVE

Let's meet Marlowe.

Mr. Frost, if you're nasty.

The apartment was dark, but there was some dawn light coming from the large window across my tiny kitchen and larger-but-also-tiny living room.

The window is the best part of the apartment, and it's completely incongruous because it literally doesn't belong there. What it should be is a blank wall. What I turned it into is a view from at least 20 stories up, not 5. It's actually Roc's view. He doesn't know it, but the last time I was over at his place—a gorgeous two-bedroom in one of those massive towers by the Bay Bridge—I performed a minor Working to mirror his view onto my blank wall.

Through it, you can see the whole of the San Francisco Bay, the Bay Bridge that leads to the East Bay and Mount Diablo (yep, real mountain name), and even a sliver of Alcatraz off to the left. And beyond that Marin, which is absolutely beautiful. Right then, the water was a shimmery light blue with a streak of fiery orange across it from the sun rising in the east, off to the right.

For all its faults… man, there's some gorgeous stuff in San Francisco.

The tiny kitchen was fairly bare, aside from a large combo coffee/espresso machine, which, aside from my work computer, is honestly the most expensive thing in the apartment. There was also a spice rack, various knives I'd picked up over the years, and a few left-out cups and dishes from meals I'd had the last few days. Despite being tiny, there was an attempt at a kitchen island that was just big enough to house a small countertop that served as the sitting/eating area.

There was a large TV on the right side of the living room that I'd gotten from someone moving out on the second floor, and a deep sectional sofa on the left that I'd found on the street and cleaned the shit out of for three days straight. There's also a tall lamp in the far corner that I got online with my first big-boy paycheck. I've had that thing for years now, and I'm fairly certain that if there's an apocalypse it'll be that lamp and five cockroaches that survive.

Technically, I have a one-bedroom—really it's a large studio that they put a wall up in to divide the large living room into a small living room and a small bedroom. Through an opening in the wall to the right, you can see said small bedroom, which is just big enough to fit my bed (queen-sized, 'cause you can't have sleepovers on a twin), and a bathroom. Between the bedroom and the bathroom is a small linen/storage closet.

Well, what looks like a small linen/storage closet.

I went to the counter and hit several buttons on the coffee machine. It began to make noises that are nonsensical to me aside from that they eventually produce coffee. I grabbed two slices of bread, tried a few times, and finally managed to slot them into the toaster.

Then I leaned heavily on the counter and tried to breathe deeply.

Next—the Phone Booth.

I twisted my right hand, and a small coin appeared in my palm, pulled from my Guild bank vault. It was made of burnished silver and bore on one side the insignia of the Workers of the West—a pair of open hands superimposed over a map image of California, Oregon, Washington, and

Nevada—and on the other side a set of traditional Instruments: a ring, a pocket watch, and a sword belt with a scabbarded sword.

I focused on the coin, letting it fill my thoughts, and two numbers popped into my mind's eye—a silvery forty-three and a golden twenty-nine. That was what I had in the vault. Which isn't really a vault, but a small metal drawer kind of like a postbox I'd set up years ago right after I got my Work Cert. Every Worker has one—some actually are vaults. We can store anything we want in there, but it's primarily where we store the coins that allow for Worker transactions. The Guild deposits them directly in there when we do a job, or if we convert Blissful money. The conversion fee is a total rip-off, though, and the exchange rate is god-awful right now.

You can use the coins in the real world if you want, but it's tricky. They don't have any intrinsic value outside the Worker world, and they just fill with whatever amount and denomination the person you're giving them to expects. So if you aren't careful, someone might think you just handed them a nickel. Or, that you handed them a million dollars. Both are tricky situations to talk yourself out of.

All I needed for the Phone Booth, though, was a single silver piece, so I let the numbers fade away and pocketed the coin.

I grabbed the now-full mug of coffee from the coffee machine—a novelty Harry Potter Marauder's Map mug that reveals the map when heated—and slathered an excessive amount of butter on my toast. I then shoved one of the pieces of toast almost entirely into my mouth.

Chewing thickly and washing the toast down with coffee, I moved around the island and across the kitchen to the linen closet. I took the silver coin and pressed it against the door. It took me longer than it should have to focus hard enough to make the transaction, but, finally, the door shifted imperceptibly.

The coin sank slowly into the wood, until fully submerged.

I pushed the door handle in, instead of pulling the door out. A yawning black void opened up in front of me; what should have been a closet full of innocuous folded sheets, board games, and sundry living necessities, was now an empty abyss.

I breathed deeply and then let the air out in a long, anxious stream.

I really hope he's home.

I stepped into the void and the darkness swirled, giving a strange kind of imitation of movement. The door jerked away behind me and then closed with a sharp snap. I was left in complete darkness, something that had taken me quite a while to get used to as a teenager.

"Marlowe Frost," I said slowly and clearly. There was a long pause, and then a chime sounded. After a few more seconds, a disembodied voice came out of the void.

"Cicero?" the voice asked. "Do you know what time it is?"

"Too early," I said, unable to keep the fatigue from coming through in my voice and making me curt. "I need to talk."

There was another pause.

"You there, Marlowe?" I asked.

A tense moment of sudden worry on my part, and then:

"Is this to do with what happened last night in Hayes Valley?"

A chill went down my back.

"How do you know about that?"

There was another pause, and Marlowe didn't answer the question.

"Do not leave your apartment and do not respond to any other incoming calls. Read the Worker Daily."

The darkness shifted, and the connection went dead.

My pulse pounding in my ears now, I raised a shaky hand to the darkness and flicked it to the right. Everything spun, and when it settled again, a small desk appeared in front of me, with a screen that floated in nothingness above it. I had seen Marlowe do the same thing, except for him it was always a hefty old tome.

As I had the thought, the disembodied screen flickered and became book-like—almost like a sort of e-reader. I shook my head and waved my hand in alarm, and it quickly returned to its original form.

My pulse thumped loudly in my ears. It had been a long time since I'd done something like that.

The Phone Booth is part of the Space Between Spaces, technically—though a walled-off pocket of it safeguarded by the Guild. When a Worker's in there, he or she can shape it however they see fit, save for restrictions that make it impossible to summon a Terror or any of the other baddies we deal with. Wrathful, Predators, Spyders, the Envious… all the things that end up becoming the wide variety of Blissful legends and nightmares we've largely wiped out. Those things still pop up when enough Blissful believe in them and bring them out of the Space Between Spaces, but Workers aren't allowed to summon them.

That was when I remembered the symbol on the candle in the house in Hayes Valley.

Someone had *summoned* that Terror.

And gotten away with it.

It wasn't out of the realm of possibility that it was a prank gone wrong. Like I keep saying, some Workers aren't… all there. It's happened before that people have played tricks on unsuspecting Blissful. There's been a whole rash of it recently in the younger generation—it started when they realized they could post the reactions on social media and go viral. The Guild cracked down on the most egregious examples, but you still see it pop up, especially with people who manage to stay anonymous. The WOTW (Workers of the West) do what they can, but it's never enough.

For the moment, I put the thought out of my mind. I was too tired to think about it, and I didn't want to follow where it led. At least not yet. If it had been an intentional manifestation instead of just a Terror pulled in accidentally by the family…

"Nope, not thinking about it," I said.

I focused back on the floating screen. I swiped a finger across it, and a common OS desktop appeared. Again, that was unique to me. It just makes the most sense to my brain to interact with the Feed the way I'd interact with a laptop. Like I said, Marlowe sees it as a book. One Zoomer I've done jobs with before claims he gets a TikTok scroll.

I pulled up the Worker Feed. The Feed is the gateway to all news related to the Worker world, both local and global. You don't have to be in the Phone Booth to access it—a Worker can pull the Feed up just about anywhere—but it's nice to have it there where there are no distractions.

The stuff that shows up on the Feed is a mix of real-world news and everything you wouldn't be able to find in a Blissful newspaper. You can definitely find some of it on Twitter (now X, I guess?) and Reddit, maybe even Substack, but those all get scrubbed every other day by some full-time WOTW member whose job it is to maintain the Separation.

You can find just about anything on the Feed, though. Bulletins submitted by Workers looking to sell things they can't (or shouldn't) sell to the Blissful, requests for services, announcements, questions, answers to deep Worker lore, and, most importantly for what I needed at that moment, the Worker Daily, which is really the only universal Worker newspaper.

I opened it, tapped the news section, and there, front and center, was the story to which Marlowe must have been referring.

I put my face in my hands and swore. I ate the last large bite of my toast and took another fortifying swig of coffee. The food and caffeine were helping, but it was going to be a long day.

The piece was headed by a picture of the Painted Lady in Hayes Valley—or at least the mangled state I'd left it in after banishing the Terror. The whole front door as well as half of the front-facing facade had been blown off and lay strewn in smoking pieces across the street. The gaping hole further exposed the destruction I'd done to the interior of the house, and there was also clearly a portion of the roof missing where I'd pulled the lightning down.

In a typical job, I would have cleaned all of that up, including wiping the minds of the family and disposing of the candle. But, obviously, I hadn't been able to do that this time around.

Across the image, superimposed in bright gold letters, were the words "Terror Clean-up Gone Wrong—Accident or Stunt?"

"Fuzzy shit balls," I muttered, turning away from the article and running my free hand vigorously through my dirty, matted hair.

"Perhaps not the most eloquent summary, but certainly does capture the essence."

I spun and clapped eyes on a late middle-aged man in gold-rimmed glasses who was watching me from about a dozen feet away. He was illuminated by a sourceless light that came from above and before him, and I knew he was seeing me the same way. There did not appear to be anything around him, which was typical—you can only ever see the person, not their surroundings, in a Phone Booth. Otherwise, I would look like I was surrounded by a number of slightly crooked shelves and an embarrassing lack of spare towels.

"Marlowe," I said, gesturing to the news bulletin. "I don't—I can't—"

"I know," he said. He took a few steps forward and stopped. It was as close as he could come—for whatever reason, you can't get closer than about six feet to another person in a Booth. He adjusted his glasses and then smoothed his vest. Despite the early hour, he was already wearing gray slacks, a freshly pressed button down, a vest, and smart brown Oxfords with a broguing pattern on them. His gray hair had been combed back so that it left his forehead clear, though it stuck up slightly in the back.

The only concession he seemed to have made to the early hour was that he did not have on a tie and had left the top button of his shirt undone.

"Have you started sleeping in that?" I asked.

"Do not change the subject," Marlowe said.

"So yes, you slept in it."

"Tell me what happened, Cicero."

I took a deep breath and did.

The first part of the story was easy to tell. It was an almost routine case, up until the dying part. After that, though, was when things got interesting.

"And then... " I faltered. I knew that Marlowe knew that there was something more, and that if I didn't tell him, the old bastard would call me on it. I also knew that once I said it out loud it would be real. Once I said what had happened, even though I in no way had intended it to happen, did not even know how it had happened, there was no going back.

Marlowe didn't prompt me, though. He just watched me, with his sharp eyes staring out from behind his gold-rimmed glasses. His grizzled eyebrows were drawn in concentration, and all of his considerable intellect was clearly trained on me.

It was Marlowe. I had to tell him. If I couldn't tell him… then I had bigger problems.

"And then one of the claws detached and fell. It speared me, right through the chest." I indicated the spot with my hand, and as I did I remembered the sensation and winced slightly, though there was no pain left. "I knew it was bad. Right away. I knew it was really bad. I fell, and then everything went black. And I…"

I looked at Marlowe again, looked him straight in the eye.

"And then I woke up in a morgue. I woke up on an autopsy table, right before they were about to start cutting."

Something flickered behind Marlowe's eyes, and the man blinked. He paused for a moment before responding, and it was clear to me that he was trying to keep his composure. "Tell me now and tell me true. Did you do anything to intentionally make this happen?"

I breathed in and out, licked my lips, and once more looked Marlowe straight in the eye. "I have not, nor will I ever, seek the Dark or the Old. I have always only ever wanted to Work, and it is more than enough for me. I did not do this intentionally."

Marlowe continued to watch me, and I felt like I was a small boy again. He hadn't looked at me that way since he had passed me from Worker training and told me I was ready to test for my Work Cert. Hell, even before that; the last time I can remember was when he caught me in a lie about a Working I'd done as a teenager to steal some of his booze.

That penetrating stare had left such an impression on me that I hadn't lied to him since.

"I believe you," he said finally.

I let out a massive breath I hadn't realized I'd been holding. I then took several more, shakily and too quickly.

"Stay calm," Marlowe said. "We need to decide what to do next."

"I'm not crazy, am I?" I asked. "I—I didn't mean to do it, I swear. You can check all my tattoos, I don't have anything that could—"

"I don't need to check them," Marlowe said. "I believe you. When you woke—what do you remember? How did you arrive at your apartment?"

"I... Marlowe, John McMillin was at the morgue. And someone else, a woman I don't know. She sounded official, though."

Something else occurred to me, something that I hadn't put together at the time but that, looking back, stuck out quite obviously. "I think… she was giving him orders, actually."

"Did they identify you? Did they see your face?""

"No. And I had no identification on me that the Blissful could use, I sent my wallet and my phone back to the apartment with my work stuff. It's all on my bed. But they know I went after the contract—I claimed it and confirmed it, Marlowe."

"They know you claimed the contract, but they do not know you were at the house last night," he said. "If you were not identified, then McMillin was likely there to do so, as much as to confirm your death. But before we continue, please, let me help you. Turn around and hold still."

He held up a hand and I knew what he was offering. I nodded, turned around, and looked straight up into the black void, exposing the back of my head.

A wave of cool relief washed over me, and then I felt the cuts and bruises from my fight with the Terror begin to itch. They wriggled and then began to close, seemingly on their own. It was a maddening sensation, like icy-cold sunscreen getting sprayed all over your body, but I forced myself to hold still until it passed.

"Thanks," I said, turning back. Like I said earlier (I think I said it—well, if not, I'm saying it now) Marlowe's a Stitcher, which is the Worker version of a doctor. He's a doctor in real life, too, and that's how he discovered his ability to Work, healing things that should have been impossible to heal. He's semi-retired now, but he still has a private practice and teaches and works with a bunch of groups around the Bay. He has special permission to Work on the Blissful who seek him out in his clinical practice under special supervision, and he provides the same service to Workers when they need it.

"It's been a long time since I've had to do that for you," Marlowe said softly. Almost sadly, it seemed.

"I know," I replied. "Did you find anything?"

Marlowe shook his head. "No. There is no evidence of any foreign tampering. No Work clings to you, nor any evidence of the Terror. For all intents and purposes, you have always been alive. If you hadn't told me otherwise, I would not have known you had died last night."

I remember feeling disappointed. I'd been hoping that he'd find some sort of clue buried somewhere deep inside me that would help start to unravel what was going on.

"Back, then, to the matter at hand," Marlowe said. "They know you claimed the job, but they do not know that you are the Worker who was there last night."

"You said that—who else would have been there, though?"

"I am certain that they think it was you. But they do not know. Come, read the article again. Quickly, please."

I did, speeding through the details.

"Result of a contract gone wrong... claimed the previous evening... no identified suspects. Christ, you're right—there aren't any names."

"Language," Marlowe said. "Now, this is your way through. We need to buy time to understand what has happened, and time to establish plausible deniability."

"If I wasn't there last night, then where—?"

"You were visiting with me," Marlowe said smoothly. "You left work and instead of 'porting to Hayes Valley, you came to visit me, before returning to your apartment. You have just woken up and are on your way to work."

I was too tired to fully take it in, but Marlowe isn't some criminal mastermind. The fact he had a plan ready to go to explain away illegal activity should have rang some alarm bells for me. It didn't, though—at least not immediately.

"They'll know I didn't go through the lobby," I said. "They'll poke holes in that story as soon as they get access to the footage."

"If the footage is intact, then yes. But it will take them time. And with time we may replace it, or think of something else."

"But I can't go to work anyway," I said. "I need sleep. I'm a zombie. Literally. But also, you know, figuratively. If I go into work I'll fall on my face halfway through the day."

"Yes," Marlowe said grimly. "Well, we will have to ensure that you do not. But you must promise me that you will come to me as soon as you can, once you have made an appearance. And that you will not look into this any further without speaking with me first."

"But I—what if they come find me at work?" I asked.

"Then you answer their questions with what I just said. You came to see me. We spoke about old times, and you wanted to brush up on Working techniques before going after the Terror. They can't place you at the house or the morgue. Go to work like you usually would, stay as long as you must, and then come straight to me. Will you promise to do that?"

Finally, I started to realize that there was something that I was missing.

"What do you know about all of this, Marlowe?" I asked.

He shook his head. "Not now."

"But you know something."

"Not now, Cicero."

My tired brain began catching up, the combination of food, caffeine, and Marlowe's Working helping me stumble back to some semblance of my normal cognitive abilities.

"Why aren't you surprised?" I asked. I put my coffee cup down on the desk, shook my head, and ran my hands through my hair again, thinking hard. "Why aren't you telling to go along with the enforcers? You always tell me to play by the rules. Why aren't you telling me to turn myself in and trust that this'll all get sorted out?"

Marlowe did not respond immediately, but something in his expression softened, and he looked at me with a worrying kind of sympathy.

"We have not spoken recently," he said. "There is… much to discuss."

"So tell me."

"We do not have time, Cicero."

"I just fucking died, Marlowe! Make time!"

Marlowe held up a hand to forestall any additional outbursts and spoke in a quick, firm tone that he had used a number of times with teenage me but never adult me. "I have told you I will not speak about it here. I know that this is much to take in. I do not know everything that is happening. But something is happening. And when you come to see me, we will discuss it. Right now we do not have the time to do so. You need to go to work. You need to live a normal day in your normal life, as if nothing has changed, to avoid drawing suspicion. It is of utmost importance. Do you understand me?"

For a moment I wavered on the edge of cursing at him again, but his tone and his demeanor were too serious. There really was something going on that I didn't understand.

"Fine," I said. "Fine. But how the hell am I going to make it through a workday? I barely made it back here. I haven't slept. The only reason I can stand right now is because I'm caffeinated, and that's not gonna last long."

Marlowe took a breath and then sighed. "There is a way."

It took me a minute, and then I realized what he was suggesting.

"No," I said. "No—the last time I—Marlowe, you were the one who told me never to do it again! You said it was like taking a handful of Adderall instead of just studying for the test!"

Marlowe continued to watch me grimly.

"No," I repeated. "You were right. There has to be something else."

"The last time it was improperly administered," Marlowe said. "My direct advice to you was that you should never use it without proper supervision. This time, you will have supervision, as well as proper embedding. The goal is to get you through this day with energy and to avoid any suspicions that might set you up for official questioning by the Workers of the West. The Guild is required to represent you, but that does not mean the WOTW will let this go. Unless you can think of a better option, I believe this to be best. You need to be seen at work, and you need to have all your wits about you in case they come to question you."

I shook my head in disbelief. "Marlowe, why are you doing this? You don't need to be involved. Maybe I should just turn myself in. Isn't that the right thing to do? Isn't that—?"

"No!"

He said the word so forcefully that I actually took a startled step back. If we had been in a real room, the word would have echoed. He was looking at me with an unnerving intensity. His lips were drawn tight in a thin line. He looked upset with himself, but also as if he were fighting some kind of internal battle.

A sharp buzz interrupted the moment. The buzz became a faint, repetitive ringing. We both looked back behind me, toward where the door to my linen closet was in reality.

"My alarm," I said. "Seven."

I turned back. "Marlowe, you're really starting to freak me out."

He looked to be standing on the edge of a mental precipice trying to convince himself to step off, but unable to do so. Finally, he grimaced and shook his head, clearly agitated.

"Come to me this afternoon," he said.

I wanted to protest again, but something in his lined face ended the conversation. I glanced again at the Feed—at the glowing article.

"They are considering it a suspected Raising," Marlowe said. I looked back at him—he had followed my gaze to the floating screen. And just like he'd always seemed able to do, he'd astutely read my mind. "There is a reason it is forbidden. And there is a reason no one attempts it now that it has been banned."

"But I didn't attempt it! It just happened! What I did was impossible. Something went seriously wrong, and I need someone to help me with it. The Guild will—"

"If you are convicted, the Guild will turn you over to the Workers of the West. You will be given to a special group of men who will take you to a special room, out of and into which no one can 'port. Once you are in that room, all who know you will forget you. Inside that room, they will dismantle you, piece by piece. They will take those pieces and burn and disfigure their edges so that they cannot be sewn back together. They will then enclose those pieces in threefold boxes of oak, lead, and slate, and carry the boxes to the ends of the earth, where they too will be burned. What ashes and slag remain will then be mixed with the blood of animals, and the mixture will be spread across the world's oceans."

I stared at him in horror.

"That's—that's not... Marlowe, what are you talking about?"

"You have stumbled on something I wish you never had," he said, and I was further shocked to see his eyes welling with emotion. "Cicero, you must trust me. Please. I would not wish that fate on my worst enemy, and you are far, far more dear to me than that. Come to me this afternoon. I will explain all that I can. But for now, you must escape suspicion. Do you understand me?"

I stared at him, trying desperately to process what was happening.

It couldn't be true. I hadn't done anything!

But... Marlowe. This was Marlowe. This was the man who had taken me in off the streets. Fed and clothed me. Brought me back to being something like an actual person. Brought me back to sanity.

I trusted him. I had to.

"Okay," I said aloud. "Okay. But tonight, you tell me everything."

A visible wave of relief washed over the older man's face. "Yes. After the mania has worn off and you have the rest your body needs. You remember what will happen?"

"Yes," I said, bracing myself. "You really think this is a good idea?"

"I think it is the best idea we have," Marlowe said, frowning. "Remember, you have not seen the news, you are unaware of what has happened. We will embed you with the right phrasing, and that should be enough. I know of no other way to get you through your day. And, should you be confronted, no other way to help you fortify your mind, not if you are as exhausted as you look."

"I'm even more exhausted than I look."

"Then this is the way," Marlowe said. "They may very well come for you at work. The fact they have not made it to your apartment means that there is still some doubt and they do not have Guild permission to apprehend you. For all that the Guild can be troublesome, they hold to the Workers' Rights and will stymie the WOTW without direct evidence of your presence at the house last night, which it would appear they do not have. Remember the story—you consulted with me, and then you went home. Fill in the gaps with your regular nightly routine. We don't have much time. Cling to this phrasing: I will have a normal day. Embed it in your thoughts. Remember how important that is."

He reached behind his back, back into his reality, and pulled out a thin mahogany cane with an ornate head. One of his conduits, to aid the golden spectacles he wore.

"Be safe," he said. "Be careful. And stay alive this time."

Not as reassuring as I think he wanted it to be.

Part Six

High as a Hoe, it's off to Work I Go

I need to explain what a mania Working is.

If you know what mania is, you're halfway there. For those who don't, it's an elevated mood that makes you feel like you can't do anything wrong. Like everything is exciting. Like there are golden, shining moments of possibility waiting to be discovered under every rock and around every river bend. Or, you know, under every cracked coffee mug and around every grimy street corner, since this is more of an urban story.

A mania Working then is something that produces an artificial version of mania. It isn't strictly forbidden but it's... let's say 'frowned upon'.

Remember, the primary law all Workers can't break is the Separation, a strict mandate to keep everything we do secret unless officially sanctioned. Anything that breaks that law is a criminal offense.

That being said, anything that doesn't *technically* break that law (or the other major Worker laws about, you know, killing people and other fairly obviously bad stuff) is *technically* legal.

There's a whole subclass of Workings that falls into that category. A lot of good stuff. And a mania Working is one of them.

I can't remember mania Workings being a big thing before a decade or so ago when I was in Blissful college. I'm sure Workers have used a version of them throughout history, though. I mean, if Isaac Newton wasn't using it to dream up all of Calculus then I'm a ham sandwich.

But it's the Worker equivalent of Adderall, or speed, or your favorite brand of methamphetamine. It'll boost you up, but, if you aren't careful, it'll smack you right back down when it wears off. And things can go off the rails real quick. The only time I've ever used it before this past week was to pull an all-nighter for a big final exam.

To be fair, I did ace the exam.

But I also banged the TA proctoring it in a janitor's closet afterwards, and then set fire to a small tree outside the lecture hall on a dare.

The TA had a jock boyfriend who was less than thrilled. I almost got expelled for the tree. I had to hide from the lacrosse team for the rest of the semester and I was on academic probation for suspected arson.

Lessons were learned.

I also crashed hard when it finally wore off, back at Marlowe's place, where I was living at the time. And on the way back there, I'd for some reason gone down Clement Street, bought a live chicken, plucked it, and set it free in Marlowe's garden. I tried to deny said buying and plucking upon waking, but given I was covered in incriminating feathers like some medieval ne'er-do-well, you could say I'd officially fowled myself.

That was a good pun. Don't pretend it wasn't.

What I hadn't done on that occasion was embed a proper guiding principle. I'd gone with 'I will succeed in all my endeavors', which sounds harmless enough but is way too broad and unspecific. Hence the successful seduction of a coupled-up TA in addition to acing a very tricky Stats exam. Which, by the way, no one else aced, so it looked like I'd cheated my way through it, and I had to retake the damn thing anyway.

It did ensure that both I and the TA 'succeeded in our endeavors' several times whilst in said closet, though. She asked a few people to give me her number. A large part of why I had to hide from her boyfriend for the rest of the semester.

Just some things to keep in mind if you ever have a chance to give a mania Working a go.

Marlowe made me swear not to use it again, and never to put any such Working on myself instead of having someone else do it for me. He's the straight-and-narrow type. You can see some of that based on our last interaction. Which makes the fact that it was he who recommended the mania Working this time around… well, it shows you how serious he thought the situation was.

But also, he's a doctor. And if a doctor tells you to take some fun-time meds… well fuck it, let the good times roll.

So, when I left the Phone Booth that morning, I was running through life like I'd done enough coke to kill an elephant. Not a small elephant either, but one of the big ones that knock down trees and have tusks the size of pythons.

I was *amped*.

I was showered, shaved, and dressed within ten minutes. And as a bonus, I made the bed and threw all the dirty dishes in the sink.

My work bag had indeed ended up on the bed, just as I'd told Marlowe and just as I'd intended when I'd sent it home before the trip to Hayes Valley. I checked it, repacked it with a couple of extra folders, and then slid it over to the front door. I made and drank one more cup of coffee, though I definitely didn't need it.

I had to, you see. Drink more coffee. It was part of my usual morning routine, and I had promised to have a normal day and do my usual routine. At that point, of course, I couldn't remember who I'd promised that to or even why I'd promised it, but those details were unimportant. The promising itself was what mattered.

I touched the tattoo on my upper right arm, the one that allows me to manipulate my appearance. Instead of relaxing it, I mentally contracted it, like a muscle. Slowly, the office-based persona of Cicero James flowed over me. My eyesight blurred and I put my glasses on. My shoulders dropped slightly, and I gained a few pounds of desk-bound office-worker flab. My leather jacket became a drab gray peacoat, and my boots became brown Oxfords. My t-shirt morphed into a respectable button-up.

You might be asking if I needed to change my appearance. I didn't—and I don't, technically, ever need to. But everything Workers do is about belief. And the easiest way to hide in plain sight is to believe you are hidden in plain sight. And the easiest way for me to do that is to believe I'm a nerdy analyst with nothing to hide except maybe a stash of weed gummies. And the easiest way to believe that is to look like a nerdy analyst with nothing to hide except maybe a stash of weed gummies.

Despite the change, I stepped out into the hall feeling lighter than air. There was no fatigue left in my body. The very thought of fatigue was a distant memory.

I could do anything. It was a beautiful day outside. I hadn't been to Sutro Tower in ages, the view from there is gorgeous and—

No. Normal day.

I locked my door and walked purposefully down the hall to the elevator, a peppy pepped-up pep in my step. I pushed the call button and waited patiently. I looked at the digital icon above the elevator; it was at one.

Flick.

The number now said five.

Huh, that had happened fast.

A bell dinged; the doors opened; I walked inside.

Someone called out to me from down the hall to hold the door. That seemed like something I would agree to do as part of normal life, so I held out a hand. The shouter rounded the corner; it was a young woman named Anandini. She saw me and paused awkwardly, as if thinking about taking the next elevator. She grimaced and joined me anyway.

Anandini lives on my floor, at the other end of the corridor. She's a software engineer at a local tech company and a second-generation immigrant with very proud Indian parents I met once in that same elevator. I gave them a recommendation for a dinner spot around the corner. They knocked on my door later that evening and gave me an excessively large mug of chai in thanks, along with explicit instructions on how to correctly drink said chai. It was quite endearing, actually. And her dad, Dev, has a simply glorious mustache.

That's not why things were awkward, though. Things were awkward because Anandini and I had been enjoying vigorous, casual adult exercise sessions together at irregular but satisfying intervals, and when her parents found out about it the next morning—try keeping anything from an Indian parent when they really want to know something, I dare you—they returned to scold me in very harsh terms and demand I return the chai. They swore to find her a nice Indian boy, forbade me from recommending either her or them any further restaurants, and Anandini and I hadn't spoken since.

"Hi, CJ," she said, with a false cheeriness that I would have picked up on at any other time. She left it there and we lapsed into what would have been an awkward silence if I'd been in the right mind to remember that it made sense for there to be an awkward silence.

"Good morning," I said brightly. "Great day, isn't it? I think I'm going to have a normal day."

Her eyebrows rose slowly up her forehead, and she turned to examine me with a strange look. I had to stop myself from checking to see if I had suddenly morphed into a sea urchin. It made no sense to check for that anyway, because why would I have morphed into a sea urchin, you know? It's not what I would have done on a normal day, and I was having the normalest of normal days.

Surprised—she looked surprised. But also concerned? I couldn't tell. My grasp on emotions, usually fairly good, was in that moment absolutely horrendous.

I began to rock back and forth on my heels. Not so much that I looked like a crazy person, but enough that it was clearly noticeable. I realized that this was a non-normal thing to do and thought that a good compromise would be to clasp my hands behind my back while I swayed. Because normal people do that, right? And so I did that, even though it made me look like an overgrown child waiting eagerly for a ride at Disneyland.

"How... have you been?" Anandini asked.

The part of me that's the usual me was now just a tiny node of consciousness way in the back of my brain. That little node finally managed to send a flare up to the manic me to remind him that this situation should be supremely awkward. The tiny me couldn't share more than that, though, because it was so small and had used up all its effort of will, and it went back to sleep.

"I'm gooood," I said, nodding. Then I realized I was still nodding several seconds later and decided I should stop. I couldn't, however, stop myself from saying, "How've you been? Gone down to the gym since the last time?"

Her mouth opened slightly, and she blinked several times.

"Anandini.exe has failed," I said, pointing at her and winking. "Need a hard reboot, I think."

She stared at me for a full second and then barked out a laugh that seemed to surprise her as much as it surprised me. "Yeah, I guess."

The elevator dinged and the light for the ground floor lit up.

"Gotta go do my normal routine," I said, moving toward the door, completely oblivious as to the situation I had just created. "What are you doing this weekend?"

Something in the back of my mind twinged again—the little me. Really annoying. Had I said something wrong? I didn't think so. I was just being polite. That little voice was just a nuisance.

"Oh—I—uh… I'm busy tonight, but—"

"Maybe catch you in the gym again?"

She blushed slightly. "Uh—yeah, maybe." She seemed to catch hold of herself then and said, "Maybe you see me at Alchemist instead. You go there, right?"

"Yeah, definitely go there," I said, remembering the bar. "Usually Fridays."

The elevator doors opened. I walked through.

"Have a good day!" I called back over my shoulder. I caught one last glimpse of her watching me, bemused, and I felt that small twinge again, but I brushed it aside. I couldn't be diverted now, I had important office things to go and do on this normal Friday.

On Fridays, I usually take an Uber to work instead of the bus. I pulled my phone out and opened the app. The driver was already approaching. That was funny—I must have called him when I was upstairs in the apartment. I couldn't remember doing it. Oh well.

The guard at the security desk waved and said good morning.

Flick.

I was in the Uber, and we were pulling up to the Protoline building.

A ping came up again from my lower self. That shouldn't have happened. I wasn't supposed to be losing time like that. But before I could focus on it as something that needed addressing, I was getting out of the Uber, thanking the driver, and walking toward the building.

I didn't see anyone I knew on my way in and up the stairs, for which I am now, looking back, very grateful. I usually avoid the elevator and take the stairs to get some extra exercise before sitting at a desk all day long, so it was in keeping with my "normal" routine.

Got to the Protoline floor, dropped off my bag. Pulled out my laptop. Whistled part of the theme song to the sitcom "New Girl". Messed it up and decided to turn it into the theme song from "Friends". Then I did the clapping bit to the "Friends" theme and lost the train of it all and started smacking my lips to make small, wet popping noises.

An alarm went off on my phone. It was a reminder that said "9 am—Golden Gate".

Was I supposed to be at the Golden Gate Bridge???

Oh, no. Oh no no no no no.

Little me nudged big me, and I remembered it was the name of a conference room.

Right. Of course.

I left my desk holding my laptop and went to the conference room titled "Golden Gate", where we did the Friday analytics meetings, at which I was supposed to present.

Once I was there, I looked at my watch, which now looked like a simple, sturdy Timex again. It read 8:23 am. The meeting was at 9, that was what the reminder had been for.

Guess I'll wait.

FLICK.

I jerked violently as though I'd fallen from a great height. I caught myself on the arms of the conference room chair I was now sitting in.

I looked down—my watch now read 8:50 am. I looked up and blinked several times. The lights in the office had come on fully, and people were moving around outside. A twinge of panic came from somewhere deep inside me that I couldn't understand.

The time between 8:23 and 8:50 had not been necessary; I had done a minor Working to skip it.

I was Working when I shouldn't be.

Panic rose in me again, but big me quashed it.

Something's wrong you need to figure out what is wrong what is…

I had no cares or worries. All was well with life and the world. I was having a normal day.

I looked out the window. What a nice day! I smiled broadly.

I stood up from where I'd been sitting, opened my laptop, logged in, and connected to the screen display that would show my slide deck. I then walked over to the door and opened it.

Arick, my boss, was outside, talking animatedly with Erica, my office crush, and two other young women. He seemed to be telling a story, and I felt a pang of annoyance. With the clarity of mania, though, I took in the expressions on the faces of the young women and realized that they were actually interested in what he was saying. I looked at Arick, and the vision of my boss shifted. The man was balding, in his early

50s, and 30 pounds overweight. He also stood straight, dressed well, had no self-consciousness about any of the first three things I had listed, and truly seemed to enjoy life. He was telling his story with animated language that was engaging and persuasive.

I walked over to the group and watched him, fascinated.

"And then," Arick said, "we went over the side of the rapids, and, oh my God, I was scared shitless. I swear, I almost dove over the side myself. My wife was laughing her ass off!"

The two women I didn't know laughed and nodded encouragingly; Erica saw me and gestured for me to join them.

"What happened then?" I heard myself ask.

Arick turned, saw me, and immediately opened the circle to bring me in. "Oh, James!" he exclaimed. "Perfect timing, you'll love this—"

The elevator dinged, and the doors slid open. Three people walked out slowly but assuredly, looking around the office as if trying to memorize it.

Little me knew immediately who they were.

Big mania me thought, "Oh look, people!"

John McMillin was the first out of the elevator, and he bore a large bruise on the side of his face right where I'd hit him with the memory wipe the night before. Beside him was another man I knew, though who had not been on the scene last night. Or perhaps he had been and I just hadn't seen him. His name was Jamal Henry, and he was another enforcer. He was tall, black, clean-cut, and the kind of in-shape that you notice regardless of clothing. He and McMillin were both wearing button-down shirts and dark slacks. Fancier than you usually see in a tech office, outside of the Finance department, but not so fancy that they stood out completely.

I'd run into Jamal Henry a few times while working for the Guild and had actually done a job with him and a few others about a year before, the last group job I'd done. I liked him, despite my general suspicion of all Workers, particularly enforcers and WOTW reps. Even before I somehow died and came back, I'd always been leery about interacting with enforcers. Call it a guilty conscience. I'd had my fair share of run-ins with Blissful cops when I was younger, before I started Working, and that wariness had transferred to Worker enforcers.

Behind them was a woman. She looked to be mid-30s, was of middling height at best, and had auburn-brown hair cut short and brushed out of her face in a way that emphasized clean, low-maintenance function over form. She wore a pantsuit and functional heels that wouldn't have looked out of place on an exec in the exact building in which we were standing. She was also strikingly thin, so much so that her cheekbones stood out prominently and she looked almost gaunt. If she were a hundred pounds soaking wet, I'd have been surprised.

She swept an unblinking gaze over the office as she walked out of the elevator. From that gaze alone, I had no doubt that she was in charge, despite the near-foot difference in her height and the men's, and the nearly one hundred pounds of muscle Jamal had on her.

McMillin was the first to notice me. He paused and his eyes widened, and then he nudged Jamal and motioned my way. Jamal nodded and took the lead, McMillin and the woman falling in behind him.

Arick, Erica, and the other two women were all staring at the new arrivals.

"Good morning," Henry said.

Another twinge of anxiety bubbled up and popped from the little me sitting somewhere in my subconscious. Big me again ignored it. I was performing my routine. This was nothing more than a typical Friday. I had no idea why these three people were there. I knew McMillin and Jamal, but I wouldn't have expected them to be here today, and I'd act as if I didn't know them since we were around Blissful. I hadn't done anything strange last night. I had gone home, talked with Marlowe, gotten a good night's rest, and now was ready to give my presentation before going to work a job in Hayes Valley.

"Hi there," Arick said, gregariously striding forward and extending a hand. The contrast between him and Jamal was fascinating. It was like seeing the leads of a cop show and a tech mockumentary meet in a weird crossover episode.

"You folks look lost, can I help direct you?" Arick asked.

"I think we're in the right place, actually," Jamal said, shifting his gaze to me. I looked back, confused, and let a small amount of anxiety bubble up to my face. That was what would happen naturally, after all. That's what I'd be thinking on a normal day—why were they there for me? Why would enforcers ever be at my place of work in broad daylight?

"Here about the conference?" I asked, making something up on the spot. The words came out of my mouth before I could give them any thought, and once they were out I thought they would more or less do.

Jamal's brow furrowed for a brief moment—not in confusion, but in concentration. He was examining me, silently, and it looked like he wasn't seeing what he'd expected.

"Yes. The conference."

It was the female Worker who had spoken, and I knew immediately from the voice it was the same woman from the morgue the night before. Jamal took a step back, ceding her the floor. She did not move forward to take Arick's proffered hand, and he caught the hint and dropped it.

"We're sorry to barge in like this, but we've been talking with Mr. James about the Modern Analytics conference in December, we were just in the building to see a few clients. Figured we'd drop in and see if there's a way to convince him it's worth coming to. He managed to escape from us the last time, but we're dying to have him."

Well. How cheeky of her.

She locked eyes on me, and a pang of warning came from little me, and this time big me definitely agreed. It wasn't a Worker thing. Sometimes you just meet people that you know right away are going to either get their way or make your life hell until they do.

"Ahhh," Arick said. This was something he could completely understand. He was a former Sales rep, and a very successful one. I'd be willing to bet rather heavily that he'd done the drop-in prospecting we-happened-to-be-here sales pitch dozens of times himself. "I appreciate the hustle! I'm Arick Anderson, I didn't catch your names?"

McMillin and Jamal introduced themselves.

"Mallory," the woman said. "Mallory Shrike."

This time she did step forward and shake Arick's hand, and as she did another ding went off in my head, but this time it came from neither small me nor big me. It was something external. I couldn't figure out what it was, though.

"We're actually about to head into a meeting," I said, looking at my watch. "Maybe we do this afterward? Arick, do you think—?"

I stopped. Arick's light blue eyes had glazed over slightly, and there was a very slight hint of deep color in them. Almost… violet. It flashed and then disappeared.

They dropped hands. Arick smiled broadly and waved vaguely. "Oh no, no need to worry about that, James. I have enough to catch up on with Kumar and Joshua today. You said the deck's all set up?"

I nodded. "Yes, but didn't you want to go over—?"

"It's fine, it's fine," he said, waving again. All kinds of alarm bells were going off in my head, and little me was making a lot of noise that was confusing big me. This wasn't normal anymore. Arick always wanted me to open the meeting—he'd had me open the meeting every Friday since he'd taken over the manager role. And he always had a dozen questions about the numbers. Good questions, actually. He couldn't put the numbers together himself, but he knew what they meant, and his tech bro demeanor dropped away as soon as we were sitting in a conference room looking at them together.

"Are you sure?"

"Yes, completely! Just come in when you're done. You'll bring him back in one piece?"

"I don't know if we can promise that," the woman said.

"Hah!" Arick said. "All right, at least leave the juicy bits for me, OK?"

"Certainly," she said, flashing her lips-only smile once more.

I was watching Arick carefully, but nothing else about his demeanor had changed. The strange color is his eyes had not reappeared, and his hard-charging gregarious affability had not been blunted in the slightest.

"Get a good deal out of 'em, James," he said, with a heavily exaggerated wink. "Oh, and we have Kumar on deck for a speaker position, if you're looking for someone. Our resident Data Scientist. Spoke last year at Dreamforce."

"Mmm," the woman—Shrike—said.

"All right then," Arick said, clapping his hands together and rubbing them quickly. "Gotta get in there."

He walked over to the room I'd set up. Two other men were in there now, Ben and Timothy, and they had dialed in the aforementioned Kumar and Joshua on the large conference room screen at the end of the table. Kumar, who had just returned from a trip back home, had a cheerful Zoom background of an Indian town behind him.

Erica and the two women I didn't know headed back to their desks. Erica caught my eye as she left, and there was a question there, with a note of concern. I smiled calmly back at her, shook my head in a 'don't worry about it—not a big deal' kind of way, and then turned back to Jamal and McMillin, who were watching me with neutral, stony expressions that looked like they'd been lifted out of a Law and Order episode.

"Is there a place we can talk?" Jamal asked. McMillin was glaring at me sullenly, and I realized that they had agreed to let Jamal take the lead. I don't think McMillin had forgiven me yet for the bruise, even though he wouldn't remember me giving it to him.

Normal day. What would happen on a normal day if this was going on?

Easy. Play along. I'm innocent.

"Oh. Yeah. How about Potrero Hill?"

I gestured with my thumb toward another conference room on the other side of the common working space that was dark and empty. A few more people had filtered into the office by then and were looking curiously at the two tall men and the smartly dressed Mallory Shrike.

"That works," Jamal said.

He started walking, and McMillin lagged behind, waiting for me. I fell in behind Jamal, and McMillin and Mallory Shrike fell in behind me.

A moment of panic threatened to overwhelm me, but then Marlowe's Working took over again and all emotion washed away, down the drain that led to the small me, who was no doubt drowning but who I couldn't be particularly bothered with at the moment.

This was no problem. I was an eager and attentive member of the Guild. I was helpful. I wanted to see what was the matter and help them do their jobs. Hell, maybe there was a job in it for me, after all. Another contract, another opportunity to Work.

Flick.

We were in the conference room, and I was sitting on the far side of the desk. McMillin was pulling the blinds across the window.

Fuck. Fuck fuck fuck fuck—what the hell is happening???

It was getting easier to silence the buzzing.

I'd had a steak sandwich last night for dinner. I'd watched an episode of The Office in the background. I'd done a load of laundry. Marlowe and I had spoken about what to remember when approaching a Terror that's grabbed hold of a physical building. I'd gone to bed. I hadn't slept well, though, but that's life sometimes, you know?

"Jamal," I said. "It's been a minute."

"It has," he replied shortly. His tone was polite, but he wouldn't meet my eyes.

"Not since that sinkhole that opened up near Coit Tower, right?"

"I think that's about right, Cicero," he said, leaning back cross-armed against the side of the door, conspicuously blocking the room's only exit. He did meet my eyes then, but his gaze was flat, just like his tone of voice. "Heard you've been keeping busy since then. Mostly solo jobs."

"Soured a bit on group Work after that one," I said. "Not a big fan of other people putting my life in jeopardy. But you know, takin' any contract I can find that lets me get my hands dirty. Just picked one up yesterday, actually, looking forward to getting to it tonight."

Immediately, everyone's gaze sharpened and locked onto me. McMillin had been adjusting himself in one of the chairs and froze; Mallory Shrike, standing at the head of the conference table, watched me with a veiled expression.

"Did I say something?" I asked, looking between them. "If I didn't, I think you might have all collectively just smelled a fart. Wasn't me, I promise."

Routine. All routine. I make jokes in tense and uneasy times.

"Mr. James," Shrike said, "did you check the news this morning?"

I paused as if considering this, then looked over at Jamal, then McMillin, and then back at her. "I did not, I was running late. Why? Something I can help with? Clean-up job?"

She watched me for a long moment and then walked slowly around the side of the conference table. Her steps were slow and deliberate, and her gaze stayed on me the entire time. It should have made me uncomfortable, and this is where I made my first real mistake. Because things were about to become very non-normal, and I was stuck in normal mode.

I smiled politely at her as she approached.

She pulled out the chair closest to me and slowly sat. She leaned forward, resting her hands on her knees, and continued to hold my gaze.

"You elected to take a Worker contract yesterday morning for a job near Alamo Square, correct?"

I continued smiling benignly, and let my eyebrows climb my forehead as if this were completely new to me.

No! No, it isn't completely new to you!
Huh?
You know about the job, idiot! YOU NEED TO GET THIS RIGHT!

Oh, right.

"I took the contract out, yes," I said. "It's open until tonight, right? Is it closed?"

Shrike glanced at McMillin. "Yes. It's closed."

I followed her look over to McMillin, and then looked over at Jamal, too, before focusing back on her. "Is that what this is about? Is something wrong with the contract?"

She watched me for a long moment.

"Mr. James, I'm going to need you to tell us where you were between the hours of 7 pm and 2 am last night."

I let my eyebrows rise again, and then I remembered Anandini's reaction in the elevator only about an hour earlier. That had been a good expression of surprise. I decided to use that.

I let my eyes go wide, blinked a few times, and let my mouth fall slightly open. I then closed it and put on a thinking expression, making sure to furrow my brow. Yes, that was good.

"I—well, I was here until six-thirty, I think, and then I went home."

"Home?" Shrike asked. I nodded, and she reached out with her right hand and flourished it. A folder appeared in her hand, slim but certainly not empty. I caught sight of my name marked on the cover. She set it down on the conference room table and flipped it open. "You live at 3280 Beale Street, apartment 525, correct?"

That was my real current address, not the old one.

"Yes," I said, careful to stumble just slightly over the answer.

Stick to your routine. Don't embellish. You have to get this right!

"I will," I said, rolling my shoulder and flicking my chin as if fighting off a small buzzing insect that wouldn't leave me alone.

I realized they were all staring at me.

"I will admit to having trouble sleeping," I said. "There's a presentation this morning..."

I looked down and sighed.

"Look, I need this job. It pays for living in the city, and I can't Work full-time. I'm having trouble sleeping, have been all week, and I went home last night to try and relax and psych myself up for the job today. I claimed the contract, but it was available until tonight, so I figured I'd do the presentation today and then hit it tonight when everything was off my mind. It's been a few weeks since the last contract I was able to claim, and I wanted to do this one right."

I looked back over at Henry. "You remember the last time, right, Jamal? I'm good at this kind of job. Terrors are my thing."

It was true. The last time I had worked with Jamal may have been the last time I'd worked with a full crew, but it was also a time I had saved the day. After one of the crew went crazy—like I mentioned, lost track of reality and started pulling stones and rebar out of the fucking buildings around us—I'd gotten trapped with the Terror all on my own inside Coit Tower, and I'd taken it down before the rest of them had even had a chance to get to me.

Jamal nodded and glanced at Shrike. "It's true," he said. "He did it by the book, and he did it basically single-handedly."

She took a moment to absorb this, and then she reached inside her coat and took something out of the inner breast pocket.

She set it on the table with a careful yet decisive movement. It was a piece of paper. Well, not really paper—it was more like parchment, which I've only ever seen in really old books that Marlowe keeps in his library. She pulled back her hand, leaving the folded parchment where she'd placed it. I looked blankly down at it, and then back up at her.

"You go antiquing?" I asked.

She was not diverted.

"You dropped your… thing," I said, pointing at it.

"Take it," Shrike said.

I hesitated for a moment, looking between her and the two men. None of them moved, but all of their eyes were focused on me. Jamal, at least, seemed to acknowledge that this was unusual with a small frown, so at least I wasn't the only one feeling that, but he didn't look like he was going to intervene. McMillin just kept boring holes in my head with his eyes.

I reached out to touch the parchment, and as I did the little me managed to nudge the big manic me hard enough that I realized I did not want to touch it.

I had my left hand out, the hand that has the tempest tattoo, which was currently hidden up my work sleeve and curled around my wrist and forearm. I let energy flow through the tattoo to the tips of my fingers. A glove of air encompassed my hand, thin enough to be practically invisible.

I held the page up, careful to do so in a way that didn't show the very slim barrier between my fingers and the parchment.

Nothing happened.

Both Shrike and McMillin seemed to deflate slightly.

I think in that moment I had them. Whatever that parchment was, it had to have been some kind of test, and I had gotten around it. There was a look in Shrike's eyes that said she thought that maybe this lead had been a waste of her time after all.

"Can I ask what's going on?" I said. "Did something happen?"

McMillin and Henry exchanged a look, but neither they nor Shrike answered the question.

"Can anyone corroborate your story about last night?" Shrike asked instead. The way she phrased it, though, made it seem like she was only going through the motions.

I scented victory. So I launched into the prepared spiel.

"I uh… I didn't have any company, if that's what you're asking," I said, intentionally being awkward. "But I did meet up with my old sponsor, Marlowe Frost. Sometime around eight, I think. Just to go over what I was planning. Like I said, I wanted to do it right, and he…"

I trailed off as a chill fell over the room that was entirely unanticipated. Shrike's attention sharpened and honed back in on me. She became very still, and I caught motion out of the corner of my eye. Had McMillin's hand moved closer to his side, where he kept his Ruiner?

It was clear that I was suddenly back up at the top of their suspect list, and I had no idea why. Little me started to panic, but big me refused to let it show in my face, just as Marlowe and I had intended with the mania Working.

Little me was overreacting. We were still doing great, Mania Me was sure of it.

"Marlowe Frost? The… renowned Stitcher?" Shrike asked. It felt like she had wanted to assign him a different label.

Huh. Well, that was surprising. She was interested in Marlowe?

He was weird this morning. He knows something about all of this.

"That's him," I said.

She examined me for another moment, then unlinked her hands and leaned back in her chair, crossing one thin leg over the other. I noticed as she did that one of her nails was a bright violet color, but only one of them. Looking at it made me feel strangely queasy, so I stopped.

"And what did you say you discussed?" she asked.

"The job," I repeated.

"I thought you said Terrors are your specialty? Why did you need to consult with Mr. Frost about a job involving one? Are you that close that you would consult him on a confidential Guild contract?"

I swallowed and cleared my throat. "This one looked like it was attached to a house. Tricky. Residential neighborhood—don't want anything to go wrong in a spot like that. So I wanted to be sure to get a second opinion. And he's my sponsor—and registered with the Guild. I… the contract didn't say anything about confidentiality."

"Mmm," Shrike said, noncommittally. "Talk about anything else?"

I cleared my throat again, and I started to realize that something was wrong. I don't know how long it had been growing, but finally the something that the little me had been yammering on about broke through to the big me.

SHE'S WORKING YOU!

I was getting… tired. That wasn't right. Even big me knew that wasn't right. I shouldn't be getting tired, the mania should last for another few hours at least.

Shrike's fingernail continued to shine with that strange violet light.

I could almost feel dark circles being drawn under my eyes. My head was becoming heavier and heavier. As the exhaustion of the night before began to wash over me, I tried desperately to hold on to the mania Working, but it slipped away. Abruptly, the big me and little me reversed, and the manic, happy-go-lucky CJ was replaced by the exhausted, panicking Cicero James.

She had sliced through Marlowe's Working. Either that or she had picked it apart as easily as a parent working out a knot in a child's shoelace.

"What did we... sorry?"

"Did you talk with Marlowe Frost about anything else, Mr. James?"

"Uh... well, work-life balance, I guess."

She raised an eyebrow.

"Work-life balance," she repeated, every syllable dripping with skepticism.

"Yeah," I said lamely. "Important."

Her eyes were spearing me. Anxiety began to eat me up, and doubts crept into my mind and nagged at me from the edges of my consciousness. Had I somehow given up the game? Was it something I'd said? Something I'd done?

"Is... the job still available?" I asked in a last-ditch attempt to continue sounding normal.

Shrike smiled slowly, the motion pulling her gaunt face weirdly sideways. "No. No, it isn't."

She nodded to McMillin, who, I realized far too late, had strapped on his Ruiner.

McMillin was out of his chair and in my face before I could even attempt to understand what was happening. He picked me up and slammed me face-down onto the tabletop, his Ruiner flaring with bright red light to lend him supernatural strength. My ring gave an echoing flare, trying to protect me, but it was still severely depleted—I'd forgotten in my haze that morning to refresh my Instruments—and the impact against the table clacked my teeth together and forced the breath out of my lungs in a sharp, devastating rush. I began coughing and gasping.

"Jesus Christ!" Jamal exclaimed. "McMillin! What the hell are you doing?!"

"Hold him," Shrike said coolly. "Henry, stand back."

Even though my cheek was pressed down hard against the tabletop, I was able to see through a watery haze of tears Jamal look between McMillin and Shrike, and then down at me. There was a clear look of shock in his eyes that said that he hadn't known this was going to happen and that he wanted it to stop immediately.

I knew I liked him.

Shrike ignored him, though, and instead walked around the side of the table so that she was even with my head. She was short enough that she was only a few inches away from me when she leaned over and said, softly, "You were so close. So close to convincing me that you aren't involved in all this. But then you said the one thing that made it impossible for me to believe you."

She leaned in closer and spoke right into my ear.

"You said, 'Marlowe Frost'."

That made no sense. That made no sense at all.

"What the hell do you want with Marlowe?" I managed to choke out. McMillin still had me pinned in place, his hand with the Ruiner now around the back of my neck so that all I could do was writhe around ineffectually in its grip. The glove, clearly replenished with energy since the night before, continued glowing bright red.

"McMillin, Shrike," Jamal said, sweat glistening on his forehead now in the dim office lighting. "Stop it. Right now. Let him up!"

"Be quiet, Henry," McMillin snarled.

"Let him up!" Jamal repeated. When neither McMillin nor Shrike responded, he strode forward and grabbed McMillin's shoulder.

Shrike skittered away from me. Something happened that I couldn't see, since McMillin was crushing my face down into the hard surface of the conference room desk. There was a sizzling sound and then the sharp smell of ozone.

A pause, a beat of silence, and then I heard the heavy sound of a body falling to the floor. As he fell, Jamal came back into my view.

His dark eyes were wide and staring; his mouth was slightly open.

For a really bad moment, I thought he was dead. The situation was so bizarre and unexpected that my body had gone into full fight-or-flight mode, and I was so pumped full of adrenaline, despite being held immobile, that I was beyond keyed up. I was so wired that I was biased toward assuming that everything was just the worst it could possibly be.

But then I realized that the enforcer was simply stunned. His eyes were glazed over and unfocused, but his chest was moving up and down.

The sound of Shrike's heels striking the solid floor as she rounded the table toward the downed enforcer filled the small room. She knelt, her clothing hanging loosely, and reached out a hand. She touched the center of his forehead with a thin finger.

The finger with the long violet nail.

It looked almost like a talon, now—it had grown from its original noticeable but inoffensive form into something several inches long. It was also now encrusted with previously concealed stones that sparkled with a brilliant intensity.

Conduit, I remember thinking. *It's her conduit.*

"You will forget," she said calmly. The talon flared with violet light, and the tiny, embedded gemstones sparkled.

Jamal moaned and rolled his head.

Shrike stood and took a step back. "Stand," she said. Though her finger was no longer touching Jamal's forehead, it flared again, and a small spot of bright white on Jamal's dark skin, the exact spot where she had touched him, flared in response.

Jamal obeyed, eyes still glazed over and mouth still hanging open. Once he was standing, she stepped closer again. "You will listen to Enforcer McMillin and obey his and my commands for the next hour. After that, you will go home and be ill with food poisoning until this evening. All you will remember is that McMillin and I correctly questioned the suspect Cicero James and that you had to leave early. You will report for work as usual at your next shift."

The light in her talon disappeared, and she staggered slightly, catching herself against the table. I knew the signs—the Working she had just performed had taken a huge amount of energy out of her, and she hadn't been able to draw it from one of her Instruments.

How the hell had she managed to do that to a full Worker?

Making someone do what you want—aside from being entirely illegal—is ridiculously difficult. It's a pure battle of wills. You're forcing a reality onto them in which they believe that they are completely yours to command. There're no half-measures with something like that. You break the person you're Working on, and you bind them to you for however long you want it to happen. Usually they bounce back, but not always.

It's easier to do to a Blissful, but aside from being, like I said, il-fucking-legal, it's nearly impossible to do to a Worker, especially one who's ready for it. She had to have caught Jamal in a moment of weakness, and she had to be very strong.

But you also need special tools for it. A special conduit.

It had to be the talon. I had never seen a conduit like that before—but then again, I was the only one I knew of who tattooed conduits onto my body instead of using an implement the way that old school Workers like Marlowe tell you to do it. There are no rules about that kind of thing—all that matters is that you believe in what you use enough for it to work.

And goddamn did she apparently believe in hers.

"Mr. James," Shrike said. Her face was slightly gray, and she was sweating, but her eyes remained bright and sharp and they drilled right into me. "Tell me about Marlowe Frost. What did the two of you really talk about last night?"

Wait. So she believed the lie I'd told them about going home?

My mind suddenly reeled again, and my view of the whole confrontation shifted.

This… was this not about me?

Marlowe. She wanted Marlowe. Did she think… did she think Marlowe had done something?

Does she think he Raised me?

But that didn't make any sense either, if she didn't think I'd been at the house.

I was completely lost. What the hell was the right thing to say?

I was starting to sweat profusely, and McMillin was leaning on me more heavily than he needed to, so I was gasping for breath. I also had a headache coming on from stress and fatigue and now lack of blood flow, and somehow I'd banged my elbow again and it was throbbing violently.

The mania Working was almost entirely suspended, and I was exhausted once more. I had no idea what to say. The only thing I could think to do in that moment was the Worker equivalent of lawyering up.

"I want my Guild rep," I managed to gasp. "I'm not saying anything without him."

My Guild rep, Brandon Perkins, is a short, energetic man, as affable as he is forgetful. He would have been absolutely no help in that situation. But I still had the right to demand that he be present for any official questioning. I was a fully registered Guild member, and they—

"Turn him over," Shrike said.

McMillin and Jamal both grabbed me and flipped me so that my stomach was facing the ceiling. They weren't gentle about it. I was slammed into the table with enough force to push the air out of my lungs, and I gasped and spluttered like a fish fresh out of the ocean. My back made a loud bang against the table that, in an ideal world, would have alerted the office to what was happening, but a bright red line had sprung up around the conference room door that looked to be some kind of Working meant to lock it and keep any inconvenient sounds from crossing the threshold.

I racked my brain for what to do next. My hands itched to ball into fists and ready the tattoo Workings I had hidden up my sleeves. But once I opened that box, there was no going back. Attacking an enforcer, even in this situation, would make me the Worker version of a felon. And if I ran, I'd be a felon at large, and other Workers would come after me. It would be my word against theirs. I didn't even know if I could escape by Working my way free anyway. I might be able to take them by surprise, but even if I could, I wasn't going to kill them, and once they reported me then I'd be in real shit.

But wasn't I already?

If you leave you won't know what they want with Marlowe.

But if I stay, will she use that talon on me?

"Let me be clear, so that we can be certain there are no misunderstandings," Shrike said. She stood close to the table, leaning over me. There was no maniacal glint in her eyes, nor was she smiling. She was stony-faced and frowning, like a parent forced to watch a child undergo the process of setting a broken bone, knowing it was necessary but distasteful. "Someone was Raised last night. Someone at the same house you were supposed to be Working at. A house that, when we examined it, had clearly been the site of a battle between a Worker and a Terror."

Raised. OK. They still thought I—or someone—had been Raised.

"That's impossible," I managed to say, reverting to playing dumb. "That's—no one's done that in centuries. And even if someone did perform a Raising, it wasn't me!"

"We don't think it was you who did the Raising, Mr. James."

Shrike was staring at me with frightening intensity, and I was staring back, but I knew I looked nowhere near as self-possessed as she did.

So that was it. They thought Marlowe had Raised me.

I'd completely walked into it. By saying I'd spoken with Marlowe last night, I'd connected myself to him. They would have found out anyway that he was my sponsor if they'd looked deep enough, but Marlowe and I hadn't been in touch formally for a while now. Informally, yeah, but it would be easy to miss our connection unless you dug deep enough, and I'm far from the only stray that Marlowe has taken in over the years. He's known for it.

But the doubts I'd started having that morning began to creep back in.

Had I been Raised? Had Marlowe done it?

That kind of Working is completely off the grid. It's the worst kind of forbidden. Anything that smacks of what the Blissful might think of as Necromancy has long since been banned in civilized Worker society. Anything that goes so blatantly against nature is off the table.

Could Marlowe have… would he have done that?

And could he have done it without me even knowing?

"We know you were at the house last night, James," Shrike said. "We know that you were taken from the scene by Blissful EMTs and that you died en route to the SF morgue. And yet here you are, alive and, quite literally, kicking."

Without any other good ideas, I stuck with the story I'd been telling.

"I wasn't there," I said. "I didn't even go the job! I was home!"

Shrike continued to stare at me, to watch me for signs of something I couldn't begin to fathom. What was she thinking?

"I wasn't there!" I repeated, more desperately. "I'll swear it any way you want me to, but that's the last thing I'm saying unless you put me in a room with my rep. Or a judge. Hell, drag me back to the Twilight House and let's make this all official, huh?"

It was a wild gamble on my part, and as I met Shrike's gaze, I knew it hadn't worked.

"There will be no Guild rep," she said softly. "There will be no judge." She clenched her jaw, a motion that rippled the muscles in her gaunt cheeks. "Because this never happened."

Which was ominous as all fuck.

"Just let me go then," I said. "It's fine. Just let me go and I'll go. I get it, if someone's out there Raising people, then it's serious. But I swear I don't know anything about it. It wasn't me—I didn't get Raised. I had nothing to do with this. I swear it."

Shrike reached inside her pantsuit coat again and pulled out something small, something that fit entirely concealed in her hand.

"I wish I could believe you," she said, still in that soft tone that was somehow so much worse than anger would have been. She sounded almost... resigned. "But you don't understand the magnitude of what you've stepped into. Of what Marlowe is trying to make happen. I know you were at that house last night. I know you were at the morgue as well. I know you died and came back. I know that you won't go to the Guild because what they'll do is far worse than anything I could do to you here in this room. And I know, too, that you won't turn on your sponsor. So, Cicero James. What are we going to do?"

"I'm not—!"

She slapped her hand over my mouth.

Something small and hard fell from her hand onto my tongue. At first, I thought it was a cough drop or some candy. Which was odd enough. Maybe she had gotten it out of her pocket to use herself and forgotten it was in there when she had gone to quiet me?

But then the candy began to move.

I reacted on pure animal instinct. I bucked wildly on the table and shook my head from side to side, trying to push her hand away from my mouth, trying to spit out whatever it was that was moving in there. McMillin and Jamal held me down, firmly, and Shrike climbed practically on top of me, straddling my legs and pressing her hand down over my mouth with all of her weight so that I had no chance of wriggling free.

The thing in my mouth began to grow, and I felt sharp spindly legs sprout from the hard candy center. It grew like some horrifying just-add-water insect sponge, and I could feel it moving toward the back of my throat, sinking little hooks into my tongue to pull itself forward.

I completely lost it. The human part of me just left, and the animal underneath took full control. I snarled and tried to bite the thing in half—I pushed and lashed at it with my tongue—I cleared my throat so violently that I brought up acid, but nothing worked. The thing set its sharp hooked legs more firmly into the roof of my mouth and the back of my throat.

I began to gag and even heard myself making pleading noises, but there was nothing I could do and nothing my tormentors seemed ready to do for me. At the last moment, I remembered the stored Workings in the tattoos across my palms and opened my fists to let them out, but my mind was too far gone, and, with no direction, the energy simply flared and faded.

The bug in my throat sliced into something, and my whole body went ridged, and then slack.

Darkness began to swirl down on me, and the last thing I saw was Shrike's violet nail pressing down against my forehead.

Part Seven

Doing a 'Memento' impression.
If you don't get the reference,
trust me, it's a good one.
And 'Memento' is a great Christopher
Nolan movie that you should go watch.

I woke with a shout, thrashing wildly against my sheets. I scrambled to my feet and flew across the room before I knew what I was doing. I grabbed the curtains and wrenched them open with the unnecessary force of blind panic.

Light streamed in, illuminating my bedroom via the stolen view from Roc's apartment. The sun was just beginning to set over the Pacific Ocean, to the west of the Bay.

I recoiled from the light with a yelp, shielding my eyes. I was gasping for breath, but slowly I realized that I was home and that I was alone. I was covered in sweat, despite the temperate room, and I couldn't seem to catch my breath. I continued to pull in deep, gasping lungfuls of air for several moments.

I was also buck-ass naked again.

How had that happened? How had I gotten back to my apartment? The last thing I remembered...

What *did* I remember? I... I remembered going to work that morning. I remembered speaking with Marlowe. I remembered the events of the night before.

But what had happened at work?

The Working. Marlowe put me in a mania.

Had it worked? I didn't remember a thing after talking with Marlowe in the Phone Booth. No—wait—I remembered brief flashes. Getting to the office, setting up the room. The strange timeslips, the Workings that I wasn't supposed to be doing.

Everything else was blank.

"What did I…?"

I grimaced. My throat was sore and felt strangely wooly, the way it does the morning after drinking too much. I hoped I wasn't coming down with some kind of cold. Something was going around, and I was the last one I knew of who hadn't had it yet.

Or hell, maybe it was COVID. That seemed to be the kind of week I was having.

A faint buzz came from the other room. My phone—on silent but vibrating.

I pulled on a pair of gym shorts and went out into the main room of the apartment. My phone was where I usually put it after getting home from work, next to the door in a small carved wooden bowl I'd found at an antique store. Beside it, hung up nicely, was my work coat and my Protoline-branded backpack.

I must have come home on autopilot, driven by the manic state.

Shit—had I completely zoned out and run that way the whole day?

I grabbed my phone and turned it over. Half a dozen texts and three missed calls.

Aw, hell.

I was supposed to have gone to Marlowe's after work. Why hadn't I? Had I just autopiloted my way back to the apartment?

I swiped up to see the notifications. Two of the missed calls were from Marlowe—one from three hours ago and one from thirty minutes ago. The call from thirty minutes ago had an accompanying voicemail.

Trying to orient myself, I tapped open the text messages first. One was from Marlowe and said simply "Call when possible." The other five were from three different people—Erica, from work, Anandini, who lived down the hall, and my friend Roc.

The text from Roc I had expected. The other two I really hadn't.

I opened the text from Erica first, hoping it would give me some kind of clue as to what had happened between arriving at work and waking up in bed.

<<Great work on the presentation today! I think Arick really liked it. Thanks again for letting me sit in, and it was so fun to grab coffee afterward.>>

And then:

<<We should get a real drink soon.>>

I stared at that text for a full minute, reading and re-reading it. Several dozen permutations of what had happened, how it had happened, and what it meant that it had happened, all ran through my head faster than Tom Cruise down a long hallway.

Aside from the fact it was the hot girl from the office who'd texted me—which is a hard detail to overlook, lemme tell you—it filled in several crucial details. Firstly, that I'd given the presentation and had no memory of it. Secondly, that the presentation had gone well and Arick had liked it. Arick, while certainly the friendliest person I knew, was also the toughest boss to impress with a presentation, partly because he was so good at them and expected everyone else to be good at them too. Arick also didn't *like* work. He either hated it or loved it.

Which, I suppose, meant he'd loved it.

And then the really interesting part: apparently, Erica and I had grabbed coffee. What the hell had we talked about? What had I *said?* I couldn't remember anything. Had I mentioned anything I shouldn't have?

And then there was the final line.

<<*We should get a real drink soon.*>>

Remembering the TA in my last mania story, you'll understand why I was suddenly very worried about what may or may not have happened between me and a woman I work with.

We'd gotten coffee together. After work, on a Friday afternoon. And now she was dropping hints about wanting to get a 'real' drink.

If there had been… overtures… did that mean they had been well received?

Had I just gone on a coffee date with Erica Masters?

Without remembering a goddamn second of it?

I sat with that thought for a long moment, letting it ring through my mind. I wanted to be excited, but I also really didn't know if I should be. Finally, unable to deal with it in the face of more pressing problems, I swiped the message away and opened the next one, from Anandini.

<<*Hey CJ! I'm not going to make it to Alchemist tomorrow night, I've got work friends going to a new club opening in the Castro. Not sure it's your scene, but looks like fun. Big Round Five is gonna be playing, if you know them. You should come!*>>

Club opening. The same one Roc was trying to get me to go to?

At this rate, I wouldn't be going anyway. I needed to see Marlowe, and I still needed to figure out what had happened the night before. I also needed to be on the alert for any enforcers coming to ask me questions. I couldn't believe that they hadn't been to see me yet. Marlowe had been convinced they would come for me at work, but surely I would remember that. Or someone would have mentioned it.

I swiped that message away too, and then opened Roc's.

<<you fuckin' stealth rizzler>>

<<i need the details immediately>>

It took me a minute to realize that this meant Roc knew about me getting coffee with Erica. He often waxed poetical about her... traits.

I texted him back.

<<No idea what you're talking about.>>

Immediately, response bubbles popped up.

<<typical cj, man of mystery. you're telling me tomorrow night>>

I shook my head. I couldn't focus on that right now.

I typed back a shrug emoji, hoping it would come across as non-committal but satisfy Roc's need for a response, and swiped the texts away.

I pulled up the voicemails and tapped the one from Marlowe.

"Hello, Cicero," said Marlowe's voice. It was friendly and casually cheerful, and sounded exactly like one old friend calling another. "I'm calling to check in about what we discussed last night. I think we agreed on next steps, but perhaps we misunderstood each other. I'm here now, looks like I may have missed you. Give me a ring when you have a chance."

I grimaced and hung up. "Give me a ring?" I muttered under my breath. I didn't think I'd ever heard Marlowe say that. It made me think of the Phone Booth, though, which always chimed whenever someone… whenever someone joined a call.

I glanced over at the door to the linen closet.

Huh.

I hurried over to the door, breathed deeply to clear my mind, and placed my hand against the wood. A small space cleared on the door, showing an empty blackness. Since I wasn't making a call, I didn't need a coin, but it also meant I wouldn't be going inside.

After a moment, gold type scrawled across the face, and the Feed popped up on the right-hand side, scrolling through the day's news. I touched the writing and pulled it out toward me. The Feed popped out into 3-D, surrounding me in a ring of partially see-through images and scrolling texts.

There were no messages from Marlowe. His message hadn't been some kind of obscure code, I'd just jumped to a random association. I sighed and was about to swipe it all away and go back to my phone, but then I glanced over at the Feed and saw that the top story was now a bulletin notification about an emergency Guild meeting.

Tonight.

> **NOTICE**: The monthly meeting of the unionized Workers of the West has been moved to this evening, and will now be a mandatory emergency meeting for all registered Workers of the SFBA chapter of the Worker's Guild. It is requested that you attend this meeting in person. If you are unable to attend in person, please attend via Worker Web connection, which will be toll-free this evening from 7 pm to 9 pm Pacific Standard Time. If you are unable to attend entirely, please be sure to contact your Union Rep immediately upon receipt of this message to arrange an alternative time and manner of communication.

My hands had gone cold, and I ran one of them absently over my face. They were calling everyone in.

What else would you expect? You were fucking Raised! It really happened!

That tickled something in the back of my mind, but I shook my head to force the feeling away. It felt like the memory of a dream, not something real. Maybe it was what had woken me up?

Raised. It was looking more and more likely that that was what had happened. I'd only ever heard rumors about shit like that. And I'd never heard of someone doing it to *themselves*. Hell, I didn't even know if that was possible.

I needed to talk to someone smarter than me.

I could still go to Marlowe's. But would he be there or would he be at the meeting? And the meeting was in an hour. If I was going, then I'd have to leave and go straight there, I wouldn't have time to go to Marlowe's on the way.

I pulled out my phone and saw another text from Roc excoriating me for holding back the details he craved. I ignored it, brought up Contacts, and tapped Marlowe's name. The phone rang as I continued to scroll through the Feed. I stopped—I had a notification from the Guild, marked urgent. Not as urgent as the first notification, but that had been an emergency notification. This was just a standard Worker message.

I clicked it open and read it quickly.

Mr. Cicero James,

We regret to inform you that the job you elected to perform has been canceled. You will be offered the opportunity to sign up for

the first new job that is posted that meets
the same criteria as your canceled job. We
apologize for the inconvenience. If you
would like to claim a currently open posting,
please feel free to do so.

Sincerely,
Rashida Walker

It then provided a link to the list of open Worker jobs. I didn't click it—I didn't need to.

Well, officially canceled. Were they trying to pretend it had never happened?

I went back to the Feed, searching for the story from that morning.

It was gone, disappeared as if it had never been. While the phone continued to ring, I directed the Feed to show me the story that Marlowe had shown me, with the picture of the house and the write-up about what they thought had happened.

Nothing came up.

The Feed showed other stories about Hayes Valley from a couple of months ago, and a few from years prior, but nothing current.

The ringing stopped, and Marlowe's phone went to voicemail.

"Shit," I hissed, turning away from the Feed and pacing over to the couch. I perched on the sectional armrest as I listened to Marlowe's recorded voice.

"Hello, you have reached Marlowe Frost. If you are calling about a medical emergency, please hang up and call—"

I groaned and rubbed my temples. I'd forgotten how ridiculously long Marlowe's answering message was.

"—if you are calling in regards to a speaking engagement or a guest lecture response, please reach out to—"

"Jesus, Marlowe, we get it, let me leave a message already."

"—if you are seeking—"

"Dammit, Marlowe!"

I pulled the phone away from my ear and took a deep breath. I played pretend waiting room music in my head to calm myself. Shouting at a piece of technology was not going to get me anywhere, except maybe to a store for a new phone.

OK—I was calm. So calm.

So *goddamn* calm.

I put the phone back to my ear.

"—and I will call you back as soon as possible. Thank you."

BEEP.

"Hi, Marlowe," I said, adopting a friendly and offhand tone similar to what Marlowe had used when he had left his message for me. "This is Cicero, calling you back."

I grimaced at having to use my first name, but it was what Marlowe called me.

"Look, I'm sorry about missing our meeting earlier today, I came home right after work, completely on autopilot. Must have been... following my regular routine. Just completely forgot. Hope I can make it up to you and find a new time. Call me back when you get this."

I hung up and stared out the window at the setting sun throwing dazzling light across the San Francisco Bay. The stunning beauty of the late summer sunset was lost on me as I tried to piece together what had happened and what to do.

Well, they didn't come to see me at work, I thought. But they must be onto me. Maybe they were watching me and just saw me go through the day and that was it.

I wasn't one for optimism, though, and the situation wasn't lining up. They knew someone had been Raised, they had to know. That had to be what the emergency meeting that evening was all about, why they'd scrubbed all evidence of the job, and even scrubbed the news from the Feed, which was something I'd never seen before.

It was only a matter of time. They were going to come after me. I shifted on the arm of my sofa so that I could more properly look out my fake window at the view.

My thoughts trailed off. A tenuous calm settled over me. I could feel my pulse slowing, and the quiet of my apartment pressed in on me from all sides. It wasn't a bad kind of quiet. It was almost soothing in a way.

But in the calm, the thought I hadn't had time to fully consider bubbled up in my mind.

I'd died. I'd *died*. I knew I had. I remembered it all vividly. Much more vividly now than I had upon first returning. I remembered the scimitar-like claw falling from the ceiling, remembered the shock and the pain and the inability to even stand. I remembered the look on the kid's face, the distant scream of his grandmother, and then how everything had gone black.

And then the shock of waking up. Waking up completely whole and healed.

Raised. No one had been Raised in centuries.

I turned to look at the Phone Booth. The door still had the black window with the Feed and the Worker Web interface pulled up. I took a step toward it, then stopped. Something told me not to trust it. Something told me that there was something wrong.

Could they be watching?

The thought bubbled up from a newly tapped mental wellspring of paranoia. I wasn't quite certain where it had come from, but I felt it very strongly. I live in the 21st century, I know all about surveillance programs. The Workers of the West isn't supposed to do any of that, but, hell, neither is the US government, technically, and what the NSA can do with a bug is nothing compared to what a cadre of Workers can do if they really put their minds to it.

The Guild was supposed to protect me and my right to privacy, but who knew how far that went. It was the Workers of the West, the governing body of all Workers this side of the country, that I was concerned about. Enforcers work for the Workers of the West, not for the Guild, though the Guild controls all licensing and registration of Workers, as well as the collection, posting, and fulfillment of Worker contracts.

The WOTW was who would come for me.

Is that why Marlowe wanted to talk at his place?

I have an apartment—Marlowe has a mansion. He lives in Seacliff, which is a bougie suburb-in-a-city on the northwest tip of the San Francisco Peninsula. Marlowe inherited the house from his father, who passed away when he was young. After his professional success, he rebuilt the house from the ground up with all of the Worker bells and whistles that make a place secure. His place can't be found on any map, can't be 'ported into without special permission, and can't even be visited unless you're given the specific address by Marlowe himself.

Ironically, Blissful can walk up and knock on the door anytime they want. Marlowe finds you all funny and engaging, especially the ones who want to talk about various gods and messiahs. I once caught him debating a Mormon in his bathrobe.

Marlowe was wearing the bathrobe, not the Mormon.

All of which is to say that if there was any place that should be safe and secure, it was Marlowe's.

I looked at my phone. The official Worker meeting was in fifty minutes. It would take me fifteen to get there by 'porting, which is the only way to get to the Twilight House. Another fifteen to walk to the meeting place.

It's a Worker city. You'll see.

But I had time before I had to leave, if I was planning on attending.

I glanced over at the kitchen island. I thought for a moment, and then walked over and rested my hands on the smooth countertop surface. I closed my eyes and believed that the island was transformed—that it was a large bookshelf made of stone and wood, and that it held a row of thick leather-bound books at just about eye level with gold lettering on them.

Energy drained out of me, and I shivered. I opened my eyes and stepped back.

The island had transformed just as I had imagined. It was now no longer a kitchen island but a bookshelf that stretched almost to the ceiling, full to bursting with books of every size, binding, and age. Half of them had come from Marlowe as part of my training, and though I had insisted at the time that I wouldn't need them—all of the information is available via the Worker Web now—in that moment I was very glad that I had them.

The books I was thinking of in particular were slightly below eye level, and they covered an entire shelf all by themselves. The gold lettering they bore on their spines read:

The Compendium of Materia Magi

I ran my hands over the dozens of volumes, finally coming to rest on one that had the letter R embossed on the upper spine. I pulled the book out of its slot and turned with it, walking toward the couch. I waved my hand back at the bookshelf and it became a kitchen island once more, convinced that it was and had always been a kitchen island. I sat and opened the book to the beginning and thumbed over to *Ra*.

I found it. It was difficult to miss. An entire five pages were devoted to the subject of Raising.

I skimmed first, reading quickly. The text moved with my eyes, revealing more text in each line before I got to the next—something that had made me extremely motion-sick when I'd first encountered it during my apprenticeship. Marlowe had insisted I persist, though, and now I was glad he had, because the reading went by extremely quickly, which was the intention of the Working.

Here's what I read:

Raising the Dead was once considered an art and has been practiced throughout most of recorded history. There is evidence of it throughout all major civilizations, perhaps most prominently in Egypt in the form of mummification.

What is today called Raising (colloquialisms - see page 235 of book C-D), the practice has been banned in all modern Worker societies as of 1023 Worker Common Date, or 1994 Common Era (also AD). It has been historically conflated with Necromancy (practice of, see page 369 of book N) but is not considered the same. While some proto-Worker societies practiced Raising as part of Necromancy, it was very often a corrupted and impure version meant to raise and enslave a dead body via simple reanimation. Raising the Dead is the holistic retrieval of a newly deceased soul from its path through the Space Between Spaces on its way to a final resting place (for information on the Seven Heavens, Thirteen Hells, and Final Destinations, see page 524 of book S, page 739 of book T, and page 691 of book F).

Since the practice has been outlawed by every major society (the last being the Workers of Atlantic Africa, headquartered in Nigeria, which passed restrictions in 1023 WCD or 1994 CE/AD), there has been no major research into this Working. What research has been done, specifically on how to accomplish a Raising of the Dead, has been stricken from this book as well as all other areas of public Worker consumption. Information is still available to the Guild in the Hidden Mysteries.

I skimmed several more paragraphs detailing the history of the practice. There's some seriously evil shit in there. People Raising slaves to keep them in eternal bondage even after they'd died; medical experimentation; 'research' into the afterlife of people of different faiths.

You get the idea. It's illegal for good reason.

I went to a paragraph at the end of the page, which read:

It is important to note that Raising of the Dead is performed by an external source and cannot be performed by the Worked on themselves. For more information on Resurrection, and the subcategory of Self-Resurrection, please see—

And that was where the passage cut off. It didn't stop, it just ended, in mid-sentence. I had never seen that before in my entire time using the Compendium.

And then, as I watched, the sentence began to disappear, one letter at a time, as if someone were deleting it in real time.

I shouted in alarm and stood up violently, sending the book spinning across the room, where it landed with a thud on the floor. The page remained open and facing me, and I stared in shock as the words disappeared, erasing the sentence until there was no mention of self-resurrection left.

Heart pounding in my chest, I picked the book up again and quickly flipped through the pages, all of which moved but didn't seem to be spontaneously deleting themselves.

I found 'Resurrection.'

That passage was much shorter than the one about Raising. I read it furiously, looking for any mention of *self-resurrection* but finding none. It referenced Raising the Dead as the main source of information and noted that resurrection was a religious term, while Raising of the Dead was the preferred Worker terminology, and then just referred the reader back to the passage about Raising.

The passage that was currently being edited.

My phone buzzed and I quickly grabbed it. There was a single message on the screen.

<<*Attend the meeting. Speak to no one about last night until you see me.*>>

It was from Marlowe.

PART EIGHT

THE TWILIGHT HOUSE

I looked at my watch, heart rate spiking. 6:35 pm. Shit—I'd spent longer looking at the Compendium than I'd meant to.

Go to the meeting. Go to the meeting?

I shook my head and swore in several colorful varieties, pacing back and forth across the kitchen. I opened my library again, shoved the Compendium book back into place, and then let the library return to being a kitchen countertop. I ran my hand along the cool tile surface, trying to slow my racing heart. I cracked my knuckles, rolled my shoulders.

Going to the meeting seemed like a horrible idea. It seemed like the perfect opportunity to walk into what was a completely obvious trap.

They were gathering together all Workers. They had to think that anyone who *didn't* show up would be one of their suspects. If I *did* show up, they would have me trapped.

Were the people editing the Compendium part of the WOTW? Who else would have that ability? Once they had all the Workers together, were they going to question everyone? Were they going to ask for alibis for the night before? The fake one Marlowe and I had agreed on was serviceable, but it was hardly foolproof and would completely fall apart if they managed to question us independently.

I sent a text back to Marlowe.

<<Will you be there?>>

While I waited for a response, I grabbed my leather jacket, ate several handfuls of trail mix to appease my growling stomach, downed a glass of water, and checked my

Instruments. They were all in place, though barely half full. Usually they fill while I sleep, feeding off the order of my apartment and the Circle I have inscribed beneath my bed, but it seemed that I hadn't had more than a couple hours of sleep after getting home. I could quick-charge them, but even that would take more time than I had.

My watch had the most energy to spare. I carefully siphoned some off into the ring and the band.

I breathed out a harsh sigh, shaking my head. The sun was setting outside my window, and I was standing in a kind of transitional dusky light.

"Fuck it," I said.

I moved toward the door, grabbing my wallet and keys. I looked at my phone—no response from Marlowe. I paused at the threshold of my apartment, propping the heavy door open with my booted foot.

All Workers were going to be there. *All* Workers.

Hades Jackson.

Hades is a Worker who specializes in answers to questions you aren't supposed to ask. He communes with the dead, dispatches souls who have been trapped on this side of the Space Between Spaces, and trades favors with anyone who needs answers they can't get through… reputable means. He isn't really a friend—I'm not sure he has friends—but I've been to him a few times when prepping for a job, and I think he likes me.

Marlowe told me not to talk to anyone before him.

But I don't often do what I'm told. And if anyone outside Marlowe knew something about Raising, it would be Hades.

I looked at my watch again—6:41.

"Shit."

I stepped out fully into the hall and let the door swing shut. I took the elevator down, walked through the lobby, and came out onto the sidewalk.

I didn't take the time to call a car. I didn't need to—where I was going wasn't a physical location. At least not one that can be plotted on a map for an Uber to get to.

I hurried down the slight hill outside my apartment building, moving in the direction of the Salesforce Tower that dominates the city skyline these days. There was an alley only a few blocks away that was perfect for 'porting, one that I use all the time.

I ran my fingers along the metal face of my watch, glancing down at it. I needed fifteen minutes to get there. Maybe slightly more at the moment, since so many Workers would be 'porting in.

I ducked into the short, dirty alleyway and breathed out slowly, focusing. There weren't many people passing by on the street, so it shouldn't be a difficult transition.

I glanced at my watch, hit the first of the pushers on the side, and let the Working take hold. The alleyway sealed itself off, though the sound of traffic kept coming through the blank gray light that now covered the entrance. The sky darkened in patches, like drops of ink falling on clean paper. The ink spots ran together and closed in around me, and I channeled belief through the watch. This was easier than the 'port I'd done the previous night since I knew exactly where I was going and the gateway was kept perpetually open.

The hand in the small subdial in the larger watch face ticked—once, twice, thrice—and the minute hand of the main dial jumped forward.

The alley winked away completely, and then reappeared, this time with subtle differences. The bricks were now longer, and a gray-and-tan color instead of an industrial red-and-gray covered in grime. The alleyway itself was shorter, and it ended fairly abruptly in a stone wall several feet in front of me. The changes weren't alarming, though—they were expected.

I was in the Twilight House.

I turned around and stepped out into a long, narrow lane lined with two dozen or so similar alleyways. To my left, at the end of the lane, was a large park that was both manicured and wild in perfect proportion—the other entrance to the House, if you weren't close enough to an alleyway to use one. Easier to go through parks in some ways, if you're drawing on raw chaos. Alleys are more ordered, though, with varying touches of decay. Better for the kind of structured energy you can store in an Instrument.

The sky above was in perfect twilight, bright enough to see by but dark enough to cast shadows. If I could have seen the horizon, I would have seen a tiny sliver of sun just peaking over the western hills, and a moon in the sky in the east.

To be expected—it's always twilight in the House.

It isn't really a house, though, it's a city. I don't know why they call it a House, it's something metaphorical or allegorical or whimsical or bibliographical or... I don't know. And it isn't the only Worker city—but it is one of the most famous, and it's the central Worker hub for the government of the Workers of the West. Marlowe's explained how it exists to me several times, but most of the details just flat-out refuse to stick in my head, so I'll just give you the basics: the House, like all Worker cities, is sequestered in a pocket of reality that melds the Space Between Spaces with the real world. It's impossible to enter from the real world and impossible to leave from inside the House, unless you 'port through what we call Port Street.

In terms of time, it's always fifteen minutes (give or take a couple either way depending on how many people are coming and going) to 'port to the Twilight House, from any park or alleyway in the western US. In terms of space, I have no idea where it is, aside from that it's somewhere in Northern California. I'm sure someone knows, but not me. Same for any Worker city. Every registered Worker can get in as long as they're in good standing and they've been there before, but you have to 'port in. "Been there before" is the key to a lot of 'porting. You generally need to know where you're going, or it'll take a lot more energy to make sure you don't end up somewhere you don't wanna be.

Anyway—that night in particular, I was very obviously not the only Worker running late. There was a veritable flood of latecomers popping into existence from other alleyways and from around trees and bushes in the park at the end of the lane. It was misty that evening, or foggy, I don't really know the difference, and it made the appearing people feel ominous and shadowy in the twilight setting. Everything always seems more mysterious in the House.

I turned right, away from the park and toward the end of the lane. A few strides later, I had emerged out into a wide and well-kept town square.

I'd seen it all before, of course, but I still paused for a moment to take it in. Every time I come to the House, I feel… something. I'm not sentimental, but the House is… special. Any Worker based in the West will tell you the same. It's full of impossibilities—there are buildings there that shouldn't be possible, buildings that *aren't* possible, except that the builders believed them to be possible and so they are. Towers attached to inns nestled next to wattle-and-daub apartments straight out of Elizabethan England. Adobe brick houses from the American southwest. Log cabins, Mediterranean single-level homes with wide courtyards and olive trees. Flagstone streets that inexplicably ascend next to perfectly flat pavement roads. Modern glass-and-metal townhouses that wouldn't have been out of place in any number of close-to-the-city suburbs. And out further toward the edge of the House there are even ranch-style homes and a few castles that dot the hills— European mostly but also one Shogunate-era Japanese one that I love. The center of town, though, is all of a single piece, and the closer you get to the true center the closer you get to architecture that is made of soaring towers of tan, white, and light-red stone with a decidedly Romanesque flavor. There's a gorgeous clock tower, too.

It's an audacious city. It's bold and outrageous and somehow it all blends into one piece.

It's… well, it's what a lot of real-world cities wish they could be.

I walked down Clemon Boulevard outside Port Street toward the center of town. A few dozen other Workers were walking along with me in loose groups, and there were more out in front of us and still more coming up behind. Some of them I knew by sight, though I wasn't sure of their names. A group of them, young men who looked like tech bros wearing Patagonia vests over jeans and henleys, were speculating about the reason we'd all been called in.

"What do you think?"

"About the meeting?"

"No, about the stock market. Yeah, dude, the meeting."

"No idea. Just saw the notification."

Another of them chimed in.

"Annoying it's last minute."

"Oh that's right, you had that thing tonight didn't you?"

"Yeah man, anniversary. I had to make an excuse to Jenny."

"You gotta wife her up like I did," said another of the men. "Can share anything with a spouse, remember."

"We aren't in the 50s, Pete, you don't wife a woman up too early these days. They're more scared of marriage than we are."

The man speaking was chubby and had a boyish grin. The other men laughed along with his joke. I thought vaguely that I knew him, and the name Gordon Yang bubbled up from somewhere in my mind. Maybe I'd done a job with him at some point.

The conversation turned to jokes and jabs about the modern dating market, which was mostly just repackaged bits from popular standup comedians. I fell back and started listening in on a conversation between a pair of elderly women. Both had full heads of gray hair but carried themselves well and stepped lively.

"It's that job I was telling you about," one of them was saying. "The one I sent you the Feed article about that disappeared."

"You sure you didn't just send the wrong link again?"

"Carol, I keep telling you, links aren't a thing on the Feed, that's social media."

The woman, apparently Carol, rolled her eyes. "It's the same thing, Sue."

"It's different, you old biddy."

Carol cackled and slapped Sue's arm. They segued into talking about various social media platforms and I separated from them.

So other people had noticed the article disappearing.

Other Workers were joining us on our way through the House. Very few people actually live in the House, but lots of people maintain homes there. Technically we all have a home there, though I've never claimed mine. It's a malleable space, so, in theory, we could put ten or twenty times as many of us in there and we would all fit without even making a dent.

But, surrounded by Workers all day every day? No thanks.

I didn't hear anything else interesting as we made the rest of the way to what some of us call the Bowl and what others call the Meeting Place. It's on the side of a central hill with a paved courtyard in the middle of the House called the Twilight Plaza. There's power in calling things what they literally are, hence 'Meeting Place', but the thing also looks like a bowl scooped out of the tall hillside that serves as the center of the Twilight House, with all the important buildings centered around it. Everything there is Romanesque architecture and green lawns and old trees—it's gorgeous if that's your thing. The Bowl/Meeting Place is essentially a large partially covered amphitheater built into the side of the hill, and it's where we gather for (surprise surprise) meetings. There are other buildings if it's raining or snowing—which happens, since the House mirrors the seasons out in the real world—but that evening was tolerably warm, and so to the Bowl we went.

I glanced at my watch as I joined the crowd walking down one of the main stone corridors into the Bowl. 7:03. The meeting was definitely going to start late, but I should have expected that. Given the last-minute nature of the request—or demand, really—to attend the meeting, there wasn't much else people could do aside from show up whenever they were able.

When we emerged from the corridor into the amphitheater itself, I scanned the Bowl. It's big and grand, like a decently sized concert venue, with stone steps and a stage at the bottom, and surrounded by tan-and-white stone walls. The seats are all worn stone with low back rests, which is actually more comfortable than it sounds, but still not comfortable enough to justify long meetings, which is why we usually keep these sorts of things short.

I noticed several people I knew. Some of them saw me and waved; I waved back but didn't make any effort to join them.

None of them were Marlowe.

I reached into my pocket as I sat close to the edge of one of the stone benches, away from where others might pass me or try to engage me in conversation. I looked at my phone, hoping that maybe I'd received a message before I'd entered the city—which, since it technically doesn't exist, is quite beyond the reach of cellphone towers.

There were no new messages.

Motion caught my eye, and I looked up. My heart skipped and then started beating faster. There were men and women in enforcer uniforms stepping into place around the edge of the Bowl on the top row of the amphitheater. All of them had Ruiners at their waists that were easily accessible. They were watching the crowd carefully, and there were many more of them than I had seen in a long time—several dozen at least.

Other Workers had noticed them too, and they were either eyeing them or making comments about them to their neighbors. The enforcers, for their part, were just standing there, scanning the crowd and looking tense while trying to pretend they weren't.

Several minutes passed while we waited. Sitting there I could see the bare sliver of sun over the hills slightly off to the left of the stage. It lit the Bowl decently well, but not entirely, so small working lights also shone along the steps and stone walls of the amphitheater.

More time passed, and soon almost the entire amphitheater had filled up, which meant there were several thousand of us in attendance. There were wide Feed screens to the back right and back left of the Bowl that would share everything with those who hadn't been able to attend in person. But it looked like a combination of curiosity and worry had driven a decent number of us to come into the House in person to see what all the fuss was about. I don't know officially how many of us there are out here in the west, but the number usually cited is somewhere in the neighborhood of ten thousand actively registered with the Guild. It's not required to be registered, and there's definitely a bunch of us who live off-grid and have nothing to do with the Blissful world, so the all-in number is anyone's guess.

Workers are an anarchic bunch—we have a healthy distrust of authority, but we've been around long enough to know that we can't live completely lawlessly. We have a loose governing structure, and a few ironclad rules that we call the Code, as well as a list of Workers' Rights maintained by the Guild. The head of the Workers of the West is a position we call the Steward—he's like a governor, and we vote on who gets to fill the position every year sometime in November. The current Steward is a man named Kaj Van Sant, and he's been Steward for four years running.

I'm telling you this because he's the one who finally started the meeting.

He walked up on stage and the lights in the floor and walls dimmed slightly, and everyone quieted down and looked his way.

"Good evening," he said. His voice is accented slightly with European vowels and a clipped cadence—I vaguely think German, though the 'Van' could make him Dutch or something else, I guess. Most of us like him pretty well. He has a strong, debonair shock of gray-white hair that is always well-coiffed, a wiry body with a paunch that shows he runs but still drinks wine and eats bread, and a seemingly endless wardrobe of well-fitted button-down shirts that he often rolls up to the elbow. He also has very clear gray eyes. Those are all the physical details I can think of. Fill the rest in yourself.

Go wild. Give him a wart and a leer if that tickles your fancy. Maybe a false eye and a limp.

There was a general round of murmured greeting in return, which Kaj paused to receive with a raised hand, a small smile, and a tilt of his head.

"Thank you all for coming this evening. I will get straight to the point and leave out the pleasantries, as I am certain everyone is eager to get back to their regular lives. There is other business to attend to, but we will leave it to our next calendar gathering set for the beginning of next month."

I was paying close attention now. As soon as Van Sant had come out on stage, my nerves had ramped right back up, and I suddenly felt as jumpy as a rabbit in coyote territory. I noticed movement off to the side of the amphitheater stage, in the partially covered backstage area.

I felt a thrill go through me but had no idea why. A woman was standing there that I didn't know. She had brown-auburn hair and wore a dark navy pantsuit, which made her stand out because Workers don't usually wear formal clothing. Again, anarchic bunch. Much more likely to see us in anything from leisurewear to old paint-stained Led Zeppelin t-shirts (depends on the generation). This woman, by contrast, looked like she'd stepped out of a cable TV cop show. She wore an enforcer badge on her chest, and I caught a glint of something on one of her nails. She wasn't wearing a Ruiner and didn't seem to have one holstered at her hip.

Something about her seemed…

I coughed suddenly, a hacking whole-body cough that came out of nowhere. The people sitting to both my right and left looked at me askance, and I managed to squeeze an apology out at them as I tried to suppress the sounds coming from my throat. I covered up the bottom half of my face with the front of my black t-shirt and waved apologetically in that universal sign of "sorry about this—weird, isn't it!"

The fit passed as quickly as it had come, and I managed to tune back in to what Van Sant was saying. I didn't think much about the coughing at that point.

"I will not sugarcoat the news. Some of you may have heard rumors already, which is part of why we decided to call this meeting. Some of you may even have seen a news story this morning about a recent job that went awry. You may also have seen that story disappear."

There was a small murmur of conversation between neighbors, and the hairs on the back of my neck did that trying-to-stand-on-end thing.

He had just admitted the story had been pulled. I wasn't sure what I had expected, but a bald-faced truth hadn't been it.

"That story was pulled at my request," Van Sant continued, looking uncomfortable and slightly ashamed. If it was an act, it was a convincing one.

There was more murmuring and shifting as Van Sant let the statement land. He nodded and grimaced and then said, "It will be up again as soon as this meeting has ended. The only difference will be an addendum with additional details— namely, that the Worker who was involved is now wanted by the Workers of the West for a most serious crime."

There was some murmuring at this. I waited for the other shoe to drop.

"There is evidence that this Worker perished on the job... and then was Raised shortly thereafter."

A moment of dead silence, and then conversation exploded.

"Raised? Did he say *Raised?*"

"That can't be right—that's some medieval shit, right?"

"Jesus. That's… wow."

"No wonder they called us in!"

Electricity buzzed through my body, but I didn't let my anxiety rise to the surface. I put on what I thought was a decently plausible look of shock. Since I wasn't sitting next to anyone I knew, I was able to avoid any awkward conversation and didn't have to force anything verbal.

Marlowe had better know what the fuck he's doing telling me to be here.

Van Sant hadn't named the Worker. Did that mean they didn't know it was me? There had been those two enforcers at the morgue, McMillin and—

My brain seemed to short out, and I twitched and blinked several times. There had been another Worker there, hadn't there? McMillin hadn't been there on his own. Who had it——?

The short happened again, and I shook more intensely. My heart started to beat too quickly—I was panicking. What was going on?

Calm. Marlowe wouldn't have told me to come if he didn't have a plan.

They didn't know it was me. That had to be it. If they'd known it was me, I wouldn't just be sitting there, I'd be surrounded and on my way to a cell. I was at the meeting to show that I didn't have anything to worry about. No worries at all—why wouldn't I be there? I was innocent. Someone had been Raised? How crazy! Wow!

Van Sant let the buzz of conversation continue for a full minute, and then he lifted a hand for silence. It was slow in returning, but his reputation was such that once people had exhausted their immediate questions, they were eager to turn back to him for further details.

During that time, I again scanned the crowd for Marlowe and again managed to confirm he wasn't there, unless he was hiding under the stage or in a bush somewhere. There was also no sign of Hades Jackson, but that was more to be expected. Hades didn't usually attend the meetings themselves—but he always made sure he was in the House when there was a big event that would involve foot traffic going by his place.

"This is indeed a serious crime," Van Sant said. "As this occurred in San Francisco, it falls on the purview of the Workers of the West to look into the matter. We have the promised help of the Guild in bringing this matter to a close, and they will stand ready to assist the accused Worker with representation once they are apprehended."

They. He keeps saying 'they' instead of 'he'. Is he being intentionally vague, or do they really not know it was me? Do they have other suspects?

"We have already begun conducting interviews on persons of interest. Please rest assured that the Worker who stands accused of this crime will be apprehended."

There was more murmuring at this point, but it was subdued. Most people seemed to be more intrigued than worried. After all, Raising in and of itself isn't dangerous. It's one of the most severely restricted Workings, but it's also something that's exciting to think about. Like robbing a bank. Everyone knows it's wrong and it would be bad to do because if everyone did it society would stop functioning. But if you *could* pull it off and get away with it....

Van Sant seemed to have caught on to the sly note of interest and curiosity creeping into the crowd, though, and was ready with his next comment:

"I would further like to remind everyone that the penalty for Raising is... unpleasant."

The general murmuring cut off, and a more solemn air descended. There were grim expressions on the faces of the older Workers, while the younger generation tended more toward interest and curiosity.

I realized that a lot of the younger Workers, like me before Marlowe clued me in, didn't actually know the details of the punishment for a Raising. That's how long it had been since someone had been Raised.

I'd experience it firsthand if they found me. They would tear me to pieces, burn me, send me to the edges of the earth, and all the rest of it. And if I had unconsciously done a Working that had brought me back once, what if it happened again? What if my body slowly, over hundreds of years, tried to make its way back together? Would I feel it? Would I be conscious all that time?

Panic began to overtake me, and I quickly stamped down on my thoughts. It's a trick most Workers learn early on. When your thoughts can change reality, you learn to clamp down hard on fear and panic. If you go too far down that road, you can end up manifesting those fears and leaving an opening for something to crawl out of the Space Between Spaces.

I told myself to focus. I was there for a reason. Marlowe wouldn't have told me to come if it were a trap. Marlowe never did anything spuriously. He hadn't told me to come to his house, hadn't told me to go on the run—he had told me to come to this meeting. It had to be the same reason he'd told me to go to work. It had to be. The best way to avoid suspicion was to act as if there were no reason for anyone to be suspicious. They didn't know it was me—hell, they hadn't even come to interview me at work.

The back of my throat spasmed again, and another violent coughing fit clamped down on my chest. I managed to cut it off more quickly this time, but I also started to worry. I wondered again if maybe I was coming down with something.

"I would like to remind everyone as well," Van Sant said, "that the Ten Prohibitions are taken very seriously. We will be sure to use the fullest extent of our power to enforce the Worker Code, by which you all have sworn to abide. Workers have survived millennia, and we have not seen a Golden Age like this since the turn of the Enlightenment. What we have is in large part due to the laws set in place—the Code that we follow, which includes the Prohibitions. There are reasons that certain Workings are banned, and if anyone would like reminders as to those reasons, I have written several excellent books on it myself, all of which are available at fine booksellers throughout the Twilight House."

Van Sant smiled cheekily, and the Workers let out an appreciative chuckle at the longstanding joke, dissipating some of the tension. Van Sant had come to prominence as an author and historian before running for Steward, and he had indeed written some of the best non-Compendium books on Working and Worker law and history of the last few decades. Rumor was that he had even contributed several dozen passage updates to the Compendium itself, which is a rare thing.

"Now," Van Sant said, becoming serious again, "before we get you all back to your busy lives, there is one more matter of business. Before you leave, the Workers of the West Enforcers, in attendance tonight, are here to take voluntary alibis via Truth Catcher."

There was a renewed rustling at this point and more than a little grumbling but no outright protests. A chill washed over me. I bit the inside of my cheek and began to pick at the skin along the sides of my thumbs with the nails of my index fingers.

I didn't *have* an alibi. Not one I could give a Truth Catcher.

A ringing filled my ears that was loud enough to drown out the rest of what Van Sant said to the crowd. I caught the tone—soothing, making apologies for the overreach, general politician gobbledygook—and I knew that they would all go along with it. It wasn't required—anyone could refuse—but it was the easiest way to prove your innocence, and any Worker could elect to speak into a Truth Catcher to clear themselves of wrongdoing. If you didn't, you remained on the quickly narrowing suspect list.

For something like a Raising, a breaking of one of the chief Prohibitions, I had no doubt that everyone in the whole goddamn House would just give the alibi so that they could be done with it, which would officially put me even more squarely on the enforcers' radar.

I looked around frantically. All exits were lined with enforcers. None of them were wearing their Ruiners, but they all had them stashed at their belts and I knew how quickly they could strap them on.

Fuck fuck fuck fuck FUCK FUCK FUCK—

"I do not ask this of you lightly," Van Sant said. I managed to focus back on the man and what he was saying. To his credit, he did sound regretful. "It is no one's intention to pry into your private lives. You need not tell us anything revealing—and should you wish to give a statement in private, you may of course do so. All of your answers will be witnessed by a third party in accordance with the Workers' Rights, and all alibis confirmed by the Truth Catcher will be considered ironclad."

There were a few stalwarts who shouted something out on the far side of the crowd—I couldn't hear the words, but it appeared Van Sant did. He nodded and held up a pacifying hand.

"I completely understand your objections. This is a very special circumstance. One who has broken one of the Ten Prohibitions may well be willing to break others. The prohibition against controlling the will of another Worker, for example, or, to be entirely blunt, the prohibition against killing another Worker."

Silence greeted this. Even I had to admit he had a good point. Because at that moment I was willing to do some pretty crazy shit.

"As such, we are acting proactively to determine who we can rule out as a suspect. We want nothing more than to avoid casting aspersions on anyone who should be above suspicion. Anything you admit to will be privileged, as under the Worker Code, and you have the right of refusal. The Guild has already agreed to this step, and though representatives will be provided to all those who request them, it has been agreed that measures should be taken to bring this to a conclusion quickly and efficiently."

"And, as such, I am happy to be the first to give my alibi."

There was a smaller murmur here, one of grudging approval.

He gestured offstage and an enforcer came forward bearing a small metal globe made of an antique-looking gold. The globe shone with a faint blue light along lines of runic language that helped hold the Working in the device.

Truth Catchers aren't rare, but they aren't common. They're hard to make and maintain, and there are strict rules about when they can be used and when they can't be, and only official Workers of the West enforcers are allowed to carry them. They're all registered and tracked, too, so that no one can take one for personal use. They're damn useful when you aren't on the run from the law. Almost everyone who can use them to clear themselves does. They can't be duped, and as long as the asker words the question correctly, they're basically infallible.

And I mean that literally—Truth Catchers are *never* wrong. The sky is blue, the grass is green, and Truth Catchers know exactly what you mean.

Should I run for it? *Could* I run for it?

I stood with the rest of the crowd—mechanically, just imitating what everyone else was doing. In fact, my thoughts were telling me frantically to do anything *but* stand—to run, race, dash, sprint, pick a verb, any verb—but I knew I couldn't. They'd pick me out.

If I have to fight, I need to wait until the last minute, when I'm at the front of the line with the enforcer and the Truth Catcher. And I can opt out. Yes—I'll just have to opt out.

It was the only answer. They couldn't compel me to use the Truth Catcher. It would put me on the list for refusing, but that was better than telling a lie and being caught, in which case they would just take me in for questioning anyway.

It would be better to avoid that whole thing, though. Was there a way?

I was going around in mental circles and I knew it.

Marlowe told me to come. He had to know this was a possibility. Why the hell would he tell me to come? Did he send me another message after I got into the House?

I shuffled toward the end of the row of stone seats along with the rest of the crowd, scanning the walls. Every exit was manned by enforcers—two here, three there, a half dozen in the big central archway. There are a dozen or so exits to the Bowl, but they were all covered.

Something sharp pricked my thumb. I flinched and jerked my hand up and away from whatever it was. There was a spot of blood on the skin, just below the nail.

What the hell had that been?

I looked around the floor and the seats as I continued to shuffle along with the crowd. There didn't appear to be anything obvious. It had felt almost like some kind of insect bite.

I shook my thumb and sucked at the drop of blood. I glanced around one more time and finally caught sight of a tiny white dot almost out of my line of sight, a few steps behind me now.

I apologized to an older couple and let them go in front of me. I crouched down—the white dot was a multi-sided star.

I'd seen one of them before.

Marlowe.

I reached for it, and as soon as the tips of my fingers touched it, it began to unfold like the tightly furled bud of a flower.

There were only two words on it—a name.

Jamal Henry

I stared down at it for several seconds, and then the word faded, and the paper began to fall apart, like thin paper in water. I let it fall from my fingers; it was gone before it hit the ground.

I stood and looked around frantically while trying to pretend I wasn't looking around frantically. I scanned everyone I could see, trying to find Marlowe. If he was present, he sure as hell was hiding and hiding well.

I looked around to see if anyone had noticed. Luckily, no one seemed to be paying me any attention. Even if they were, I probably just looked like I had been checking a bootlace or something. Kaj Van Sant had left the stage after very conspicuously taking the Truth Catcher test himself, and along with him had gone all the others who had lined the stage, including the woman with the strange nail that I had clocked earlier. Something about her still made me think… I don't know. I coughed absently and focused again.

Jamal Henry.

The rest of the amphitheater had mostly emptied to the aisles at that point, everyone making their way up and out past the enforcers with the Truth Catchers. I was starting to look like a straggler, and I needed to figure out what I was going to do.

If Marlowe sent that note….

Jamal—I knew him. An enforcer. I remembered him from the last group job I'd done, a Terror manifestation at Coit Tower that had infected the whole building and required more than one Worker to handle. Jamal had been the enforcer assigned to the case since we'd had to shut the building down to deal with it. Why the hell had his name been on a piece of paper sent to me?

Was Jamal even *there*?

I scanned the line of exits and felt a small jolt as I recognized the tall, dark enforcer. He wasn't hard to find— he's handsome as all hell and several inches taller than most people. He was one of the enforcers holding a Truth Catcher, taking the alibis of the Workers filing out of the Meeting Place.

I was a drowning man searching for a lifeline. Walking deliberately toward an enforcer I only partially knew felt like suicide. But someone—*dear God, I hope it was Marlowe*—seemed to want me to go to him. I had no reason to believe that Jamal would do anything differently from any of the other enforcers, and no reason to expect that I would be able to pass the Truth Catcher with a lie just because Jamal was holding it. That wasn't how Truth Catchers worked.

But maybe the exit Jamal was stationed at was the one with the quickest line to Port Street. Maybe Marlowe was helping me get out as quickly as possible. Maybe I was supposed to force my way past Jamal? The line in front of him did look shorter since it was toward the side of the Bowl, and maybe…

I began to shuffle in that direction. My heart raced in my chest and my mind continued to whirl. I checked my Instruments, shifting them on my wrists and finger. They were all conspicuously visible, as is tradition in a Worker gathering—everyone exposes their Instruments, otherwise it's kind of like you're concealed carrying them—and though they weren't as full as I wanted them to be, definitely not for a fight against an enforcer with a goddamn Ruiner, I'd be able to use them if I needed to.

I cycled through my tattoos. I had the Muse of Fire and Storm tattoos on my palms, of course, and I had several more over the rest of my body, some of which you're familiar with now.

None of them, though, are quotes that translate easily to "lie convincingly to an enforcer".

There was one that might help. One that I have only ever used once. One that I desperately did not want to use again, because there would be no turning back from using it.

Note to self, get a Houdini quote about escaping tight spots or some shit.

I found myself at the back of the line leading up to Jamal, with nowhere else to go. I was fifth in line. The older couple I'd let by was ahead of me. The woman spoke something into the metal orb covered in runes, and the blue light turned white, then blue again.

Truth.

Jamal stepped aside and gestured for her to pass, then turned to her husband.

It was only Jamal and one other Worker at the exit, and Jamal was the one holding the orb—the other enforcer was the required third-party witnesser, and he was recording the names of the Workers, their alibis, and the color the orb changed. That guy was someone I didn't know, but he was middle-aged, balding, and had a pronounced beer gut.

I ascended the last step up and was on level ground. The older man spoke into the orb and it turned white, then back to blue. Another truth.

Three people before me now.

I just had to refuse the Truth Catcher. That was it. Simple. I'd just have to take my chances.

But what if they took me into custody right then and there? What if I was the only one in the whole goddamn amphitheater who had a reason not to just say the truth about what they had been doing last night during the Raising?

There was one other option. The tattoo along my collarbone.

I ground my back teeth together. The only time I'd used it, it hadn't worked at all the way I'd intended it to. I'd gotten it as a Working I'd meant to give me clarity and willpower. I'd gotten it on my collarbone because tattoos there fucking *hurt*, and it's helpful to have pain in the process of inscribing and storing a tricky Working.

But the one time I'd used it, it had opened the Space Between Spaces. And that's… well, it's not as bad as getting Raised, but it's up there.

I was second in line now. I touched the black lettering through my shirt and brought it to mind.

*There are more things in Heaven and Earth,
Horatio, than are dreamt of in your philosophy.*

I know, it's an overused Hamlet line. But it's still a banger. And I'd set it with the intention of clearing my mind, making it easier to think. Turns out it does a whole lot more than that.

Standing in line, I thought to myself, I could use it. I could slip into the Space Between Spaces if I dared. Like a dark kind of 'porting. But if I opened the Space, I risked letting in something horrible right into the heart of the Twilight House. And if I went into it, I'd be at risk of said horrible things taking me and preventing me from ever coming out.

Terrors aren't the worst thing in the Space Between Spaces.

I took another step forward. My turn was next.

I stilled my mind. It was what might have to happen. I invested some of my willpower into the tattoo and felt warmth spread from my collarbone all throughout my chest. I knew that beneath my shirt the black ink had turned a softly glowing red-gold.

"I was bouldering up in the Presidio," I heard the young woman in front of me say. The globe turned white, and the man standing next to Jamal made a note on his pad of paper. That struck me as funny, suddenly—that he was taking manual notes. With everything we can do with Working, nothing beats a pen and paper.

I stepped forward, ready to pull the rip cord and officially become Suspect Number #1. But before I could act, Jamal locked eyes with me. Something passed between us that gave me pause. I couldn't put my finger on what it was or why it had happened, but it was more than just recognition of someone who he had Worked with before. Jamal seemed to be recognizing me for... something else.

The enforcer glanced sideways with only his eyes—not moving his head, not shifting his stance. His partner was still looking down at his notepaper. I followed Jamal's glance and understood 0% what he was glancing at. Jamal then focused back on me, very pointedly, and I, already in a near panic, started to freak out.

Did Jamal know? *Did he know?*

Jamal raised the golden Truth Catcher orb. I glanced down at it, and then back up at him. The concealed tattoo was hot on my upper chest.

"Where were you last night between the hours of 7 pm and 2 am?" Jamal asked, deep voice very clear and words perfectly articulated. No getting around that question.

His eyes flicked again to his partner. I followed the look. The other man was still gazing down at his pad of paper. The pause lengthened, and Jamal shifted his gaze back to me and widened his eyes in a "put it together!" kind of expression.

I guess I'm an idiot because I still didn't get it.

Jamal's eyes got even wider, and he glanced again at his partner and then back at me.

No—not his partner. The pad of paper.

He was looking at his partner's notes.

I locked eyes with Jamal again and realized that somehow, for some reason, he was helping me. My brain raced with options. I had no idea what he was trying to tell me, but it was clear that it was something.

He doesn't want me to refuse. He wants me to say something.

"Nothing to worry about," Jamal said brusquely as the pause lengthened, starting to become noticeable. "Just state the truth and we'll take care of the rest."

State the truth. State the…

"I was at work at 6 pm," I said, sticking to the truth as much as I could. "And then I left."

The orb glowed white, confirming the partial truth I'd just told.

"And after work?" Jamal asked.

His partner, eyes focused on his paper, did not see Jamal flick a finger toward the nearby wall. A crack in the stone amphitheater suddenly widened, and there was a sharp *snap!* sound as a bit of wall settled alarmingly. Several people in the general vicinity jumped, but no one more obviously than Jamal's partner. The man stood up from his stool and turned around as if he'd heard Death itself call him out by name. He clutched his paper to his chest and stared at the wall, his other hand dropping to the Ruiner at his side as if he might unholster it.

"Whoa!" Jamal said quickly, crossing to lay a hand on his partner's shoulder. "Steady, Everett. Steady. Everything's fine."

The partner, apparently quite shaken, tried to collect himself.

"I'm sorry, Henry. Still getting over the… I'm sorry."

"It's all right," Jamal said. "It's all right."

"Where were we with…?"

"He's good," Jamal said, holding up the orb, which was still glowing white from the half-truth I had told. "He went home after work."

"Ah, I see. Thanks, Henry."

"Good," Jamal said shortly. He lowered the orb, which was back to glowing blue, and twisted it. The light snapped off. "Then we're done."

"Yes, of course. Name?"

"Cicero James."

The partner flipped his papers over, wrote my name on another sheet, and then nodded. Jamal motioned for me to go ahead and continue on out of the amphitheater, giving me another significant look that I interpreted as "act naturally and don't do anything stupid."

I moved forward with more than a slight feeling of unreality. I couldn't understand what had just happened or—equally as important—*why* it had happened.

Why the hell would rule-following enforcer role model I'm-not-angry-just-disappointed Jamal Henry stick his neck out for me?

Is he working with Marlowe?

Working with Marlowe *on what???* And how the hell did Marlowe have influence over an *enforcer?* Marlowe wasn't some mob boss who could lean on the Guild or the WOTW to make them do what he wanted them to.

I made it out of the long passageway without being followed or called back. I expected the entire time to hear someone shout my name, or, worse, run after me and tackle me to the ground, but it didn't happen. I wanted nothing more than to break into a run and make a dash for Port Street, but I forced myself to walk slowly, following the crowd.

Outside the Meeting Place, still feeling strangely disconnected from myself, I turned back.

No one had followed me out of the Bowl. There were no enforcers eyeing me suspiciously, no partially concealed figures with glowing red eyes leering at me from the shadows.

I should get out while I can.

But if I'd really escaped notice…

I glanced toward one of the streets a bunch of Workers were walking down. The Room of Dawn and Dusk was over in that direction, on Jackdaw Lane. If I knew Hades Jackson, he'd be there. It was his bar, after all. At least currently.

I looked back at the amphitheater one more time. I'd been one of the last people out of the Bowl, and, aside from a few other stragglers, there was no one behind me. Officially, I had just given a Catcher-verified alibi, witnessed by two enforcers.

Was I safe? Did I have time to see Hades?

I need answers.

That thought was top of mind, and it continued to float there above the stew of other thoughts and emotions, bumping up against the top of my skull with a dull, achy consistency. The twilight sky cast everything in shadow and mirrored the indeterminate nature of my thoughts.

There was too much happening that I didn't understand. And I was putting too much store in Marlowe having the answers. Whatever was going on, he knew something about it, and he hadn't filled me in. He was hiding something. And now he was pulling strings I'd had no idea he could pull. Maybe for good reason, but it still made me feel very uneasy.

Hades might have answers, too. If anyone knew something about Raising, it would be him. Hell, considering someone was *actively editing* the Compendium, this might be my best chance to get information from a source I could more or less trust. Who knew how long my alibi would stick? Unless I got really lucky, they would come to question me eventually, and there was no escaping that. This might be my last time to freely walk about the Twilight House for a while.

Well then. To Hades I go.

Part Nine

Hades Jackson

and the Room of Dawn and Dusk

Feeling reckless but resolved, I hurried toward one of the side streets outside the Bowl, following behind a pack of young men that included some of those I'd followed in from Port Street earlier. They seemed to have had the same general idea as me: to visit Jackdaw Lane and not waste a trip to the Twilight House.

I got there quickly—despite its peculiarities, the Twilight House is fairly concentrated, and all of the places you really want to visit are basically located in the same square set of several blocks around the big central hill and all of the official buildings.

The bar itself is a two-story affair, like everything on Jackdaw Lane, with a shop, bar, or restaurant on the bottom and an apartment for the owners above. It has a large wooden sign across the front that proclaims "The Room of Dawn and Dusk" in large gold letters superimposed on a sunset and sunrise melding into one another in a spray of pink, crimson, indigo, and violet. It's been around for as long as anyone can remember, and it's a celebration of the power found in transitions. Dawn and dusk are excellent times for Working, along with high noon and the witching hour.

Hades is the current owner. He is not the first, nor will he be the last. He's had it for the past few years, but rumor is that the bar has been around almost as long as the House itself.

I've never been there when the owner was anyone else, though.

Also, I should clarify—the bar is named after the two people who work there. Ownership passes from Worker to Worker and has for generations—but there have only ever been two people who work in the bar. And I use the term "people" loosely. From what I've heard, they've always been there, and no one knows exactly who or what they are. They may actually be older than the bar itself, and some say they're from the Space Between Spaces. They aren't like Terrors or the Wrathful or any of the baddies we get called in to deal, but they aren't human. At least, I don't think they are. But then again maybe they were once, and enough Workers cemented them in their thoughts and beliefs over the years as something more and so they became that.

Hades is the main draw of the bar these days, but they remain a close second. If you're looking for information, you go to Hades. If you're looking for a boon, for something no one else can help you get, you go to Dawn. And then Dusk finds you for payment.

I opened the door and stepped into the anteroom. All of the windows were boarded up and have been ever since I first came there. Two men were waiting, both several inches north of six feet and easily several slabs of high-quality muscle over two hundred pounds. They both also wore a full complement of Instruments on their right hands, in the traditional mode— a band, a watch, and a ring. Theirs were all heavier-duty than mine—thick leather reinforced with metal, solid tungsten rings, watches of the chunky diving-to-the-depths variety— and clearly meant for power, not finesse.

One of them held out a hand. "Hold," he said. He held up an orb, very similar to a Truth Catcher but different enough to be considered legal for non-enforcer use. There isn't really a name for it, but you could call it an Intent Detector maybe. They're rare but not impossible to obtain for someone like Hades Jackson. "Name and business."

I cleared my throat and spoke clearly. "Cicero James. Here to speak with Hades Jackson."

The orb's light turned from green to yellow. It didn't go so far as to prove that I was telling the truth, but the knock-off Catcher was saying I had no ill intent.

"Are you aware of the rules of this establishment?" the second man asked, peering at me with dark eyes that spoke of a strong will and a consciousness completely at peace with doing violence to those he felt deserved it.

I glanced at the large stone plaque engraved with bronze on the wall to my left. It was extremely worn with age, but the words were still as clear as if they had been newly carved. I had no need to read them, as I'd seen them a dozen times, but I did so anyway.

ENTER HERE AND ALL WONDERS SHALL CEASE
AND MIRACLES FADE.

GLAMOR AND ILLUSION SHALL BE STRIPPED AWAY,
AND ONLY TRUTH SHALL REMAIN.

FOR THIS IS HALLOWED GROUND,
AND SHALL BE HALLOWED GROUND,

FROM THE SETTING OF THIS FIRST DAY
TO THE BREAKING OF THE LAST.

A shiver went down my back. It's a special feature of the Room: once you cross the threshold, you can't Work until you leave again. There are stories that the Room was the first building built in the Twilight House, and that its grounds were consecrated along with the founding of the wider city as a haven for those who had fled there, facing persecution in the east. There are stories too that it was originally a meeting place for the Native American medicine men who were the proto-Workers of the continent, but who had been replaced by European-born Workers the same way that settlers had colonized the rest of North America.

Maybe that's who Dawn and Dusk really are.

It wasn't the first time I'd had that thought.

"I am aware," I said. The two large men nodded and stepped aside.

Entering the Room is always jarring. Crossing the threshold brought me into a smaller bubble of reality within the larger one holding the Twilight House. The ground of the bar was not wooden or stone, but dirt and grass. Behind me, the door stood completely on its own, disconnected from any walls or ceiling. Around it and beyond it were the rolling, grassy hills of a western plain straight out of a cowboy movie.

There was a rising sun just beneath the horizon to the east and a setting sun just beneath the horizon to the west. The sky above was striated with clouds that were lit gold and crimson, violet and indigo. Fifty feet from the door was a wooden bar, and between it and the door were about two dozen wooden tables with wooden chairs. The bar itself was made of a gorgeous dark wood, and it circled a massive tree that towered above the plain, spreading its limbs out over all of the clustered tables. Built into the trunk of the tree were several dozen shelves, upon which you could find any liquor imaginable, including, I'd been told, many that hadn't been heard of in the outside world in almost a hundred years.

I braced myself. Right on cue, waves of cold and heat washed over me. My sight flickered, then returned, and then so too did my hearing, as if a subwoofer in my head had been switched suddenly off and then back on. My nose stuffed and then cleared; my clothes seemed too heavy, and then too light, as if I were wearing nothing.

It was part of whatever Working had been woven into the consecration of the ground. It had only become stronger over the years with each new Worker who believed in the effect and expected it upon entering. It was a wiping away of whatever it is that makes us Workers. It takes quite a lot of getting used to, but when you do get used to it, there's a kind of peace in it. Like setting down a heavy load and letting yourself rest for a while.

Anyway, I had expected that part. What I had not expected was the sudden spasm in the back of my throat and sinuses.

I began to cough violently, and I had to lean against the doorframe to keep myself standing upright. I felt something shift, and I thought vaguely that there must be a really gnarly clot of phlegm stuck somewhere back there. I really was coming down with something. I bent over and spat out onto the ground of the grassland plain.

A bolus of phlegm hit the ground—pink, yellow, and red.

I stared at it for a long moment.

Red. Bloody. That didn't make any sense.

I touched my throat and swallowed—no pain. I took a deep breath—no pain. And no further urge to cough.

Immediate thoughts of cancer and rare Ebola-adjacent diseases sprang to mind, even though I was protected against things like that by my ring. Anything truly life-threatening shouldn't be able to touch me. The common cold or something lower level could sneak through, but nothing like cancer or viral meningitis or… whatever.

And yet I'd just spat out a wad of blood and mucus.

Well, I was going to see Marlowe anyway—I could have him check me out. There was no use worrying until then.

I coughed again when I thought of Marlowe, and an image came to me of the woman with the strange talon finger that I had seen at the Meeting Place. I shook my head, not sure what it meant, and looked around.

The Room was sparsely populated. There were about a dozen Workers, mostly the tech bro group, who had come after the meeting. I scanned the tables as I walked toward the bar but saw no sign of Hades. I glanced over to the far left, beyond the tables, to where there was a second freestanding door, one that led upstairs to Hades' private rooms. I had never been through that door, and I knew that I—or any Worker—would be an absolute fool to try to gain entry without permission.

It was possible that he was on the other side of the tree that marked the center of the Room—there were more tables back there along with bar games—but that seemed unlikely. I made my way to the bar itself, ignoring the tech bro Workers who had just ordered a round of drinks and retreated to a set of tables off to one side. Pitchers were already appearing on the tables they had appropriated, and beer was flowing freely from several of the taps behind the bar, disappearing into thin air, and then reappearing to pour into glasses that had materialized on their tables.

I stepped up to the counter, the strip of dirt that lined the bar crunching beneath my boots to announce my presence.

Dusk turned and locked eyes on me. He's a tall man, but not imposingly so, thin and sinewy, and always wearing a gray linen shirt, brown pants of some indeterminate material, and a thick wool vest, usually dark brown or black. That night he was wearing a tight skull cap over his bald head, black leather. His skin is a dark copper color, and his eyes are like fresh honey—golden-brown fading to amber. He smells like sandalwood and trail dust.

"Cicero James," he said softly, approaching me. He has an accent that I have never been able to place, and it gives his words a kind of weight. His jaw is thick and heavy enough to crack a walnut, and he keeps a permanent scruff across his hollow cheeks and strong chin that's dark brown with a few dignified patches of gray.

"Dusk," I said. I had never introduced myself to him, nor ever been introduced, but Dusk had known my name ever since I had first set foot in the Room. It was the same with everyone.

"What can we do for you this evening, Cicero James?" Dusk asked. He leaned forward slightly on the counter of the bar and gestured behind him with his head. I glanced back at the rows and rows of bottles.

"House bourbon," I said. "Just a single. Neat."

Dusk nodded and began to turn.

"And," I said, "a chat with Hades."

I flourished my hand and withdrew two coins from my vault, which was up the street back outside the bar, somewhere in the Worker's Bank. The first coin was silver, for the drink; the second coin was gold, the price to pay for an audience with Hades Jackson.

Dusk looked at the coins, and then at me. "And is there anything else you would wish to purchase this evening? Something that comes at a different price?"

I suppressed a shiver. I had the sudden thought that I could ask Dusk himself to explain the Raising. Hell, I might even be able to ask him to make it all go away, and he'd talk to Dawn and maybe they'd actually be able to do it.

But if Dawn granted the boon, Dusk would collect the payment. Something of equal value. And in this case that might turn out to be one hell of a bill.

It was a last resort. I had never done it—made an exchange with them—but I had heard stories from people who had. Some of the deals had been wildly successful, and the asker had gladly paid the price. Others had been absolutely ruined— and swore the boon had been nowhere worth the cost.

I could do it. And now might be my chance.

I haven't even spoken to Marlowe yet. There might be a simple way out of this.

"No," I said slowly and carefully. "No, I do not wish to purchase anything else."

Dusk nodded and smiled with just his mouth—his lips closed, his eyes unchanging. He looked neither disappointed nor relieved. "Very well."

He motioned to his left, to an unoccupied table. On the table there had appeared a blue rose that floated unsupported. It glowed faintly. "Please have a seat, and Hades will meet you soon. Your drink will be delivered to your table."

I nodded, thanked the man, or whatever he was, and walked over. A glass rose slowly out of the hardwood table and then filled with an amber liquid. I took a sip and let it burn the back of my throat. I swallowed, waiting to feel pain from the earlier coughing fit, but there wasn't any. That made me more worried, not less.

As I waited, I thought. Now that I was here, what was I going to ask? Hades swore to confidentiality in all of his dealings, and I had no reason to suspect he had ever broken that confidentiality. But did it hold for something as important as breaking one of the Ten Prohibitions? It might. It might not.

I decided to approach it in a roundabout manner. Yes. Maybe I was there to sniff out a job. Maybe I was there to see if there was a way to get to the Raised Worker myself, bring him in.

That might just work.

"Cicero James," said a warm, rough voice. "What a surprise."

I stood and turned. Hades Jackson held out his hand, and I clasped and shook it. The hand was rough and warm too.

Hades Jackson is about my height, maybe an inch taller, and he has black hair that falls in a thick wave around his head and down the back of his neck. He has rough, leathery skin that puts him north of forty but makes it impossible to say exactly how old he is, though I've always had a feeling that he isn't as old as he pretends to be. That day he was wearing his customary leather duster along with black jeans. Under the duster was a dark button-up shirt with swirling designs and a charcoal-gray vest.

The most striking aspect of his appearance, though—as always—was his mismatched eyes: one of pale blue, and one a deep midnight-black flecked with green.

"May I?" he asked, gesturing to a chair at the table. It was a formality since he owned the chair and the table and everything else, but he's polite to a fault until he isn't. I nodded, and he sat. As soon as his ass hit the seat, the blue rose disappeared, winking out of existence as if it had never been. "What can I do for you?" he rasped. "Last I remember, you had to speak to a little ghosty about a missing locket. How did that all go?"

"Better than expected," I said, honestly. "Tonight, though, I wanna ask about... well, did you go to the meeting? I didn't see you there."

His eyes narrowed, and some of his affability drained away. "You've bought three answers to three questions, Cicero James," he said. "Do not make the mistake of trying to trick me into giving you a fourth. Your tongue may be silver, but I am only seduced by gold. Speak plainly."

I grimaced and took another sip of whisky.

He was right—that had been stupid. At least Hades was feeling charitable and in something like a good mood. If he hadn't been, he might have answered the question and counted it as one of the three I'd bought with my precious coin.

"I'm here about the Worker who was Raised," I said, watching the other man's expression carefully. "The one who caused the emergency meeting this evening."

As I would have expected, Hades kept his expression neutral and gave away nothing. His mismatched eyes gleamed in the twilight, and his thin-lipped mouth stayed shut. He did not blink but focused on me with a hungry-wolf intensity.

I continued. "I need to know about Raising. I don't want to know how to do it, I just need to know enough to track down who may have been the one to perform it."

I wanted to go on, but I stopped myself, watching him carefully. I didn't want to ask a question yet—I had to be sure what I did ask would be answered.

Hades nodded slowly as he absorbed what I'd said.

"A fine line," he said slowly. Then he smiled—a wide, toothy grin that showed a line of crooked, yellowing teeth. "You always bring me the most interesting topics," he said. He chuckled then, seeming to enjoy himself, and then he waved a hand and another glass appeared on the table, this one full with nearly three times as much amber liquid as had come in mine. Hades grabbed the glass and tossed it back in one, then shook his head, smiled widely again with his thin lips and yellow teeth, and leaned in, his mismatched eyes wide and almost seeming to glow in the bar's half-light.

"You may continue. I will only summon shades to answer that which is within the Code and the Appendices as lawful to answer. If they cannot answer, you may ask again."

I had to struggle to keep myself from reacting. That was a *very* generous offer. Why was Hades in such a good mood?

It didn't matter. I was getting what I wanted, and I would be a fool not to take advantage of it. It was about time I came upon some good luck.

"We have a deal," I said, holding out my hand. Hades smiled again and shook it. There was a tiny flash of blue flame above our clasped hands, and a tingling across the back of my neck.

"We have a deal," Hades repeated. He leaned back in his chair, mismatched eyes watching me hungrily. "Ask, Cicero James. Ask and I shall answer."

I paused. What should I start with? What was most important?

The pause lengthened, and I knew I had to fill it. Hades is not known for his patience, especially not once he has been engaged.

If he can't answer, he'll tell me. I need to know about Raising, start there.

"What is needed to perform a Raising?"

Hades considered this for a moment and then nodded slowly. He raised his hand toward the seat to his right, my left. The outline of a shape appeared, insubstantial but present. I suppressed a shiver. I had seen Hades do this before, but it was always eerie.

He was calling up a shade of one of the dead.

It wasn't Raising—he wasn't bringing them back—and therefore it was technically legal. It's damn hard to do, though, which is why almost everyone goes to him for it. I don't know of anyone else who can do it the way he does, in fact. It's a big part of how he got his name. And why everyone knows that if you need a question answered… you go to Hades Jackson. Because he can ask the dead themselves.

A charge filled the air, as if an electric field had suddenly sprung into existence around the table. The muscles in my arms and legs began to jump and twitch in response, and I clenched my jaw against the eerie feeling, trying to hold myself still.

"Speak, dear shade, of Raising," Hades said softly. "Speak of requirements and execution."

The shade gave no sign that it had heard him, and for a moment I thought whatever Hades had done hadn't worked. We sat there in silence, the shadowy figure floating and my teeth on edge from the strange otherworldly electricity coursing through me. But then slowly a ringing seemed to rise in my ears, and the world began to vibrate in strangely rhythmic pulses.

I glanced around. No one else in the Room seemed to have noticed anything. The tech bros were engaged with their beer and a game of shuffleboard, and the few other patrons who were in attendance were speaking with each other, apparently completely oblivious as to what was happening at the table between Hades and me.

Only one person, a short young woman in a dark windbreaker, was glancing over at us, but her eyes slid past even as I looked her way, and she did not look back.

I'd seen this happen before. The living mind does not want to look upon the dead, and it will blind you to them unless you consciously fight to see them.

"Listen," Hades said.

I jerked my head back around. His eyes were fixed on the shade.

I looked at the faintly black outline, which was now vibrating, splintering, and reforming.

"Life may be stolen from Death three days after a soul has gone to the undiscovered country," said a voice. "Thrice the cock must crow, thrice must darkness fall. Then does Death grow complacent, and from him many may trifles be taken."

The voice was straight from an old *Tales of the Crypt* rerun. As if that creepy basement-dwelling half-dead skeleton narrator had popped into existence three feet away from me. Childhood me was both thrilled and appalled.

After I got over that, I managed to realize that what it had said didn't make any sense. I'd risen much sooner than three days after dying. Did that mean it hadn't been a Raising at all? Or did that mean somehow someone had found a new way to Raise people?

"The moon must be high, and there must be gathered Workers three. The Miracle shall only be performed to satisfaction with sacrifice—life for life. An animal will do, but one of innocence it must be. Of sheep, a lamb or ewe. If thou canst use a man, seven days after the soul moves on may the ceremony be performed… if a woman, young and pure, eleven. At thirty days, thou must usest a newborn mewling babe. Beyond that, I know no more."

"And this is the only way?" Hades asked. "Know you no other?"

The shape became even more indistinct, fading back out of existence. Hades reached out and snatched closed his fist in midair, between him and the shade. The fading stopped, and there was a mighty groan as if chains held in rotting wood had been pulled tight.

After a long moment, a final sentence came.

"No other ways to me have e'er been spoke. No other ways by me have e'er been known."

Hades nodded and said, "Then sleep again, dear shade. Find thy rest."

There was a deep sigh, and the hazy, indistinct shape disappeared. The feeling of the electric current faded with it, and I was able to fully relax my hands and jaw again.

Hades breathed deeply as if he were drinking in something that only he could sense. He let that breath out and seemed to be invigorated. He looked back at me, his mismatched eyes wide so that I could see whites all the way around the irises. His pupils were slightly dilated as if he were intoxicated. I had a feeling it was from more than just the whiskey.

"The first question has been answered," he said. "Ask the second."

I was suddenly thinking very quickly. If that shade was right, then I hadn't been Raised at all. Could it be wrong? I didn't know. But I did know that Hades, as part of our bargain, would not lie, and to ask him if the shade had lied would be to insult him.

So if the shade was right and I *hadn't* been Raised... then what the hell had happened?

Maybe that was the next question. Why not? Worst that could happen was that Hades would simply refuse to answer it.

I had to word it correctly, though.

Haltingly, I said the following:

"What happened… to the Worker who died last night… at the house in Hayes Valley… after he was killed by the Terror that had infested it?"

Hades's eyes narrowed, and I did my best to keep my face blank. It was a perfectly plausible question given what I'd shared I'd been trying to get.

He leaned back, and this time spoke himself.

"The Worker who died last night was taken to a morgue. After several hours, he woke."

I didn't react, but I came damn close.

How did he know that? Who had he been speaking to?

I took a shallow breath and tried to remind myself that Hades Jackson was in the business of knowing. He could summon a shade any time he wanted to for his own purposes.

And I *had* ended up in a morgue. The shades were the remaining imprints of those who had died. No one had died in that house last night aside from me, but I hadn't been the only dead guy at the morgue, I was sure of that.

Hades knew somehow. Maybe it was a shade, or maybe someone else had been asking questions and exchanging information.

And then another possibility came to me. If I had been dead for several hours before returning… had *I* been a shade?

I had no memory of what had happened between when the Terror had speared me and when I'd woken up in the morgue. If I'd been a shade, if I'd gone somewhere or nowhere or anywhere, I had no memory of it.

Did Hades?

I suddenly had a thousand new questions to ask, but I bit my tongue and took a deep breath to keep myself from asking them.

I had one left. My second question hadn't worked out the way I'd wanted it to. I'd been hoping for something like "he was Raised." I hadn't wanted where I'd literally gone.

What if I took a shot?

"I desire clarity on my second answer," I said, making sure to phrase it as a statement.

The left side of Hades's wide mouth curved up in a slow smile that again revealed his yellow wolfish teeth. "You may have it," he said. "But tread carefully. My patience only stretches so far."

I thought quickly about what road might make the most sense to follow. I wanted to know everything, but what mattered in that moment was getting clear on the event itself. The metaphysical happenings between dying and waking would have to wait.

"Please explain further what you mean by 'he awoke'," I said finally. I desperately wanted to be more clear, but I couldn't think of a way without asking another question. The 'awoke' part was the part that mattered, though. Was it a figure of speech or had I just been sleeping? Had I died or just… hibernated somehow? That could help me.

"The Worker who died last night was not Raised," Hades said slowly, his eyes locked on mine. "He simply woke when his body was again able to support consciousness."

A thrill raced through me. It wasn't exactly what I had been hoping for, but it was definitely a breadcrumb on the right trail.

Not Raised. Not Raised!

Without thinking, I asked, "How is that possible? You can't just wake from death."

I snapped my mouth shut so hard that my teeth clacked, but the damage had already been done. Hades was already nodding. He raised his hand, this time to the other chair at the table. The shade-summoning process repeated itself, with an indistinct shadow appearing in the chair, without dimension or depth but with a sense of weight that vibrated the air around us and this time left a metallic taste in my mouth instead of a vibrating electricity.

"Speak of the dead," Hades commanded the shade. "Once one has crossed over, is it possible to return fully to life if one is not Raised?"

There was a long silence, and then a deep bass voice said simply, "It is not possible. If one crosses over, one is bound, through means foul or fair. An exchange must be made."

Hades nodded, as if that settled things, and raised a hand to dismiss the shade. "Wait," I hissed. "Wait!"

But the shade was already fading, and soon there was nothing left but an empty bar chair.

"That can't be it," I said, leaning forward. "I need to know more!"

"Our business tonight is at an end, Cicero James," Hades said. He pushed back from the table and stood. I stood as well and rounded the table, reaching out to stop him. Hades shot me a glare that stopped me dead in my tracks. I suddenly remembered where I was and that I was powerless, while Hades, as current owner of the Room, had access to all its power. He was not bound by its rules for patrons; he had full access to his Working ability, while I, for all intents and purposes, was no more a Worker than one of the Blissful until I left.

"Please," I said. "I need to know more."

Hades stared at me for a long moment, and then his expression changed. His narrowed mismatched eyes relaxed, and he briefly pursed his lips as if shrugging with them.

"We will see each other again soon, I think," he said, his rasping voice making the statement sound like both a threat and a promise. "You are welcome to return tomorrow night to ask more. But tonight, our business is concluded."

He took a step toward me and said in a lower voice, "*We are finished.*" He flicked his eyes back at the bar, where Dusk was still visible, now serving one of the tech bros who was wearing a blue fleece vest. "Though you may try your luck by other means."

I swallowed, again considering it. Finally, I shook my head.

"No. No, there has to be another way."

Hades met my gaze again. "Don't be a stranger, Cicero James. You are one of my favorite customers. You always ask such... *invigorating* questions." He turned to go and then stopped once more.

"This I will give you," he said, "not out of charity but out of curiosity. You were followed here, and you are being watched. Have you noticed?"

My heart skittered and skipped a few beats. My surprise and panic must have shown on my face, because as soon as I realized I had frozen, Hades chuckled softly. "You need to be more observant. The woman at the table by the door—she followed you in and no doubt will follow you out. I have not seen her before, but she carries a type of Ruiner with her. It is hidden, and unusual, but I can feel it in here, the same way I can feel your Instruments, useless though they are inside the Room."

Hades watched me for another moment. "Be careful, Cicero James. I wish to speak with you again in the flesh before I speak with you as a shade."

He left, and I tried to rein in my racing thoughts.

Part Ten

I Confront My Stalker

I walked toward the entrance/exit of the Room of Dawn and Dusk as naturally as I could. I did not want to give any indication to the woman Hades had pointed out that he had just told me about her, partly because I had no idea what I was going to do about it yet.

It wasn't something that Hades would lie about—Hades didn't lie. He would sometimes conceal the truth, or omit it if that suited him, but his whole reputation was based on the premise that when he said something straight out, everyone could take it as gospel.

If Hades said there was someone following me, then there was someone following me.

I realized when I was several paces away from the freestanding door that I was still holding my drink glass. I blinked a few times, shook my head, and placed the glass as calmly as I could on an empty table. It was a heavy glass, and I remember it making a satisfying thunk against the wood. Funny the things you notice when you're in a heightened state.

I glanced over at the young woman in the dark windbreaker that I had noticed earlier looking at Hades and me. She was who Hades had meant, the only woman sitting by the door, and directly in my path so that I'd have to pass by her as I left. She was sipping a clear liquid cocktail that could have just been water. I did no more than casually glance her way, though—I've had more than my share of practice at being discreet in interesting situations, unfortunately, and staring at the person you're trying to observe is not ideal.

I walked straight to the tall wooden door, opened it, and walked out. As always, leaving the Room was just as jarring as entering it. The process by which my Working was stifled upon entering the Room was reversed, so that I felt a wave of heat and then one of cold, and then all my senses seemed to dial back up. I became hyper-aware of the world around me again, and sweat beaded on my forehead as if I'd just broken a fever.

I shook my head and wiped my hand across my face, then blinked several times, taking a moment to adjust. The bouncers waited patiently, watching me but not making any moves to help. I have to imagine they're pretty used to that whole process.

"Get what you came for?" one of them asked.

"More or less," I answered. The first man nodded and the second one grunted in a way that seemed to acknowledge the underlying truth of how I had responded—that people never really get everything they want in the Room of Dawn and Dusk, though they are occasionally lucky enough to get what they need.

I crossed the anteroom back to the door that opened onto the street. It was darker outside now, but there was still a glimmer of light on the ring of hills surrounding the House. It was as close to real night as the Twilight House ever came.

There were a few streetlights that had been lit, old-school lanterns with flickering flames inside them instead of electric lights. Their illumination was watery and half-hearted.

I walked down the street slowly enough so as not to lose my tail, who I assumed was still following me and therefore would make her way out of the Room soon. I wanted to get a good look at her if I could manage it before I lost her.

A few moments later, I heard the door open again. Jackdaw Lane is narrow enough and at that point was empty enough that there weren't many other noises to cover the sound up, aside from two men further down the lane bidding against each other for someone's business, offering deals for their respective establishments.

I turned a corner, down a side alley that I thought would eventually take me back to Port Street by a slightly different route from the one I'd arrived by. I paused just inside the mouth of the street, pressing myself against the brick wall of one of the buildings. I listened hard, trying to hear footsteps. The two men up the road were bickering now, offering a free beer and a free appetizer respectively to whomever they were trying to persuade, and their banter temporarily drowned out any smaller sounds.

I drew on my band and felt a welcome rush of heat that told me my Working ability was back after leaving the Room. I hated being without it, and I sucked in more energy than I probably needed to before breathing it out and letting it fade my appearance, blurring me to any curious eyes. It didn't make me invisible, but in the semi-darkness it did make me essentially see-through as long as I stayed fairly still.

I held onto the belief that I was insubstantial and unnoticeable as strongly as I could, knowing that, if Hades were telling the truth, the woman following me was looking for me directly, and if the Working was shaky, her concentration might break through it.

I leaned slowly out around the corner, careful not to make any sharp movements. For a moment, I thought the street behind me was empty, but then I saw someone standing off to one side, looking up and down Jackdaw Lane as if trying to determine which way to go.

She was a few dozen yards away, but close enough that I could make out basic features. She was short, or so it seemed—several inches shorter than me, at least. She had thick, shoulder-length hair that was either dirty blonde or light brown, pulled back behind her head and out of her face in a functional kind of way, without much regard for how it looked. She had a sharp jaw and high cheekbones that made her look almost elf-like, and fair skin that looked tanned by the sun.

I quickly checked her hands—nothing on them. No ring, no band, no watch.

Hades had said she had a concealed Ruiner. Was that her only Instrument? Was she an enforcer? I couldn't see her ears from where I stood—it was possible she had earrings she used as rings, or piercings elsewhere, which was becoming more common. Her windbreaker sleeves covered her upper arms, and her pants covered her legs—they might be concealing a band as well. In addition to the dark windbreaker, she was wearing muted, worn sneakers, tight black pants, and a loose green shirt.

She ran her hand agitatedly through her hair and then muttered something to herself. She looked up the street the other way, shook her head, and then turned the way I had gone, apparently deciding (correctly) that I had headed in the general direction of Port Street.

I slowly pulled back into the side alley and let go of my belief in the concealment Working so that I didn't drain too much energy from my still-depleted band.

OK, so I was being followed. That wasn't... ideal. What was I gonna do about it?

I glanced down the alley and saw that it twisted out of sight. Was there another end to it? That turn went in the general direction of Port Street.

One way to find out.

I hurried off, dodging wooden boxes and various detritus that I assumed had been left there by the restaurants and bars that lined Jackdaw. I rounded the first twist, then a second, and then found myself at a dead end in the form of a brick wall.

"Shit."

I walked up and placed a hand against the gritty, grimy brick. Several ideas ran through my mind, from rearranging the bricks to just blasting through them, but before I could settle on any one method, I noticed a small mark on a brick just above my head and off to the right. It was a small oval eye with a runic shape in the center, like a pupil.

A Working signature. This wall was part of one of the buildings.

"Shit! Shit shit shit—"

I whirled back around. I could still attempt to blast my way through, but it would take a hell of a lot of mental fortitude to overcome the belief embedded in the wall that was no doubt making it sturdy and solidly connected to the buildings on either side of it. Like I mentioned back at the morgue—making something think it's a wall is one of the easier types of Workings, and it's hard to undo. The energy I'd have to expend to force a contradictory belief on the wall—or just blast through it, if I even could—would draw more attention than just that of the woman following me. If I'd had more time, I might have been able to pick the belief apart like pulling strings in a complicated knot, but that could take hours. Even if I ended up getting lucky, it would have taken at least twenty, maybe thirty minutes to make significant headway.

OK—dead end. Go back.

I hurried back up the alley, thinking that maybe I would get lucky and the woman would rush past and not see it, or that she had gone a different direction already.

I slowed as I neared the entrance and pushed myself up against the side of one of the buildings before pulling more energy from my band and performing the same Working as before to make me insubstantial. I was about to poke my head around the corner again when I heard footsteps moving in my direction.

Two sets of footsteps.

"Over here!" I heard someone say under their breath. I had the sudden impression that whoever it was was waving to attract the attention of someone else further up the lane.

I readied myself for a fight. If all else failed, I would fight my way through to Port Street. I had no idea who these people were, but I was willing to bet they were people I didn't want in control of me. I couldn't let them take me into custody, not after hearing what I had from Hades Jackson. I hadn't been Raised—I was innocent of that, at least, and I needed time to figure out what had really happened in order to clear my name. There had to be some kind of evidence to prove it, something that I could present to the Guild to show that whatever had happened hadn't been intentional, that it hadn't been my fault.

I balled my hands into fists, easing my tattoos down from my forearms and into my palms, readying them for use.

"Jamal!" hissed the same voice.

I froze.

The enforcer chose that exact moment to walk into my range of vision. His large, heavy boots were the other set of footsteps I'd been hearing.

I got lucky. Hidden as I was in the shadows of the alley in my insubstantiality Working, the enforcer's eyes slid right past me. I wasn't as lucky as I could have been, though—because Jamal began walking toward the side street and met the young woman not ten feet from the entrance. I clung to the shadows, barely daring to breathe, and listened to them exchange a hurried, whispered conversation.

"Did you lose him?"

"Fuck you, did I lose him," the woman hissed back, glaring at him. "He went to the Room of Dawn and Dusk and met with Hades, then he came out here."

"And then you lost him."

"I did not lose him."

"Then where is he?"

I beat back the urge to step out dramatically and say "Tah dah!"

Why were they chasing me? Why had Jamal let me go only to come after me now? Was it a setup of some kind?

"He's on his way to Port Street," the woman said. "I'm sure of it."

Jamal nodded. "So you lost him."

"Say it one more time, Jamal," she hissed. "Go on!"

She stepped forward threateningly, which I found comical despite the situation, considering that she was at least a foot shorter than him.

"What did he talk with Hades about?" Jamal asked.

"I don't know. Hades doesn't allow eavesdroppers, you know that. He summoned two shades, though. I think James engaged him, the typical three questions. It got pretty tense toward the end. I think he wanted more answers than Hades was willing to give."

I took a step back, trying to put more distance between me and them, but I was so engrossed in eavesdropping that I didn't look where I was putting my foot, and I accidentally kicked a dislodged chunk of brick.

Immediately, both Jamal and the woman turned toward the alley. I felt a huge weight fall on me as they stared straight at me and my Working tried to sustain itself despite their concentrated efforts to see me, and their belief that they *could* see me. My belief that I was insubstantial met up against them and held, but it was unsustainable, and the Working would crack even if I didn't let it fall—it would simply consume all of the energy in my band.

I made a snap decision and decided to force a confrontation.

I dropped the illusion and strode forward, emerging dramatically from the shadows. I let some of the energy in my right-hand flare out, and a flash of flame whooshed around my head and shoulders. I let the tempest Working in my left-hand release a slight wind, which whipped my hair up and swirled the dust at my feet.

Both Jamal and the woman jumped, startled.

"Whoa!" Jamal said, holding up his hands, neither of which, I noted, bore a Ruiner.

"Jesus H. Christ!" the woman swore. She looked much more ready for a fight—she had pulled out a long, thin piece of wood from somewhere on her body and was holding it protectively in front of her. Her other hand was beneath her windbreaker clutching something at her waist. Likely the Ruiner she had concealed.

The thin bit of wood took me by surprise. I hadn't seen a wand in ages. What a throwback.

"Now would be the time to explain why you're following me," I said.

I let more energy flow through the tattoos on my palms, and flame sparked around my right fist while electricity crackled and flashed in white-gold branchings around my left.

"James!" Jamal said, insistent but not raising his voice. He was still holding his hands out and up as if to show me he meant no harm. He glanced quickly up and down the street, as if worried that we would be seen or heard.

That gave me pause.

"Marlowe sent us, you idiot," the woman said, still watching me intensely and holding her wand at the ready.

The words weren't at all what I had expected to hear, and so they didn't quite register at first the right way in my brain. Then a few gears clunked into place, and lights and whistles started going off as my thoughts caught up to what she'd said.

"*Marlowe?* Why—why would he *send* you? Why isn't he here himself?"

"He's under suspicion for last night," Jamal said quickly but calmly, still showing me his open palms as if I were a skittish horse. "We'll explain—just, take it easy. Think it through. Why would I help you get out of the Meeting Place only to ambush you now?"

I watched the enforcer for a long moment, and then let the energy dissipate from my hands. The flames and the lightning winked out, leaving us all once more in semi-darkness, and the wind blew itself out as well, settling the hair back flat on my head.

"All right, fuckin' Goku," the woman said, moving forward. "Move!"

I took several steps into the alley, and Jamal and the woman joined me. They both looked back down the lane one last time and then, apparently satisfied with what they had or hadn't seen, turned to me.

"We need to get you out of here," Jamal said. "Marlowe's at his place."

"No," I said. "Explanations first. I'm not going anywhere until you tell me who this is and how you started working with Marlowe. And just generally what the hell is going on."

The woman glanced at Jamal. He sighed, nodded, and then glanced back out into the Lane once more.

"Kori Clark," she said. She didn't stick out her hand to shake or anything, but she did slip her wand back up her sleeve, which I took as an indication that she was at least temporarily willing not to try and curse me or anything else witchy.

"Kori Clark?" I asked. "Do you have a superhero identity or something? That's the most Marvel-sounding name I've ever heard."

"Yeah, I'm Shut The Fuck Up Girl and my power is kicking you in the balls until you shut the fuck up."

I stared at her.

"I don't think I'm going to like you," I said.

"KC, watch the Lane," Jamal said.

"KC? Please tell me your middle name is Francis or Franny or something," I said. "Is your uncle a colonel?"

She shot me a scathing look. "No finger-licking good here, Sissy-row." She turned away and went to the mouth of the street.

I opened my mouth to snap out a riposte, but Jamal put a hand on my chest and held me back. "Leave it," the bigger man said. "We need to do this quickly."

I pursed my lips and focused on the enforcer. "OK. Talk."

Jamal shook his head. "I don't even know half the time. Look, Marlowe's the one you'll want to hear the answers from. He... didn't want you to be a part of this. Not unless you wanted to be. He wanted you to have that choice. And he said first and foremost to pass on an apology that that choice was taken away from you."

I watched Jamal's face carefully, trying to detect any hint of a lie. He seemed earnest enough. And why would he lie? Like he said, he'd just helped me escape an official WOTW investigation. I grunted. "Well, that definitely sounds like Marlowe."

"Doesn't it just."

I took half a second to mentally reappraise Jamal. We didn't run in the same circles, but he was about my age and there was something about him that seemed familiar. We hadn't been in the Academy together—even considering how short my time there had been after being home-schooled by Marlowe—and I really could only remember doing the one job with him. I'd seen him at meetings and things, but that's all.

He must be another one of Marlowe's students. That must be how they met, and now he's working with him on… something. Or maybe Marlowe's calling in a favor?

Marlowe tends to pick a certain type of person to take under his wing. People who want to do the right thing but hate being told how to do it. I wouldn't have expected an enforcer to have been one of his pupils, but, given that Jamal was now helping me evade the WOTW, I supposed he was exactly the kind of person Marlowe would have picked.

"Fine—so he'll tell me more when we get to him," I said. "But why are you working with him? And what's Kentucky Fried Chicken doing following me?"

"Marlowe recruited us a few months ago," Jamal said. He held up a hand, seeing the questions in my eyes already. "He'll tell you. I can't. It's… dangerous. And we aren't safe here. *You* aren't safe here."

"Do you know what happened to me?" I asked quickly. "Does that have to do with whatever it is Marlowe's up to?"

Jamal shook his head. "I don't know. I'm still catching up on everything. All I know is that something happened— something we've been waiting for. Not for it to happen to *you*, but for it to happen to someone. One of about a dozen names.

You were on the list. Pretty low on the list, honestly. Which is why no one approached you earlier."

"A list?"

Jamal nodded but did not elaborate further.

My thoughts immediately began spinning again. Marlowe had known something. He had known and that was why he had told me to come to his house after work, but I hadn't and so Marlowe had had to send Jamal and this Kori person to bring me in.

"Why isn't Marlowe here?" I asked again. "What is he wanted for—what could they possibly have on him? Isn't he like, Worker Role Model of the Year or something?"

I was still struggling to reconcile the image of my teacher and mentor with that of someone apparently under active investigation by the Workers of the West.

"We're not completely sure," Jamal said. "Or at least we weren't until last night. I don't know what happened, even— I'm... I could have sworn I was on duty for it, but I was sick earlier today, I'm still catching up on everything."

"But he's under suspicion."

"Yes. They think he's the one who Raised you."

My heart did a double beat, hearing him say the words out loud, and my adrenaline spiked. He was saying it straight out. And regardless of the fact he said he was working with Marlowe, I didn't like anyone saying it, especially not a WOTW enforcer.

"I wasn't Raised," I said. "That's what Hades just told me. In order to be Raised there have to be certain things in place, and a certain time period—none of that was there for me. It was something else. I don't even know if I technically *died*."

Jamal was watching me closely. I couldn't tell what he was thinking.

"Are you sure that's what Hades said?"

"No, I just said it while we were telling each other important information to be funny."

Jamal rolled his eyes and crossed his arms, standing up to his full height and looking suddenly menacing.

Jesus, dude is a goddamn tree.

I threw my hands up. "It's fuckin' Hades, man! You never know *for sure* for sure, but yeah, it's about as certain as I've ever felt leaving the Room. The shades said it straight out."

Jamal was still looking at me with an inscrutable expression, which I found much more suspicious than if he had shown some kind of reaction. What did he know?

"The sarcasm is unnecessary and somewhat hurtful," Jamal said, "given the fact I'm risking my career to keep you out of WOTW hands."

I closed my eyes and rubbed my temples. "Yeah, fine, you're right, you're right, I felt that as soon as I said it. My bad. Habit. Just kicks in, you know?"

"I'll give it a pass this time."

"OK, thanks."

"Only time, though, you got it?"

"Understood, chief."

Kori turned back into the side street. "Are you done bro-ing each other? Can we go?"

"Almost," Jamal said. Then, to me, "They're reviewing the alibis tonight. We need to get you out before they get to yours. We got you through on a technicality, and I'm not sure it'll hold up for very long, given that you're the Worker who claimed the job."

"You sure they didn't get to him already? Before the meeting?" Kori asked, eyeing me like a potentially rabid dog who had been bit but had yet to start foaming at the mouth.

"They didn't," I said. "Marlowe thought they'd come for me at work, but they didn't. I don't remember much of the day, though—Marlowe gave me a manic Working to get me through it."

Jamal frowned.

"Yeah, yeah, it's risky and not exactly Guild-approved, I know," I said. "But I had just, you know, come back from the *dead,* though, and there was no way I was going to make it through the day on coffee and deep breathing."

I heard a snort and glanced over at Kori, who was smirking.

"I... no one spoke to you?" Jamal asked.

His eyes flickered with a strange glint of violet.

"Uh… KFC, do his eyes usually do that?" I asked.

"Do what?" she asked, ignoring the barbed nickname.

Jamal blinked and shook his head, then put a hand to his temple and rubbed with a thick, muscular finger. His eyes returned to their natural rich, dark brown, and he blinked several more times. I looked significantly at Kori, who now looked alarmed.

"What was that there, boss?" I asked Jamal, my anxiety mounting.

Violet... why does that make me think…?

An image of the woman who had been on the stage with Kaj Van Sant at the Meeting Place came to mind. I frowned. "Hey—do you know who that lady was up on the stage tonight? She had a finger like a..."

I made a gesture with my hands, suddenly unable to find the word. It seemed to all be slipping out of my head, like water through a sieve.

"Talon," I heard Kori say. The word seemed to come from far away, though. Another coughing fit hit me, and I doubled over with the force of it. It was worse than any of the previous episodes, and this time it felt as if there were a lump in the back of my throat that I couldn't clear—some kind of ball that I couldn't swallow around and couldn't cough up.

I felt a sharp pain in my knees and realized I'd fallen. I braced myself with my hands against the ground and heard sounds of alarm from both Jamal and Kori. Jamal reached down to hold my shoulders, and something sharp sizzled and cracked and jumped from me to him, something that produced a cutting violet light. Jamal cried out and grabbed at his temples, his eyes flashing unnatural colors once more. Kori left her post at the alley entranceway and rushed back to us, then stood there looking indecisive, clearly unsure what had happened and how she was supposed to help.

She turned to Jamal first. She threw a hand into her jacket and pulled out a modified Ruiner. It was brown leather, fingerless, and had a ring on the middle finger. She then pulled the thin wand out of her sleeve with her gloved hand and began muttering words under her breath. She grabbed Jamal by the shoulder, something she could only do since he was slumped over holding his head in his hands, and held her wand up in front of his face. She continued chanting, speaking faster and faster so that whatever language it was that was rolling out of her mouth came blisteringly quick and furious, cracking and spitting as if she were a hissing cat.

The violet light in Jamal's eyes disappeared. He drew in a deep, shuddering breath and then seemed to focus on Kori again, fully back in his right mind.

"They got to him. Damn. Damn! I was there!"

"What?"

"It was Shrike."

"Who the fuck is Shrike?" Kori asked.

"She's some kind of WA consultant, she came in and pulled rank on Smith this morning. She was there. She wants to use him to get to Marlowe, she put a—she *put something in him.*"

My coughing fit had begun to subside, at least enough that I was able to follow all of this, but I was still having trouble breathing. I crawled forward and managed to sit/lean against the nearest wall, where I continued to wheeze and clutch at my chest.

"We need to get it out," Jamal said. "We need to get it out *now.*"

Kori shook her head frantically. "We should wait for Marlowe. Marlowe should do it. We don't have any idea what it is or what taking it out could do."

"No," Jamal said. "We can't take him to Marlowe while it's still in him. It'll lead her right to him, and it'll burrow through the mansion's defenses. She'll be able to get in."

I continued to watch them both with very wide eyes. Parts of the conversation had begun to slip away from me as I was now having trouble taking a full breath, but what I *was* following was alarming me greatly. I began to shake my head and try to stand.

"Hold him," Jamal said.

Kori grimaced, and then leapt on me like a cat on a rat. I fought against her, but the coughing fit had left me weak, and she, it turned out, was freakishly strong.

Jamal pulled his Ruiner from its holster at his hip, slipping his hand into it in an easy, practiced motion and strapping the black leather wristband securely into place. I redoubled my efforts to escape, but I couldn't manage to lock my thoughts onto any Workings long enough to ready them.

I looked at the Ruiner and felt something shift inside my throat. For the first time since it had been implanted, I was conscious of it being a *thing*, and the realization came to me that that *thing* didn't want the Ruiner to get close to it.

That changed everything. All rational thought left my mind as I truly realized that there was something *inside* me. In my throat, in the top back of my throat, maybe even in my *brain*—

GET IT OUT GET IT OUT GET IT OUT!!!

The words did not come from my mouth, but I apparently thought them so loudly that Kori and Jamal both winced and recoiled.

"Hold him!" Jamal repeated.

Kori clamped back down on my arms and threw herself across my torso, leaving my head and neck exposed. Jamal, grim-faced and jaw set, lifted the hand with his Ruiner and closed it in a quick, practiced motion. The rings lit up with a cool green light, and my coughing subsided. Then the metal lines that ran from the fingers to the back of the hand glowed a hot red, and I felt a searing sensation in the back of my throat.

I screamed, but the sound didn't go anywhere. Kori was muttering again under her breath, speaking faster than a human tongue and lips should be able to move.

Something in the back of my throat split, and I couldn't scream anymore. There was something moving, something scrambling for purchase, sinking tiny claws into whatever it could find in an effort to remain inside me.

Memories of the past few days—images, sounds, sensations—all flickered through my mind as if I were feeling them there and then. And then more—memories of sensations from months ago, from years ago, from the whole spectrum of my life. I was cold, I was hot, I was tired, I was elated, I was at a beach, I was walking through the rain. I knew that it wasn't really happening—some core essence that was purely *me* knew that it was all wrong—but it all felt shockingly real.

"Got it!" I heard someone say, but I couldn't tell if it was a memory or if it was actually happening. I couldn't breathe, something was blocking my throat and I was choking—my mouth was wide open, so wide that I felt as though my jaw might dislocate, like my whole mouth might unhinge and open like a snake's. Jamal's hand was on my throat, and the Ruiner was glowing red in front of my eyes—

There was a tearing sensation in the back of my throat, and something came loose. I coughed and choked, and Jamal twisted his wrist and closed his fist.

A mass of blood, phlegm, and metal shot from my open mouth past my hyperextended jaw. It flew across the narrow side street and slammed into the wall opposite, splattering a disgusting mix of bodily fluids in several directions. In the center of it was a metal centipede—an ugly, segmented, horrific *thing* with dozens of legs that clawed and grasped.

I bent over and began coughing and hacking. Blood, phlegm, and saliva all pooled on the ground beneath me, and my throat felt as though it had been split in two. But I could breathe. Finally, I could breathe. Air whistled in through my mouth like the sweetest thing I had ever tasted; the freshest, cleanest drink of cold water on a hot summer's day.

I fell back, gasping. Jamal knelt beside me.

"Easy, easy," he said. "You can breathe? Nod if you can breathe."

I nodded several times, still gasping and clutching at my throat. Kori had hurried over to the centipede thing, which was still wrapped in red light and scrabbling around trying to free itself from Jamal's hold. Jamal's Ruiner still glowed with echoing bands of crimson light, and though the thing twisted and turned violently, it could not escape.

"What is it?" Jamal asked over his shoulder.

"Fuck if I know," Kori said. "It wants to get the hell out of here, though."

"Seal it up. We're taking it with us."

"That does *not* seem like a good idea," she said, glancing back. "It looks like some kind of tracker, in addition to whatever else it's supposed to be."

"It is," Jamal said, his tone and expression dark. "Shrike planted it."

"How did she manage that?"

"I don't know, but I was there. She wiped my memory. It hasn't all come back yet."

"What?"

Jamal glanced at her, and Kori stared at him for a long moment, apparently unsure what to do with this information. Finally, she said, "How do you remember now?"

"The bug," he said. "The Workings on both of us interfered with each other and the one on me must have shorted out. There's probably some kind of Working on that thing that impels it to remember everything—that hit against whatever Shrike put on me that made me forget. That's my best guess, at least."

My world spun, and I slumped to the side.

"Shit!" Kori exclaimed. Jamal grabbed me before my head could hit the ground.

"James," Jamal said, sitting me back upright. "James, can you hear me?"

Everything was going in and out of focus. I nodded, but it seemed like I was doing so from very far away, as if I were controlling an avatar with some kind of broken game controller that responded on a delay and kept trying to make me turn left.

I looked down and realized I had lost a decent amount of blood. I tried to open my mouth to speak, but the only thing that came out was a croak. A spike of pain rushed up the back of my head and rang through my skull as if I were a bell that had been struck by a massive mallet.

And then I heard a noise—somewhere far off in the distance. At first, I couldn't tell if I was imagining it since I'd just been thinking about ringing bells, but then both Kori and Jamal reacted to it too, turning to look back at the entrance to the alley.

"Is that an alarm?" Kori asked.

Jamal looked down at me, then looked back at the struggling centipede buried in the wall, still trying to escape. Then he looked back at Kori. "Do you think—?"

The alarm became louder as something else picked it up. It was an electronic blaring sound, like a firehouse klaxon.

"She knows we took it out," Jamal said. "Somehow she knows. We have to go. *Now*."

Kori hurried over to me and grabbed up one of my arms and threw it around her shoulder. She was several inches shorter than me, so that part was fairly easy, but when I tried to stand, my legs wobbled and almost gave out and the bulk of my weight fell on her. She caught me with a grunt and managed to keep us both standing, but it was clearly a strain. "Little help here!" she managed to gasp at Jamal.

"I need to head them off," he said quickly. "I need to keep my cover intact. I'll lead them away from Port Street—but you need to get him there so he can get out and get to Marlowe."

"I can barely stand with him!" she gasped. "How are we gonna get to Port Street?"

Jamal turned to me. "Can you make yourself lighter?"

I still couldn't speak, but I was fairly certain I could Work. I nodded and began pulling energy from my band. It doesn't take much effort to make yourself a few pounds lighter or heavier, but it's a logarithmic function of effort, and for every extra pound it becomes increasingly more difficult. The most I've ever managed is about thirty pounds either way before it became unsustainable for more than about a minute. So, I mentally aimed for about half that and hoped it would be enough.

Kori felt the change and lifted my arm higher around her shoulders. "We'll make it work," she grunted, taking my weight as best she could. "What about that thing?"

She gestured to the centipede with her chin. Jamal considered it for half a second, then strode forward and slammed his Ruiner-clad hand into it. There was a flare of red light, the sound of a deep percussive impact, and then a metallic crunch. Impact cracks spread through the wall from where Jamal had crushed the thing. Or at least where I thought he had crushed the thing—when he pulled back, it was revealed to still be intact but not moving and clearly dead. Whatever enchantment it had held seemed to have been snuffed out.

I gestured to it and then gestured to myself and Kori, trying to form words but unable to get them out through my brutalized throat.

Jamal and Kori both looked at me, then after a moment seemed to understand.

"You don't think it's still tracking, do you?" Kori asked Jamal.

"No," he said. "James is right—take it, get it to Marlowe."

Jamal plucked it out of the wall using the strength of the Ruiner, turned, and tossed it to Kori. She caught it with the hand not supporting me—and also wearing her modified Ruiner—and then twisted her wrist and it disappeared. It was the same kind of motion I use to access my vault, so I assumed that she had put it in hers.

"Go," Jamal said. He was already moving toward the entrance to the alleyway. "They'll be on their way here, it'll be the last place that tracker sent a signal from. I'll bring them in. If you see me in the House again, you don't know me. Worse—I'm a threat. You have ten minutes tops. Get to Port Street."

He left the alley, running up the Lane the way that I had come from the Meeting Place. Kori and I followed, and then went the opposite direction.

Curious heads were peeking out of bars and restaurants along the Lane, and I knew that soon enough the street would be filled with an interested crowd. My knees still didn't want to lock properly, and so I was stumbling about like a clown on stilts, but with Kori's help I managed to make it down the street. As we went, my head began to steady, and I was able to take more of my own weight. The problem was that my throat was swollen and closing up again, and though I could wheeze in enough air to function, I couldn't take a full enough breath to support running or any seriously aerobic activity, which kept me light-headed and floppy-limbed.

We heard a commotion behind us as we reached the end of the street, and we turned back to see Jamal leading a group of enforcers down Jackdaw Lane, checking bars and restaurants as they went, calming the people who were looking out into the street and asking them to go back inside.

Kori and I shambled on, both of us breathing heavily. My head had begun to spin again, and I had to lean more heavily on her, slowing us down. The energy in my band was slowly draining away as well, and there was only so much longer that I would be able to keep my weight reduced.

We made it down another street, and one more, and then we were on the long boulevard, Clemon, that eventually led to Port Street, with its alleyways and park. We weren't the only ones heading that way—it appeared that about two dozen other Workers who had stayed after the meeting had also decided that now was an excellent time to Irish Goodbye their way out of the Twilight House.

"Hurry," Kori grunted. "We have to get through before they close the street."

I was confused by that until I saw what she must have already seen: enforcers hurrying down Clemon from the direction opposite us.

Of course. The alarm had told them that something was happening in the city, and they were closing off Port Street to keep whomever it was that might have triggered the alarm from fleeing. Whoever it was that had, say, found and destroyed an illegal tracking bug planted by a WOTW official. The same someone who, quite rightly it turned out, might be the Raised worker trying to make a getaway.

"Can you stand on your own yet?" Kori asked.

"Yes," I managed to croak. What little energy I had in my ring was doing its job and slowly helping me heal. That plus adrenaline gave me the strength to hold myself steady.

She held out her hand and flourished it. The metal centipede appeared again. She grabbed my hand and forced the bug into my fist.

"Go," she said quickly. "I'll draw them off. Go!"

"Wait," I croaked painfully at her. "Wait, they'll chase you!"

"That's the point, dummy."

She helped me the last couple of steps and then pulled her wand out of her sleeve and started shouting at the enforcers. She pushed me away so that I staggered forward under my own weight while she stepped out into the middle of the street, far enough away that it looked like she might have hit me by accident while hurrying by.

Immediately, the enforcers locked onto her, and half a dozen of them began moving in her direction, shouting at her to stay where she was and raising Ruiners.

"Over here!" she called. "He's over here!"

She was pointing back the way we'd come, around a tight corner that the enforcers wouldn't be able to see around until they got there.

That seemed to surprise them—they went from suspecting her to suspecting something beyond her, and the five or six of them rushing over hurried after her as she moved off the way she was motioning.

I hobbled along past them as quickly as I could, dragging one hand along the wall to keep myself steady and standing.

Two enforcers had stayed behind. One of them was further up the street herding people back the way they'd come. The other was standing between me and Port Street. There was a Ruiner on his left hand, and he was waving to the trickle of Workers that had gotten past the others, telling us to turn back.

"Everyone, please stay where you are! We believe that the Worker we were looking for is in the House and may be trying to escape. Please, until further notice, Port Street will be closed! Thank you for understanding!"

Two or three Workers closest to the top of the street began to protest.

"I gave my alibi to the Truth Catcher, you have no right to hold me!"

"So did I—I've never heard of anything like this!"

"I understand," the enforcer said, though his eyes were wide and he seemed to realize he was in danger of quickly losing control of the situation. He seemed fairly young. "Please, just wait for a few minutes while we sort this all out."

I inched forward toward the man's right side, where he was further away from the wall. My throat was feeling better and better as my ring fed energy back into my body. I could take a deep enough breath now to walk on my own without holding onto the wall, which was certainly a step in the right direction.

I glanced down the street.

The first 'porting alleyway was a dozen paces away. I could make it if I had a distraction.

I breathed deeply, focused on the Muse of Fire, and squeezed my right hand into a fist, pressing my fingers into the tattoo. I locked my gaze onto a public metal garbage can on the other side of the street and believed fiercely that it was suddenly full of heat.

The trashcan issued a loud metallic BANG as the metal sides expanded. The sound ripped through the street, and everyone's heads jerked in that direction. The enforcer spun, brandishing his Ruiner, and that caused a further outcry from the gathered crowd, similar to what you might expect people to do if a Blissful cop started wildly brandishing a gun.

In the confusion and behind the enforcer's back, I slipped down the street, keeping to the shadows as much as I could. I drew on the last of the energy in my band to make myself as insubstantial as possible, believing as deeply as I could that no one was noticing me, that even if they saw me they weren't really *seeing* me.

I took about half a dozen steps, and then the last of the energy in the band ran out and I became fully visible again.

"Hey!" someone shouted. "Why does he get to go?"

I didn't pause to look back or see if the enforcer was turning to come after me. I rushed toward the nearest alleyway, the exertion causing my throat to spasm and me to wheeze and hack as I tried to breathe. I squeezed the top pusher on the side of my watch, fixed an alleyway in my mind that I knew well, close to Marlowe in the Richmond district of San Francisco, and then stared hard at the subdial as I dove into the alleyway.

One.

The entrance to the alleyway grayed out, though I could still hear through it the sounds of pursuit. There was more shouting from the few Workers who wanted to get back into the alleys, and the enforcer was shouting "Stop! Stay where you are!"

Two.

I could hear the man's boots pounding on the paved street, the sound growing louder as he ran in my direction. I forced my belief through the watch and clutched the metal bug tight.

Three.

The bubble in space and time that is the Twilight House popped, and I was thrown violently back into reality.

Part Eleven

Marlowe Mansion

Not haunted, like Luigi's

I spun out in an alleyway at the intersection of 6th and California in the Inner Richmond, a city-suburb on the west side of San Francisco. It was fully dark now, and as I staggered out between a house and a laundromat, I took a fuller look at my watch: 9:43. Between the meeting, my trip to the Room, and then the travel back to the real world, that seemed about right.

A wave of cold washed over me and my legs went weak. I only managed to hold myself up by putting a hand against a gritty concrete wall and forcing my knees to lock through sheer force of will. I started coughing again and brought up another bolus of blood, phlegm, and saliva that I spat onto the ground. My head ached, and I was having trouble concentrating.

The one thought left in my head was *'Get to Marlowe.'*

I left the alleyway, trying not to weave and wobble too much on the uneven sidewalk that tilted downward toward California. I was certain that there had to be an alley closer to Marlowe's house, which was a dozen blocks away or more from where I was, but I hadn't found one that fit quite as well as the one I'd just used. One of the problems with rich neighborhoods is that they tend to get rid of alleyways, and their parks are too structured—manicured, even. That makes it harder to travel directly to them. I'd lived at that intersection of 6th and California for several months after graduating from

Blissful college. I'd used that alleyway often enough that I could 'port to and from it in my sleep, which was almost certainly why it had come to mind as I had fled the House.

Marlowe.

The thought of walking the rest of the way to my former mentor's house felt like contemplating climbing Everest. The thought of calling a rideshare and trying to convince them to take me, bloody and coughing, in the still-recent age of COVID, did not seem feasible either. Hell, if I tried it, they might even call the cops. Not that the cops of San Francisco are known to be overly responsive these days, but, considering my recent luck, I might be the one call they did follow up on. And if they decided to hold me, I'd be easy pickings for whoever wanted to find me.

My mind shook, and a series of memories previously held restricted were jarred loose and bubbled up into my conscious mind. Now that the bug was out of my system, I could remember McMillin, Jamal, and that woman—Shrike, right?—coming to see me at the Protoline offices. The memories expanded until they were so large that I staggered under their weight and had to sit down on the uneven curb, amidst patches of birdshit and old gum.

My mind focused primarily on the woman. She had Worked on another Worker—and not just on me, but also on Jamal, an enforcer and a direct representative of the WOTW. Had she done the same to McMillin? It was completely against the Code, not to mention the Guild-protected list of Workers' Rights. And who was she? Why had she been up on stage with Kaj Van Sant at the emergency meeting that evening? She'd had an enforcer badge. But hadn't Jamal said she was some kind of consultant?

Too many questions with no answers. I took a calming breath and pulled more energy from the solid metal ring on my finger. It was nearly ice-cold now, and I knew the energy in it was almost drained again. If I had wanted to, I could have broken it and pulled all the remaining energy out in a single rush, but that would have rendered the ring completely useless, and I would have had to make another one. The slow drain was working well enough. If I was lucky, I might be able to work on filling it as I made my way to Marlowe's.

A bus pulled up to the intersection with a large number 1 in the window, and I realized abruptly that that was the answer to my transportation problem. With a pained groan and much cracking of joints, I pulled myself to my feet and hurried over, waving a hand over my head. The bus driver saw me and blessedly waited.

I boarded the back of the bus, pressing my phone, which I still had in the inner pocket of my jacket, against the Clipper scanner. The scanner dinged in recognition, and I fell into a nearby seat that someone had vandalized with a stylized yellow-and-purple graffiti signature.

I still had blood on my shirt, but I pulled my leather bomber jacket as close around me as I could to hide it. I couldn't hide all of it, and I knew I had to look pretty bad just generally, but it was the best I could do. There were about a dozen other people on the bus, and I thought for a moment that they would say something to or about me, but after an initial round of wary glances, they all looked away and concerned themselves with their phones, or looking out the window. I breathed as slowly and evenly as I could, trying to hold back another coughing fit.

The bus lurched forward, then abruptly stopped again, and I nearly slid out of the hard plastic seat. I maneuvered myself so that I was braced more securely, then sat back. The bus lurched forward again, this time officially down California toward the Outer Richmond.

My racing heart began to calm, and exhaustion slowly crept in and laid down over me like a blanket. I only remembered then that I still hadn't gotten a full night's sleep, just the nap that had been forced on me after I'd gotten back home that afternoon from work.

I could remember the whole day's events now, and, slowly, with nothing else to do, I began to unpack and review them. I could remember the woman—Mallory Shrike—interrogating me. I could remember McMillin holding me down. I could remember them Working Jamal and then putting the bug in my throat. I could remember leaving the room under their instruction, giving my presentation, talking with Roc afterward and getting coffee with Erica, and then going home.

I remembered it all as if I were watching it on a TV show, though, or like it was a stage play. I knew the main character was supposed to represent me, knew it had *been* me, and I even remembered the sensations the character had felt—the taste of the coffee I'd drunk, the scratchy quality of my throat during the presentation, no doubt the aftereffect of the implantation of Shrike's bug—but my conscious mind hadn't been online during any of it. So as the memories came back to me, I reviewed them like a football player watching game tape after a concussion.

Against the Code, something in the back of my head muttered. I started to push the thought away but stopped. It returned, and I examined it with growing interest.

Against the Code.

What they had done to me wasn't something that any Worker was allowed to do to another. It was part of the Ten Prohibitions. The First Prohibition was that no Worker was ever to kill another Worker. Harming one of the Blissful was covered in the Third Prohibition. One of the ones in the middle was the one about Raising. And the Second Prohibition very clearly stated "No Worker shall Work on another Worker without their consent."

Versions of the Code bind all Workers everywhere. Workers all came together around the end of WWII and ratified the Code, which is a little like our version of the Geneva Convention. The Code details what Workers can and cannot do, and the Workers of the World, as well as all affiliate Worker groups (like the Workers of the West, which covers the westernmost part of North America), ratified it. There are only a few hundred thousand Workers in the whole world, so it's much easier to wrangle us all than it is to convince the UN to do something, for example, which represents billions.

The Prohibitions are part of the Worker Code, and anyone who wants to Work in the real world has to swear to follow the Code and then register with the Guild. The Guild has an accompanying bill of Worker's Rights that balance out the Code—the right to mental and bodily autonomy, for example—and in cases like this, both the Code and the Rights would say that what had happened to me earlier that day was illegal.

Very, *very* illegal.

And McMillin had gone along with it. Which almost worried me more. He wasn't a pleasant person, but he wasn't dirty, as far as I knew. Or at least, he hadn't shown any obvious signs of it until all of this.

Shrike. Mallory Shrike. I'd never heard of her before, and apparently neither had Jamal.

Where had she come from? Had she been called in specifically because of what had happened to me? Did she run around the country handling Raising cases? And how was she important enough for McMillin to be comfortable not only taking orders from her but flagrantly breaking the Code and the Rights with her there to see it?

I had no proof that they had done it—not proof I could take to anyone important. It was my word against theirs. Jamal would be taken more seriously, but if he was concerned about blowing his cover on whatever he was working on with Marlowe, then there was no way that he would come forward, at least not now. I could use a Truth Catcher, I supposed— turn myself in and swear before a judge that I had been coerced.

But she worked with the enforcers. She and McMillin both did. And they hadn't seemed the least bit worried about doing what they'd done to Jamal, much less to me. And unless Shrike had somehow Worked on McMillin before they'd come to the Protoline office, then McMillin was in on it too and just as willing to get his hands dirty as she was.

Was he the only enforcer working with her? Were there others?

My phone buzzed in my pocket. I pulled it out and saw a message from Roc Holliday.

<<cj. do I look better in red or blue. i know you know.>>

The banality of the text made me feel suddenly ten times wearier. Ordinary life was continuing on around me as I dealt with something so far above what I had been prepared to deal with just twenty-four hours before.

<<Blue>> I texted back, though I really had no idea. Roc is one of those people who will badger you until you give him an answer, so even if you don't have an answer it's easier just to make something up and give him one. It was probably no more than an opener anyway to get me talking to him— something his follow-up text confirmed.

<<i knew you knew. where you at, man. kristi's tonight, you in? i need the download on how the coffee with erica went (!!!)>>

Kristi's is a bar in SOMA, close to Roc's apartment. He calls it his 'safe space,' which is tongue-in-cheek Roc-speak for the only place he never picks anyone up so that he can always go back there and know the bartenders have his back. It's in an old basement and Speakeasy-themed.

<<btw—remember, club opening tomorrow night. it's gonna be insane. need u there.>>

I looked at that text for a long moment, wondering why it seemed to have jostled another thought loose in my head. I was so tired that it took another bus stop before I realized what it was, though.

Anandini. That's the club opening she mentioned—and she knew someone from Protoline who was going to be there. Did she mean Roc?

I wasn't really surprised. If you played the Six Degrees of Separation game with Roc, I'm fairly certain he'd be at most three degrees away from any even slightly attractive single woman in the English-speaking world, and probably the non-English-speaking world as well.

Before I had a chance to respond, I saw a street sign for 30th out the window and with a jolt realized I hadn't asked for a stop. I scrambled around and pulled the yellow stop-requested cord and a pleasant ding sounded through the bus, along with a digital female voice that declared "Stop requested." The driver, about to keep going, grumbled something under his breath and instead let the bus settle to a full stop.

The doors opened with a loud accompanying hiss of air, and I pulled myself to my feet and stumbled as much as walked off the bus. I managed to make it to the sidewalk without falling on my face, but it was a near thing. No one on the bus offered to help me off. I didn't blame them. You don't mess with people who are bloody in SF. Good Samaritans aren't really incentivized anymore. More likely to get in trouble for a good deed than a bad deed these days.

The bus drove off, and I lowered myself onto a nearby condo complex stone barrier that was about knee-height and didn't appear too dirty. I took several deep breaths of night air. There was a chill, steady wind coming in from the west, off the Pacific Ocean, which wasn't that far away from where I was. I could hear some kids laughing in an apartment across California. Cars whizzed by along the wide street at irregular intervals.

I knew I had to keep moving, but I couldn't force myself to carry on yet. I set myself an allowance of a dozen deep breaths, and with each one I forced myself to breathe progressively deeper. I drew on what was left of the energy in my ring and concentrated all of it on my throat. I felt the swelling reduce as if a cold ice cube were being applied to the inflamed skin, and then my muscles and skin wriggled uncomfortably as they knit together faster than nature would have done on its own.

And then the ring went completely cold and dead, all its energy drained.

My throat got angry again, but not as angry as it had been. It was still sore, but I felt like I'd be able to use it for more than just croaking at people, like some swamp witch's toad.

I thought briefly about trying to refill the ring, but, looking around, there were no obvious signs of chaos to draw on and I had nowhere near enough energy to put things in order to generate power that way. I had my lighter in my pocket and could create a spark, but I would need more than that in my currently exhausted state. I'd have to set up a ritual when I had time, unless I could find something on the way. Or I could use Marlowe's Circle once I got to his place.

My dozen breaths up, I pushed myself back to my feet and started walking again. This time I was able to move and breathe without coughing, and I took advantage of the fact by striding more determinedly down the street toward Marlowe's house.

As soon as I was off California and beyond the Sea Cliff entrance (two stone pillars that have the imprint of clam shells on them and proudly proclaim 'Sea Cliff') I began to feel more confident. I continued to scan the shadows as I went, but there did not appear to be any threats, supernatural or otherwise, to impede my progress. It appeared that I had escaped the House and any pursuit clean.

I hadn't been to Marlowe's place in years. His practice is closer to the UCSF medical center, which works well since he sometimes guest lectures. He tends to meet me and all his other former pupils out at various coffee shops and parks around the city instead of at his house. Marlowe loves a good park.

My mind turned inward again. What did he know about all of this? Why did they want Marlowe and why had Jamal and Kori spoken about him as if they were... working with him. Maybe even *for* him.

There were too many questions and not enough answers, and as I thought it all through again my pace began to slow.

My former teacher hadn't given any indication earlier that morning that he was anything other than the Marlowe I'd always known, and yet this whole time he'd been working on something secret with who knew how many others. Something that had included a list of names—a list with *my* name—that he'd never told me about.

What do they want with him? Is he dangerous?

That rang hollow to me. I couldn't fit an image in my mind of Marlowe as anything other than a firm yet kindly teacher. Thinking about him being involved in some kind of illegal activity... what the hell would he even be involved in? Treating his patients too well? I had never heard a bad word spoken about the man, and everyone seemed to know him and hold him in high esteem. Hell, people spoke about him in hushed tones as if he were some kind of living legend.

I turned a corner and walked up a slight hilly incline, past two rather large houses that I, at least, would classify as mansions. At the top of the hill, I went around another bend, and there was Marlowe's house.

It was exactly as I remembered it, and exactly as it had been when I had first arrived there as a disreputable youth.

The mansion itself was three stories tall, with a main central building and two wings. It was built into the side and top of a hill so that the third story was a high crest overlooking the Bay, which began only a few hundred feet away off the steep side of one of the neighborhood's eponymous sea cliffs. One of the wings of the house went along the hill moving upward, while the other curved down and became a circular base that seemed to anchor the structure on the lowest part of the incline. I knew that that was where the library was—and that the bedrooms were in the upper wing, while the central area was kept for living, dining, and formal occasions.

A green-gray metal fence ringed the property, lined up with the sidewalk, and that was my next obstacle. It was perhaps ten feet high, with ornamental swirls atop each thin metal post that culminated in ornamental points that I knew from unfortunate experience were quite un-ornamentally sharp. The fence looked easy enough to climb, but if anyone were foolish enough to try it, they would find out quite quickly that it was impossible. Marlowe's Workings are always subtle when it comes to that kind of thing, so you wouldn't know you were being thwarted unless you were a Worker really looking for it, but believe me when I say you wouldn't make it over. I tried several times in my early teenage years.

Marlowe has a garden in the back of his house, but the front is carefully constructed and manicured so as not to appear the least bit garden-like. A lot of Worker houses are like that—you don't want people using the park connection to suddenly show up on your lawn. Marlowe's garden in back has a single entrance and exit that is intentionally less cultivated, but it's under a special Working so that you need a key to access it via 'porting. I hadn't used it in years, and there was a good chance he'd changed the key. Which was fair— and I wouldn't have used it anyway. It's quite rude to simply 'port into someone's home, even if you can.

Still caught up in my thoughts—more so than I would have liked to be, but to an understandable degree given the circumstances—I forced a long breath out and stepped up to the gate in the long metal fence. There was a black box with a white button on the left side. I pressed the button and heard as well as felt a buzz that indicated the signal had gone through. For a moment, nothing happened. Then a voice spoke up, cool and male.

"You are no longer scrawny, but you still have the look of being up to nothing good."

I rolled my eyes. "Let me in, Luis, he wants to see me."

"There's no need to take that tone with me. In fact, there's no need to take any tone with me. I control the doors here and he trusts me to let in whomever I deem worthy and exclude whomever I deem unworthy."

"I know where he keeps your skull and fingerbones, Luis," I said. "Don't make me come up there and shake you."

"How *dare* you threaten me?" the voice demanded. "You have no right—"

The gate buzzed again. Marlowe's voice sounded in the air around me, drowning out that of his spirit familiar. "Cicero— I'm very glad you've made it. Come in, please. We are in the library."

"We?" I asked, but it was too late—the connection had been cut, and Marlowe was gone. The gate swung open silently on well-oiled hinges.

"I still think you're a shiftless rube," said the disembodied voice of Jacob Luis.

"I still think you're a nosy shit-eater, but you don't see me going on about it," I growled back through gritted teeth.

The door to the gate began to swing closed again on me, but I caught it before it could. Jacob Luis grumbled something inaudible, and then his voice cut out with a snap like when a burning log pops in a fireplace.

I paused for a moment, on the threshold of the estate. I felt, perhaps irrationally, but, considering how everything had gone so far perhaps not *entirely* irrationally, that taking the next step would be moving forward into something from which I could not turn back. I don't know if I'm the only one who gets those feelings sometimes, but I got one of them in that moment. The feeling like you're on the edge of a high cliff, the wind whipping you on all sides, and if you take a wrong step you might fall.

I looked back out into the night. Nothing but darkness and stillness and the distant sound of the ocean. Somewhere, people searching for me.

I stepped inside and let the gate close the rest of the way.

I walked up a gently curving tan-stone path that cut across the sweeping front lawn and beautifully constructed courtyard with matching stone fountain. It led me to a set of tall, solid, light-wood double doors at the front of the house, both carved with arched indents and strongly graven designs of knots and flowers. They opened before I even raised a hand to knock.

"Welcome back, kid," said a new voice, warmer and much kinder than Jacob Luis's. A small puff of wind blew against the back of my neck and I smiled slightly, turning back to look. Behind me was a tiny wisp of sapphire-blue light—it was barely visible, even in the darkness, because we were outside the house.

"Good to see you, Calliope," I said, genuinely meaning it. Her laughter and a sense of pleased excitement rang through the air. She, like Luis, is a bound spirit from the Space Between Spaces. Not everything that comes through from the other side is dangerous—there are a bunch of things that are harmless, even beneficial. Every tale you've heard about water nymphs and sprites and muses—they're all stories about creatures like Calliope that made their way through, summoned by some Blissful endeavor.

Her name is Calliope, like one of the ancient Greek Muses, but the Muses aren't real—no more real than vampires or the Devil or six-legged dogs that can whistle Yankee Doodle. But if you believe in anything long enough and hard enough, you can convince yourself that there really is something out there like it, and you leave a space open for that something to manifest into reality. Calliope—and Jacob Luis, for different and darker reasons—was born that way, back when Marlowe was in med school and trying desperately to write a song for a young boy he was treating, who loved music and who was dying. Marlowe has never told me the story himself, but the way Calliope tells it, she just popped into existence and found Marlowe, still new to Working back then, staring at her. He asked her if she was Calliope, one of the ancient Greek Muses. The chief muse, if I remember correctly. She responded that she could be if he wanted her to be, and so she became an imitation of her. She helped him finish the song, and then she asked to stay with him. Marlowe petitioned the Guild, and they were bound together. She'll be with him until the day he dies, at which point she'll pass back into the Space Between Spaces.

Jacob Luis is… well, he's what the Blissful would call a demon. A fire demon, I suppose. He's one of what we call the Wrathful, entities that are formed in the Space Between Spaces as a byproduct of people's anger. Like Terrors, they're born out of intense repeated emotion, in this case blind, self-righteous fury. Rage, more specifically—the kind of blind rage that sucks energy out of you. His full name, he says, is Jacob Luis, though why he chose that no one seems to know. Some Wrathful were once people who died but whose shades refused to pass on and so got trapped in the Space Between Spaces. It's possible that's what happened to Jacob Luis and that it's his real name from when he was alive. He was bound to the mansion by Marlowe's father, Christopher Frost. Luis made a wager with the elder Mr. Frost and lost. Wrathful do that—they make hasty decisions and can get lured into bets that allow Workers to bind them. He was bound in service to the Frost family for a period of one hundred years. To hold him, he was forced to relinquish his skull and fingerbones, which all Wrathful have for reasons I've never entirely understood—or maybe I knew at one point and now I've forgotten. You have those, the Wrathful have to listen to you. You lose 'em or give 'em back, the Wrathful can get loose. You destroy 'em, you destroy the Wrathful.

Don't feel too bad for Luis, though. If Marlowe's father had lost the wager, Luis would have won the right to peel the man's skin from his body and roast him over a charcoal fire before consuming him piece by piece.

That's how Marlowe tells the story, at least.

Having encountered other Wrathful… yeah. I believe it.

"How is he?" I asked Calliope as I turned back to the door. I stepped forward, crossed the threshold, and felt a tingling across my skin as the protective Working that Marlowe had embedded into his home—partly using Jacob Luis's power—washed over me, confirmed me as an acceptable guest, and then passed on.

"Luis? Dreadful as always," Calliope said, popping into existence near my ear. Inside, and therefore closer to Marlowe, she was much more substantial, and she looked like a young woman, about six inches tall, and the sparkling color of a bright blue sapphire.

"Marlowe," I replied with a small grin. "Why would I ask about Luis? He's always the same."

Calliope laughed—a sound like the sweet tinkling of bells. "You have no idea. He's actually much better than when we first came. Trust me."

"That's… alarming," I said. "You never told me that."

"A girl has to keep some secrets to parcel out over the years," she said.

We stopped just inside the mansion's foyer.

While I had remembered the outside of the mansion well enough, I had somehow forgotten how grand the inside is. The entrance hall has a high vaulted ceiling, and directly across from the double-door entrance and foyer is a staircase that ascends the curved reception hall and becomes a long walkway on the second floor, leading to the third story and the rest of the house. Straight ahead, past the stairs and below the walkway, is an entrance to the main living area of the house, including a kitchen and a large entertaining room currently home to a long, ornate dining table. There's another room off to the side of it that I couldn't see right then, but that's filled with paintings and books and art. There's also not a TV or computer in sight. Something that drove teenage me absolutely insane while I was living there.

I looked to my left, down another corridor lined with several large and tasteful paintings, mostly of impressionist landscapes. At the end of that corridor was another set of stairs, short and narrow, that led down to the large library where Marlowe spent the vast majority of his time.

"He's worried," Calliope said, following my gaze. "About you."

I glanced up at her, feeling my exhaustion again. "He's been keeping secrets, Calliope."

"Everyone keeps secrets," she said. "He's been working hard to try to find a creative solution to all of this. I've been helping him as best I can, but there's only so much I can do."

I almost asked her for more, but now that I was within spitting distance of Marlowe himself, I decided to wait and ask him directly.

"He said 'we' are in the study—who else is here?"

Calliope paused before answering. "You should go and see."

I frowned at her. She shrugged apologetically. I sighed and began walking down the corridor to the library. I tried to ignore as I did the memories I had of doing the same thing each evening to deliver to Marlowe my summary of the day's work. I shook my head, straightened my shoulders, and cleared my throat. I grimaced—pain. I could talk, but I still wasn't fully healed. I touched my pocket where I had stored the bug that Kori had passed to me before leading the enforcers away.

There were questions that needed to be answered, and I was no longer a child who was bringing his homework to be evaluated by his teacher. Marlowe was up to something, into something, and he owed me answers. I tried to cling to that.

I stepped down the half-dozen stairs at the end of the hall and pushed through the doors.

The library was laid out in a wide heptagonal shape, with a high ceiling and walls covered in books and artifacts. Straight across from the door was a tall window and a wide writing desk that was piled with several volumes of the Compendium of Materia Magi open to several different subjects. There was a Worker Feed as well, above the desk and to the right, scrolling automatically through several of the latest news articles and apparently searching for key phrases. I couldn't make out details from where I stood, but I was certain that there would be something on there about what had happened that evening in the Twilight House—and if there wasn't yet, then there would be by tomorrow.

Every other wall was more or less covered in books. The few places without books were small alcoves that contained stone sculptures, metal trinkets, or wood carvings, and one other window. Many of the books were like the Compendium—Worked so that they could be revised and expanded through official means on official release schedules. The other window, smaller and narrower than the first, was set in the middle of an archway made of books. Beneath that archway, seated in front of the frosted window, were two large, comfortable leather armchairs and one cushioned window seat. The stone floor was covered with a large, detailed rug of muted red, tan, and black wool that hid a large and very ornate set of runes carved in the floor. Those runes were part of the protection that Marlowe had expanded on after inheriting the place, and there were other sets throughout the house.

There was music playing, an old vinyl album of some American standard by Tony Bennett. It came softly from the corner of the room. The lights were on and spilled a comfortable golden glow over the scene.

And standing in the center of the room, speaking to two seated figures in the chairs by the frosted side window, was Marlowe Frost.

He always looks taller and more vibrant in person. He's an old man, in truth—in his early 70s—but he stands straight and tall and strides purposefully when he walks. He has the gray hair and sagging skin of age, but a sinewy body and gnarled hands that have not lost their strength. Always clean-shaven, in the every-day rain-or-shine manner of men of his generation, and his hair is shockingly thick for his age, completely slate gray, and well-combed in front but unceasingly rebellious in back. He almost always wears a button-up shirt with the sleeves rolled up to expose his forearms, a pair of fitted slacks that he can easily move in, and brown leather brogues.

As I entered, he turned and looked at me through his gold-rimmed glasses, his one concession to old age.

"Cicero," he said, with an obvious tone of relief.

I nodded. "Marlowe. Looks like we've got some things to talk about."

"We do indeed," he said. "Thank goodness you're safe."

I couldn't help it—I immediately felt calmer. Being there, in the soft golden light, hearing his music, seeing him, knowing that this place, at least, was safe and whole and sequestered from the storm that had gathered outside… the amount of relief I felt almost choked me up.

It sounds silly, I know. I really do get it. But… I never had a home growing up. Not like most people. What happened to me, what made me a Worker… it isn't important to get into the details, but it wasn't… fun. It wasn't pleasant. And the only real light in my life that pulled me out of the darkness was Marlowe Frost and his hard-headed insistence that I could be better than I was.

Anyway. Enough sentimentality. Making myself sick.

The two other people in the room were people I didn't know. They were both seated in the high-backed leather chairs by the frosted side window under the book arch, and they stood as I entered, examining me with long, significant looks. One was a tall, athletic Asian woman in a light gray hoodie, dark leggings, and running shoes; the other was a shorter bespectacled Caucasian man with a bold nose and perfectly coiffed dirty-blonde hair. The man was wearing clothing on the opposite end of the spectrum from the woman: a perfectly fitted vest-and-slacks combo that made him look a bit like a late-20s version of Marlowe, and he immediately put me in mind of either a lawyer or an accountant.

Marlowe strode forward, gesturing for me to come further into the room. He removed his glasses and slipped them into one of his pockets. "Good to see you, my boy," he said, holding out one of his strong, gnarled hands. I grasped it and shook it firmly. Marlowe grabbed my shoulder with his other hand and smiled a hard smile.

"I'm so sorry for all you've gone through since last night," he said. "I feel I only know bits and pieces of it, but I've at least heard the official account of what happened in the Twilight House—Jamal is still with the enforcers, but Kori was able to send word just a few moments ago and share that you'd made it out. I'm very glad."

"She also told us to pass on a message," one of the others said, the young man. He was resting his hands lightly on the back of the chair he'd recently vacated. "It was, 'Neener neener, saved your life, you little wiener.'"

The young woman rolled her eyes and folded her arms across her chest.

"Yes," Marlowe said. "That was indeed part of the message."

He took a step back and held out his hand toward the other two. "Cicero James, please meet Paulina Grace and Atticus Eriksson."

They both nodded in acknowledgment.

"Hi," I said tersely before turning back to Marlowe. "Let's talk. Privately."

The twinkle in Marlowe's eye dimmed. He nodded slowly. "We may speak privately if you wish, but please be assured that both Ms. Grace and Mr. Eriksson are fully aware of the situation and what has happened. You may speak openly in front of them if you wish."

"I don't wish," I said. My flood of relief at seeing Marlowe had quickly ebbed. If anything, now that I was there and felt finally somewhat safe, it was harder for me to hold back.

My still-healing throat took that moment to twitch and send a jolt of pain through me, and I grimaced and started coughing again. I tried to take a full breath, but that just made it worse, and I staggered over to place my hands on a nearby desk, feeling lightheaded. Marlowe quickly came to me and grabbed hold of my arm to help me to stay upright. I felt a wave of heat prickle through me as the old Stitcher scanned me for injury.

"What has happened to your throat?" Marlowe demanded when the heat reached that spot. "Come here at once."

The mentor became a doctor, a change that I had seen happen many times before, and I knew that there was no denying him. I was led to a chair—one of the two in the archway alcove. The young man—Atticus—was sent to fetch a glass of water, and the young woman—Paulina—was sent to check the Worker Feed to see if they had received any more communications from Kori and Jamal.

"Looks like Kori didn't manage to tell you everything," I croaked, easing back into the chair and trying to take slow, calming breaths.

"It would appear not," Marlowe said, feeling my throat in a quick, practiced manner. He'd taken his gold-rimmed glasses back out of his pocket and placed them once more upon the bridge of his nose. "Open your mouth," he said.

I did—Marlowe took one look and hissed a breath out through his teeth. He pulled back long enough to look me in the eye.

"May I fix this?" he asked.

I nodded and slipped my ring off my finger. There was no energy left in it, but it might still try to react when Marlowe Worked on me, which would risk breaking it.

Marlowe placed his hands on either side of my face and stared deeply into my eyes. I have been stitched by Marlowe many times before, but the process has never stopped being slightly unnerving. Marlowe's bright eyes speared right through me and seemed to see everything that made me up. He tilted his head to one side after a moment and then nodded to himself.

"You are healed," he said simply, stating a belief. Heat rushed into me, and the belief pressed down on me. I consciously lowered my mental defenses to let my body accept it.

The wound in my throat immediately closed up and smoothed over, leaving not even a scar behind. All pain ceased, and I was able to finally take a full and completely unobstructed breath. The heat dissipated and a slight chill washed over me, even though most of the energy for the stitching had come from Marlowe. The man didn't show the slightest sign of fatigue and hadn't even needed to use a breaking or ordering to generate power. Then again, he'd been doing this all his life, and I'd seen him Work truly miraculous things before. I've joked occasionally that he could probably convince a broken bone to heal just by winking at it.

"Better?" he asked. I nodded. "Good. Good."

He straightened up, again removed his glasses, and took a step back. "Now—what happened? Clearly, I need to hear it from you directly. Please spare no detail."

I looked up into Marlowe's eyes and for a brief moment considered holding back parts of the full story. After everything I had gone through in the last 24 hours, I had no idea who to trust anymore. Marlowe hadn't been entirely open and honest with me, so why should I be open and honest with him?

But those thoughts, born of resentment, passed quickly. He had promised to tell me what I needed to know. I owed him the chance to share the details. I was tired and hurt and I wasn't thinking clearly. If I couldn't trust Marlowe, then my problems ran much deeper.

I sighed, then glanced over at Paulina and Atticus, the first now scanning the Worker Feed and the second setting down a glass of water and a clear glass pitcher on a nearby desk.

Marlowe seemed to sense and understand my reluctance.

"Privacy, then," he said, calmly but firmly. "Ms. Grace, Mr. Eriksson—please give us the room." The two glanced at each other.

"Fair enough," Paulina said, turning away from the Feed in the corner and pulling up a personal version of her own with a flick of her wrist. It moved with her and she continued scanning it as she left. "I'll let you know when the news hits. Or if we get word from Jamal."

"I'll be just outside," Atticus said. He had a clipped, precise way of talking that seemed intentional, as if he were putting a strange bit of extra effort into being understood. Paulina seemed to be West Coast American through and through. "I'll make the call we talked about."

"Thank you, both," Marlowe said.

They left, and once the door had shut behind them, I told Marlowe everything that had happened since I'd gone to Hayes Valley the evening before.

I started off slowly, but before long it was all coming out of me. Everything from my confrontation with the Terror to the details of my waking in the morgue. My interrogation under Shrike at the Protoline office. The process of the bug implantation. Waking at my apartment, realizing I'd lost half a day. Going to the Twilight House, Jamal getting me out of the Meeting Place. Going to Hades and getting some partial answers. Meeting Jamal and KC, and then escaping the House.

Marlowe asked very few questions. Mostly he just listened with a serious expression, and at one point he moved to the second of the two leather chairs, the one opposite me, and sat.

Finally, it was over.

I felt like poison had been drawn out of me, and I was exhausted all over again.

"Thank you," Marlowe said. "It would seem that it is time to tell you what it appears I should have told you several months ago."

PART TWELVE

SO, WAS I RAISED OR WASN'T I?

Marlowe sat back and sighed. He had his hands clasped together in front of him and his knees spread apart. He had been leaning forward, engaged in my story. Now he seemed to be thinking it through.

"First," he said, "to reassure us both—may I see this bug that Kori gave you?"

I nodded slowly and reached into my pocket. I pulled out the bug and held it out, flat on my palm. It was hard and metal and completely lifeless, but I still felt as though it might suddenly spring to life again. Its segmented body and cruel sharp legs glinted dully. We both heard a hiss, and I looked up above to see Calliope watching from the ceiling, staring at the bug with a blazing hatred.

"What do you see in this, Calliope?" Marlowe asked immediately.

"It is dead and good that it remains so," she said, sounding like cold water boiling off a hot stove. "But there was one of the Envious trapped inside it, pulled from the Space Between Spaces. One that I have known. A male. Proud, as they all are, but this one especially so. Obsessed with hoarding knowledge."

"What was he before he was bound?"

"A hunter," she said. "He roamed the plains of your Midwest and drank the blood of bison. He lived in them and cursed the hunters who slew him in their skins. Several dozen fell under his sway before he was taken back to the Space Between Spaces."

"Has he been brought back since?"

"I do not know. It would have been inadvisable to do so... even in a construct as tightly confined as this one."

Marlowe turned back to me.

"It was the woman you spoke of who planted this, correct?"

"Yes. The woman with the talon."

Marlowe looked troubled. There was a frown line creasing the center of his forehead—a line that was well-used and graven deeply. He stared off into space as if searching his memory for anything related to her and what I had conveyed to him about her.

"Her name—Mallory Shrike?"

"That's what Jamal said," I replied.

Marlowe shook his head. "I have never heard of her. I have not had much contact with the Workers of America. Someone with the ability to control a spirit such as what Calliope has described cannot be unversed in the deeper and darker strains of Working that take many years to master, though. The Dark and the Old. And the kind of Work she did on both you and Mr. Henry... something here is strange."

"The... this thing is dead, though, right?" I asked, holding out the bug once more, offering it halfway between Marlowe and Calliope. "Or, not dead but sent back."

Marlowe nodded. "I feel no Working still in place upon it. Mr. Henry did well. Few things can stand up to a Ruiner properly used."

He glanced up at Calliope. She was still blazing brightly but seemed to be calming down.

"I can cross over to see if I can find him in the Space Between Spaces," she said, "but there would have been some indication of his escape if he had been left behind after the destruction of the construct to which he was bound."

Marlowe nodded. "Then let us assume he has been returned."

I felt part of the weight lift off of me. At least that was dealt with. I wasn't being tracked anymore, and there wasn't some malicious manifestation wandering around the Twilight House—or worse, loose in the real world—that we'd have to track down. I laid the bug on a nearby desk, glad to be rid of it.

"Now," Marlowe said, "to the matter at hand."

I felt a prickle of apprehension go down my spine, like the light touch of a cold finger.

"I wasn't Raised," I said. I wasn't sure why, but it felt very important to state that right at the beginning. "The shades confirmed it, and the Compendium says Workers can't Raise themselves anyway. The rules about Raising seem clear—and I don't fit the bill."

"It would seem that you do not," Marlowe said. His hands were still clasped in front of him and he was watching me thoughtfully. "I must admit, though, that even I thought you had been Raised. And I must also insist that there is still a chance that you were. We all thought that that was how it might begin."

"That… what would begin?"

"Something that has consumed me for several months now," Marlowe said slowly. "I am sorry to say that I do not know exactly what happened to you. There is one thing that seems both likely and unlikely. Much of what we will have to do next hangs on that point."

"I need to know something, first, Marlowe," I said. "And I need you to tell me straight out."

I expected a different reaction from the one I got. Instead of asking me what I meant or looking politely curious, he seemed to know immediately what was on my mind.

"Of course," he said, "you wish to know if it was I who did this."

Even though I'd been prepared to ask the question, hearing him say the words out loud made my heart jump in my chest. I nodded.

"I should have begun there. So much is happening that it has been difficult to keep everything in order. The answer is unequivocally 'no'. I did not attempt to Raise you, nor did I have anything to do with what has actually happened to you. I have never performed a Raising, nor will I ever perform one. I, like many others, believe that it is an act that goes against the course of nature, and that it is a practice that is rightly banned. You know that I am not generally a dogmatic man, but I do believe that certain acts stain both the actor and the one acted upon, regardless of intent. I believe that Raising is one such act."

I felt a weight fall off my shoulders. I *knew* that he was telling the truth. I could see it in his face, hear it in his voice. There wasn't any Working involved, it was just knowing him and knowing what it was when he was telling the truth.

"But they think you did it," I said.

Marlowe's expression darkened. "Perhaps," he said. "This Shrike may. But I also think she or someone else may be using the accusation of Raising as an excuse to convince the WOTW to come for me. It is one of the few things that would force their hand."

"Why?" I asked. "Marlowe, what have you gotten yourself into?"

He nodded, but held up a hand. "We will get there, I promise," he said. "But first, I think we need to fully rule out the possibility that you were Raised."

I swallowed and cleared my throat. "Sure."

"Good," Marlowe said. He took a deep breath and reset his shoulders, sitting up straight in his chair. He seemed to be marshaling his considerable cognitive abilities. "I think we can agree then that, at the very least, you were not Raised in any traditional sense. What the shades told you matches what limited information I have about Raising."

"Yes. So it *has* to be something else," I said, insisting on the point. "And they have to know that. Anyone with access to a Compendium and half a brain to check it has checked it by now and knows you can't self-Raise. And based on what I heard in the Room from Hades and his shades, I don't meet the criteria for someone else Raising me. It didn't happen three days after I died, and it definitely didn't happen later than that."

"This does not, however, exclude the possibility that someone has determined a new way to perform a Raising," Marlowe said calmly. "And the Compendium has been edited to remove even as much information as you might have read this morning. The information will have been moved to the Hidden Mysteries, to which we do not have access."

I felt that cold finger run down my spine again.

"Shouldn't the Compendium contain all known Worker knowledge not voted to be hidden?"

"It should. But it would appear that someone is editing it in real-time. The snippets are small, and they were removed quickly; but edits should not be made outside of an official reissuing, and must be confirmed, as you say, by a vote. Let us put that problem aside for the moment, though, as it is part of the larger problem and off the subject of Raising. One of two things has happened—either you *were* Raised, and the timeframe was indeed only a few hours, or something new has happened, completely unrelated to Raising."

I cleared my throat and worked moisture back into my mouth. I realized that my right leg was bouncing up and down and I intentionally stopped it. I rolled my shoulders back and unclenched my jaw, which I realized was starting to ache.

"I don't think I was Raised," I said slowly. "I don't think it fits."

Marlowe nodded. "Perhaps. But if you did have to Raise someone, and do it only a few hours after their death, how would you do it?"

I shook my head and looked off blankly into the distance. "I… I'd need a sacrifice. The shades were clear about that."

"When did you come back?" Marlowe asked. "What time?"

"A little after two in the morning," I said. "I think. I saw a clock on the way out of the morgue."

"And when did you die?"

"Sometime around seven," I said slowly. I did a quick calculation in my head. "Which means I came back… seven hours later."

My stomach lurched unpleasantly. Seven is a number that everyone believes to be significant. It's a major early prime, and almost every religion has ended up deciding that seven is a good number of gods, demons, virtues, sins, angels, muses, you name it. Anytime you see seven pop up, it's adding to the collective cultural belief of the whole world that that number is significant and has weight.

I caught Marlowe's gaze and realized he was thinking the same thing. He nodded slowly.

"Not three," Marlowe said, "but certainly another number with strong belief backing. Someone could certainly Work with that, or begin to build a Working off of it. What else?"

My thoughts swirled around, and I tried to speak through them.

"If a Working was done to Raise me, then there must still be the other ingredients for it to take place. Nothing can be given or exchanged for nothing. A sacrifice must be made—the shades were clear about that too. A soul for a soul. Based on the escalating needs of the sacrifice, it could very well be that a smaller sacrifice is actually all that is needed to do a faster Raising. And that waiting longer requires more."

Marlowe nodded again. "That is logical. The weight of effort to pull a shade back from the Space Between Spaces increases with time until it is, for all intents and purposes, impossible. And that is only for calling back shades, which is legal under the Code and which Mr. Jackson so notoriously exploits. To fully bring someone back and reincorporate them into their bodies... we must assume even more effort is necessary."

"And it must be breaking that is used—chaos," I said, my mind whirling. "Order is too slow. Something that big that fast needs sacrifice and sacrilege."

"I think that is a logical conclusion as well."

I paused for a moment and cocked my head slightly to the side. "The other ingredients seem straightforward. A pull on all five senses, to return each of them, and a breath of thought."

"Agreed. So, it *could* be possible. But now… motivation."

I turned my thoughts to that and found nothing. "I don't know, Marlowe. Why would anyone Raise me? Even if it's possible to do it, who the hell would? And why?"

Marlowe frowned again. "I don't know."

I leaned back in my chair, feeling tired again.

"I mean, if it wasn't you, then who else would give a damn?" I asked, trying to find the energy to care. "No one knew I was there aside from the Guild when I accepted the contract, and even then they didn't know when I was going to go. No one was there when it happened. No one knew I was in the morgue until Shrike and McMillin showed up to investigate, and that's when I woke up."

"This does seem to be the largest hole," Marlowe said.

"The key premise of Raising is death," I said slowly, rotating the problem in my mind, looking at it from all angles. "The key premise is that the soul leaves the body and needs to be retrieved from the Space Between Spaces, or wherever, and brought back. What if... I never left? What if I died but never crossed over?"

Marlowe nodded, watching me carefully. "This leads us down the second path, the path that I and the others have been investigating. At least, a version of what we have been mulling over. What do you remember from the experience? What did you perceive?"

"Nothing," I said. "Nothing until I came back. Or... woke up, I guess. And then… pain."

I flinched at the memory as it came back to me. "Yeah. Lots of pain. And then euphoria, and then just… confusion. I couldn't remember what had happened at first."

"And do you have any memory loss from before the event?" Marlowe asked, very much, I supposed, as he would ask one of his patients about their medical history. Marlowe had always been good at asking questions.

I paused and thought again, then shook my head. "No," I said. "No, I remember it all. Right up until I fell and then everything went black."

Marlowe paused, then asked, "When you woke, you retrieved your Instruments?"

I nodded and raised my hands to show my ring, watch, and band. "They took them off me when I got to the morgue, I guess. I didn't wake up with them on. I almost left without them, but I saw them when I was running out."

"Yes, yes you did tell me that," Marlowe said, reminding himself as he leaned back again, looking up into the air as if there might be a low-hanging answer there, hovering just above our heads. "And... hmm. I suppose I did not ask this, though. You have all of your Instruments—do you have all of your tattoos?"

I opened my mouth to say that of course I did, but I stopped myself. I didn't know for sure that I had them—I wasn't in the habit of checking, to be honest. They had always just been there.

Marlowe saw the realization flit across my face and stood. "Very well, let's have a look."

I got to my feet and pulled off my jacket, then my shirt. I unbuckled my belt and lowered my jeans as well, keeping my underwear in place but exposing my thighs. I held out my arms and looked down.

My palms, my forearms, my shoulders, my clavicle, and my thighs were all marked with black writing. I turned slowly to show Marlowe my back, and when I had turned back around, he nodded. Calliope fluttered down from where she had been watching the proceedings and flicked around me several times in quick succession, too.

"Nine," Marlowe said. "Is that correct?"

"Yes," I said. "All here. And none new since I died."

"And all still in working condition," Calliope confirmed. "I can feel the potential in them."

"Could any of them be construed as implying resurrection?" Marlowe asked her.

She stopped her twirling and flew up to stand on Marlowe's shoulder, leaning against his neck. "Not that I can see," she said. "If you really squinted and looked at it sideways, maybe the one on your chest, Cicero, the one about heaven and earth. But you'd have to use a hell of a lot of power to make that out to be a Raising Working."

I felt a thrill of anxious energy but didn't say anything. I hadn't told them about that tattoo and what it did. I was still trying to figure out what to do about it.

Marlowe didn't seem to notice, though, or at least he didn't ask me any questions about it. After scanning the tattoos once more, he nodded, apparently satisfied. I moved to put my shirt back on, but as I did Marlowe suddenly held out a hand. "Wait."

I froze. "What? Did you find something?"

Marlowe's eyes were crossing my body, flying back and forth. "Where were you injured by the Terror? You said that it struck you in the chest, but I see no scarring. And yet when you came here this evening, you were clearly injured by the bug Shrike implanted and not able to heal on your own. You are not and have never been a self-healer."

"I woke up without any scarring at all," I said slowly. "That was part of what was so strange."

"Your ring," Marlowe said next. An idea seemed to have come to him. "When you picked it up, it was still intact? There was still energy stored inside it? It wasn't broken or in any way damaged."

"Yes… all of my Instruments had energy. Barely any, but they hadn't broken. They were still functional."

Marlowe breathed in deeply and seemed, if possible, to become even more focused—but not on me. He turned away and crossed toward the center of the room, looking at something internal, absentmindedly scratching his neck as he did.

"It might be real after all," I heard him mutter.

Calliope had fluttered up into the air and was staring at me now, in a way that made me uncomfortable. What was going on?

"The death wound healed," she said, more to Marlowe than to me.

Marlowe nodded, still facing away. "One of the key signs."

"You're starting to freak me out a little bit," I said.

Calliope didn't respond, and it didn't appear at first as if Marlowe had even heard me. He continued to look away, his face hidden along with any expression that might have given an indication as to his thoughts. He ran a gnarled hand through his hair, further fluffing it up in the back, and then turned back to me.

An unnerving intensity seemed to have infused him, as if Marlowe was no longer looking at me but looking at something inside me, something I represented, and was invigorated by it.

"My boy," Marlowe said slowly. "I don't know how best to tell you what I need to. I... I am not often at a loss for words."

I looked between him and Calliope.

"Just say it," I said. "Whatever it is, just say it."

Marlowe opened his mouth but paused again.

"Tell him," Calliope urged. When he still hesitated, she flew over to him and repeated herself. "Tell him, Marlowe!"

"We can't know for sure," he said. "It is only a guess—it has only ever been a hypothesis. We don't have the full text yet, that is the whole point of tomorrow night."

"But it *fits*!" she said. "And even if it's not true, it's possible, right? And you owe it to him to talk it through. You're right, you know you are."

"Enough," I said, stepping forward. "Just tell me. Whatever it is."

Marlowe considered me for another long minute, and then finally said:

"Have you ever heard of the Immortals?"

Part Thirteen

There can be only one!

Really, though.

I stared at Marlowe for a long moment.

"You mean… the bad Henry Cavil movie from like a decade ago?"

Marlowe blinked and then let out a short laugh. A smile broke across his face, and he shook his head. "No—no, I do not mean that. I mean the chain of Workers going back several centuries, if not millennia, that have found themselves immortal."

I just stared at him blankly. "Marlowe, I have no idea what you're talking about."

"I am not surprised," Marlowe said. "Come over here, please."

He turned and walked across the room to the desk under the large window covered by two long midnight-blue drapes with golden rope tassels. He waved his hands, and several large tomes flew off the desk and back up to their various places on the library bookshelves.

One book, however, remained behind. It was thick and bound in worn, cracked black leather. I could make out gold letters on the spine but couldn't quite see what they spelled out. The pages of the book were made of thick parchment instead of paper, also significantly worn with age. Unlike the Compendium, this book looked to be just a book. An old book, certainly, but, from what I could see of the pages as Marlowe flipped through them, there was no moving text, no swirling images, and no shifting paragraphs. Ordinarily, that would have been considered a flaw. Now, with the Compendium being edited, I felt strangely relieved.

Marlowe found the page he was looking for and held the book out to me.

"Please read," he said.

I walked forward slowly and looked down at the indicated page. It looked to be a sub-chapter of some larger passage.

The Immortal and the Relevance of the Gifts

As previously stated by this author in the first volume of these Works, the Prime Gifts are thought to open the way through which the Immortal must walk. In a sense, the Immortal is him or herself the final Gift, or perhaps the first. As all Gifts have given birth to various Worker legends that exist to this day, so too is there a lesser-known and more obscure myth of the Immortal—or, more specifically, the chain of Immortals that lies unbroken from antiquity to modern time. Similar to the previously discussed myths and legends around certain deities, and messianic figures that at one time held the Prime Gifts, there are underlying themes common to all faith traditions that relate back to the Immortal. These legends have been passed down by proto-Workers across all cultures—shamen, medicine men, druids, and so forth.

I stopped reading and looked up at Marlowe. Marlowe looked back at me over his gold-rimmed glasses, which he had placed back on his nose in order to read the text. His face was expressionless, and his eyes were calculating, as if he were taking in my reaction to what I had just read.

"Where is this going, Marlowe?" I asked. My heart was thumping loudly in my ears, and I was having a hard time taking a full breath.

"Please keep reading," Marlowe said. "Another page will do, I think."

I looked back down, turned one of the thick parchment pages, and continued reading the cramped black text. It appeared handwritten, but very clearly and precisely.

Unlike those who have the ability to win and therefore earn the right to bear the Prime Gifts that we have heretofore identified, the Worker who becomes the Immortal does not choose their Gift. They remain unaware of their potential until it is awakened, though there are certain patterns to each Immortal that this author has previously detailed. For a fuller discussion, please see the first volume of these works, The Eternal Cycle.

The innate ability or seed of immortality is extremely rare, and as such most Workers do not believe it exists, or that immortality is simply a Blissful legend rather than something with which legitimate Workers should concern themselves. Those who do believe have most often throughout history seen it as something dark and unnatural, akin to the practice of the Old and the Dark, which misses the mark.

Instead, the birth of the Immortal signifies a great turning in the world, including the re-emergence of the Gifts. This leads us to conclude that the Gifts are bound to the Immortal, and that only through the Gifts can the Immortal reach the Eternal and make the Choice that will conclude the current Cycle and begin the next. Until this is done, the Gifts shall persist, and the Immortal will remain bound to life. Given enough time, the Immortal will continue to awaken from death once reassembled, their bodies clean of all signs of that which killed them. This author has collected in the first volume of this work many of the competing theories as to how this may be possible, but there has been no consensus throughout history and therefore the truth remains a mystery.

I stopped reading, even though there were several more paragraphs on that page and the one after it. There was a ringing in my ears.

Marlowe surely didn't mean to say that *I* was...

I looked back up and saw him watching me very closely with those bright, intense eyes of his, unblinking. He was waiting for my reaction.

I stepped away from the desk and turned back to the middle of the room. I didn't know where I was going, but I knew I had to move. I felt suddenly trapped, as if I were in a room barely taller than my head with walls pressing in against my shoulders.

"Cicero!" I heard Calliope call out. I heard Marlowe say something as well, but I was already across the room and had thrown open the library doors. They banged off the walls outside with a loud, echoing slam, and both Paulina Grace and Atticus Eriksson, who were waiting outside the room, jumped. I rushed past them as they exclaimed at me, words that passed over me like wind, ruffling me but leaving no impression.

I hurried through the halls of the house. Some part of me recognized that I was hurrying down the corridors of my youth and caught sight of various features—scuff marks that had never been buffed out, missing chips of paint—that were probably invisible to anyone who hadn't lived there. I turned corners blindly, feeling a need to leave, to *get out*, that was so overpowering that everything else simply fell away.

The next thing I'm aware of remembering is sitting in the garden, breathing in the cold night air. A mist had descended—or maybe a fog, like I said I'm not clear on the difference—and the heat of the warm fall day had completely dissipated.

The garden in the back of Marlowe's house is lined with tall, thin trees, and there's a large, sprawling magnolia in the center, around the trunk of which is set a wide wooden bench. There are stone walkways through the garden that are lined with soft golden lights that illuminate at dusk and extinguish at dawn. Not Working, just technology—Marlowe entertains people there and has thrown parties throughout his life for social functions that are often non-Worker events. I was forced to attend several such events while I lived with him. I snuck my first drink at one of those parties actually—a beer that I stubbornly forced myself to finish despite the fact it tasted exactly like what I imagine chilled horse piss tastes like.

There's another bench, this one stone, farther away from the house, near the 'porting entrance, which is set back in a large spray of flowering bushes I've never been able to remember the name of. That was the bench I'd fled to, and where I found myself when the sense of claustrophobia lifted enough for me to come back to myself.

I sat there for several minutes, just breathing. My head was spinning, and I didn't know what to do, much less what to think.

I reached into my leather jacket and pulled out my wallet. I opened it and pulled out a dime and a quarter. I put the wallet away and pulled out my lighter, flicked it for a spark of chaos, and then twirled the dime and quarter in my hand.

They disappeared, and in their place appeared a single cigarette. I clicked the lighter again and took a drag, pulling the smoke into my lungs. It burned, much more than I'd anticipated. I coughed, surprised, and then remembered that I hadn't filled my ring, and so the normal protection my lungs enjoyed was absent.

"Shit," I muttered, and I put the cigarette out against the hard stone of the bench, then twirled the stub in my fingers and sent it into my vault to deal with later. Marlowe would kill me if I left it lying around his garden.

Immortal.

The thought rattled around inside my head.

The book was right, there were stories about things like that, but none of them were supposed to be real. I'd never paid much attention to them because they were so obviously fantastical. It wasn't something that you could actually do, make yourself immortal. It was like flying or stopping time— a myth, an idea that was fun to think about but that could never be true. One of the great Worker myths that just didn't happen.

I heard the door to the house open and looked up to see Marlowe slowly making his way into the garden, backlit by a spray of golden light. The sapphire flash that was Calliope was no longer with him, and it appeared that Paulina and Atticus had stayed behind as well. He examined the garden slowly and methodically until he found me. He nodded to himself and then began unhurriedly walking toward me, his hands clasped behind his back. He looked at the garden as he went, seeming to enjoy it, looking up at the branches of the large magnolia tree and breathing in deeply the cold night air.

A slash of fiery light appeared just above and to the left of my sightline. I closed my eyes and took a deep breath, then slowly let it out.

"Hello, Luis," I said.

"Was he mean to you?" the bound Wrathful asked. "He's mean to me. If you set me free, I can do something about it."

"You've been trying to get me to free you for half my life, Luis," I said wearily. "Do you really think I'll change my mind and do it now?"

Jacob Luis gave a heavy sigh that sounded like leaves crackling and then disappeared again with a sullen grumble and a sharp pop.

Marlowe crossed the last of the garden and stopped several feet away. "Would it be too much to request to sit with you?" he asked.

I shifted over. Marlowe came and sat beside me, a respectful distance away, as if I were a skittish horse in danger of bolting.

"I don't like where this is going, Marlowe," I said. I felt incredibly weary, and I remembered again that I hadn't slept in almost forty-eight hours, aside from the enchanted nap that Shrike's Working had forced on me. And who knew if that had actually been restful or not—real sleep is notoriously tricky to force via Working. You can knock someone unconscious no problem, but that's not exactly restful. The mind isn't something you can just switch on and off.

"I'm sure," Marlowe said simply. "And I owe you another apology."

I looked over at him sharply.

"It was never my intention to pull you into this," he continued. "I... perhaps I should have been more open with you. But you have built yourself a life, and I am incredibly proud of you for doing so. I did not wish to disrupt it without good reason."

I nodded slowly. "Right. Jamal said something about that."

Marlowe sighed and leaned forward, clasping his hands between his legs. "If we continue and I share with you what I have been working on and what has been happening, then there is no going back, Cicero. I have been very careful to keep this separate from my relationship with you. With all my pupils, for that matter, though with you in particular because you were one of the names that came up during our research. I… must be honest, I had hoped that if all of this were true, it would not be you who was chosen. Not because I feel you cannot handle it, nor because I feel you are a poor choice. I hoped it because I know that you have always wished to live an anonymous and uncomplicated life, after what you experienced in childhood. This is dangerous, secret, and… complicated."

I sat in silence for a long moment, just trying to absorb everything. After a while, I asked, "How long have you known that I was on this… list?"

Marlowe nodded, mostly to himself, as if he had prepared an answer to this question knowing that I would ask it. "It came to my knowledge several months ago now that something was about to begin. There are certain signs that the same author you have just read has detailed out, or refers to. Shortly thereafter, the pages you read tonight came into my possession, and though we have only been able to decipher and read some of them, what we have gleaned was enough to generate a list of names of potential Immortals. There were about two dozen."

"They have to be all across the world, though."

"Some of them are international," Marlowe confirmed. "But the bulk of them were in the United States, in one of several major cities, including San Francisco."

"How the hell did you narrow it down to only two dozen names?"

"The Immortal that begins what Gallimand calls the Eternal Cycle is always born in a city on the border of order and chaos, in one of the great world powers of the age. The higher the disparity in a given city and country—the wider the gap between the ordered and joyous lives of some and the chaotic and desperate lives of others—the more likely it is for that to be the location. Chicago and New York were of course on our radar, as well as Atlanta. There are several foreign cities too, as I said, but largely it was thought that the wealth gap, rising crime and violence, partisan division, and the worldwide reach of technology… well, it seemed strongly possible that this could be the epicenter of the next Cycle."

I leaned forward and put my head in my hands. I dug my fingers into my temples—my head was pounding, and I felt a truly horrible headache coming on.

"And you think it's *me*?" I asked, looking up. "I… how?"

Marlowe frowned and even showed a flash of frustration. Not at me, but at some thought he seemed to be having. "I do not know," he said, and then I understood. For Marlowe, not knowing something important is almost sinful.

"We do not have enough information. The only reliable source we have is what we have deciphered of Gallimand's writings, but the larger Works have been… suppressed. There are others involved who do not wish to see the signs or acknowledge that the current Cycle is ending and the next is set to begin. Imagine that we are in winter and that the current year must end before the next year can begin and bring about spring. And that there are those who profit off of winter and wish to extend it indefinitely."

"But I don't want this," I said, ignoring the rest of what he'd said. That all felt too big, too important to handle just yet. "Give it to someone else on the list. I don't want it. Take it away, I'll give it to whoever wants it. Whoever you think is best."

Marlowe's face was grim. "I do not believe that to be possible," he said.

"Well, then what the fuck am I supposed to be doing with it?" I asked, anger mounting in me to cover for my panic. "What the fuck have I stepped in?"

Marlowe again looked frustrated. "I do not know. Not entirely. The Works are not nearly as complete as they were when they were written. What does seem clear is that the Immortal plays an important part in the Eternal Cycle. The implication has been that he or she can in some way rebalance the world in order to begin the Cycle anew."

I stared at him for a long time, unable to comprehend.

"Marlowe, I have a hard time deciding which streaming service to pay for. Last month I thought seriously about giving van life a try. I pirate movies because going to movie theaters is like three times as expensive as it was when I was a kid. I'm unmarried, I have no kids—who the hell am I to *rebalance the world?* Marlowe… I'm not your guy. This is… I had delusions of grandeur when I was younger, but I think I've proved I'm not built for that."

"You have many excellent qualities, Cicero," Marlowe said. "And you have always been more capable than you know."

"Don't do that, Marlowe. I gave up being special. I didn't end up being a doctor or an astronaut or the President or anything like that. I got to be a Worker, and that's more than enough for me. My life is boring now, and I *like* that. I'm making up for all the epically non-boring shit I had to go through as a kid."

Marlowe was nodding, and for a moment he couldn't meet my eyes. When he began to respond, he continued looking down at the ground.

"I am sorry, Cicero," he said. "I do not have the answers for you. I... have never hidden my respect for you. Both for your abilities as a Worker and for the integrity you have adopted as the man you have become. Your resilience, in particular, I have always admired. What we are doing, what is happening... it is important. Not just to us, but to everyone. But… I know you. And I care for you, deeply. And if you wish to leave, then I will attempt to find a way for you to do that. Tonight. And tomorrow you can begin a new life, and leave this behind as best you can while I try to find a way to take this burden from you and give it to another."

He did look at me then, and I knew that he was serious. I knew that he was willing to help me run if that's what I said I wanted. Despite any consequences, he was willing to put me first. I knew it wasn't just me, either. I'd heard rumors of how he'd helped his other pupils. He would spit in the face of God and the Devil both if it meant giving the people he cared about a say in how they wanted to live their lives.

We sat in silence for a long moment, listening to the breeze in the leaves of the magnolia tree and the just-audible sound of the Pacific Ocean crashing on Baker Beach in the distance.

"There's no way for me to stay here in SF, is there?" I asked finally.

"Not if you wish to remain uninvolved. If you want to be involved, I can protect you. Otherwise, if you stay, they will come for you. We are not the only ones looking for the Immortal, especially not now that word has gotten out about your awakening. We can fight them—we *are* fighting them—but the stakes are unimaginably high, and you may not survive what is to come if they find you. You will live, but… there are ways to make you wish you could die. I have made my peace with what I might have to sacrifice, as have the others working with me. But that was my choice, and theirs. You have not had a chance to make a choice, yet."

I shook my head and looked away. "This is all absurd. Have you ever thought that that book is, I don't know, completely batshit? Just, you know, wrong? About everything?"

"I certainly have," he said. "In fact, I still have my doubts. But I hope to lay them to rest as of tomorrow night."

"What's tomorrow night?"

Marlowe shook his head. "You cannot know that unless you join us."

I threw my hands in the air, then stood and began to pace. "This is ridiculous! If it concerns me and what you're telling me I'm supposed to be doing—or not doing—or, hell, I don't even know—then you owe me an answer!"

Marlowe was completely unruffled by my outburst. "If you join us," he said, "I will answer whatever you would like. But if you are going to run, then you may already know too much, and I will tell you nothing further."

I turned away. I stared at a cluster of gnats dancing over a small dip in the garden that had filled with water. Silence rang in my head. There were too many thoughts. Too much to absorb. I just couldn't… wrap my arms around it all.

But Marlowe was saying there might be answers. There might be a way out. And if there was a way out, I wanted to know about it.

To rebalance the world…

I thought about where I'd been that morning. Appearing in the Tenderloin, seeing the devastation there. I thought about the news coming in from all around the world, every day another step closer to war in who knew how many countries. Every day another corruption scandal. Every day another religious or political or sectarian divide exploding into violence. Every day another threat to humanity. A never-ending row of hydra heads.

Was all of that because things were… unbalanced?

Could I actually *do* something about it?

"If I choose to help, what happens?"

I could feel him watching me. "If you choose to help, then I will share with you what we've been working on. There is much to do."

"Would I be involved?" I asked. I was looking off into the distance, past the garden, out into the dark landscape that mirrored the black night sky. Images of my life were flashing before my eyes. Half in the world of Working and half in the world of the Blissful. "Not protected and coddled. Would I be a full part of whatever this is?"

"Not at first," Marlowe said. "But eventually, yes."

I continued to stare off into the distance. Something was shifting inside me. Slowly but inevitably. I felt as though I had been waiting for this for years—this exact moment. I felt as though I stood on the precipice of doing something that might truly matter for the first time in my life, and yet I knew nothing about what it was or what it entailed.

"Am I really immortal?" I asked softly.

The older man shifted on the stone bench, and I heard the sound of him fixing the line of his fitted slacks so that they fell correctly over his shoes.

"Yes, I believe you are."

"And that is part of all of this? It's... part of... fixing things?"

"There is too much I do not know and that I must still find out. But if what we have discovered so far is corroborated tomorrow night... then yes. Yes, if you wish to be, you could be a very important part of this."

I nodded. I took a deep breath and then finally turned back to face him.

"Are you on the right side?" I asked. There had been too many questions lately about who my former mentor really was. Too many revelations about the reach he had, and about the enemies he had apparently made. I didn't invest the words with any kind of Working to try to force the truth from him— I knew Marlowe would be able to resist it even if I did. Instead, I simply looked into his face, openly and honestly, and asked the question.

Marlowe blinked several times and then smiled slightly, and the ghost of an expression that I thought might be pride flitted across his face before fading. He then seemed to turn inward and truly consider the question. He was silent for several seconds, looking very serious—long enough that I had time to listen to an owl hoot in the distance and a chorus of nighttime insects chirp back and forth at each other, an unseen world unconcerned with our weighty conversation.

Finally, he said, "I am on the side of this world and this life continuing. I am on the side of redemption and hope and choice. And I believe that to be the right side."

I nodded, not blinking. I took a few steps back toward Marlowe and held out my hand. Marlowe broke eye contact long enough to clasp it, and then he looked back up.

"Then we're on the same side," I said. "Tell me the rest of it. I'm in."

PART FOURTEEN

GAIUS GALLIMAND

A light sparked in Marlowe's eyes. A light I'd seen before and knew well: the light of unyielding determination. And with Marlowe, when he's devoted to something, when he has that light in his eyes, he can turn tides and shake stars.

"Very well."

He twirled his hand and pulled from thin air what looked to be the same leather book that had been on his desk in the library.

"First, you deserve a copy of this."

He handed me the book, and I took it. There was golden lettering embossed on the cover.

The Collected Works of Gaius Gallimand
Vol. 1-7

The author's name seemed vaguely familiar, but I didn't know why.

"Gallimand," I said. "Who is he?"

"A Worker scholar," Marlowe said, "who lived nearly five centuries ago. He was quite popular for most of his life, but then universally discredited when he published this. His work was banned and confiscated. It was not only unpopular but considered offensive and anti-Worker. It wasn't until a few years after writing and distributing the first edition of this book that it became clear that nearly everything he wrote in it was correct—or so I believe, and so did others at the time.

There was still so much anger around it, though, that Worker governments at the time had the books collected and tightly controlled. What had not already been burned or hidden was taken from the general Working populace."

I looked back down at the book. It didn't look all that deadly. No blood dripping down the cover or ghostly screams rising from its pages. I opened the worn leather cover. Inside was the same thick parchment paper I'd seen in the library— not Worked like modern paper was so that it could be updated and edited to replace previous editions.

I flipped through the pages, the vast majority of which were blank.

"Did people find it offensive because he published an empty book?" I asked, holding it up.

"Not quite," Marlowe said. "Gallimand tried to protect his work when it became clear he and it were being hunted. After being pilloried for the first run of his Works, he wrote and circulated a second edition—several dozen carefully protected copies sent to those he thought would be his allies. This is one of those second edition copies—or, more specifically, the one that I have is, and what you hold is a copy of *that* copy, stripped of the protections that made it dangerous to handle. Gallimand himself Worked the pages of the original copy so that they could only be read by certain people, and he used several ciphers to further conceal them. As you can see, we were able to begin deciphering the third volume, titled 'Gifts', but we have not yet found the key to the other sections, nor to the rest of the Gifts volume."

"But what *is* in here—these are his original words?" I asked.

I realized I was holding the book gingerly, as if just by touching it I might hurt it. In my defense, it was the oldest thing I'd ever held, even if it was only technically a copy.

"The words are original," Marlowe said. "But please do not be too concerned with the care of that particular book. Like I said, it is a copy. I have the original safely stored and have made several copies like this one that are Worked so that they will mirror any deciphering we make to the original copy."

He held out his hand for the book, and I passed it back. He opened it and turned swiftly to the back page and then presented it to me again. What he'd turned to was an insert detailing the titles of each of the volumes the book professed to hold. There were seven of them. The section that was the most complete was 'Volume 3: Gifts'.

"Is there a plan to fill in the other volumes?" I asked.

Marlowe shook his head. "That is what we are working on. As I said, the full book was banned outright, and most copies of the original print run were destroyed. He was a very well-respected man prior to its publication—a historian, a philosopher, and one of the revolutionaries who participated in what was a Renaissance of both the Worker and Blissful worlds—but when he published this, he was ridiculed and marked as a danger to Worker society. It tainted the rest of his life's reputation, and he became a pariah in all serious scholarly circles. The credit for his more popular contributions was reassigned to several of his less savory contemporaries, who were only too happy to accept it."

"He sounds unfortunate, not dangerous."

"At first," Marlowe said. "But then the predictions he made in the final volume of these Works began to come true, and he became not just some easily ignored crackpot but a dangerous prophet. Turn back to that final page."

I did, and this time saw that the seventh volume was titled *Predictions and Prophecies*. The first volume, Volume One, was titled...

"The Eternal Cycle," I muttered.

"Yes. Does that sound familiar?" Marlowe asked, watching my reaction. "Aside from our conversations this evening, of course."

"It does, but I don't know why."

"If you'd had a proper Worker education at the Academy in the Twilight House, they would have told you that it's the central belief of an old, dangerous Worker religion. It is also the first volume of Gallimand's Works. All volumes were banned, but it is *The Eternal Cycle* that is perhaps best known and also hardest to find. All others proceed from it, but without an original copy of the *Cycle*, the other volumes are but pieces of a puzzle with no coherent whole. The third volume, as you've seen, references details in the first volume several times. I think it is safe to assume the other volumes do as well."

"You must know something about it, though. Otherwise, why would you be interested in it?"

"I know more than most," Marlowe said, nodding. "Though not nearly enough. What I do know is enough to have piqued my interest, even before the *Gifts* volume was deciphered. You see, the premise of the *Cycle* is that once every few hundred years, the world needs to be… rebalanced. And that if it isn't, everything descends into darkness and chaos. The world ends."

I remember feeling a chill at how easily he said those words.

"A nice cheerful end?" I asked. "Chaos brought about by cute puppies in sweaters and otters wearing bowties? Just too many cute things running around and *oh no, so much chaos*, guess we'll just have to pet them all?"

Marlowe gave me a small, polite smile. "Unlikely. I do not know the details. The first volume may not even touch on it—

in fact, I suspect that the full details are only mentioned in volume six. Look," he pointed again.

I did—volume six was titled *The Breaking of the Wheel.*

"Well, puppies can break wheels if they try really hard."

"These puppies would be more along the lines of hellhounds," Marlowe said. "And all manner of other beasts that are present in the collected religions of the world."

I snorted, thinking Marlowe had made a joke. The old man was not laughing, though.

"That stuff isn't real," I said. "Not unless someone manifests it. Vampires, werewolves, shapeshifters—those things haven't existed for centuries. They're just runaway beliefs that latch on to the communities that believe in them, and then feed off of those people until they become real. Most of the time they're Wrathful or Terrors or the Envious. Spyders, Dopples, all the stuff we deal with, just wearing different faces and names. Besides, Workers have killed almost all of the old stories off."

"Ideas cannot be killed," Marlowe said, speaking as if correcting me on a wrong answer on an exam. "Neither can beliefs. There is a reason that every religion in the world believes in similar versions of the same stories. There is a reason that the story of monsters that drink the blood of innocents exists in Europe, Asia, Africa, and the Americas entirely independently. Why snakes and lions and birds of prey lend their fangs and claws and wings to gods and devils all over the world. The primal fears and flaws of humanity will never be entirely outgrown, and will always re-emerge. And I believe this too is something that Gallimand writes about."

Marlowe motioned again to the book, and I saw another volume—Volume 4—titled *The Creatures of the In-between: the Beast, the Demon, and the God.*

"So he's some kind of Zarathustra/Nostradamus mashup who just knows everything?"

"I believe he was a scholar," Marlowe said. "As well a very shrewd historian. He was drawn to the Cycle by an interest in understanding it, and only after he found out everything he did did he attempt to share his findings with the larger Worker world."

"But where're the rest of the pages?" I asked, holding the book up again. "Without them, there's no way to know for sure if it's all legit."

Marlowe sighed. "Unfortunately, original copies are exceedingly rare. Assembling them is a difficult task. These books... they were not meant to be found. And even when found, they are not meant to be read except by those Gallimand intended to read them."

"But you really think this Cycle is real?"

Marlowe frowned. "That is the right question. There is always the possibility that all of this is nothing more than academic. That Gallimand truly was daft in his old age and claiming knowledge he did not actually possess. However..."

He motioned again to the book.

"This has convinced me that there is something more that we must understand."

"What are the... Gifts?" I asked.

Marlowe nodded and leaned forward, talking with his hands the way he did when diving deep into an explanation.

"There are rumors of several dozen, it would appear, and though Gallimand did his best to chronicle them, he very specifically states that the most important, and potentially the only true Gifts, are called the Prime Gifts, of which there are only five and that, he claims, have existed since the dawn of time. Gallimand claims they need to be 'won' to be used, and that once they are won they are bound to the person who won them until another wins them in turn."

I opened the book again and began leafing through the Gifts volume. I saw again that same cramped handwriting and several chapter subtitles, some of which had paragraphs of text beneath them and some of which had only a few lines.

"*The Gift of Transference…. The Gift of Time…* Marlowe, these are all impossible."

"It would certainly appear that way," he said. "I believed so too. And then we found one."

I looked up sharply. "What?"

"Yes. We found one."

"And you… won it? It works?"

"No," Marlowe sighed. "We are not certain what it means to 'win' one of the Gifts. That part of the book we have yet to translate."

"Translate?"

"Indeed," Marlowe said, reaching over and flipping several more pages. About halfway through the third volume, after several blank pages when the cramped writing reappeared, the words were entirely indecipherable, and I realized it was written in some sort of code. "There are several ciphers used in the book. We are working to translate what we have so that we can unlock the Gift we have recovered."

"All right. But if you found one of these things—what does it do?"

Marlowe's eyes seemed to shine with a bright, eager light. "It is the Gift of Transference," he said. "Completely spontaneous travel, without time dilation."

I couldn't help it—I felt a soaring sensation in my stomach.

"That's crazy, Marlowe," is what I said out loud. "Spontaneous transference without any loss of time or equivalent exchange… no one's been able to do that."

"I am equally skeptical," Marlowe said. "But the location of the Gift was just as detailed in the book, and once we were able to decode it and follow the admittedly difficult path Gallimand set for us, we found it. When we decode the rest of the instructions, there is a good chance we can determine how to use it, and also search for more of the Gifts."

My head was starting to spin. There was too much new information that I was being asked to absorb. Too many things that I hadn't known or even considered possible were now racing around my brain, fighting each other for space.

Immortal.

That word above all kept ringing in my ears. It didn't feel real still. Despite having gone through it, and now Marlowe telling me all of this, I felt like the ground on which I'd built my life was being rearranged beneath me, and I wasn't sure I'd be able to keep my balance.

"Are you certain, Marlowe?" I asked, suddenly backtracking again. "I don't feel... there's nothing special about me. I'm a decent Worker, but that's… I'm not *important*. I never have been. I wasn't even worth sticking around for when I was a kid."

Marlowe raised a hand and rested it on my shoulder.

"I'm going too quickly," he said softly. "I apologize."

"No, it's not that," I protested, despite the fact it absolutely was.

"I do not know for sure that all of this is true," he said. "There is one obvious way to test the theory that you truly are immortal, but I do not think it ideal."

An image of Marlowe stabbing me in a very polite and clinical manner to see what would happen flashed through my mind.

"My hope is that there are answers in the first volume of the Works, but even that might only provide a small piece of the puzzle. What I do know is that you should be dead, and you are not. For whatever reason that miracle occurred, I am grateful."

He squeezed my shoulder, and I cleared my throat and had to look away into the garden. Marlowe removed his hand and didn't speak again. After several moments, I broke the silence.

"So not only am I suddenly immortal," I said softly, "but I might also be a sign that the end of the world is coming?"

Marlowe frowned. "It would appear so."

"And what happens if we don't do what we need to do for everything to... rebalance?"

"The implication is... catastrophe."

I tried to mentally fit more of the puzzle together, but the pieces still wouldn't line up.

"But then why are people coming after *you* for looking into this? Why all the secrecy? If this is something that's supposed to happen, if it's a natural cycle, who is trying to prevent it? And *why*? Shouldn't everyone be worried about it? Shouldn't we be getting Van Sant and the Workers of the West and the Guild and... shouldn't *everyone* care about this?"

Marlowe's expression darkened, in a way I did not think I had seen before. There was a stoniness to it, and a deadness to his usually bright eyes.

"There are always those who wish to subvert the natural working of the world," he said. "There are always those who think they know better and that they can and should impose their desires on reality. And there are those who have power and wish to gather more—and fear, quite rightly, that change will bring about their downfall."

I began to ask another question, but before I could get it out of my mouth, there was a rustle in the leaves behind us.

Part Fifteen

Gettin' the Whole Gang Together

Marlowe and I both stood quickly. I balled my hands into fists and relaxed my prepared Workings from my forearms down to my palms. Marlowe took his gold-rimmed glasses from his pocket and settled them on the bridge of his nose; the glass in them flashed and seemed to sparkle.

Jamal Henry, tall, broad and breathing heavily, emerged from around the corner of a large hedge in the direction of the 'porting entrance to the garden. He walked several steps toward us before he looked where he was going, and when he finally saw us standing there, prepared for a fight, he jerked and pulled up short.

"DAH! Oh, Jesus! Wow. Jesus *Christ*. You scared the *hell* out of me."

Marlowe stepped forward and removed his glasses. He held out a gnarled hand. "Jamal! My sincere apologies—we were not expecting you. Are you well?"

"I'm fine. I just—need a minute." The enforcer leaned against a nearby trellis and wiped a shaking hand across his forehead. "Jesus, Mary, Joseph, and all of their carpenter friends."

I realized that he wasn't running a hand over his forehead after all but massaging his temples. My own headache came back with a wicked throb, and I winced and grabbed at my temples as well.

Marlowe caught the motion between us both and took charge. "Sit—both of you," he said. We did as told, sitting side-by-side on the stone bench like schoolboys who had been caught tracking mud into the headmaster's house.

Jamal removed his Ruiner, and I removed my ring. Marlowe swept us with a wave of heat that prickled our skins and then a Working that drove away our pain.

"Something remained attached to you from a previous Working," Marlowe said, concerned. "It is gone now, but whoever placed it is strong. Our mysterious Ms. Shrike?"

"Mallory Shrike," Jamal confirmed, standing up and cracking his neck, a darker, healthier color coming back into his cheeks. "I learned some more about her."

"Good," Marlowe said. "Let's—"

There was another shuffling of leaves and then a pop as someone else entered the garden through the 'porting entrance.

Jamal and I immediately pushed in front of Marlowe.

Kori Clark rounded the corner, and, very similar to Jamal, cried out in alarm and jumped nearly a foot in the air when she saw us standing there.

"SHIT! Wow—Fuck a duck—what the *hell* are you doing standing there? Are you just waiting to give innocent people fucking aneurysms?"

"Aneurysms are not caused by sudden shock," Marlowe said, smiling slightly. "A hemorrhagic stroke, perhaps, caused by an existing aneurysm, though, could make sense."

"Fine—whatever Marlowe just said, you want to give me that?"

"Where've you been?" Jamal asked, looking at her suspiciously.

"Doing my job, Stretch," she said. "Jesus, you're way too intimidating to just be standing around in the dark waiting for little girls to show up."

I snorted in spite of myself. She rounded on me.

"Don't think you're all innocent either. Just 'cause Batman is out here being ominous doesn't mean you get to do it too, Robin."

"Enough," Marlowe said before I could respond. "Ms. Clark, do you have information for us?"

"'Course I do," she said, as if it were the most obvious thing in the world. "Where do you want me to expound?"

"The library would seem the appropriate place," Marlowe said. "Let's all go, and we'll hear what you have to say."

I saw Kori pause, and then she very deliberately looked straight at me. "All of us?" she asked. She looked back at Marlowe. "Are we a boy band now? Just inviting in pretty faces to pad the ranks? He's not one of us."

"Aw, you really think I'm the pretty one?" I asked.

She scoffed. "You clearly aren't the brains."

"You just don't stop talking, do you?" I asked.

"You just don't stop being annoying, do you?"

"What's your problem? I've known Marlowe way longer than you have—if anyone's got a right to be part of something, it's me."

"You don't know anything about me," she sneered.

I took a step toward her, my ears ringing. "And you don't know anything about me."

"I know you're a little snot who's had us running around all night 'cause you're in over your head and can't take care of your own shit."

"Well, you look like how bad fish smell, when was the last time you showered?"

Kori took an aggressive step forward that echoed mine, her face a thunderhead of anger.

"Enough!" Marlowe barked. She stopped where she was, looking at me with an expression of deep animosity. But we both seemed to know what that tone meant—Marlowe did not very often bark orders, but when he did, it meant he'd lost patience with something he found entirely childish and he would countenance it no further.

"Come," Marlowe said in his normal tone of voice. "Into the house."

Jamal gave us an annoyingly superior 'stop being foolish' look and followed Marlowe as he moved off.

Kori gave me one last critical side-eye.

"Like what you see?" I asked.

She clearly wanted to respond to the taunt, but she glanced toward Marlowe, who was not very distant, and apparently changed her mind.

"Welcome to the party, Sissy-row. Try not to die."

She stalked off after Jamal and Marlowe.

"That would appear to be the least of my problems," I muttered.

We all followed Marlowe back through the wide glass garden doors, through the large entertaining hall, and down the corridor and short set of stairs into the library. Inside were waiting the two people from earlier—Paulina and Atticus. Paulina was on one of the ladders searching for something on one of the higher shelves; Atticus was in the corner pouring over a volume of the Compendium of Materia Magi. They both looked around when the doors opened, and there was a flash of sapphire light that signaled Calliope's presence as well.

The little faux-muse hurried down from the ceiling chandelier where she usually perched and dropped onto Marlowe's shoulder. "How did it go?" she asked in a stage whisper that could be heard by all of us. "You left with one and came back with three, somehow they're multiplying."

"Inferior copies to be sure," I said.

"2.0 is always better than 1.0," Jamal said.

"Not even a little bit true. Matthew McFadden is dreamy, but Colin Firth is Mr. Darcy."

I heard a small laugh, and I glanced over at Atticus. The young man was smirking as he resettled his tortoise-shell-frame glasses on his nose and looked up from the Compendium.

"We have reports from both Mr. Henry and Ms. Clark to review," Marlowe said. "Mr. Henry was about to share his with Mr. James and me in the garden just now when Ms. Clark returned, and I thought it would be best to bring us all together to listen and then discuss next steps. Mr. Henry, would you like to begin?"

Jamal cleared his throat and stepped forward, clasping his hands behind his back. He looked like a soldier at parade rest.

"There will be an increased enforcer presence at the Palace gala tomorrow tonight. Smith has officially assigned me to be in attendance, along with the group we discussed before. Ratcliffe and Schmidt are still leading. There's a chance Smith is sympathetic to our cause, but I haven't been able to feel him out completely. Marlowe is still widely regarded as an upstanding member of the Worker community, and if the reports against him weren't coming from this particular source, I think they'd be dismissed out of hand. As it is, we now know that the woman who arrived to investigate Cicero's death—or, well—"

He paused and waved vaguely at me.

"My dramatic return?" I suggested. "My dastardly refusal to go quietly into that long goodnight? My Jesus Christ Superstar rendition without the ABBA songs?"

Atticus snorted again.

"Yes, that," Jamal said, returning his hand behind his back. "The woman who came to investigate it is a consultant from the WA. Her name is Mallory Shrike. I hadn't heard of her until yesterday, but people I trust know her reputation. She's... she could be trouble."

"The WA—you mean the Workers of America?" Kori asked.

"No, the other WA," I said, "Welders Anonymous, it's a great group, you should look into it."

"I hear they're open to all joiners," Atticus said.

I looked at him. He raised an eyebrow at me.

How exciting. I'd made a friend.

"Focus, please," Marlowe said. "Thank you, Mr. Henry. I haven't heard of this Mallory Shrike before this evening, which... concerns me. She isn't one of the players I had on the board, but, clearly, if she is here and she is tracking all of this then she must be seriously considered."

"If she's from the WA, then we have more heat on us than we were expecting," Jamal said grimly. "She's trying to bait you, Marlowe. Smith was implying it heavily, but he couldn't say it right out for the obvious reason that you *are* officially a person of interest. And I agree. We have to step very carefully here."

"If all goes to plan tomorrow night, then we may have better evidence to provide Smith as well as others," he said, pacing toward the window. When he turned back, he was looking down, deep in thought. After a few seconds of silence, he said. "How did she arrive so soon after Cicero's event? How was she ready for it and able to respond so quickly?"

"We can't be the only ones who've noticed the signs and created a list of potential Immortals," Paulina said. "I mean... we know we aren't." Her voice was light and feminine, but her tone was dark. She had descended the ladder and was leaning back against it now, in a casual way that belied the kind of comfortable relationship with her own body that only trained athletes have. "If Shrike and the WA have one of the original books, too…. If I were them, I'd be looking for the signs everywhere."

"She was at the Palace tonight," Kori said. She had dropped her backpack into one of the chairs closest to the door and was squatting comfortably next to it. I clocked that as weird, but it seemed to be in keeping with the 'I do things my own way' nature of her character. I don't know why, but it annoyed me. She couldn't just sit in the chair like a regular person?

"Have you seen her before?" Jamal asked.

"First time up close. But someone said her name. Skinny, kinda brown/red hair, purple nail."

Jamal and I looked at each other.

"That's her," I said.

"Then she was there—she and half a dozen enforcer-types," Kori continued. "Only the enforcer-types weren't typical enforcers. They had enforcer badges, but they were different from the usual badges."

"Private contractors," Jamal said. "The WA uses them sometimes. They're not part of the official government body. She's a consultant, and I'd be willing to bet the others are too."

"What exactly does she consult on?" Paulina asked.

"Special interest cases. Which is code for 'strange coincidences no one else wants to deal with.' Puts her right in our path. Especially if Kori's seen her skulking around the Palace."

"You mean the Palace of Fine Arts?" I asked.

There was a pause in the conversation and several looks were exchanged. Atticus put his hands in his pockets and sucked his top lip into his mouth. Paulina made a small clicking sound with her tongue before looking over at Marlowe. Both Kori and Jamal were watching me with evaluating expressions.

Marlowe watched me for a long moment. The conversation we'd had in the garden seemed to fill the space between us, and I still wonder what was going through his mind. I wonder if even then he was trying to find another way to move forward, another option. The silence lengthened, but we were all waiting for Marlowe to fill it.

Finally, he spoke.

"We believe that the first page of *The Eternal Cycle* will be auctioned off tomorrow night at the annual Workers of the West Arts and Culture Exhibition. This year the event will be held in the Palace of Fine Arts, alongside a Blissful auction."

The others all shifted as he spoke, and the mood in the room changed. As if Marlowe had spoken something out loud that they weren't used to acknowledging in the presence of outsiders. I took a moment to let the words sink in, and then I glanced around the room at the expressions on the faces of the others.

"And you're thinking about… buying it?"

Paulina pursed her lips and raised an eyebrow.

"Ah," I said. "You're thinking about *stealing* it."

Kori and Jamal both glanced back at Paulina, who blinked several times and shifted guiltily.

I looked back at Marlowe.

"Stealing? You condone this behavior? You're not the man I remember growing up with."

"I don't condone it," Marlowe said with a heavy sigh. "If there were a way to legitimately pay for and acquire the page, then that is what the plan would be. But the cost at auction is worth more than this house and every gold piece I have and can borrow. It is an extremely rare artifact and expected to draw… significant interest."

"Why the hell are the WA letting it go up for auction, then?" I asked. "If it's real and this Shrike lady represents the

WA, why aren't they listening to her and just taking it down or away or something?"

"It's privately owned by the Artifacts and Antiques Trading Company," Atticus said. I pegged his slight Southern accent as a Louisiana drawl, and it made the name of the company stand out loud and clear.

"Ahhh," I said. Even I had heard of them. They deal in Worker artifacts and have been around for hundreds of years. They also have a reputation for being very professional and particularly… harsh with anyone who crosses them.

They are definitely not people you want to rob.

"We also don't think most people take the Gallimand Works seriously, at least from a content perspective," Atticus continued. "In fact, we still think it highly likely that, while Shrike is homed in on the Works, we don't know how much she actually believes in them herself. Based on what Jamal's said, she doesn't seem nearly as interested in them—or you— as she is in Marlowe."

Jamal and I exchanged a glance.

"She did seem to think Marlowe was the one pulling the strings to make me… immortal."

I tripped over the word, still not used to it. It seemed entirely too grand. I was just a small-time Worker who did consulting jobs. Hell, I had a day job at a tech company like a garden variety Blissful. It made absolutely no sense that this was happening to me.

My mind shook, and I crushed the thoughts down and out. I couldn't think about them in detail or I'd crack. Couldn't think about any of it or I'd end up squashed under a mountain of imposter syndrome.

"She did think you had been Raised," Jamal said. "When she questioned you. And I agree, she's fixated on Marlowe. But the more people who look into the Hayes Valley job, the more they are going to be looking into you *and* Marlowe. Still, Shrike is convinced that Marlowe is… orchestrating everything. Which, to be fair, he has been."

"Fuck me if I want to be fair to that bitch," Kori said.

Marlowe turned to her and raised both eyebrows.

She grimaced and seemed to shrink back.

"I would prefer not to be fair to that oh-so-dastardly woman," she said in an unenthusiastic monotone. She shot a flat stare at Marlowe. He nodded. When he turned away, she crossed her eyes and stuck her tongue out at his back.

"In any case," Jamal said, "the best information I have is that she's still working under the assumption Marlowe Raised James. She elevated it all the way to Smith. She didn't reference Gallimand or anything, so I don't know if she's reading from the same hymn book we are or if she's just got it out for whoever believes in it all. Over my head now. Smith still isn't buying it, but we have to take any report like that seriously. James's alibi is holding up better than we'd hoped, but it won't stop them from bringing him in if something else happens. There will be additional enforcers on standby tomorrow night for the exhibition, and I'm willing to bet Shrike and her people will be there too. Maybe not in an official capacity, but at least around."

"Which means we now have two objectives for tomorrow night," Marlowe said. Everyone's attention sharpened and shifted back to him. "Get the book and avoid providing the WOTW or Ms. Shrike with a reason to apprehend us. Which means we revert to Plan A."

I did not expect the sudden reaction that came from those words, but there certainly was one. Both Paulina and Kori made sounds of objection. Jamal looked down and shook his head. Atticus seemed to be the only one who had seen this coming—he simply nodded and readjusted his glasses, frowning slightly.

"This is already complicated enough, Marlowe," Paulina said. "We all agreed on Plan B and it's what we've been working on for the past week. We can't go changing things now, it's too risky as it is."

"Absolutely," Jamal added. "One thing at a time. Plan B is good, it'll work, and we should stick to it. You don't need to be there."

Marlowe held up a hand and they both fell silent. "I understand your concerns. But our hand has been forced. We *must* keep up appearances and show we have nothing to worry about and nothing to hide. And we also have Cicero's help as necessary."

"But he's not one of us!" Kori snapped, pointing at me. "Sure, we rescued him, we helped him out, that's all fine. But just because he can't die doesn't mean he's automatically a part of this. This is bigger than him or any other name on that list—it always has been."

The words rang in the air for several long seconds, and they seemed to echo particularly loudly in my head.

"Mr. James is an excellent Worker," Marlowe began. "He—"

"Marlowe," I said. "It's fine."

All eyes flicked over to me.

"Look, I haven't slept in two days," I said, letting the deep weariness I felt come through in my voice. "I went to do a job last night and I died. I fucking *died*. And then I woke up on an autopsy table in a morgue, and I've been doing everything I can to keep it together since then. I know you've got something going on here, and I know there's something important about it, but all I want to know is what's happening to me. And the answers are in this book, I guess. So, at least until we have this page and know more, I *am* a part of this. Whatever needs to happen, I'll help make it happen. And then when we get the answers, if you want me out and we can figure out how to make that happen, then I'm on board. I'll just go back to my life."

There was a pause as everyone took this in. I was surprised that Marlowe did not speak up, but he seemed to be reading the room and giving everyone time to think and react.

"Look, is the compromise that I stay here and wait for you all to get back?" I asked, looking around. " You seem like you've got this all nailed down. I don't need to be in the way and messing everything up."

"My point exactly," Paulina said. "No offense. You seem like a decent guy. Marlowe says good things about you, and I know you wouldn't be here if he didn't think you were trustworthy. But we already have a plan, and it's been ready since before you came."

Atticus cleared his throat and shifted in his seat. "Well," he said, "there is one thing."

"Something new?" Marlowe asked, looking concerned.

"Yes and no," Atticus said, turning back to the desk he was still at and pulling out a stack of papers on which he seemed to have been making notes in a clean, slanted hand. He turned back with it and held it out to Marlowe, who took it and examined it.

"This is supplemental research I've been doing, looking into anything I could find on Gallimand. It turns out he was... well, let's just say what we all know, he was an eccentric. After his publication and subsequent persecution, as we all know, he became paranoid. His notes were transferred into languages or codes that could only be broken by ciphers or read by those that he intended to read them, which we know from the Gifts volume that we have. Some of it is fairly simple, and the original copies of the pages—where they survived—do not all have those Workings on them. But most of the truly original copies are lost, and the second run of copies, after Gallimand's persecution began… almost all have significant protections. More significant than we may have realized. In fact, we may have gotten very lucky with the one Marlowe found originally."

He pulled out another piece of paper, handling it much more gingerly. He passed this one to Marlowe too. It was old and weathered and looked to have been carefully cut from a book. The page was almost crumbling, and I saw a small mark at the top that I assumed was some kind of preservation Working that Atticus had believed into the page.

"What's it say?" Jamal asked. Marlowe was reading it, his eyes moving from side to side. His expression gave away nothing. Finally, he lowered the page and handed it back to Atticus.

"Thank you," he said. "It is very good that you found this."

Atticus nodded, looking mildly pleased with himself.

"Ms. Clark," Marlowe said, "last week you shared with us that the page had arrived in a large crate, and out of the crate was taken a heavy carrying case with clear windows that contained the page itself. Do I have that right?"

"Yes," Kori said. "But we're planning to pick the case, we don't have to worry about it."

Atticus shook his head. "That unfortunately doesn't solve our problem. One of the protections that Gallimand began putting on the pages of his Works was that only those sympathetic to his cause could handle them. Specifically, it would appear that outside of a very short list of people who have long since died, only the Immortal or one of what he calls 'the Gifted' could touch them and reveal what they say. At least, that is what this seems to say," he gestured to the page he had provided Marlowe. "The page coming up for auction was traced through Venice, Prague, London, New York, and now here. It is from a second-run copy, which we all knew, but much more heavily protected than the book we have. In addition to being written in code, the page cannot be touched or handled. All attempts to do so have resulted in… well, it appears the results are unpleasant."

A long pause.

"Fuck me," Kori said. "Are you serious? We were about to walk in there and try to steal something that no one knew until *today* we couldn't even *touch*?"

"We didn't even know officially that the page was going to be here until last week," Paulina said, clearly trying to sound reasonable and lower the temperature in the room. "This is why we have the go-no-go meeting tomorrow morning. This is why Atticus and I have been doing additional research. If we don't feel good about the plan tomorrow morning—the plan and *all* the details—then we call it off. That has always been the deal. Right, Marlowe?"

"That is right, Ms. Grace," Marlowe said calmly. He did not look at Paulina, though, nor did he look at any of the others. He was very clearly thinking about something else.

"Great, because I don't feel good about this now," Kori said. "We've got this woman from the WA breathing down our necks, we've got heat on Marlowe because they know he's connected to you," she motioned to me as if I were some piece of questionable overpriced art that she just couldn't wrap her head around, "and now we can't even touch the thing we're supposed to be stealing. There's way too much going on now."

"It can still work," Jamal said.

"It's possible," Paulina said. "We can take it out in the case it came in. If no one can touch it, then they have to be ready to transport it for the winner of the auction anyway. We just find out how they're planning to do it and use that."

"It's possible to get James in there," Jamal said. "But they'll be watching him—and you too, Marlowe, which is why we didn't have you coming originally. Smith was clear that one wrong move by either of you and he'll have to acquiesce to Shrike's demands to bring you both in for questioning. You're still the only leads they have in what they're still considering a Raising. If you make the slightest slip-up, they'll be on you. Unless we can give them another suspect or lay a false trail or something. But we'd need someone like Hobb for that."

"Who's Hobb?" I asked.

"He's already working on it," Kori said. "And a cover identity for James. It won't be ready by tomorrow, though. Not if we want it done right."

"But they won't be arrested just for walking in, will they?" Atticus asked. "That's what you're saying, right, Jamal? Cicero will be under suspicion, and he'll be watched, but they'll be watching Marlowe too, and neither of them will be arrested or taken in for questioning?"

Jamal nodded. "Not by the WOTW, as long as they don't do anything suspicious. Who knows what Shrike is planning, though? But yes, Smith briefed us all before I came back here. They're not to be detained. Not yet, at least."

"I'm standing right here," I said, raising a hand. "I'm not invisible as well as immortal, am I?"

"We never figured out a way to get past the inner guards," Atticus said, completely ignoring me. He had his hand on his chin and was looking off into the middle distance. "People, not systems. Systems we can fool. People, we either subdue or convince."

"We still might need to do both," Jamal said darkly.

"I told you, we need Hobb," Kori said.

"We don't need Hobb," Paulina retorted.

"*Who is Hobb?*" I asked.

"Please be silent," Marlowe said.

It was a sign of all our respect for him that when he asked for it, silence fell immediately. He was still looking down at the floor, and his eyes were still darting from here to there as if he were focusing on things that only he could see, pieces to an invisible puzzle that he was mentally fitting together. After several seconds of silence, he nodded and looked up. He took several steps forward so that he was in the center of the room with all of us arrayed around him.

"I understand your frustration, your fear, and your anxiety. I understand that what I have asked of you is not easy and that what proof I have been able to share with you has been scant. I know that you are here as much on faith in me as anything I have shared with you. But I must implore you to follow me through on this journey. Think through what has happened, what we are seeing happen before our very eyes. We know that Gallimand's predictions held true centuries ago. We know now that there is a faction rising within the WA that seeks again to suppress knowledge of what he knew, and that that faction is willing to violate the Code and Worker's Rights in service of their goal. More, we know that outside forces are pushing to stop the Cycle altogether—to break the wheel that has been turning for all time."

He turned to me.

"And we have an Immortal walking among us."

I had to look away. I could feel the others watching me, and I don't think I've ever felt like more of a fraud. I hate when things are expected of me. I hate it. I've let too many people down in my life, and there I was with some impossible standard they were already trying to make me measure up to. I remember hoping desperately that once we got the page we'd find some way to change things. Or maybe we'd find some way to prove that this was all wrong, that I wasn't who they were looking for. That I really had been Raised by some fluke coincidence and the Immortal was someone else on this list they had.

"I know you do not know him," Marlowe continued. "But I do. And I ask you to trust me in this as you have trusted me so far, that Cicero James is a good man and an asset. We do not know what his role in all of this might be, but we must find out. There are answers in the Works, and this is the first page we have found that could help us truly unravel what we do not yet know. There is a crisis coming, and Workers must stand and face it, as we have done for millennia, or else our world and the world of the Blissful will both be in grave danger. What that danger is we must discover. The answer is nearly within our grasp."

He paused. No one seemed to feel like speaking. He nodded.

"Ms. Grace is correct—we are not yet committed. We will meet tomorrow morning for the go-no-go meeting. However, this is the final plan for which I advocate:

"Mr. James's presence is the most straightforward method for retrieving the page, and we should bring him along with us tomorrow night. To add a layer of extra security, we should register his ticket under a false identity, and we should use the back exit route to access the storage room. Both will require Hobb."

Paulina threw up her hands and then crossed her arms, but Marlowe held out a hand to her before she could voice her thoughts. "I know that Hobb has questionable motives. But he is loyal when bought. And we'll need his contacts and his… less than savory abilities. He already knows the details. Ms. Clark, can you arrange it with him?"

"He won't do it on less than twenty-four hours' notice," she said, shaking her head. "It's too tight a window."

"Can we make it worth his while?" Marlowe asked.

Kori sighed and scratched at her chest. "I can try. No promises, though."

"Thank you." He looked around again at the gathered group. "I do not believe in coincidence. We have found that there is additional protection on the page we need at the same moment that the method of getting around that protection has been delivered to us in the form of Mr. James. There are other interested parties who may wish to obtain the page before we do, and the information it contains may be lost to us. The window is open, and our path appears, while treacherous, navigable. We must walk it while we have the chance to do so."

I remember sitting there listening to him and thinking a) great speech, deserved an Oscar nod, and b) why on earth would any of them trust me enough to go through with this plan?

I don't usually play nice with others. I like distance. My parents were gone by the time I was ten—the event that made me a Worker took them. The only person I've ever really trusted since then has been Marlowe, and boy did that take time.

So I don't expect other people to trust me either. Mutually assured distrustation. I expect distrust as the default factory setting, with an optional anger expansion pack thrown in if you're willing to spend a little bit more. Kori—her reaction to me was what I expected from everyone. What I felt most comfortable with, honestly.

But I guess that's what makes Marlowe special. People trust him. He believes in what he says, and that helps other people believe in it too.

So when he finished and I looked around the room expecting rolling eyes and shaking heads, I saw various expressions of deep thought. It ran the gamut, of course—Jamal was still his stoic self, and I'm fairly certain he'd have done whatever Marlowe asked of him, speech or no speech. And Kori's face was surly and sullen. But they all seemed to be seriously considering the points Marlowe had made.

I just wanted to go to sleep.

"We have the meeting in the morning," Marlowe said. "10 am sharp. Everyone has a lot to think about, and there are still things to do. Please, feel free to stay in the guest rooms if you would like. Otherwise, I will see you all tomorrow morning."

That was all Kori needed—she stood, grabbed her backpack, and walked out the door. Everyone watched her go and listened to her footsteps retreat up the stairs and down the hall.

Jamal stood next and said, "Goodnight, everyone." He left too, his booted feet making deeper and steadier sounds.

Not seeing any further reason to stay, I stood next and said something similar—I can't remember what words I used. I'm lucky I was still conscious at that point.

I left the library while Paulina and Atticus were still talking with Marlowe and made my way to the front door, following Jamal who had just gone through it. I put my hand on the handle and stopped. I thought about going back to my tiny, overpriced apartment. I thought about being alone and then having to make my way back in the morning. I thought about everything that could happen between the two locations, going both ways.

I looked up the staircase that would lead me to the third floor and the guest rooms.

Calliope appeared in a flash of sapphire light.

"He had Jacob Luis make up your old room," she said. "The clothes you left are there, too."

I let go of the cool metal door handle and stumbled in the direction of the stairs.

I made it up to the room, and it was exactly the way I remembered it. He hadn't changed a thing since I'd last been there. The bed was still in the same place, the sheets and pillows were the same freshly laundered green-and-gray linen. My old clothes were in the drawers, and the bed was as soft and warm as it had always been.

I was asleep before my head even hit the pillows, of which there were still far too many.

PART SIXTEEN

Go? No Go? Bogo?

I woke to the sound of birds chirping outside my window. I groaned and rolled over, covering my eyes to block out a bar of sunlight streaming across the bed.

I'd slept in my clothes, and I felt like it. I sighed, opened my eyes, and blinked several times, staring up at the ceiling. I lifted my chin and looked at the large, ornate clock on the wall across from the bed.

I slowly realized it was nine in the morning. I'd slept nearly eleven hours straight.

I sat up, working out a kink in my neck, and moved to the edge of the bed. I found myself looking out the window. I could see the garden. The bird I'd heard singing was on an eave just outside, cheerfully building a nest and whistling while it worked. A scrub jay—blue and gray and black. Beyond it, the garden was washed in early morning sunlight. The fog/mist from last night had dissipated, and it was again one of the rare sunny days in San Francisco.

Two in a row—lucky.

My head was blessedly empty, but I knew it couldn't stay that way. I closed my eyes and listened to the natural sounds of morning, trying to hold onto them for as long as I could. I remember that moment very clearly—that was the last moment of calm before the rush of everything that led up to me writing this for you.

For several moments, I just breathed. I just sat there with my eyes closed, feeling the warmth of the sun on my skin, hearing nothing but birdsong and—very distant, just on the edge of hearing—the sound of the waves of the Bay lapping against the shore of Baker Beach.

Wow my life had changed. Remember that idiot back at the beginning of all of this? That idiot who thought his time spent going into an office with air conditioning and free coffee and easy requirements about putting numbers in a computer wasn't absolutely grand?

That started me thinking, because of course it did. My brain had done some processing during the night—some desperately, desperately needed processing.

I looked over at my nightstand and saw the book Marlowe had given me the night before. The copy of Gallimand's Works. I had to have brought it up with me, or else Luis or Calliope or someone had brought it up for me. It was next to my phone, which the same someone must have taken out of my pocket and plugged in to charge. I could see a few more messages from Roc and one from Anandini.

How far away that side of my life seemed to me now.

I'd died and come back. If no one had Raised me, then I was immortal.

Was I? Really?

I stood and walked over to the desk, staring down at the book with its worn black leather cover and gold lettering.

There was a ribbon of green cloth sticking out of the top. Someone had marked one of the pages for me, toward the end of the book, in the mostly empty last volume. I grabbed the book, flipped to the marked page, and started reading.

A final word:

The emergence of the Immortal begins again the Cycle,
ending the Fourth Season of the previous Cycle and beginning

the First Season of the next. The Immortal heralds a time of chaos and strife, and until his or her work is done, he or she shall not die. The Immortal shall feel pain, and the rending of their flesh and the flaying of their soul, but they shall not pass from this world into the Eternal until their work is done. As such, it must be remembered that when an Immortal dies, they are resurrected only once their body is replaced and whole. If they are dismembered, they will not return until the pieces of their body are reassembled. If they are drowned, they will not return until their lungs once more are clear of water. If they are burned, they will not return until their body cools.

Those who oppose the Immortal have used this in the past to delay the beginning of the next Cycle, leading to famine, disease, and death. Those who bear the Gifts must stand by the Immortal in his or her time of need so that they are not delayed. As spring must follow winter, so must one Cycle be allowed to follow after the other.

"Jesus Christ," I muttered. "What a fucking thing to wake up to."

I dropped the book back down on the bedside table, where it made a solid *thwack*. I put my head in my hands.

I didn't know what to do with any of that. I still don't, to be honest. What the hell do you do when you find out that there are people out there who might be thinking about drowning you or burning you or dismembering you or… I mean, what do you *do?*

I stood up and ran my fingers through my hair, which had become a greasy halo around my head. I looked back over at the clock on the wall. It was made of wood and metal without a hint of plastic, a small pendulum clock with brassy gears and internal works that hummed along easily, ticking time away.

It was about fifteen minutes after nine. The meeting that Marlowe and everyone else had talked about the night before was supposed to be at ten, downstairs in the library.

What was everyone going to say?

Guess I should go down and find out.

I sniffed myself.

Oof, but a shower first. *Definitely* a shower first.

I walked across the room to the door and looked out into the hallway. It was deserted. I could hear voices coming from the direction of the third-floor landing that led to the stairs and the lower levels of the house. People were in the kitchen. I could smell coffee and toast and something cooking. Bacon. My mouth watered, and I realized that, on top of barely sleeping for forty-eight hours, I'd also barely eaten.

Across the hallway—which was lined with other doors that led to other guest rooms—was the large guest bathroom. It had four sinks, and beyond them two separate rooms, one with a toilet and one with a shower. The doors were all open; no one else was using any of the facilities.

I sniffed myself again and reconfirmed my decision. If I didn't shower, I'd overpower the coffee and the bacon, and they'd kick me out of the house on sheer principle.

I showered, I shaved, I shat. Not in that order. A shocking amount of dirt and grime came off of me in the process. Fifteen minutes later, mostly revived and smelling like

Marlowe's fancy tea tree and coconut oil soap, I made my way downstairs.

Once past the third-floor landing, I started being able to make out distinct words in the conversation floating up from the kitchen. I only heard snatches, and as much as I'd have liked to eavesdrop on bits of juicy gossip or overhear them talking shit about me so I knew where I stood, it was all very mundane.

"No way they trade him," Jamal was saying. "Not with the new reserve QB rule. The Niners can't end up the way they did last year."

"It's certainly statistically unlikely," Atticus responded. "You know, I've been working on a model that I'd like to get your thoughts on to help us better predict—"

"I'm not helping you gamble, Atticus," Jamal responded firmly.

"I know you hate them, but you need to give them a try," Paulina was saying. "I can't believe I tried an apple fritter before you did."

"I just wanna keep making those dumplings you showed me last weekend. They were so good I wanted to slap you." Kori, I assumed.

I descended the stairs and walked through the wide archway into the living room and kitchen, beyond which were the large glass wall and doors that led to the garden, glowing with warm, buttery sunlight. The room had polished wooden floors stained a dark gray and several tasteful rugs under the couches and chairs. Everyone was clustered around the kitchen island, which was more like a kitchen continent, with two sinks, an insert for chairs, a large stovetop with six burners, and a metal vent built into the granite surface that lowered itself down into the island when it wasn't needed. It's what most kitchen islands aspire to be when they grow up.

They didn't notice me at first, and I hesitated in the arched entryway. A sapphire flash that was Calliope popped in and out of the scene, as well as a crimson flash that was Jacob Luis, though he seemed to hover on the periphery as if he both wanted and didn't want to be included. Coffee had been made and set on the counter in a large French Press, and next to it was a pot of tea. There was also a plate of buttered toast, a swiftly dwindling stack of bacon, a cast iron skillet of eggs and hash browns, and several bowls of chopped fruit and fresh berries.

Kori noticed me first, before I could make the decision to deliberately walk into the room, or, like I was contemplating, skip breakfast entirely to avoid socializing, despite my ferociously growling stomach. But Kori looked up as she took a long sip of her coffee and caught sight of me before I could turn to leave.

I blinked and looked off to the side, breaking eye contact. Then, shaking my head at myself and very close to muttering disparaging remarks under my breath, I looked back, my lips pressed in a tight line, trying not to challenge her but just to meet her gaze.

She watched me for a moment over the rim of her white coffee cup. She has clear blue eyes with bits of yellow in them; from a distance, they blend into a light green. The conversation continued on around her.

I don't know how long that moment lasted, but it seemed like a pivotal one, so I held it. Looking back, it was probably only a handful of seconds, but it felt longer. It felt as if I were being fully evaluated. Not just as a Worker or potential collaborator in their grand schemes, but as a person. As if she were looking at me in the full, sober light of day and trying to divine the quality of my soul.

She was the one who broke the moment. She took a breath and sighed it out through her nose. She then gave me one last up-and-down look, taking in my second-day-worn clothing but clean and still-wet hair. Then she tilted her head very slightly to one side, shrugged with her eyebrows, and raised her white coffee mug a few inches.

Coffee? she was asking.

I swallowed and nodded, stepping into the room.

She turned and grabbed another mug and said something to the now orange-yellow cluster of sparks that was Jacob Luis. The bound Wrathful paused, grew a weak-jawed face that looked at her with deepest loathing, and then glided over to the nearly empty French Press and set about heating what was left and adding more grounds and water.

My boots made hollow sounds on the wood floor, and I realized that the others had taken off their shoes and left them by the entryway. I took another step, then stopped. Jamal, Atticus, and Paulina stopped talking and looked around, catching sight of me. I gave a short, awkward wave—a single jerk of my hand.

"'Morning," was what came out of my mouth.

"Certainly is," Paulina responded. She was by far the most put-together of the group—she no longer wore workout attire, but instead had put on a light layer of makeup, washed and lightly styled her hair, and wore a light gray shirt under a white denim jacket above form-fitting navy jeans. She seemed much more calm and accepting of my presence than she had the night before. I wondered how much of that was the effect of sleep.

I knelt and unlaced my boots, pulled them off, and slid them over in line with the others' shoes. When I straightened again, I saw Jamal smile very slightly and nod his approval— a single bob of the head.

I walked forward in the silence, and it was awkward. Really, really awkward.

So. I broke the tension.

"Has anyone told Jamal he's wearing a shirt that's two sizes too small for him? Or are we waiting until he's had his coffee?"

Atticus, who had just taken a sip from his mug, choked, spitting out a spray of tea which, luckily, was directed away from the rest of the group. Paulina forced her lips into a tight line and raised her eyebrows so high that they almost climbed into her hair, before raising her own cup in front of her mouth and taking a very long, very deliberate sip. Kori barked a laugh and pointed a finger at the enforcer. "Yo, I *told* you," she said.

"James!" Calliope hissed, flying across the room in an instant and revolving into her tiny pixie form, hands on perfectly shaped hips and head cocked to the side, eyes literally blazing. "That is completely inappropriate!"

The effect of her scolding, though, was ruined when Jamal bent forward and flexed his considerable chest, which was, indeed, very visible in the well-fitted black t-shirt he was wearing. "Well, if you got it, flaunt it," he said.

"I don't mind it," Paulina said with a coy smile.

"Neither do I," Atticus said with a wider one.

"No, but is it really that bad?" Jamal asked.

"I mean, did you ask permission first or did you just steal it from the grade school lost and found?" I asked.

Atticus and Kori laughed. Paulina looked torn, like she wanted to laugh too but didn't want to hurt Jamal's feelings.

"That's enough out of you," Jamal said, pointing a thick finger at me. "If you like your teeth the way they are, you'll be nice."

I walked toward the kitchen island. "Why, what're you gonna do to my teeth? Don't try to eat them, they aren't mints, I swear."

Jamal met me halfway and punched my arm in a bro-friendly way.

I feigned pain, grabbed my arm, and cried out "Abuse! Hazing! I'm being hazed!" and dramatically fell to the floor.

Atticus legitimately cackled. Jamal rolled his eyes and picked me up by my t-shirt like a misbehaving pet. "Get your coffee, drama queen."

"I expect curtsies next time," I said. "Long may I reign."

"I don't see what was funny about any of that," Jacob Luis said, popping out of existence at the countertop and popping back in with a freshly brewed cup of coffee that he set on the ledge of the island closest to me with a disembodied hand.

"Yeah, well, you think it's funny when puppies get hurt," Paulina said darkly.

"Ah, yes. Cute things in pain. Very good," Jacob Luis said.

"I'm glad Marlowe keeps him on a tight leash," Jamal muttered, eyeing the ball of flame.

"Ah, man, I needed that," Kori said, wiping tears from her eyes. "All right. Well, you're cooler than I thought you were. You can have bacon."

She grabbed the plate, turned it, and sent it sliding across the granite countertop. I stepped up to the island just in time to catch it.

It smelled like heaven.

I grabbed a few pieces and took a sip of coffee. The coffee was the perfect temperature, and I took a bigger gulp, trying to ignore Luis's look of disappointment that it hadn't been hot enough to burn my tongue. The little demon liked playing tricks within the bounds of his contract, but he had a hard time judging what would actually hurt people. It was almost endearing. He was, all things considered, a highly ineffectual demon, which was part of how I suspect Marlowe's father had managed to bind him to the family.

"Good to meet you all with coffee and food," I said. "I... was a bit out of it last night."

"I think we all were," Paulina said. She smiled at me, and that was the first time I realized exactly how pretty she was. Which, in addition to the fact she could be a sportswear model, suddenly made her stand out much more significantly in my mind. "You slept well?"

"Like the dead," I said without thinking. I paused, took another sip of coffee, and added, "which I guess I should stop saying, 'cause, hey, my life just got real fuckin' weird."

Atticus laughed again, a short and wry "hah", and Jamal grunted in agreement. Kori was focused on a bowl of yogurt, berries, and granola now and seemed to have forgotten I existed. Paulina's smile faded slightly, but when she saw me looking at her she brought it back.

"How'd everyone else sleep?" I asked. I don't remember being overly interested in continuing the conversation, but I do remember wanting very badly to talk. To anyone about anything. That's how I process things—talk talk talk. In case you haven't caught on to that yet. And if I can't talk about the problem itself, talking about anything else works.

"Slept well," Jamal said, nodding decisively in a very alpha male sort of way. "Went home."

"He's got that square pillow thing," Paulina said. "Big ol' neck doesn't fit on a regular person pillow." Her eyes lit up as she mocked him, and she held her gaze on him a moment longer than necessary.

"Yeah, yeah," Jamal said, rolling his eyes.

"It's true, though," Kori said. "You shoulda seen him a year or two back when he was still scrawny. And could use regular person pillows."

"The pillow is because I sleep on my side, not because I started working out."

"*Started working out,*" Paulina, Atticus, and Kori all said at the same time, in a very poor imitation of Arnold Schwarzenegger. Kori did a halfway decent Mr. Olympia pose, and Atticus put the piece of toast he was working on in his mouth and flexed both of his biceps, which together barely equaled one of Jamal's.

"Y'all are put here to test me, and it shows," Jamal said.

It was strange seeing them be so friendly with each other. Like I've said before, Workers are an eclectic bunch. There are Workers who hang out together and are friendly, and definitely Workers who do jobs together, but the madness we all face in moments of high stress, and the signs of it that show through in our ordinary lives, usually make it pretty hard to sustain friendships.

And yet here they all were, chatting and drinking coffee.

It felt... normal.

"So you've all known each other for a while," I said, after swallowing an embarrassingly large mouthful of bacon. There was a chorus of nods in response.

"Through Marlowe mostly," Paulina said. When she spoke, the others seemed to cede her the floor. She has that kind of personality—you want to listen when she speaks. "I was first. I was doing research at Cal into ancient texts. One of them turned out to be a Worker account of history that had been lost and Worked so that the Blissful thought it was a recounting of the fall of Rome. There are so few personal accounts of Workers before the Reformation, I decided to do my best to piece together what I could. Which, to be honest, wasn't much until I came across several accounts of Gallimand. I felt like I'd heard the name before but couldn't place it—"

"I felt the same," I said quickly. "Where's it from?"

"That's the thing," Atticus said. "We don't know. It doesn't seem like anyone knows, actually."

"Which is why it interested me," Paulina said. She had her arms crossed over her chest and was looking down at the granite island countertop. "So I reached out to an old mentor of mine, who put me in touch with Marlowe. When he found out what I had, he asked to meet. After that, I walked him through what I'd discovered, and he showed me the book he'd managed to obtain. And then he—in his very Marlowe way—asked me if I wanted to be a part of this."

I nodded. "Part of Team Immortal? If you don't have a name yet, that's my recommendation."

There was a long silence, and I realized I'd stepped on a conversational landmine.

"Ah, never mind," I said quickly.

"It's just that—" Atticus began.

"You aren't in the club yet," Kori said bluntly. Her stone-face was back, and her eyes were once again very intense and unblinking. She was the shortest and slightest of the entire group, but there was something about her that seemed more solid than the others, and it was only partly physical. She has a stillness to her, an almost deadly calm.

Look, I'll come right out and say it—I knew then, and I know now:

Don't fuck with Kori.

"Fair enough," I said, drinking more coffee. I was starting to really feel alive again, my brain firing on all cylinders now that I'd had food and caffeine and a night of solid sleep. Everything that had happened was going through my mind all over again, but in a way that was ordered and measured. It felt like I'd hired a mental cleaning crew to pick up after me while I was out, and now everything was neatly filed and easy to examine piece by piece.

I looked at my watch. 9:47.

"Thirteen minutes," I said. "Just so everyone knows since we're all thinking about it."

Jamal grunted again and drank more tea. "I forgot you just say whatever's in your head when things get quiet."

"Only when everyone is clearly thinking what I'm thinking and it just needs to be said. Look, I know we're about to get into it all, and it's fine if you want to wait until Marlowe's here. I'm just... trying to get my bearings. It sounds like you've all been living with this for a while, and I just got here. And apparently I'm supposed to… be playing a part."

Kori continued to look at me with her stone face, but Paulina was nodding. I focused on her. "I don't usually Work with others," I said. "Jamal was there on the last crew job I took, and it… let's say it soured me on the idea. Pretty permanently."

"Understandably so," Jamal said grimly. His tone put an end to any need for further explanation, but he did helpfully add, "But it wasn't James's fault. In fact, he saved three other Workers that night from an idiot we never should have brought along."

I swallowed, pushing the memories away. "Thanks, Jamal." Another moment of silence, and then I shrugged and continued. "So, yeah. I don't know what this all is, but I guess I get the general details. And, look, I'm not interested in being in if you all don't want me here. So, before we go into this whole thing, just level with me. Is this something I want to be a part of? Is this something *you* want me to be a part of?"

As hard as it was for me, I stopped talking and just waited. I don't know, but I was nervous. My heart was pounding and my palms were sweating. Even though I was half hoping they'd say I should just shove off and find another port in the storm.

"You don't want to be a part of this," Paulina said slowly. She was frowning, a small line creasing the space between her eyes and her lips pulling down at the corners. "I don't think any of us would be part of this if we could have stayed out, now that it's all happening."

She glanced around for confirmation, and I saw a haunted look appear in a number of eyes. Thinking about it still sends chills down my back. If I'd known then what they were all talking about, I don't know if I would have gone forward. But, that was the whole point of the secrecy. And the whole point of me writing this to you.

Horrors have to be faced. And sometimes it's better to decide to face them first, and already be committed when you stumble across them in the dark.

"But you *are* a part of it," I said. "And you aren't leaving."

Paulina looked at me, still frowning. The others all seemed to be waiting for her to speak.

"No," she said finally. "No, we aren't leaving. Someone needs to do this. And if we're the ones who have to do it, then that's the way it is. It's important."

"*Vita non est vivere sed valere vita est,*" Atticus said. He adjusted his glasses on the bridge of his nose. "Life is not just about staying alive."

"You know, I was just saying that to my barber," I said.

Jamal stifled a grin, and Atticus looked sheepish. The mood remained dour, though.

"And… do you think I can help?" I asked.

"Yes," Jamal said. He had a very serious look on his face. "Yes."

I looked around at the others to see if there were differing opinions. Kori was looking at her bowl of yogurt again, her lips pursed. Atticus looked unsure, and so did Paulina.

"Marlowe thinks you can," Paulina said. "And if you're really… immortal... well, I guess we need you. To help get the page if nothing else."

I nodded slowly. "Okay," I said. I gulped down the last of my coffee. "Okay, then."

A clock in the hallway started playing a little tune, then struck out ten thin, silvery chimes. Right as the first chime began, Marlowe appeared on the second-floor landing and made his way down the staircase, then stood in the wide arched entryway.

He looked tired—he either hadn't slept well or hadn't slept at all. Knowing Marlowe, it was likely the latter. His eyes were still bright and sharp, though, and when he saw us all standing together around the island, he paused and took in the scene.

The tenth chime died away, leaving a ringing silence in its place. "Come," he said at last, stepping back and motioning to the corridor that led down to the library. "It is time for decisions."

We went back to the library and basically resumed our positions from the night before. The room was much brighter now, with sunlight streaming in from the large window on the far side of the room, the blue drapes with the golden tassels pulled back. Most of the books had been reshelved by Jacob Luis during the night, aside from the ones that had been marked with special bookmarks to show the reader wanted to keep reading them.

Marlowe did not waste time on preamble. Once we were all assembled and the doors shut behind us, he opened his arms wide and then clapped his hands together. He was nodding and looking at each of us in turn.

"Very well," he said. "We have three things to discuss and decide today. The first: Will we bring Cicero James into our circle? The second: Will we move forward with the Palace job tonight? And the third: Will we include Mr. James in the Palace job? Are there any objections to these three topics? Questions, concerns, modifications?"

He looked around and paused for a reasonable amount of time.

I couldn't help myself—I raised my hand.

Marlowe frowned at me and said, "Yes, Cicero?"

"Is it too late to go to the bathroom?"

Marlowe smiled very slightly. "I'm afraid so," he said.

"In that case," I continued, leaning back against a nearby desk, "my next question is, after we get the book, then what?"

There were a few looks exchanged.

"Then we see just how deep the rabbit hole goes," Jamal said ominously.

I rolled my eyes.

"What?" Jamal asked, looking offended. "You can make jokes and I can't?"

"To be fair, he does look a little like the Morpheus actor," Paulina said.

"Lawrence Fishburne," Atticus muttered.

"Everyone needs to stop using 'to be fair'," Kori grumbled.

"Colloquial," Marlowe said, "but Mr. Henry is correct. Once we understand what is in Gallimand's *Eternal Cycle*, we will have a better idea of how to proceed."

I don't know if I ever really had a choice. I was still tempted to run, and I hate committing myself to things. But what else was I going to do? They were coming for me no matter what.

And it was easier to be brave in the bright light of morning than it had been the night before.

"All right," I said. "Then let's do it."

A bit of tension seemed to leave Marlowe. He nodded and looked around the room.

"Any other comments?"

Jamal shook his head, leaning up against a bookcase with his arms crossed over his chest. Paulina, sitting cross-legged in a chair, did the same. Kori didn't make any sign or motion, which I know now is her way of telling everyone to just get on with it. Atticus adjusted his glasses nervously and just watched everyone, as if trying to memorize the scene.

"Very well. The first order of business—shall we bring Cicero James into the Order?"

"Yes," Jamal said. He glanced over at me and nodded.

"Yes," Atticus said.

"Yes," Paulina said. Her voice was heavy and she was looking at me almost pityingly. "If he really is the Immortal, then he needs to be a part of this."

"No," Kori said.

Everyone looked at her. She had her arms crossed over her chest and she was scowling at the ground. The silence lengthened, and she looked up. "No," she said again. "We don't need him. We can do this without him. There are already too many of us."

"There's four of you," I said, confused. "Five, if you count Marlowe."

Kori scoffed and waved a hand. "See? He has no idea."

"I... what?"

"More will be revealed in time," Marlowe said firmly, "and not until then, Ms. Clark."

I remember thinking quite distinctly that she was going to stick her tongue out at him again, but she didn't. She made no response, and the silence lengthened until Marlowe had to break it again, prompting her.

"We need to be unanimous," he said.

"What?" I asked. "You—but everyone else said yes!"

"It always has to be unanimous," Atticus said, sounding weary. I had a sudden feeling that this wasn't the first time Kori had made a stink about something.

"He hasn't proven himself," Kori said stubbornly. "He died—great. He's immortal. So let's just keep him safe until we know what it is he's supposed to do, and then he can do it. Sure, the WA wants him. But they want *you* more, Marlowe. Shrike had him and she put a bug in him and set him loose so that he would come here and she could break your wards to get to *you*."

She looked over at me, looked at me hard and unyieldingly, and shook her head. "He hasn't proved it yet. He hasn't proved he's one of us."

"Fine," I said. "Fine! But you all still owe me answers. You owe me answers about what's happening to me. And the Gifts book gave me some, but it's all wrapped up in this crazy Gallimand's Works, and if you all believe the page going up for auction at the Palace is the one with the answers, then you owe me the chance to take a look at it."

"You can't be part of the Palace job without being part of us," Paulina said. "If something happens and Shrike gets to you again, she could use you against us."

"She won't get to me," I protested. "Not again. Not now that I know her and I'm ready."

"He should come," Atticus said. "And that'll be how he proves himself."

A silence fell as this new suggestion sank in. I could almost feel the wheels turning in everyone's heads as they thought it over.

"Deal," I said. "I'll help you get the page, and you at least let me read it so I have answers. And if I help you get it and that's enough for KFC over there, and the answers are good, then induct me into whatever cult you have going on here, Marlowe."

I turned on Kori, almost sneering at her. "Good?"

She watched me stonily for several seconds, and everyone waited for her response.

"Yeah," she said. "Yeah, if you make it back and we get the book, I'll go along with it. But I'm going to be right there with you the whole time. And if you think about making any kind of move that puts any of this—any of *us*—in jeopardy, I'll spin your head around your neck before you can say 'Exorcist', immortal or not."

The tension in the room dipped down. It didn't go away entirely—there wasn't much chance of that—but it did dial back several notches.

"Very well," Marlowe said. "It seems our first order of business has decided our second and third. Are we agreed that we will attempt to retrieve the page of Gallimand's first work, *The Eternal Cycle*, tonight with Cicero James in attendance to earn a place among us?"

"Yes.

"Yes."

"Yeah."

"Sure."

"Then we are decided," Marlowe said. "Let's get to work."

Part Seventeen

Prep Time

The next ten hours were some of the most frantic of my life.

I did my fair share of cramming back in Blissful college after my brief stint at the Worker Academy that earned me my Work Cert, but I haven't done any kind of intense studying since then. So when Marlowe and crew turned me over to Atticus, who proceeded to dump the entire Palace Job plan on me in excruciating detail, it took me about ten minutes to realize my head would likely explode before I absorbed it all.

"OK," I told Atticus. "Start over. And explain it to me like I'm five."

"Ah. All right then."

Round two was better. I was able to grasp that there were several layers to the plan, partly because the Workers of the West Arts and Culture Exhibition would be taking place alongside an actual Blissful art auction, which is how these kinds of events usually work. Workers who knew about the real event, and purchased tickets from the Artifacts and Antiques Trading Company, would be ushered into a back room that only Workers could access, and in that room there would be bidding on Worker artifacts and art from across the modern and historical worlds.

As event locations go, the expo center part of the Palace of Fine Arts is blessedly small compared to something like Moscone, which is used for the massive Dreamforce event Salesforce holds every year. It does still have several main rooms, a dozen offices, and multiple levels, though.

"Luckily," Atticus explained to me, "getting in isn't the hard part, since we all have tickets."

"We do?" I asked. I'd been imagining some kind of action movie zip line stunt, or an indestructible suitcase propped up under a metal security gate that we could then duck under. "So we're just going to walk right in?"

"Most of us," Atticus said. "Marlowe, you, Kori, Paulina, and me. Jamal will be there on duty, and he'll have access to the areas the enforcers will be checking, which includes all of the back ways between the two rooms and the different auctions. Kori will be there as Paulina's guest. She'll get in and work on getting Hobb in too, along with some of his crew, and they'll be who help you get the book. It's straightforward enough—we get in, the auction starts, the bidding on the book happens, they take the page back to the holding area but a *different* holding area than the one it was stored in initially, where the buyers can go see their pieces after the bidding ends. The page will be one of the last items—third to last, in fact, it's one of the big finale pieces. When the bidding on it closes, you get up and go to the bathroom. Jamal gets you into the back, Kori and Hobb get you to the page, you grab the page with Kori, Kori and Hobb get you out. The rest of us walk out the front door."

"Won't they notice the page is missing?"

"With luck, no." He pulled out another piece of parchment that was the same type as all of the pages in the worn black leather book with gold lettering that Marlowe had given me, except that this one bore the title "Volume One: The Eternal Cycle" at the top and looked very deliberately torn and frayed in a way I was certain matched the page to be displayed.

"You'll replace the real page with this," Atticus said.

The page was covered in very real-looking handwriting.

"How do you know what it looks like? Is this the actual writing?"

"Yes," Atticus said. "Kori was able to get in and take pictures. We're hoping the back is the same, but, honestly, if anyone suspects enough to pick it up and look at the back, we're already in the shit, and a mismatched front will be the least of our worries."

"Wait—why are we trying to steal it? Can't we just decipher this?"

Atticus shook his head. "This is gibberish. Whatever the way to read it is, it's not in the words themselves, or, if it is a cipher, it's like nothing I've ever seen before. There's also the back, like I said, which we definitely don't have. We just made up all the writing on that side, using the front as a template. No, we need the original. And what works well is that, if we're right, the original will translate for us once we get you or one of the Gifts involved, but this will stay exactly as it is, which means it should be a while before anyone notices we stole the original."

"Got it. So, simple, right? Get in, take the page, get out."

"Yes and no. There are… quite a few more details. Here are the schematics of the floor plan, let's review them first."

He pulled out several very detailed blueprints that might as well have been written in Greek and began trying to explain them to me.

A few hours later, we broke for a late lunch and joined the others in the kitchen. By then my head felt like an overpacked suitcase with random shirt sleeves and pant legs awkwardly caught in the sides and trailing out the back.

"How was your reading of the book last night?" Atticus asked.

He, Paulina, Kori, and Jamal were all around the kitchen island again. We were eating deli sandwiches from some place nearby.

"I read one page, got depressed, and stopped," I said frankly.

"Ah," Atticus said.

"What did you all think when you read it?" I asked the group at large.

"Haven't read it," Jamal said.

"Yeah, me neither," Kori said.

"Really?" I asked. "You just… didn't read it? This book you've all been talking about and planning to steal pages for… you just figured 'nah, I'm good'?"

"I figured I work with a bunch of nerds who wanna tell me about it anyway," Kori said. "Why spoil their fun?"

She winked at Atticus. He just smiled wearily and drank from his cup of tea.

"Do you know all the Gifts then?" I asked.

Kori shrugged. "Like, the gist of them."

"The bad ones too?"

She paused in the act of taking another sip of her afternoon coffee. "What?"

"Yeah, like the little ones that are supposed to start popping up that are just really inconvenient if you end up bound to them."

Kori looked at me for a long moment, trying to see if I was being serious. I kept my face as open and innocent as I could. Kori then looked at Atticus, who nodded sagely and took another sip of his tea. Kori then looked at Paulina, who spoiled it by snorting a laugh into her sandwich.

"Ah, Paulina, we had her!" I cried in mock outrage. Atticus and Jamal began to laugh, and Kori turned around and glared at them.

"You very much did not," she countered.

"What would have been one of the inconvenient gifts?" Atticus asked, looking interested.

"Fingernails that grow faster than usual but aren't hard enough to actually scratch anything. Just… long fingernails you have to trim every morning."

Atticus nodded appreciatively, and Paulina snorted again and looked slightly embarrassed.

"That's a horrible one," Kori said. "A much better one would be something like growing feathers all over your body but not wings."

"No, that doesn't work," Jamal said. "That's just inconvenient. It would be better if they got wings but only tiny ones that can just barely lift you an inch off the ground."

"Yeah," Paulina said as she swallowed a bite of her sandwich. "Yeah, that's better."

"I am going back to work now," Kori said, and she left the room.

About ten seconds passed in silence.

"What about a mole that shoots fire when you sneeze?" I asked.

In addition to eating lunch, the afternoon break was also the time that we all filled up our Instruments. I've been a little coy about some of the details of Working up until now, partly because I didn't want to exposition-dump all over you, but I'll take a minute just to give you the basics, and a few quick examples of what we did to refresh ourselves. Skip it if you don't care.

Remember, all Working is tied to belief. You can't do anything if you don't believe in it. That being said, you need energy to power those beliefs. Easiest place you can get it is from your body. But that only takes you so far, unfortunately. So, Workers have figured out how to store extra energy in our

Instruments and funnel energy more efficiently through various channels.

None of this matters if you don't believe in what you're using, which means that every Instrument is unique, like my watch, band, and ring. I made them all myself, and I made them during what we call an Order Ceremony. It's not all that different from any garden variety religious ceremony, honestly, because all religious ceremonies are, at their heart, Order Ceremonies, or at least the Blissful equivalent.

If you need quick and dirty energy, you use chaos. Out in the world, especially in a big city, there's a lot of chaos around that we can use. Think of it like fast food, though. It's quick and cheap calories. And if you're running around and need to top up, well, grab a quick burger and fries. They're tasty and they'll keep you going.

Order, though, is like a steak dinner with those little fingerling potatoes. And a rare, expensive Pinot. And tiramisu for dessert.

Order is what you want if you can take the time to have it.

At Marlowe's place, there's a wine cave. (Like I said—mansion). Anyway, he took the modest basement his father left him and converted it into an underground wine cave and storage area. It's complete with stone walls and floors and those incandescent light bulbs in fancy little wall sconces that glow the perfect shade of amber. And in the center under a cleverly removable patch of rock, is an Order Circle.

You don't need an official Circle for a ceremony, but it helps. And the repetitive use of it helps *a lot*. There are locations in the world that are natural circles, places of wonder that have been built up over hundreds if not thousands of years. There's a fairy ring I found in the middle of Big Basin once, surrounded by redwoods, and I've heard there are spots at the bottom of the Grand Canyon and in Yosemite and

Yellowstone and the Blue Ridge Mountains. It doesn't have to be natural—it can be Blissful-made but with great significance, like the altar inside Notre Dame, or the courtyard around the Ka'ba in Mecca. Being there and just *existing* naturally starts to refill you. And, in the case of Workers, it refills our Instruments, which store energy.

Marlowe's Order Circle is about as traditional as you get, which is exactly what you would expect from him. He personally uses all Academy-approved Instruments: a pure gold ring, a leather belt with an etched silver buckle, and a bronze pocket watch on a long chain made of hand-forged links. Oh, and his glasses are one of the three Academy-approved conduits—the other two are wands made of traditional woods (oak, ash, elder, willow, cedar, hazel, and hawthorn), or one of the primary gemstones (ruby, sapphire, emerald, topaz, diamond) set in a metal casing. So, really, it's not much of a surprise that his Circle is also uber-traditional.

The classic Circle (aka what Marlowe has) uses all prime numbers from two to eleven. It starts with a line down the center, lined up from north to south (the true poles, not magnetic). That's two. Then around that is an equilateral triangle that represents the three phases of the mind— conscious, unconscious, and subconscious. Then there's a five-pointed star (a pentagram) to balance the five elemental forces (earth, water, air, fire, and aether/void depending on who you ask). Around that is a heptagon to represent the seven planes of being, and finally there's a circle around the whole thing with eleven smaller circles spaced equidistant around it, each containing again all of the things I just listed.

As a Blissful, you wouldn't be able to use a Circle to do a Working or to recharge any kind of Instrument. You would, however, if you sat in the middle of one, feel an otherworldly sense of calm and well-being. When properly imbued, an

Order Circle is the epitome of balance and harmony. A Worker at the center of a circle like that is protected and about as safe as they will ever be, especially if it's made with materials the Worker believes have power.

You might be wondering why there aren't circles like that all over the place. Lots of Workers do have them, actually. I mentioned it way back several chapters ago, but I've got one under my bed, and over the course of a night it fills my Instruments and I imbue it back with energy that then keeps my apartment *mine* and makes it hard for anyone I don't want to enter without a lot of hassle. Thing is, Circles are hard to maintain unless you keep them protected, so they aren't usually in public places. Marlowe's is about as industrial-strength as you get. It's engraved in the floor and lined in gold, silver, and bronze, and studded with the five primary gems (reminder: ruby, sapphire, emerald, diamond, and golden topaz) at each of the junction points.

Oh, and get this—the shelves of the wine cellar are made of the seven traditional woods (reminder: oak, ash, elder, willow, cedar, hazel, and hawthorn). And the *wine* is all fancy, which is a great example of belief and rarity making something mean more—so even the wine on the shelves, which people believe to be valuable, adds to the power of the Circle.

Now, if you were to make a Circle in the dirt outside with nothing but lines… you can see the difference. It would *mean* a lot less—though if you were in a natural location where order and beauty have accumulated, it might still work. But, every crack and every shift would make the Circle less efficient.

Anyway—there's your exposition, and, while it certainly isn't an Academy degree, I think it's enough for you to appreciate just how awesome Marlowe's circle is and why using it for an Order Ceremony is so efficient.

Oh! And an Order Ceremony—it's a fancy term for sitting and meditating in the center of the circle. This is another great example of whatever feels the most meditative to you, that's what you should be doing. It's the Worker's belief in the meditation that is most useful. I'm sure that Marlowe does the Academy-approved breathing cycle, which is a series of breath patterns that would be pretty familiar to anyone who's done any kind of guided meditation (yoga, Buddhist temple, Catholic monastery, you name it). There's a physiological response to all of that that's supposed to be very helpful.

For me, I just lie down, stare at the ceiling, and take a little nap. I've never been able to do the breathing thing. And the nap works way better.

It took us all about fifteen minutes to completely refresh our Instruments using Marlowe's Circle—even mine, which were still nearly empty after my long, *long* day.

I'm fairly certain Jamal's version of meditation is a bodyweight workout routine since I saw him finishing one up when I came down to take my turn. When I left, it was Paulina's turn next, and I saw her start doing a stretchy yoga-type activity as I walked up the stairs. Not sure what Kori and Atticus did—it's not usually something you talk about with other Workers unless you're pretty close.

That wasn't all the prep we did, though. Because out in the world, if you need to use a conduit for something you haven't prepared, you might need to use a little chaos. And for that, you need to break something, or degrade something, and out of that breaking you get a little burst of energy that you can use like a spark to start a fire.

So Marlowe has on the way up out of the wine cave a bowl of what we call Break Sticks. They're all made of one of the seven classical woods, and they're just refined sticks. They act a lot like my lighter—by breaking them, you release just enough of a spark to perform a less structured Working. In my case, something that I don't have imbued in a tattoo, for example. For Kori, maybe some wand pattern she hasn't come up with yet.

Anyway—after I filled my Instruments and stashed a couple dozen Sticks, I went back to details with Atticus. And it wasn't long after that when I was on my way to get more coffee that I met the final member of the Palace Job crew, the by-then notorious Jensen Hobb.

He's the closest thing I think I've ever seen in real life to that kind of charming scoundrel/rogue stock character you see portrayed in movies all the time. He's tall—not as tall as Jamal, but taller than me and the others—with a glorious head of dark wavy hair and several days' worth of stubble along his perfectly shaped jawline. His skin is nicely tanned, and if I had to guess I'd say he's in his early 40s. He has a Scottish accent, and that afternoon he was drinking tea when I walked into the kitchen and found him chatting up Paulina. Apparently not for the first time.

"You know it'd be a great time. I've seen your collection; you're telling me you'd turn down tickets to Carmen?"

"I'd have a great time with the tickets, just not the company," Paulina said, with a small, tight smile. She was making herself a second half-sandwich, this one quite heavy on the pickles.

Hobb sighed and seemed ready to try a different tactic, but Atticus, who had preceded me into the room, said loudly, "Hi, Hobb! Have you been well?"

Hobb turned, and that was when I got my first full look at him. As I said, he's about as roguishly handsome as a man can be, and he has dark hazel eyes that slid right over Atticus and immediately locked onto me.

"Well well well, what do we 'av 'ere?" he asked, standing up and redirecting Atticus to the kitchen island. Atticus didn't seem much bothered by this and set about making himself a plate. He seemed particularly keen on a large Tupperware full of sausages, onions, and sauerkraut that looked like leftovers.

Jenson Hobb stepped smoothly in front of me so that the only way to the coffee and food was through him. Given that I knew nothing about him at that moment aside from the fact Paulina didn't seem to care for him and there had been some serious debate about whether or not he was trustworthy enough to be involved in the evening's events, I felt it most prudent to stop instead of trying to run him over.

He held out a hand, and I shook it.

"Paulina, love, would you mind introducing us?" he called over his shoulder.

Paulina, who had made her sandwich and was on the way to one of the living room sofas with a stack of papers, said, "James, Hobb, Hobb, James," as she passed. Hobb glanced at her, his eyes lingering on her figure in her form-fitting jeans, before he pulled his focus back to me.

"So, you're the one," Hobb said. I had a moment of panic wherein I thought wildly that somehow he knew I was immortal—that somehow someone had told him about what had happened. Hobb still had hold of the hand I'd shaken with; I balled my free hand into a fist without even thinking, summoning power into my tattoo.

Hobb glanced down, saw my fist, and then clocked my ring, my watch, my band, and even traced the black ink of the tattoos that were peeking out from the shirt I was wearing. He looked back up into my face.

"None of that needed, friend." He reached up to the collar of his own shirt and pulled it down to reveal the dark upper lines of a tattoo of his own. I felt a moment of surprise. I had never met anyone else who used tattoos as a conduit.

"I know that game," he said calmly. "No need to play it here."

I nodded slowly, and after I did he winked at me and then released my hand carefully and deliberately. He stood there still and staring, clearly waiting for me to release the energy in my balled fist before he said or did anything else.

"James."

I broke my gaze away from Hobb and looked over at Paulina, who was sitting on the couch but leaning back toward the two of us, looking concerned. "It's fine. He's repugnant, but he's fine."

I looked back at Hobb and let out a slow breath. I deliberately uncurled my fist, turning my palm to face innocently forward. Hobb followed suit, and the sense of danger that had suddenly built up around him dissipated as if it had never been. He slapped my shoulder jovially and said, "You hear that? She thinks I'm fine. I'm gonna get that embroidered somewhere. Paulina Grace thinks yours truly is F-I-N-E fine. Mmhmm."

He ran his hands over his wavy hair and then scratched the stubble on his chin, examining me once more. "Yeah, you're him," he said again. "The one we're gonna be gettin' inna that vault ta grab the page, right?"

I felt some of the tension drain out of me. That him. He didn't know about the Immortality thing. He just meant me in the context of the job.

"Yeah. Yeah, I'm him."

"Great. I like your jacket."

"Thanks," I said. "Thrift store. Real leather."

"I can tell," he said, reaching out and grabbing the collar to look at the brand. I immediately tensed again, but he did nothing more than look at the tag and then release me. "You lucky chav, this is fuckin' genuine. Not mass-manufactured crap. It's a 'one of'. 6 of 27."

He sized me up again, with a deeper consideration, then said abruptly, "Any chance I could nick it off you for a few quid?"

I glanced at Paulina, who rolled her eyes and shook her head.

"Don't think so," I said. "Pretty attached to it."

He shrugged. "Ah, well, I 'ad to ask."

He clapped a hand against my shoulder again and then started walking away, toward the entryway to the house. "I like your style. We're gonna have a lovely time tonight."

I looked at Paulina again. She just looked back at me—pointedly—and then returned to her sandwich and papers.

The rest of the crew came in and out of the house more and more frantically as day slowly faded to night. Kori seemed to run continuously back and forth to the garden and its 'port gate. Jamal left after recharging his Instruments to go to the official enforcer briefing for that evening; he was part of the detail requested by the company holding the Worker auction, the Artifacts and Antiques Trading Company.

And Paulina, it turned out, was our official liaison.

"I was invited as an honoree months back when they were putting it all together," she explained to me as she walked me through the finer details of how I would be able to find and identify the Works page in a room full of old, crumbly pages. "They know about my work with historical narratives and artifacts and they invited me to consult on the authenticity of several pieces."

"So you were the one that ID'd the Gallimand," I guessed.

"Gold star," she said with a pleased smile. "Soon as I saw it, I knew what it was. It's the first Gallimand artifact we've been able to track down."

"You don't know where any of the other ones are?"

She shook her head as she sifted through sheets of paper with row after row of antique books and other book-adjacent items on them. "No. But not for lack of trying. We have leads on about a dozen, but all still in progress. That's why this one is so important. We're behind in the race. Worse, we don't even know what race we're running. We've been forced to resort to—"

She cut off. She then very deliberately dropped the sheets she had been ruffling through and pointed a finger at me. "You're good. You got me talking."

I smiled my best smile. "No idea what you mean."

I saw her eyes light up, but then she shook her head and turned back to the table. "Pay attention. Show me the difference between these pages."

I sighed and got back to it. In spite of myself, I was starting to feel fairly nervous. Going over and over the details was helping, though, so I kept at it.

Around five, Atticus returned from his latest errand with three suits and two dresses, along with matching shoes and accessories. It was a fancy affair—the suits were tuxedos, and I for one was glad Marlowe hadn't even asked me to get my own, because I would have had no idea what I was doing.

"Please try this on at your earliest convenience," Atticus said to me when he found us in the library, passing me a black suit bag with a glossy metal hook sticking out the top. "I had to guess your size, but it should be close. Reasonably."

"You could have asked me," I said.

"Really?" he asked. "What's your suit size? And please know that 'medium' is someone who contacts the dead or an inferior way to cook a steak, not something a grown man should ever say about his clothing."

I paused.

"I withdraw the objection," I said.

He smiled at me. "Cufflinks are in the inner bag and shoes are in the bottom pocket. The bowtie is real and not a clip-on. Please do *not* attempt it—I will do it for you."

He walked away before I could say anything else, and I didn't know whether to be grateful he'd assumed—correctly—that I had no idea how to handle a bowtie or to be miffed he hadn't at least had the courtesy to check with me.

I tried it all on, except for the aforementioned bowtie, and it fit perfectly. I revised my opinion of Atticus. He was the youngest of the group—he looked like he was barely out of college—but he clearly had a good head on his shoulders.

When I returned to the library in my tux, I walked in on quite a scene already in progress.

"I'm not doing it, Marlowe. This is a hard line."

"You're doing it, Kori," Paulina said, much more forcefully than I had heard her speak up until that point. "It's a dress, not scuba gear."

"I'd rather wear scuba gear!" Kori proclaimed. She was standing on the right side of the room, opposite Paulina, who looked absolutely stunning. Paulina's dress, like my tux, fit perfectly. It was a yellow-ochre color that complemented her honey-tan skin beautifully, and it had a modest slit up one side showing a tightly muscled leg accentuated by a pair of strappy brown heels. She wore shiny hoop earrings, too, and an amber chain high on her neck. One of the earrings was thicker than the other, and I realized it was probably one of her Instruments and that I hadn't seen it before since it had been hidden by her hair.

Kori was still in her windbreaker, jeans, dirty sneakers, and the loose green shirt from the night before. She had backed as far away from Paulina and the dress bag she was holding as possible without running Bugs-Bunny-style through the library wall. Atticus was standing close to the door and following the proceedings with wide eyes. Marlowe was across the room leaning on his usual desk and watching the scene with mingled amusement and exasperation.

"Ms. Clark," Marlowe said, "how were you anticipating you would gain access to the auction without meeting the formal dress code?"

"You don't need me on the *floor*," Kori protested hotly. Her blue-and-yellow eyes were blazing furiously, and she was glaring around at everyone like a cornered animal. "I'm supposed to be in the back, getting the book, that's the whole plan!"

"The only way in is through the front door," Paulina said patiently but firmly, as if she were explaining something important to a fussy toddler. "Hobb'll come around the back but we're the ones who have to let him in. And there's a dress code. As in *dress* code."

"It's San Francisco. They'd let me in in Birkenstocks and cargo shorts!"

"God, you're infuriating! I think I know a bit more about this event than you do considering *I work with the people throwing it!*"

I realized I was standing conspicuously in the doorway and stepped forward and to the side. Thing is, I was so focused on the fight that I didn't look where I was going, and I accidentally walked into a desk and loudly tumbled a stack of books onto an uncarpeted section of floor.

Kori whirled around, eyes wide, and then she saw what I was wearing. Her gaze flew over the tux, my combed hair, my freshly shaven face, and she sneered at me as if I'd been in on some grand conspiracy with Atticus and the rest of them the whole time.

"You, too?" she asked. "You look ridiculous."

"Ignore her, you look handsome," Paulina said. I tried my manly best not to be too obviously pleased by a gorgeous woman telling me this.

"He looks like a penguin wearing a toupee," Kori said.

"Now that's just mean," Atticus said. "His hair looks very natural."

"Kori, just put the dress on," Paulina said, her tone half older sister and half stressed out mother on her last fuck to give, "or I swear to God, you're sitting this one out. It's my event, you're coming as *my guest*, and it's my call. You're not putting us all at risk because you have an irrational fear of anything that makes you look the slightest bit girly. As soon as it's over you can go roll around in a pigsty to even it all out."

"Fuck you!" Kori hissed, her thick hair almost standing on end like a cat presented with a tub of water. "I'm going—the whole reason we'll be able to grab the page is because of me and Hobb. I'm critical to the plan!"

"Hobb who looks *quite* good in a tuxedo," Atticus noted.

"And we are very grateful, Ms. Clark," Marlowe said, still seemingly hovering on the border of amusement and exasperation. "But as far as I understand it, this is the only way for you to get into the auction hall itself. Hobb and his men will be waiting, but their role is very specifically to secure us an escape route once we make it out of the room. Your route in is supposed to be through the front door."

"Make Atticus wear it and give me a suit then!" she snapped.

"I'd happily wear that dress, it's gorgeous," Atticus said. "But it's not that kind of party, it doesn't fit me, and the point is *not* to draw attention."

"Only guests are invited into the auction hall. That's intelligence that you shared with us directly, Ms. Clark. If you wish to be in the room with us—and I'd very much like you to be—then you need to look the part."

A titanic struggle was going on behind Kori's eyes.

I have no idea what the dress represented to her, and why wearing it was such a massive concession, but it clearly was. And yet she also very clearly wanted to be in the room when the time came to grab the book.

Finally, she strode forward, grabbed the dress bag forcefully from Paulina—so forcefully I was almost worried she'd rip the thing in two—and then stalked toward the door. I barely got out of the way before she ran me over, which, given the thunderous look on her face, she was clearly prepared and willing to do.

"I'm not shaving my legs!" she shouted as she left.

"*Goddammit*," Paulina snarled, racing after her. "YOU'RE SHAVING YOUR FUCKING LEGS!"

I stared open-mouthed after them until Atticus came up to me, took my bowtie, and tied it in several quick, sharp movements. "I'll never understand how you straights are attracted to that nonsense," he said archly before following them both out of the room at a safe distance.

I, without any constructive comment to make to anyone about anything, remained silent.

The rest of the day mainly consisted of Marlowe quizzing me over and over again on the details of the plan. As the sun began to set, my nerves stretched tighter and tighter until they felt like bridge cables holding up several hundred tons of weight. And, before I knew it, we were gathered in the kitchen again.

Jamal was there, despite having said earlier that he wouldn't be. He'd left his enforcer badge upstairs. He got back in time for the final meeting and decided to stay before reporting to the Palace separately as part of the plan. He seemed flustered about it, which tracks with what I know about him. He doesn't like improvising his way through things, and I'm sure he was mad at himself for leaving something as important as his badge behind.

Hobb was present in a gray coverall open at the top to reveal a blue chambray shirt, both of which had several believable stains on them that lent a credible air of authenticity. He was also still somehow the handsomest one in the room.

Atticus wore his tux like he'd been born in it. Not only did it fit him well, he was thin enough that it draped his shoulders and hips perfectly, and with his tortoiseshell glasses and perfectly coifed hair he looked like he'd walked straight out of a classic Calvin Klein ad.

Paulina and Kori had apparently reached a compromise, because Kori was wearing what looked like a fancy black jumpsuit with matching black low-heeled boots, along with a chic white patterned jacket that had 80s-esque shoulder pads in it. Her hair had also been partially pulled back on the sides, she'd put on makeup (or maybe Paulina had done it for her) and the overall effect was that she looked almost like a different person. She looked *good*. Good enough that even she looked a little pleased with it all, despite her best efforts not to. The whole thing looked very much like something Paulina would wear to an 80s party, and I suspected her closet was the outfit's point of origin, with some minor modifications to the length, hips, and bust to accommodate the differences in their respective sizes. It all looked about as fancy as the dress, though, and, strangely enough, equally feminine given the cut and the tightness of the pants.

Some really *great* tightness. In that… whole area.

Paulina was wearing the dress from before, which remained stunning, and Marlowe, his gold-rimmed glasses freshly polished, was wearing his tuxedo with a scarf layered over the top and a pair of white gloves. Where Atticus looked like he'd stepped out of Mad Men, Marlowe looked like he'd stepped out of Downton Abbey. He was freshly shaved as well, and, for once, his thick gray hair was flattened down in the back so that it appeared reasonably tame.

He was also carrying what appeared to be an ornamental walking stick, something I hadn't seen him do in a while. Thing is, it isn't just a walking stick—it's a type of Worker battery. The amber cap stores energy that he can call on and unleash through the cane itself, or use to replenish more regular Instruments. It was the same one he'd used to cast the mania Working on me, I realized, remembering back to that night.

I frowned. Something about that seemed to tap something in the back of my mind, but I couldn't pull it forward. It was like a popcorn shard in the molars of my mind.

"Perhaps you could share with us all a recap of the plan, Cicero?" Marlowe asked.

I took a breath, stood up, adjusted the lines of my tuxedo—Atticus knew what he was doing, I felt very James Bond—and cleared my throat.

"We show up to the Palace of Fine Arts using mundane means. We enter through the front; Hobb and his team go around the back an hour after we arrive. Paulina and Kori make it through to their table; Atticus and I make it through to ours. Marlowe arrives separately so that we don't look like we're all together, but Atticus and I use his guest tickets. Atticus works with him, and I'll be coming as his plus one using the alias Hobb put together so that we don't set off any alarm bells at the entrance. Atticus and I meet Marlowe inside the Worker auction when the Workers start getting ushered in, Kori pretends to be sick, and Paulina and Kori head out the other way past the bathrooms to locate the book. They send the first signal to Atticus, who meets them and helps Paulina confirm the authenticity of the page before the auction. Kori lets Hobb in. Paulina and Atticus head back, they send the second signal and I go to Jamal, who gets me through to Hobb, who gets me up the back way to where they're storing the book after it's been auctioned. I meet Kori there, I take the page, Kori replaces it with the copy we made, and then we get back to Hobb and we're out of there."

I took a deep breath, and then let it out in a rush. "And a partridge in a pear tree."

Atticus chuckled and nodded at me.

Marlowe said, "Very good. Anything else?"

"Uh…"

I thought I had covered everything.

"Go team go?"

Paulina smiled. Marlowe nodded and said, "Thank you, Cicero."

I grimaced and backed up to the edge of the circle.

Marlowe looked around at all of us one by one, and a sense of solemnity suffused the room. "What we're doing tonight is important. It will require the best of each of you. I believe you will do what needs to be done, or else I would not be advocating that we move forward. Be smart. Stick to the plan. And by tonight we'll have more answers."

There was a round of nods, but no one moved.

"Well, what are we waiting for?" I asked. "Let's go take a page out of Gallimand's book."

They all looked at me.

I stood my ground.

"I get it, things are tense, but that was a better pun than you're giving me credit for."

Jamal shook his head; Atticus, who still seemed the most receptive to my jokes, gave me a little pity smirk; Kori downright scowled.

"Let's go," Paulina said, with her leader voice.

And we went.

PART EIGHTEEN

TAKING A PAGE OUT OF GALLIMAND'S BOOK

(I'M STANDING BY THAT PUN)

The Palace of Fine Arts looked gorgeous that evening, its soaring pink-and-tan stone columns and white dome top lit from below with golden light. We arrived after sundown, somewhere around eight, just as all the lights were turned on to give the full effect. The bidding was set to start at nine, though there was a silent auction that had been going on since six, when the doors had first opened.

Marlowe led the way, with me, Atticus, Paulina, and Kori several people behind him in line. Both Paulina and Kori drew attention. Paulina embraced it—she smiled and waved openly at several men she seemed to know. Kori, on the other hand, gave off a strong 'talk to me and I'll rip your dick off' vibe that, shockingly, did not encourage conversation.

Atticus and I drew a few looks, too. As long as they're clean and they fit, tuxedos look good on most men—probably why they've survived who knows how many years now. I did feel uncomfortable, though. It was hot in that thing, the shoes were new and rubbing weird areas of my feet, and I'm usually stubbly, so the fresh shave was starting to smart in the cool night air.

Getting into the gala portion of the auction was the easy part. The tickets Marlowe and Paulina had procured got us through security without any trouble. There was nothing so prosaic as a metal detector at the front of the building, given that everyone was wearing jewelry and watches and who knew what else, and if we had a ticket it seemed a given that we weren't there to blow the place up. There was, however, a bag check for the women and a brief wand-over for the men, but we made it through both without any trouble.

The only real skullduggery was my alias, Ben Johnson.

There were Workers embedded with the security crew, which was to be expected, and they were checking everyone who showed up as a Worker on their scans. To avoid any scrutiny from anyone who wasn't already there looking for us, though, it had been decided that my ticket would go to Ben Johnson, which was the identity Hobb had arranged for me on short notice. Since the ticket was a "guest" ticket of Marlowe's, it didn't matter who I was to use it, as long as I wasn't someone who would set off a security flag.

So, Cicero James stayed behind that night, and Ben Johnson, fake ID and everything, came in his place and made it through without any challenges.

The Palace of Fine Arts is a tall, domed, Romanesque building with ceiling frescos and a small man-made lagoon surrounding the front half of it. It's been in movies so you might have seen it before. If you haven't, picture something out of Gladiator but with a Californian pink-tan color scheme and you're basically there.

Inside the expo center next to it, however, is much more modern architecture. The part that we were in was a series of exposed industrial-style rooms with ceilings several dozen feet high. That night tables lined either side of each hallway, particularly the long hallway from the entrance to the main hall, and those tables were crowded with all manner of auction items, not just art and antiques. Wine packages, baseball tickets, sponsored 3-or-4 night stays at someone's private vacation home, etc.. As we walked further in, they became mostly art and antique pieces, though, and I knew that they were fancy because they had price tags that would have made cartoon-me's eyes pop out and turn into dollar signs. Several of the paintings that were being auctioned were actually at the tables, as well as a few vases and urns. Larger items like sculptures were absent but pictured in large blow-up posters.

Once we were inside, I grabbed a mocktail (called a "Foam-a Lisa" and primarily made of grapefruit, judging by the taste) and some crab cakes. I ate hurriedly—I'd forgotten to make another sandwich before leaving and I didn't want to wait until the auction dinner.

Atticus left me and went to join Marlowe, and they slowly made their way toward the larger room at the end of the hallway. I began to follow in that direction. I stopped at a few auction items and nervously put my fake name down in spaces that were already out-bid so that I wouldn't get stuck with anything. Just writing down my name felt strange, considering that it wasn't *my* name. I would be lying if I said I wasn't tempted to outbid everyone, knowing that "Ben Johnson" didn't exist and that there would therefore be no winning bid. It would just go to the next highest bidder. I thought it would be hilarious for someone to have to keep calling Ben Johnson for every item and never get him.

I realized I was smiling to myself at the idea and had turned to look at a woman standing nearby with her husband. She noticed me smiling and looked alarmed before she grabbed her husband's arm and turned away.

Which, as you can imagine, did wonders for my self-esteem.

It was nerves. I was starting to get shaky, and my brain was throwing out thoughts that would help keep me from thinking about how ridiculously high the stakes were. But, try as I might not to think about it all, I was starting to realize I might be in over my head.

I tried to control my breathing. I glanced around once more, this time checking for Paulina and Kori. Paulina was easy to find—she had been surrounded by a group of young men and a few women, many of whom she seemed to know, and was talking with them and their dates as they all made their way down the hall and toward the main room.

Kori wasn't with her, though.

I paused. We needed Kori in the room. Was she already in there?

I turned while pretending to admire the side of a Grecian urn—at least, I hope it was Grecian, because ever since someone made me read 'Ode to a Grecian Urn' I've wanted to say I'd actually seen a Grecian urn—and saw her several dozen paces back down the hall, cornered by two young men who seemed to be without dates.

I revised my assessment as I observed the situation. They hadn't literally cornered her—someone like Paulina would have managed to extricate herself from the situation rather easily—but you could tell by the look on Kori's face that in her mind, at least, she had most *certainly* been cornered, and she was about to start kicking and scratching. She was gripping the small clutch bag Paulina had lent her far too tightly and holding closed the fancy white coat she had refused to check, even though the expo hall was much warmer than outside.

"She's just gonna bite your head off for helping," I muttered to myself.

I started to turn away, and then she looked around wildly and happened to catch my eye.

Something electric shot through me, and before I knew what I was doing I was walking over to her. She saw me coming and her eyes went even wider, and then she turned back to the two men who were talking to her and made a few more polite responses.

"So that's when I diversified into crypto," I heard one of them say.

"Hey there," I said, inserting myself and going to stand next to Kori. I didn't put my arm around her or initiate any kind of familiar contact, as I wasn't entirely certain she wouldn't just bite the offending limb off and eat it. "Lost you there for a second—who are your friends?"

I looked at the two men and realized immediately that they weren't hitting on her. They were both mid-twenties soft-bodied young men who had clearly scored a ticket to an event way above their price range and latched onto the first person they'd found who appeared to be without a group. It was just a bonus that she happened to be attractive. I quickly revised again my opinion of the situation and realized just how little experience Kori must have with social events.

"Brian and Tate," one of the men said. He was tall and wide, with glasses. He held out his hand and smiled widely—when he smiled his eyes became very thin. He had a mop of curly coppery hair that looked like it had been cut at home. "We're here with (some tech company, I forget). I'm on the Product side and Tate is in Sales. It's a platform that allows art dealers and artists to connect with…"

Ahhhh—that made even more sense. They were prospecting. Probably had a quota for business cards collected or meetings set with event attendees. This would be easy to fix.

"Great to meet you both," I said smoothly, reaching out and shaking their hands. I slipped my other hand into my pocket and twirled it, using a small amount of energy. I then pulled the hand out and said, "We have to run, but I've heard of (some tech company). Shoot me an email."

I handed over two brand new business cards that I had never seen before but that had Ben Johnson's name on them.

They were actually pretty cool, I gotta say—they had that laminated kind of material on one side, and they were matte black with gold lettering on the other. Probably because I was still thinking about the Works book. Definitely made me look way more important than I actually am.

"Oh—great! Ok, thanks, uh—Ben. Right. We'll reach out soon!"

"Great." I held my hand out in the direction around them both. Kori jumped at the opportunity to extricate herself, and soon we were both free and walking away down the long corridor.

"That was humiliating," she muttered. "They cornered me."

"They did not corner you," I said calmly. "You could have left anytime you wanted."

"They were looking at me like a piece of meat, it was disgusting."

"They were prospecting," I said, rolling my eyes. "It's a tech thing—they were trying to set up a meeting with you. They probably just saw you on your own and thought you were important because you're here with all the glitz and glamor. People get to talk to other people at social events without being considered evil. Talking to people is the whole point of why everyone else is here—we're the weird ones, not them."

I walked a few more paces before realizing she had stopped following me. I turned back, confused. She had a locked-down expression on her face. I walked a couple of steps back, more cautiously. "What?" I asked.

"I don't like attention," she said.

I should have just let it go there. But my nerves were wound so tightly that they needed something to latch onto in order to stretch back out again. And so they latched onto her, like Venom onto poor, unsuspecting Spiderman.

Looking back, I know that there's Worker backstory here. I still don't know what happened to Kori to make her a Worker. Workers don't usually share that stuff, for the obvious reason that it was so traumatic it fucked us up as kids and made us break with reality. In the moment, though, I was beyond stressed and had no room for any of what I thought of as someone else's crap. I wish I'd handled it with… I dunno, finesse. She *is* a bit of a pain in the ass, and it's really not healthy. But it's all… well, people cope how they gotta cope.

I told you I'd only share the truth, though. And here's what I actually said in the moment.

"Well, that's obviously bullshit," I said. "Everyone likes attention from the right people. I don't know, maybe next time you'll get cornered by a couple of ladies and it'll be great."

I wanted to keep going but I managed to stop myself. I would like a small amount of credit for trying to cut it off at that point.

She closed the distance between us and jabbed me in the chest with a strong finger.

"Ow," I said, more annoyed than pained.

"I don't want to be cornered by women either, you ass."

"All right, fine—I *really* don't care."

She took another step closer, staring flaming daggers straight into my eyes. I caught a whiff of her perfume and tried to ignore it.

"I get to decide who looks at me."

"Uh—no, you don't. You don't get to control other people."

Her eyes flashed. "I'm in control of everything that happens to me."

I flipped. Because I knew that that was absolutely not true. Because it's never been true in my life, as much as I've wanted it to be. As much as I've tried to believe it. I'd constructed the perfect inoffensive, discreet persona, and still shit had found me. I, who had intentionally set out to live a small and simple life, was the one who'd been thrust into the middle of all this Gallimand nonsense with no choice.

I sneered at her. "Grow up and join us in the real world. People look at people. Oh, boo hoo, I'm attractive when I make an effort and it's such a cross to bear. A couple of tech guys saw me and came over to say hi. I thought they were hitting on me—which, by the way, turns out they *weren't*, so that's embarrassing—and life is *so horrible*. Go ahead and wait here, I'll fetch you some pearls to clutch and a dainty silk handkerchief to sob into."

I turned and left, half expecting her to stop me. When she didn't, I just walked away, my ears ringing. I realized that I was irrationally angry, and I even saw myself from the outside for a brief, surreal moment. I did not regret at all the sentiment behind what I had said, but even then I had a brief moment of discomfort about how I'd said it. I pushed that emotion right back down, though, and bottled it up to come out at some inopportune future moment. I'm good at doing that. I could win an Olympic medal at doing that.

My psyche is littered with suppressed emotional IEDs that even Freud would prefer not to unearth.

I made my way straight down the hall without turning back to see if Kori was still with me. I honestly didn't give a shit in that moment.

"Cicero?"

It wasn't Kori's voice.

And they'd used my real name.

My heart thudded with shocking intensity, and my adrenals dumped raw anxiety straight into my bloodstream. So much so that when I turned around, before I could even register who had called me or any other details of the situation, I was getting ready to call down lightning from the heavens and start blasting expensive art into clouds of dust like Thanos on Snapping Day, without any concern for the consequences.

And then Erica Masters, my office crush, walked up to me.

It took my brain a full five seconds to reboot. Which for me is just… ridiculously long. That's like a staring-into-space-and-drooling level of out of it for me.

She was an absolute vision. She's pretty enough in the day-to-day office setting with minimal makeup, jeans, and a branded Protoline t-shirt. But that night she was fully made up and wearing a floor-length periwinkle dress that hugged her hips and had a tastefully revealing V-shaped neckline. I had to try very very hard not to stare directly at that neckline. I swear, the effort was fucking Herculean, and frankly I deserve a medal.

Her white-blonde hair was washed and styled up behind her head, revealing her long, thin neck and highlighting her sharp jaw. She wore sparkling earrings that were probably zirconia but certainly looked like diamonds, and her lips were accented with lipstick that highlighted them without turning them an unnatural color.

"Erica!" I exclaimed. I stepped forward, holding out my arms like an idiot, with no real idea why, my mind racing. She knew who I was—who I really was. Did it matter? I was already in the hall, that had been the main reason for the fake ID and the Ben Johnson persona. Did I care that she knew? *Should* I care? "Wow, what are you doing here?"

"Hi!" she said, and before I knew what was happening, she had stepped forward, opened her own arms, and was hugging me.

I hadn't expected that. I'd just had my arms open in a go-to gesture of surprise. But now I had a face full of Erica's soft blonde hair and I could feel her pressed against me, and my mind was legitimately blown. She smelled great—feminine and flowery. Her dress was soft as silk.

The hug lasted for a second longer than it needed to, and I was the one to pull back. Out of sheer nerves, if I'm being honest. I was having trouble breathing correctly, which was disturbing since, I don't know about you, but I've been breathing since birth and have long since passed the 10,000-hour mark supposedly required for mastery.

"Wow," I said again, and heard myself say it, and immediately hated that I'd repeated it, and then tried to find something else to say, and ended up just short-circuiting my brain. "I—you—hah! You, you, you—did not expect to see you here!"

She was looking me straight in the eye and smiling and nodding along with my babble.

"Hah—yeah—here I am! Didn't expect to see you, either. I figured I'd make an appearance before I go to this club opening tonight, Roc got me on the list. Did you hear about it? I don't know, maybe it'll be fun. Anyway, what are you doing here?"

"Uh, well, I thought I'd come down here and buy an urn for the office," I said. "We're decidedly urn-less and I know how Arick hates it when we earn less."

As soon as it came out of my mouth, I was simultaneously proud and horrified. I don't know how much of that mix of emotions showed on my face, but Erica's eyes momentarily widened and then her face broke into another beautiful white-teeth-and-adorable-dimples smile.

"That was impressively bad. Please tell me you didn't spend time thinking that up."

"Oh, not long, just most of last night," I said. "I've got another half dozen, wanna hear?"

"Absolutely not," she said, laughing and shaking her head.

"Damn, I'll have to find a captive audience somewhere else. Guess I'll just have to start making some bids on these urns in the meantime."

I was just talking. My mouth had free rein. The rest of me was disassociated and stuffed in the back of my mind and watching in a kind of awed fascination.

"Well, which one are you gonna start with?" she asked, a twinkle in her eye. "There's a big ugly gray one over there that you could stash in the office somewhere."

"You're so well-versed in the lingo," I said. "Big, ugly, gray—do you sell pottery?"

She laughed again, and I felt a swooping sensation in my stomach. That was until I noticed Kori over her shoulder staring at us both. She had a slightly stunned expression on her face, almost as if she were watching a dog walk on its hind legs.

She thinks I'm batting out of my league.

And damned if she wasn't right. But I wasn't about to let Erica know that.

Kori's expression quickly became a pointed glare when she realized I was looking at her.

Right. We were doing a thing.

"Antiques and Curios is one of my clients," Erica was saying, referencing the Blissful front company that the Worker company Artifacts and Antiques Trading uses. "They gave me a free ticket after we closed that deal the other day."

She glanced over at a display nearby, and as she did I nodded sharply to Kori and jabbed a thumb toward the door we were supposed to be making our way toward, silently telling her to go ahead. She blinked a few times and gaped at me, apparently shocked that I was giving her directions, and then she snapped her mouth shut, scowled, and stalked off toward the door, swaying slightly in the black just-over-her-ankles boots Paulina had convinced her to wear. The two tech bros from before paused from prospecting to watch her walk away.

Shit. Maybe they were hitting on her a little bit.

Did I have to apologize to Kori? Maybe. Which really pissed me off.

"Ah, that's right," I said to Erica, "I forgot you closed that deal. Congrats again. Flying solo tonight, then?"

"I came with a girlfriend, but she saw an ex and now they're getting a drink," she said, turning back to me and rolling her eyes in a way that spoke volumes. "The art world is pretty incestuous sometimes, it's kind of hard to go anywhere without running into a dozen people you know. And I don't drink, so I'm just here enjoying the fancy meal and looking at all the things I *definitely* cannot afford."

"Window shopping for things out of our price range, the real American pastime."

She laughed again and put a hand on my arm, very lightly and very properly, but there it was. I let my eyes slide past her again and saw Kori looking at me still from down the hall with a long-suffering expression. She motioned to a watch she didn't have and mouthed the words "Let's gooooo".

"You're right," Erica was saying. "Who needs baseball? The Giants suck this year anyway."

"Definitely not living up to their legacy," I said, then immediately, "Are you going to the live auction?" I motioned the direction Kori had gone and held out a hand to lightly touch her elbow.

She turned easily the way I had gestured and said, "Yes! I can't sit with you, though, I've got a ticket way in the back I think, with the other vendors they invited."

"Ah, sorry to hear that," I said, which was partly very true but also completely false because I wasn't going to be staying at the Blissful auction and would be heading into the Worker auction before any actual bidding began.

"It's fine," she said, smiling brightly, "good networking opportunity. I'm still pretty new in town, so it'll be nice to meet some more people along with prospecting. And there's a raffle, maybe I'll enter that and get lucky. Always been good at getting lucky."

"Have you?" I asked, just trying to keep the conversation going while scanning the crowd for Jamal, who was supposed to be nearby and checking in with Kori and me at the door. "What's the luckiest you've ever been?" I asked, just thinking of the first thing that came to mind to keep the conversation going.

"Probably when I fell out of that airplane without a parachute and bounced off the ground."

"Oh, cool, that sounds—" I fully processed what she was saying. I looked back at her and realized she was looking at me with a knowing little smile. "That didn't happen, did it?"

"It might have," she said. "Are you waiting for someone? It's fine if you have to go, it was good to see you—"

"Oh, no! No, I'm sorry. I just—"

I finally caught sight of Jamal over her shoulder.

"I just knew my old friend Jamal was here and I was trying to find him. Look, there he is."

I waved at Jamal, and Erica turned to look in the direction I was waving.

Jamal did his best to respond in character as professional private security, but the man will never be an actor. He didn't know who Erica was or why I was waving to acknowledge him, and improvising is *not* his strong suit.

"He looks a little mad," Erica said. "Honestly, he looks like he might arrest you."

"Private security for the event," I said, which was technically true—all the enforcers there that night were listed as private security. "He's putting on a show." I glanced back at Erica and rolled my eyes. "Big scary security guard, you know? Ready to throw out pretty girls in blue dresses that think they're gonna get lucky."

The phrasing of that sentence slipped out of my mouth whole and unedited before I could do anything about it, and only after it was out did I realize the double meaning.

Erica's expression changed so slightly that I couldn't track exactly what was different. It was as if she had suddenly decided to bucket me in a different mental category than before, though, and she paused a second longer than I would have expected before responding.

"Well, under the right circumstances, getting lucky and getting thrown around aren't mutually exclusive experiences," she replied, looking me straight in the eye.

Half a beat of shock on my part. Then, my mouth, still partially disconnected from my brain, responded on its own with:

"Well, someone ought to go find those circumstances. They're bound to be around here somewhere, right?"

Somehow I managed to maintain eye contact, and somehow I managed to smile very slightly. She looked down at my lips, and then back up at my eyes, then held my gaze for a very long, shockingly intimate, moment.

"You're fun," she said. "See you around, CJ."

And then, before I could fuck up what might just be the best round of flirting I have ever participated in since the first time I realized girls were kinda maybe not all that bad, she walked off in the direction of the auction hall.

I stood there stock-still for almost a full minute, watching her walk away and trying to figure out how I had just managed to escalate to sexy banter with Erica Masters.

A voice spoke in my ear, and I jumped.

"You are punching so far above your weight," Jamal said.

I cleared my throat and shook my head to clear it.

"You don't have to tell me," I responded.

"We're here to do a job, James."

"I know, I know! I just… I mean, look at her, man."

"I will smack you upside the head."

"Fine—fine! I'm going, I'm good, let's go."

We crossed to the door to the large room that would hold the Blissful auction, and Jamal began to lag behind me. Kori had already made her way in, it appeared, since she was no longer waiting at the *entrance* for me. I wasn't sure how much of my conversation with Erica she had seen. I felt a pang of something thinking about that but refused to examine it.

If you've ever been to a fancy dinner auction, or, hell, seen one in a movie, you'll know the general layout. Lots of round tables with large numbered paddles perched on fancy place settings; a podium at the front of the room for the auctioneer and other presenters to stand at; and a place for the goods to be displayed, off to the side where they're clearly visible in a special spotlight as they're presented.

The main difference between this auction and the handful of others I've attended by necessity through work was the fanciness. The white plates—three for each diner—were set in a small pyramid atop burnished gold chargers, and atop the plates were two bowls, I assumed for soup and salad. Each charger was surrounded by a battalion of cutlery——three forks, two spoons, a steak knife, and a butter knife.

The walls were draped in elegant swathes of gold, purple, and black fabric. The podium and stand were draped as well, and there were sporadic sprays of flowers on all sides. And whether the flowers carried real scent throughout the room or it was something fake that was being piped in, the air was slightly sweet and fresh-smelling.

There were already people milling about and sitting at various tables, older men and women primarily, but with a decent smattering of the younger San Francisco moneyed generation mixed in. Most of the latter looked like the tech people I work with every day. Everyone was dressed to the nines. All the men were wearing tuxedos, though there was some variety, with several younger men wearing patterned coats in red or blue or other bright colors instead of the traditional black. The women almost all had dresses like Paulina's, along with fashionable coats, but at least three or four had gone the Kori route and were wearing non-traditional attire like jumpsuits or pant suits that were nevertheless fancy enough to fit the dress code.

Jamal peeled off toward a small corridor that led off of the main room. That was our destination. Workers would be able to open/access the corridor and the door to the Worker auction beyond it, while the Blissful would only see a kitchen staff entrance/exit.

I stood off to the side of the door so as not to obstruct traffic and swept my eyes over the crowd. Kori was already seated, and Paulina was next to her, along with a few of the men who had been chatting to her since she'd arrived. She was here on business as well, since her ticket had come through work. I guessed that the men with her were colleagues or work acquaintances, and they seemed rather excited that she had been able to attend. Kori, as her plus one, was seated with her at the table and wasn't talking but also at least didn't seem to be attacking anyone. Kori would find herself coming down with an illness when it was time to switch rooms, and she and Paulina would get up and make their way in the opposite direction from the secret corridor and around back.

Atticus was waiting for me since our seats were together based on our guest tickets under Marlowe's name. I should explain a little bit—Atticus works with Marlowe, and my guess about him being a lawyer/accountant the first time I saw him in the library was decently close to reality. He practices medical law, and, in particular, protects Marlowe and other doctors from malpractice lawsuits and insurance fraud.

He's also an apprentice Stitcher, learning from Marlowe on the side.

Marlowe himself was nowhere to be seen, which was also part of the plan. There were people here he knew—too many—and so he couldn't leave once the auction had begun without being overly conspicuous. He was already in the Workers' room, or at least should be.

"Sit," Atticus said as I approached. I did. Unlike Paulina, Atticus didn't seem to know anyone at our table. That would make it fairly easy to leave and return in the timeframe needed.

Atticus must have caught onto the anxiety still flooding through me. "We have time," he said. "Don't worry so much, everything's going well."

The tension that had been momentarily dispelled by my completely unexpected conversation with Erica Masters had returned, creeping into my upper back and neck. I tried to loosen it by rolling my shoulders, but that didn't seem to help.

They brought us food that I remember tasting amazingly good but that I can't remember the details of at all. There was also champagne and red wine, but neither Atticus nor I had any of it.

Thirty minutes on the dot after dinner began, people dressed in muted black vests, shirts, and slacks began to appear from the side corridor and make their way around the tables, tapping select people on the shoulder and whispering something in their ears. If I hadn't been looking for them, I knew that I wouldn't have seen them. There was some kind of Working going on, and I had a suspicion it was their bands helping to make them insubstantial enough to fade into the background. They blended in perfectly with the wait staff who were also making the rounds at that same time and talking through dessert menus with the attendees.

I glanced over and saw that Jamal had taken up position guarding the corridor. He saw me glance his way and he nodded, very slightly.

The way out was secured.

One of the Worker waiters made it to our table. The eyes of everyone else seemed to slide right off of him; he came and stood by Atticus and me. "Good evening gentlemen," he said in a calm, assured manner. "Are you still interested in joining us for the Worker auction?"

We both confirmed that, yes, we were interested, and he stepped back and gestured for us to follow him. Atticus and I exchanged a glance, and then we stood and followed, making vague excuses to the few other guests at the table who saw us get up to leave. They didn't know us, so they didn't press hard by any means, and then before we knew it we were on our way down the side corridor.

I glanced back and saw Paulina and Kori stand up as well, making their own excuses and heading the other way, beyond which were the bathrooms. One of the Worker waiters seemed alarmed by their movement and held a hand out after them as if about to ask where they were going, but then Kori bent over and held a hand to her mouth, and he seemed to understand what was happening. He sighed and shook his head and moved on to the next table.

I turned back and caught Atticus's eye.

We were officially committed.

Just inside the corridor, there was a blank patch of wall out of the sight line of any Blissful. The Worker waiter leading us stopped at that blank patch and gestured us toward it, saying, "Present your tickets, please." Atticus and I pulled out our tickets and pressed them to the wall. A golden light appeared, shining through the tickets and highlighting our palms. A marking materialized—a stylized runic logo for the Art and Antiques Association, which is the branch of the Worker government that monitors and regulates companies like the Artifacts and Antiques Trading Company. That symbol faded to be replaced by the Artifacts and Antiques logo, which is an old-time clipper ship at sea, for some reason, and then the light cut out entirely.

"Welcome," the waiter said.

The blank patch of wall became partially transparent, the same way that the mouth of an alleyway grays out when you 'port, save that the gray was clear enough to partially see through.

Atticus and I stepped forward and emerged into a large circular room beyond the wall. There were two enforcers in the room, along with a pair of black-clad Worker-waiters, and beyond them was a set of stairs going up. The room was lined with pillars and various works of art that were decidedly more Worker-inclined than what was outside. There was a moving painting, a sculpture made out of Immaterial (a kind of black starry substance only found in the Space Between Spaces), a vase that depicted a Worker legend I recognized as *Alicent and the Envious,* and several other unique offerings.

Atticus and I walked to the stairs and began to ascend. The stairway turned until I realized that we were above the Blissful auction hall we'd just left, likely suspended in a bubble of reality right on top of it. At the top of the stairs, we emerged into a broad circular room lined with pillars and three levels of seats. There was a ground floor—on which we were standing—that was mostly empty, made of fancy lacquered tiles and containing rows of black chairs facing a central stage. The second level had a series of golden chairs arranged with cushions around small tables and was mostly full. The third level was made up of about a dozen box seats constructed out of some dark, elegant wood. Straight ahead, toward where all the seats and tables were pointed, was a small stage, on which had been placed a podium and presentation area very similar to what was down below in the Blissful auction hall.

There were about a dozen Workers on the ground floor, most of them men in singles or pairs. There were another three dozen or so on the second level scattered through the various tables and seats, and most of those looked to be groups or couples. On the third level, three of the box seats were full of larger parties—and a fourth held the solitary figure of Marlowe Frost.

"Up there," I muttered to Atticus, motioning toward Marlowe with my chin. He nodded, and together we walked toward a set of stairs set neatly into the side of the first level and base of the second level that would take us from the ground floor up to the box seats.

We crossed and ascended—now that we were inside the room, security seemed much more relaxed. I supposed that made sense. After all, none of the auction goods were in the room yet, and if we'd already made it in then we were "supposed" to be there.

On the third floor, we turned toward the box we had seen Marlowe in, and once we entered we saw that there was a large banquet spread of food in the center of the box. Beyond that was a row of chairs that were lined up at the front of the box, from which the auctioneer would be able to clearly see bidders and their paddles. There was also a bottle of champagne chilling in an ice bucket, a small pad that you could write messages on to request more food or drinks, and several Worker delicacies that I hadn't seen in ages, all of which were made from Immaterial. There were even several small bottles of Know-Drink, which go for a dozen gold a bottle—which is really expensive. It tastes like whatever you're craving most while you're drinking it, and a full bottle is about as alcoholic as three shots of hard liquor.

I had to exercise a lot of self-control not to take one.

"Good, you made it," Marlowe said as we entered. The box was lit with a diffuse golden light that made him look quite impressively dramatic. He looked every bit the part of an aging but upstanding member of the Worker community with his white scarf, golden spectacles, and ornamental walking cane. He pulled out his pocket watch and checked the time.

Something about the watch caught my eye, but I couldn't figure out what it was. Marlowe always wore a bronze pocket watch, one of the Academy-approved Instruments and his preference over a wristwatch. I'd seen it hundreds of times.

Tonight it looked… different, though.

I put it out of my mind—I was stressed and jumping at shadows.

"Kori and Paulina made it out the other side," I said. "Everything looks like it's going smoothly."

"Excellent," Marlowe said, gesturing for us to come into the box and close the small half-door. We did. As I stepped forward, I realized that either side of the box was open so that we could see our neighbors, though currently the boxes on either side of ours were empty.

"Jamal is with them?"

"He should be," Atticus said, adjusting his cufflinks so that they showed prominently beyond the cuffs of his tuxedo but above his band, which was a non-traditional bronze cuff studded with red and black gemstones. "We'll know soon if everything is ready."

Atticus's right cufflink was glowing a hot-metal red. I had a similar one, also glowing. Paulina, Kori, and Jamal all had matching pieces disguised as rings or, in Jamal's case, a button; they were our way of communicating without cell phones or other electronic devices that could get thrown off by the constant ethereal buzz that too much concentrated Working generates.

Once the hot-red glow turned to an ice-cold blue, it would be Atticus' and my turn to leave and make our way to the back of the expo center where Hobb and his crew should currently be securing us a way into the storage area and the room with the Gallimand page.

It was another fifteen minutes until the Worker auction began, and people continued to filter into the room. As they did, especially if they had a box seat, several of them made a point of coming over to Marlowe to say hello. Atticus knew a decent number of them as well, and I was introduced as Ben

Johnson and managed to keep mostly silent and fade into the background. A few of them talked with Marlowe at length about various medical topics, and some even thanked him for recent work.

I got more and more anxious. Sitting with nothing to do except experience the seconds ticking by was the worst form of mundane torture that could have been foisted upon me. I had to stop my leg from bouncing several times, and at one point Atticus leaned over and took the small auction item listing booklet we'd all been given away from me because I was slowly shredding it into tiny rectangular strips.

Atticus, for his part, was the perfect picture of stoicism. He shook hands and exchanged pleasantries as needed, and otherwise sat perfectly calmly, legs crossed and hands loosely clasped in his lap when he was not chatting with our visitors.

Finally, the lights flickered on and off several times, which was the cue for everyone to sit and get ready for the auction to begin. Marlowe said goodbye to the last of his visitors and took the center seat at the front of the box, making himself maximally visible. He would remain there throughout the auction to be clearly free from any hint of wrongdoing. Atticus and I sat on either side of him but slightly behind.

Our cufflinks were still red.

"They're behind schedule," Atticus said matter-of-factly, voice soft but words pointed.

"We have time," Marlowe said softly. He glanced at us both with a reassuring "hold steady" kind of look, and I felt a small amount of resolve stiffen my spine.

The auction began. The lights dimmed, and a round of applause swelled, crested, and bore with it onto the stage a short, heavyset man with a beaming smile and a perfectly square black beard. He was wearing a tuxedo with a turquoise cummerbund and dazzling sapphire cufflinks. His right tux sleeve was cut short to show a beautiful watch-and-band combo and a thick golden ring with a dazzling platinum inset that encircled his middle finger.

He took out a single monocle from one of his suit pockets and placed it carefully against his nose, then tapped his throat. "Good evening, ladies and gentlemen!"

His voice did not boom through the room as one might have expected at a sporting event, but it did carry perfectly to everyone so that it was as if he were standing a comfortable few paces before us.

"On behalf of the Artifacts and Antiques Trading Company, I would like to thank you all for your generous contributions to this evening and to the society's purpose of finding, maintaining, and restoring Old World Worker items of note and import. As a reminder, all items you see here tonight have been either sold to the Company at a fair market price or released from their country of origin after procurement, and all official documentation of such shall be in evidence for all purchasers to take home, as well as officially on file with—"

Atticus's cufflinks went from red to blue.

I breathed out a long, slow rush of air, and Atticus looked calmly over at me and nodded. I looked down at my own cufflinks—still red. They'd found the page. It was Atticus's job now to get in and help Paulina confirm the identity. Then, once the page was officially auctioned, Hobb would get Kori and me around back to grab it and replace it.

"See you both on the other side," Atticus said, standing and calmly adjusting his bow tie.

"Be smart and stay safe," Marlowe said. "Remember, get the page if you can, but not at the expense of yourself."

Atticus nodded and left so that it was just Marlowe and me alone in the box as the auctioneer continued his spiel. The words washed over me and I heard none of them—they became little more than background noise. My heart was pounding in my chest.

This wasn't anything like what I had done two nights prior. This wasn't some unconscious fluke that I could explain away to both myself and hopefully everyone else. When I'd died I hadn't had any control over what had happened next. I had simply returned, sent back from whatever there is after death like a package with incorrect postage. I hadn't asked to wake up, I hadn't asked to come back to life. I simply had. And I felt justified in holding that line, justified in feeling angry and fighting back and running from Shrike and anyone else after me because of it.

But this was about to be something very different. This was about to be a conscious and deliberate act. I would be intentionally breaking laws and stealing from a well-respected—and reputedly quite vindictive—Worker organization. If everything went perfectly, they would have no idea who had taken the page, but what ever goes perfectly? And if they found out I'd been involved and tied me to the page, then there was no amount of talking I'd be able to do to keep myself out of WOTW hands.

Marlowe reached over and touched my shoulder.

I jumped. He was looking at me over the rim of his golden glasses.

"The plan is sound," he said. "Breathe."

I must have still looked unconvinced, because he glanced toward the auctioneer, who was now rattling off starting prices for the first item of the night, and then leaned in closer.

"Take in this moment. There are precious few times in our lives when we have a real chance to put everything we are on the line and risk everything we have so that we may become everything we are meant to be. I have asked you already to take too much of this on faith—I have asked too much of you based on your trust in me. I will ask no more. But on the other side, you will be one of us—the others will accept you once you've proven yourself here. And then, we will know. You will see."

I paused for a long moment, looking at him. I looked down, pulled back, and ran my hands through my hair. "Why is this all happening? Everything just changed overnight, and I can't… I can't get my head around—"

"I know," he said. "I wish I could have better prepared you for it."

There was a stir from the crowd that broke the moment between us.

"And our first truly rare item of the night, a page from an original copy of Gaius Gallimand's *Eternal Cycle*!"

I cricked my neck with how quickly I jerked around to stare down at the stage. Being wheeled out now was a plinth with a crystal-clear glass case on top. Through the case could be seen a single page of writing, boldly titled, and written in the same cipher-coded black ink that covered the pages of the book Marlowe and the others had shared with me.

An excited murmur went through the lower crowd. The box seats, however, were largely quiet, and I looked again across the small round chamber. This time I saw a few other Workers leaning forward eagerly. Several of them were older gentlemen, and they were all watching the stage intently and holding their auction paddles ready.

I looked back at Marlowe, who seemed equally surprised.

"That was the delay from the others," I said. "The order— they switched the order."

My cufflinks turned blue.

"Go," Marlowe said. "Find Kori and figure out what is happening."

I stood, all my doubts still swirling around in my head. I got to the edge of the box and looked back. Marlowe was watching me go. His golden glasses gleamed in the dim box lighting, and the metal chain of his pocket watch winked as he shifted.

The chain. The chain was different. Why was the chain different?

Gold. Not bronze—it was gold.

"Go," Marlowe repeated.

I looked up at him.

"I'll see you after," I said.

"You will."

I turned and headed for the stairs.

PART NINETEEN

THE COMPLICATION YOU KNEW WAS COMING

I descended, hurrying while trying to appear I wasn't. Luckily, everyone was focused on bidding, which had just begun for the ancient page.

I reached the ground floor and had a moment where I forgot which way I was supposed to go. I thought back desperately to my cram sessions with Atticus and Paulina, and after a moment of utter panic that threatened to build on itself and spiral out of control, the memory of the blueprints and the plan thudded back into place in my mind.

Instead of turning left and heading toward the entrance that would take me back out to the corridor and the Blissful auction outside, I turned right and skirted around the scaffolding holding up the second- and third-story levels. There was supposed to be a wait-staff door back there, and that was where I was supposed to meet Jamal.

The panic, not entirely banished, came back to whisper in my ear:

What if he wasn't there?

"Stop it," I hissed.

I rounded the curve and saw the door, and felt an almost shamefully intense amount of relief. I was glad I was still wearing the tux jacket because I was fairly certain that my shirt was a horribly sweaty mess beneath it. Not very James Bond.

I approached the door, and an enforcer stepped out of the shadows to intercept me.

"Good evening, sir," the man said smoothly. "Can I help you with anything?"

It wasn't Jamal.

In fact, I didn't know the man at all. I thought vaguely that I might have seen him the night that I'd escaped from the Twilight House—Jesus, that had only been the night before, hadn't it?—but even then, there was no shot in hell I'd be able to guess his name or pretend to know him.

Where's Jamal? WHERE'S JAMAL?!

"Hi, yes," I said smoothly, giving my tongue the reins and letting it ride, hoping that by the end of whatever I was saying I would find where I was going. "I have a question for the wait staff—my friend is allergic to avocados, and he's got a bit of a swollen throat. Now, he's allergic to a lot of things, but we checked for most of them. I think there may have been some avocado in the ceviche, though, and I couldn't find a wait-staff member on the way down."

My mind was racing, trying to figure out what to do next. I wasn't going to be able to talk my way through the door with a food allergy. I was just buying time at best. How was I going to get through?

There was a gasp from behind me, and I looked back. A bid of one hundred thousand gold had just been made for the Gallimand page. It was a stunning amount—I don't think I've ever seen one thousand gold coins together at any one point, let alone a hundred times as much. The idea that someone had that much to spend on something that, to the bidder at least, would be nothing more than a collector's item, was enough to make me feel slightly sick.

We were running out of time. That *had* to be the final offer.

"I'm sorry, is there a problem?"

I whirled back around and almost cried out in relief. Jamal had emerged and was now standing next to the first enforcer.

"Yes!" I said. "Yes, I have a question for the wait staff about the food—my friend has a horrible… um… avocado allergy."

Jamal stared at me for half a beat—completely understandably since I think it's the worst on-the-spot excuse I've ever made up— but then he grabbed the baton and ran with it like a real champ. "I'm sorry to hear that. I'll escort you through and we can talk with the kitchen staff."

He turned to the other enforcer and said quietly, "I've got it, Tom. Box seat."

Tom's expression changed from one of skepticism to one of resignation and then finally to an oily obsequiousness that I found both unappealing and forced.

"Certainly," he said, smiling too widely. "Have a good evening, sir."

"Yes—uh, thank you."

Jamal opened the door and waited for me to enter, then let it swing shut behind us.

"You're a horrible liar."

"Well, I wasn't ready for you to not be where you were supposed to be!" I hissed. "What's happening? The page is almost auctioned off, it wasn't supposed to go for another hour!"

"Last minute change," he said, walking swiftly down a corridor that led away from both auction halls. It was long and dimly lit and culminated in a bright space with white light reflected off of stainless steel surfaces that I had to think was the kitchen. "We don't know who did it but I think we can make an educated guess."

I felt a chill—Shrike. "She's officially here?"

"None of us have seen her, but we always thought she'd be around."

"Yeah but not actively interfering. Why would she bump the book up?"

"Force us to act quickly and draw us out," Jamal said.

We emerged from the hallway into the kitchen. Given that my avocado-based complaint was entirely fabricated, we did not stop or attempt to speak with any of the cooks or waitstaff. Jamal's enforcer badge gave us a pass to go wherever we wanted, and those who did look up and see us saw the uniform first, seemed to understand and process that appropriately, and then got back to work, which there seemed to be a lot of anyway.

"It makes me way more nervous that we don't know where she is," I said. "Way, way more."

"Me too," Jamal said, turning a corner and opening another door. This led to a corridor that was of the bare industrial style one would expect in the back of an expo center. It was deserted.

"Go right," Jamal said. "There's another door with a security lock. Use this."

He produced a keycard. It looked like it was an entirely ordinary Blissful keycard, and I realized it probably was. This door had probably just led me out of the bubble in which the Worker auction was suspended, and now that I was back in regular Blissful-accessible reality, security would be Blissful-level until I got back up to the second floor where the Worker goods were held.

Then I realized Jamal hadn't followed me through the door.

"You're not coming?"

"Not anymore," he said quickly. "Someone needs to figure out where Shrike is and run interference. Paulina is meeting me. Atticus was supposed to confirm the page's authenticity, but it's up on stage now so who knows where he got to. Kori and Hobb are through the door—they'll find you. Your route is the same. Go. Fast."

He shut the door behind me, and I distinctly heard a lock latch shut.

I wasted no time hurrying down the corridor. My heart was pounding in my chest, and I could hear the blood rushing through my ears. There was a general ringing going on in my head, and the eerie silence in the corridor only seemed to amplify it.

When I got to the door—it was the only one with a keycard reader in the corridor and it was all the way at the end—I held the keycard up to the scanner. There was a red light that I assumed meant the door was locked. It blinked several times, then gave an annoyed kind of squawk and stayed red.

The intense panic I'd felt earlier came crashing back down on me like a goddamn hammer on an anvil. I forced myself to take a breath and swiped the card again. The light flashed again—once, twice, three times—and the scanner squawked a denial once more.

"Fuuuuuuck," I hissed. I looked at the keycard. I looked at the scanner. I looked around me. There were no other doors with scanners, and there was nothing else at this end of the corridor. The keycard was blank and white with a serial number written in light gray stencil on one side, and the scanner was just a beige box with the little red light.

My heart was hammering in my chest. I started having trouble breathing, and suddenly visions were flashing through my mind of Shrike and her enforcers finding me and arresting me while I stood trapped in that corner with nowhere to go. The violet color of Shrike's talon-nail shone brightly through those mental images, and I began to feel queasy. My hands were starting to shake.

So I did something very risky.

Working doesn't always play nicely with technology, mostly because technology is very rigid and goes by specific laws. If you don't know them all, then you don't know which ones are safe to push on with a belief. And if you push on the wrong one—say, make a transistor believe it should act like a capacitor—it can have a cascading effect that overloads the whole system and just blows circuits and generally leads to sparks and flames and sometimes explosions.

But I was panicked, and I knew I was on the clock, and I couldn't think of anything else to do.

So I held the keycard up to the scanner and concentrated. I reached into my pocket and grabbed one of the Break Sticks we'd all taken from Marlowe's place and quickly snapped it in two. The chaos of the breaking sparked, and I fanned it to further life. I pushed the energy out into the scanner, fixing in my mind the belief that the keycard I was holding was the one the scanner was looking for, that this keycard was sending out the right code—not the *only* code, but *one of* the right codes— and that the frequency it was detecting in no way contradicted the frequency it was expecting.

Very Return of the Jedi.

It's an old code, Mr. Scanner, but it checks out.

A lighter, more pleasant squawk rang out, and the light turned green. The distinctive chu-chunk sound of a bolt retracting came from the door.

Relief washed through me.

"Too goddamn close," I muttered.

I grabbed the handle, pulled the door open, and hurried through.

Something caught my eye—something that had fallen out of the crack between the door and the doorframe, almost as if it had been placed there. It fluttered to the ground, caught in the wind of my passing.

It was a card. A... playing card?

I reached down to grab it. As my hand came into contact with it, I felt a small wave of fatigue wash over me.

There was some kind of Working on it.

It was black and silver, with strange patterns on both sides that I had never seen before, made of sweeping lines. It had no business being crammed in a doorjamb, and I had to think someone had put it there. Was it what had locked the door?

I didn't have time to think about what it was, or who might have put it there. I shook my head and flourished my hand, sending it to my vault. I wouldn't be able to do that in the room with the artifacts, but down here, in Blissful reality, the Workings to prevent transference were loose.

On the other side of the door was a short corridor that led to the loading bay in the expo center's large open-space garage. There were several trucks parked there, all with the Antiques and Curios logo.

Good. I was in the right place. I hurried to the left, along the wall, trying to stay silent. There was another door, and in front of it were two more enforcers—or at least men wearing the black shirts and badges of enforcers. That should have been what Hobb and at least one of his team had been wearing under their coveralls.

I ducked into a patch of shadow, my breath coming in short gasps that I tried to keep quiet. Slowly, I continued forward.

One of the enforcers turned in my direction. My heart skipped several beats, but then I was able to take in his face.

It was Jenson Hobb.

I ducked out of the shadows. Hobb saw me and tapped his companion on the shoulder. The second man turned, looked me up and down, and then smirked.

"Oi, you look like a right bellend in that," he said, eyeing my tux. "Well done, bruv."

"This lovely man is Jerry," Hobb said, motioning to the second man. "Long time associate and pain in my finely shaped arse. The rest of the crew's inside. Hurry up."

They both moved aside, and I pushed through the doors behind them. There were three more of Hobb's men inside, all wearing Worker-waiter uniforms. They were standing next to a metal utility stairwell, and when they saw me they started, as if shocked.

They stared at me for a moment and then moved aside to let me through. I put their expressions out of my mind but felt their eyes on me.

As I hurried past, I saw under the stairwell several pairs of feet—the auction event staff and enforcers that Hobb and his men had replaced. Breathing quickly and feeling lightheaded, I hurried upstairs.

The second floor wasn't fancy, but it wasn't the exposed industrial style of the rest of the corridors either. It looked like a modern office hallway and had taupe walls, a recently vacuumed runner carpet down the center, and several doors lining either side.

I hurried down it, counting the doors. As I went, I felt a heaviness fall on me and then lift again, signaling I'd crossed back into the bubble holding the auction.

"Three," I said, pointing to the third door on the left. I opened it and stepped inside.

Kori spun around, brandishing her wand and modified Ruiner.

"Whoa!" I cried. "Whoa—Jesus, put that thing away before you poke my eye out with it!"

"You say that to all the boys?" she asked. I could tell her heart wasn't in it, though—her eyes were wide enough that I could see the whites all the way around her irises.

"Flatters their egos," I said.

I stepped inside and closed the door. When I did, I realized we could hear the auction taking place somewhere close by. The end of this corridor must lead to the stage on which the auctioneer was performing his rapid-fire prattle.

I glanced into a corner and saw another unconscious man, who, I supposed, had been manning the door until Kori had done what Kori does.

"They moved on to the next item?" I asked.

"Yes," she said. "This is the room where the sold items are stored—it should be here!"

Should be here?

I looked around wildly. There weren't many items to look through, though—not much had been auctioned off yet, after all, aside from what must have been the silent auction pieces. Otherwise, the room was a lot of bare shelves and blank paper tags waiting to be slapped on official purchases once they were brought in.

"What do we do?" I asked. "Where else would they have taken it?"

"There must be another room," she said. "There must be another room that we didn't know about, maybe where they keep the big-ticket items."

I looked at her, and she met my gaze.

"Jamal said Shrike is here," I said.

Her gaze went temporarily distant, then snapped back to me.

Another possibility seemed to occur to both of us at the same time.

"It's a trap."

"We need to leave. *Now*."

We both raced for the door and burst out into the corridor. We heard the sound of boots—half a dozen people were hurrying down the corridor in our direction.

They didn't look like regular enforcers, but they were all wearing Ruiners. Their uniform shirts were a dark red-purple color—maybe burgundy?—and their badges looked strange.

"Go!" I shouted.

Kori and I both ran back the way we'd come. That door opened as well, and the three men on Hobb's crew who had been waiting at the bottom of the stairs stepped out into the corridor.

I felt a flare of relief, until they spread out across the corridor.

To block our path.

"No," Kori said in apparent disbelief. "No—move!"

They did not. Instead, they walked toward us, grim looks on their faces. They all looked rough, partially shaven and heavy-lidded. Like they knew how to handle themselves in a fight.

I looked back down the hall. The enforcers were fully running for us now.

"Stop!" one of them shouted. "On WA authority, stop where you are!"

The walls seemed suddenly crushingly close. I couldn't be taken. I hadn't cleared my name yet. If they took me and held me, I might never see the light of day again.

I *would not* be taken.

My fear turned to energy and rushed into a tight ball in my stomach, and then it burst out of me in sudden action. I raised my hands, with the stored energy in my palms, and held the storm tattoo out toward Hobb's men blocking our way and the Muse of Fire tattoo out toward the burgundy-uniformed enforcers. I stuck out my foot and caught Kori, who was slightly behind me, as she tried to pass. She stumbled and fell to the floor with a cry of alarm.

I forced my belief out into the world, and light, heat, and wind exploded outward in the small, confined space. Thunder roared; heat from the flames singed my hair; lightning flashed and drew spidery lines across my vision. I let out a wordless shout as I pushed energy out with all my mental strength—forcing them all *away—away!*

After a dozen seconds, I cut the Workings off with a sharp snap, breathing heavily.

The air cleared, and I saw that Hobb's men, who'd received the storm Working, were all down on the ground and not moving, too close to Kori and me to defend themselves from my sudden attack. The burgundy enforcers, though, were mostly still standing. Only two of them were down, smoking slightly and unconscious; the other half dozen had all managed to raise their Ruiners to protect themselves from the flames.

"Hold!" someone called.

Something in my mind shook loose, and I realized I remembered the voice.

Mallory Shrike pushed her way forward from the back of the group. She was dressed in an outfit not entirely dissimilar to what she had been wearing when she had come to the Protoline office: an immaculately tailored and pressed navy pantsuit. She had an enforcer badge on her chest—but not the kind that Jamal wore. Instead, it was the same dark burgundy color as the uniform shirts the new enforcers were wearing.

WA, I remember thinking. Workers of America.

That's like seeing the FBI instead of just the local police. The Worker equivalent of Feds.

"Hold," she repeated, more calmly. Her striking cheekbones in her gaunt face were made even more skeletal by the fluorescent overhead lighting of the corridor.

I felt Kori move at my feet as she began crawling toward Hobb's unconscious men, clearly trying to reach the door and secure our exit.

The enforcer closest to Shrike caught the motion and twisted his Ruiner to activate the metal amplification bands along its sides, ready to attack.

"Kori!" I snapped.

"Stay where you are!" the enforcer shouted.

"HOLD!" Shrike shouted again.

Everyone froze once more. Shrike was at the front of the group now. The men behind her were all tall and muscled, with strong brows and very large hands, which made their brandished Ruiners look even larger.

"Hello again, Cicero James," Shrike said. "I think we need to talk."

Part Twenty

Hallway Scene

(There's always a Hallway Scene)

"I—what?"

Shrike held up her hands, and I realized that she now wore a visible set of Instruments—a stylish but functional band, ring, and watch. She was not wearing a Ruiner.

That talon, though. She has that talon.

"We need to talk," she repeated.

My mind began to race. The longer she stalled, the better chance there was that someone who had heard the commotion I had just caused would come running. That might also include Jamal and Atticus, though, who would reinforce Kori and me.

How many WA enforcers does she have with her?

Too many was the answer. We needed to get out. Fast.

"Nah, I'm good," I said.

Shrike shook her head. "You don't really have a choice, James. I've read your Guild file—I know you're skilled. But you can't take down half a dozen enforcers with Ruiners. If you try to run again, we will kill you and pick up the pieces later. You'll survive, so there's no reason not to."

A thrill ran through me. She knew. She officially knew—or at least thought she knew—that I was immortal. *And* she was right—if everything about being immortal was true, then there was nothing to lose by killing me. I'd just come back.

I glanced down at Kori.

She, however, could still die.

As I was looking at her I realized that she had landed in front of me, facing away from the enforcers, with her hands concealed. She was holding her wand, and the tip was lit with a dull white light.

She was Working.

She caught my eye and managed to impress upon me that stalling for time would be a good idea.

We couldn't 'port out of there, I knew that. Atticus had briefed me on the protections that the Company puts in place around all of its auctions and events, and 'porting protection is one of the main ones. Also, given that we were in the corridor with the room where they were storing the sold items from the auction, it made a lot of sense that not only would we be unable to 'port in or out, it was highly likely that the major Working I had just done had set off every fucking alarm in the building.

I had to trust Kori. I had to trust that she was doing something that would get us out of there.

OK. So I needed to stall.

"Considering you made me eat a bug with one of the Envious in it, I'm not much inclined to trust anything you tell me," I said, looking back up at Shrike.

"You are under the sway of a very dangerous man," she said. "I needed a way to get into Frost's mansion, past his defenses. You were the only option I had at the time."

"You're not going to convince me there's anything dangerous about Marlowe," I said.

"He'll do it on his own, eventually," she said. "Just like he did with me."

It took me a moment to realize what she was implying— and then when I did, a big flare of confusion shot right through the middle of my thoughts, scattering them like a flock of geese caught in a 4th of July fireworks show.

But no. She was lying. Marlowe had said he didn't know her. *She was trying to play me.*

"You've had nothing to do with Marlowe," I said. "He doesn't know you."

"He doesn't know Mallory Shrike," she said. "I haven't always been her."

And then my mind really started racing.

I couldn't glance back down at Kori without drawing attention to her, but I desperately wanted to see if she knew what the hell Shrike was talking about.

She's just saying things. She's just trying to make me talk to her.

"This is what is going to happen now," Shrike said, still holding up her hands. "You are going to come with me, and we are going to take this burden away from you. We are going to make you mortal again."

And *that* certainly wasn't something I had been expecting either.

"I—what?" I repeated, my usual eloquence completely gone.

An alarm began to sound somewhere. I reacted instinctively and thrust out my palms. The enforcers shouted a warning, prepping their Ruiners.

"HOLD!" Shrike cried again.

I used the distraction to glance down at Kori, and I saw that she now held something made of dozens of twisting white lines. It was still connected to the white light falling from the tip of her wand, and it was still turning and growing.

She shot me a look that clearly said, 'Keep it up.'

"You're full of shit," I snapped at Shrike. "You're holding us here until the others come."

"No," she said quickly, and I was surprised to see that the expression on her face looked… earnest. She really seemed to care that I believed her, and that caught me very much off guard. I suddenly realized that she was younger than I'd first thought. Her emaciated appearance made her look older, but something shone through her in that moment that made me think that she was about my age. A feeling that she wasn't as in control of the situation as she wanted to be.

"No, I don't want them to take you either."

"Why not?"

"Because they're fools who don't believe in Gallimand's writings."

"And you do?"

"Of course."

She reached behind her back and slowly pulled out—carefully wrapped in some kind of clear container—the page from Gallimand's *Eternal Cycle*.

If I were a gasper, I would have gasped. The reveal was masterfully done. Wonderful work.

"I've been working on deciphering Gallimand's Works ever since I left Marlowe," she said. "And all I need from you is to make this page and the others like it readable. In return, we'll help you become mortal again."

"Stop lying," I said again. "You were never with Marlowe."

"I'm not lying," she repeated, eyes boring into me. "When we met the first time, I didn't know who you were. I just thought Marlowe had performed a Raising on you in an ill-advised attempt to start the Cycle with someone he could control. Now, I think you're the real thing. Which means we have a very different kind of relationship."

I was largely ignoring the content of what she was saying because it was too confusing to think about. I was instead looking at the page she was holding and desperately wondering how to get it from her.

The alarm grew louder, and I knew we were almost out of time. I glanced down at Kori again, unable to stop myself, and I saw that the intricately woven ball between her hands was no longer twisting so violently. It seemed to be slowing down, and I realized that it must be almost ready. Kori didn't look at me; she continued to focus all of her attention on the ball.

"James. You weren't the one that this was supposed to happen to," Shrike said.

I looked back up. She had taken another step toward me.

"I know there was a list," I said. "I get it, I wasn't anyone's first choice."

"No," Shrike said. "No, *I* was everyone's first choice."

I blinked several times, and opened my mouth, then closed it, then opened it again.

"You don't need to carry this burden, James. It was meant to be me. And if you come with me now, I can take it away from you. You don't want it. Everything was in motion for the Cycle to start with me the night you took that job. And then you died and it went to you. Ever since then, you've been running, and you'll continue running. The WOTW are just the first to come after you. There is a lot more you don't know yet."

"*You're* the one who came after me," I retorted.

"Yes, to get to Marlowe—to stop him," she said.

I felt something touch my leg, and I almost jumped a foot in the air before I realized it was probably Kori, surreptitiously trying to tell me that she was ready. But suddenly *I* wasn't ready.

"Why would you want it?" I asked. "They'll just be after you, then."

"That's the price the Immortal has to bear," she said.

"That's not an answer."

I felt the touch on my ankle again—Kori more insistently trying to get my attention. I heard something down the corridor, too, then. Shrike heard it as well, footsteps coming toward us and people shouting. The alarm continued to blare, and there were other sounds too, like the sound of a large crowd moving.

Are they evacuating the building?

"I want it because the world needs to be rebalanced," Shrike said. "I want it because we have a chance to right the wrongs done to so many people. We have a chance *now*. And I know how to make it happen. I know how to make the world better. And if you help me read this," she held up the page, "and the rest of the pages we find, then you can help me do that. We can make a perfect world together."

Her violet nail gleamed. I shook my head.

"Thanks for the offer," I said. "But sounds way too good to be true."

I dropped my hand down to Kori. She slapped her hand into mine.

As soon as our skin touched, there was an explosion of white light that raced up and down the corridor. Everything seemed to slow, as if the whole world was suddenly encased in a thick, viscous fluid.

Unfortunately, she'd done the Working too hastily and had caught us in it, too.

I tried to look down at her, my head moving far too slowly. She was staring at me with her mouth partially open and her eyes wide. There was an area of unaffected air close between our bodies that was rapidly growing, where the Working was unraveling.

Kori willed the unraveling forward, and it raced over me. Abruptly, I stumbled as I resumed my usual speed.

I looked back at Shrike and her men, gasping, and saw that though they were still caught, there was violet light flaring on Shrike's hand. She was trying to break the Working.

"Let's go," Kori said, starting back the way we'd come, toward the open corridor and Hobb's still-unconscious men.

"Wait—the page!"

She pulled up short, and we both looked back at Shrike, who was still holding it in her hand.

"Can you get it?" I asked Kori.

"No," she said through gritted teeth. I realized she was sweating profusely. Her jaw was clenched so that the muscles along her face and neck were standing out. It was taking everything she had to hold the Working as it was.

I thought quickly. I could force a belief into Kori's and burrow through the Working she'd created. But if I tried and did it wrong, the whole thing might crumble.

I looked at her again, and once more we seemed to have the same thought at the same time.

"Do it," she managed to say. She began to shuffle down the corridor. "I'll check... the stairs."

I breathed in deeply and turned back. Kori's Working was unraveling, heading out from where she and I had been standing toward Shrike and her men. I had maybe a minute before it unraveled the rest of the way and Shrike was able to act.

I reached into my pocket and pulled out my lighter along with several of the Break Sticks I'd taken from Marlowe's. I breathed in and then out slowly and tensely.

I broke six of the sticks and flicked my lighter. Together, the seven points of chaos gave me enough of a concentrated spark to force a new belief through Kori's Working that I then fed with energy from my body. I tunneled through the milky air, trying to corkscrew with the grain of the pattern she'd woven and burrow close to Shrike.

I couldn't touch her. If I did, she'd be able to piggyback off my Working and attack Kori's.

I directed the burrow toward the page she was holding. I touched it; the page came free and shot through the tunnel of air back to me; I grabbed it.

The second I did, the rest of Kori's Working failed. There was a brilliant flash of violet light, and Shrike's talon suddenly struck out in all directions like a mad whip. The white lattice of the Working was sliced into a dozen sections and fell apart.

A new figure appeared behind Shrike and her men—tall, dark, and handsome.

Jamal.

Hand in his Ruiner, he punched a fist out toward the WA enforcers in their burgundy uniforms. There was a concussive *boom!* and they were all thrown forward. Several fell to the ground, including Shrike.

Shrike was also the first to recover, though, and when she did she shouted something to the others that, at the time, made absolutely no sense to me.

"Pull from Beyond!"

And that's when things got real weird.

Three of the enforcers seemed to shimmer and twist sideways, as if they had turned in a dimension that was beyond normal perception. One of them grew an arm that was like a scythe and had scimitar-like claws made of dark shadow—the same kind of appendage I had seen on the Terror that had killed me. Another suddenly crouched forward and landed on four legs. Grasping tentacles emerged from all over his body and he grew to twice his original size, bursting out of his clothing. A third man threw his arms out to either side and became pale white with red circles under his eyes. His shoulders shot out, and muscle bubbled up under his skin as if he were boiling from the inside.

They were willfully pulling from the Space Between Spaces.

They were incorporating manifestations *into* their bodies.

"That's—no," I said. I don't know who I was saying it to—maybe Kori, who I had forgotten was already gone, but I think just more so to myself. What they were doing should have been impossible. And yet, impossible or not, I was now staring at three men who were sharing bodies with a Terror, a Wrathful, and one of the Envious.

I'd never seen anything like it. It's something that we're warned about when we're training, the things from the Space Between Spaces manifesting *inside* a person. But I'd never actually seen it. And I'd never seen a Worker *intentionally* bring in a creature of the Beyond and have it share their body.

All the creatures of the Space Between Spaces want bodies. You heard some of what Calliope mentioned about it, and how Jacob Luis is controlled by his skull and fingerbones. They all want skin to walk around in, to pull into.

But who in their right mind would *invite* that?

Like I said, it should have been impossible. Before that moment, I would have sworn up and down that it was. Now I know differently. Now I know that they were twinned with creatures from the Space Between Spaces, bound to them by a twisted version of the bond Marlowe has with Calliope and Jacob Luis. It grants power, but at a terrible cost.

Sound came from behind me, and I turned, expecting another attack. It saved me, honestly, because the Envious-Worker—the one with a dozen grasping tentacles sprouting from all over his/its body—rolled forward and threw itself at me. It sailed through the space I'd been in, then landed hard on the carpet floor runner, rolling over itself in its momentum.

I looked beyond it, trying to see what noise had drawn my attention, and saw Jensen Hobb.

Anger swelled in me when I saw his traitorous face, and I struck out with my tattoo Workings again, unleashing an elemental attack.

Kori dove in front of him.

"WAIT!" she screamed.

At the last moment, I redirected my beliefs on the Envious-Worker *thing* between me and them. All of the fire and lightning I had summoned, powered by my very explicit belief that Hobb deserved to be punished, raced into the former enforcer.

He/it exploded. Slime, blood, and guts burst through the corridor. It covered everything—the walls, the ceiling, the floor, me, Kori and Hobb, and even the Terror/Worker and Wrathful/Worker back down the corridor, both of whom cried out in all-too-human shock.

I stared at what I had done.

I hadn't expected it. Workers are protected by their Instruments, and when I use my Workings on other Workers, I expect their rings to protect them from the brunt of the attack. I'd calibrated my beliefs in both tattoos to specifically be at the level of most rings. What that means is that if the Envious/Worker had been wearing a ring, it should have drained, and then there should have been just enough of my belief left over to pop him hard in the jaw, maybe even knock him out or at least send him flying backwards singed a bit.

Whatever the Envious/Worker had done to transform himself, though, it looked like he had accidentally voided the rings on his Ruiner and all accompanying protection.

And now he—it—was very dead.

There was a stunned moment of silence, and then several things happened at once.

Kori shouted, "Throw us the page!"

Hobb shouted, "I didn't know about the others!"

Shrike screamed, "Grab him!"

I glanced back just in time to see Jamal strike out with his Ruiner at a temporarily distracted WA enforcer and flatten him against the nearest wall, knocking him unconscious. The Wrathful/Worker and the Terror/Worker ran down the corridor and lunged for me.

What happened next I could never give a full blow-by-blow accounting of. What I do know is that Jamal engaged with the remaining WA enforcers, and Kori and Hobb came to my aid.

Somehow, I rolled out of the way of my attackers, the teeth and claws of the Wrathful/Worker flashing at me on one side and the scimitar-like claws of the Terror/Worker slicing past my head on the other. Kori moved up to attack them, Working raw power out of her wand.

And then there was a crackling, ripping sound. It sent chills through me that I couldn't stop, and I remembered the feeling of using the tattoo across my clavicle, the one that had somehow managed to open up a rip in reality and expose the Space Between Spaces.

I turned and saw before me the same hole that I'd made accidentally several months before—a horrible black yawning mouth that sparked with blue and silver lightning, surrounded by a nimbus that spun violently around it.

A hole in reality that led to the Space Between Spaces.

Standing in front of it was Mallory Shrike, tall and proud, eyes blazing.

"You thought you were the only one with tricks?" she asked.

Before I could respond or make a move to react, she thrust her hand out at me and her violet talon was in my face. It turned razor-sharp, and then sliced across my throat.

For a shocked moment, I just stared at her, and then the blood began to drain from my body.

My ring went ice cold on my finger, and then back to room temperature. It hadn't protected me at all. Somehow Shrike had gotten though its guard without any difficulty.

I grabbed at my throat and felt the hot liquid gushing out of the gaping wound in my neck. I tried to breathe and found I couldn't. I tried to speak but had no functioning voice box left to push words through.

I desperately pushed out with my palm tattoos again, without finesse, and tried to brutalize my way out of the situation, but the shots went wide. Everything was growing cold and distant.

My last sight was of Kori, shouting and screaming at me, being dragged bodily from the hall by Hobb; and Jamal, bloody but alive, retreating down the corridor the other way.

And then I died again, and was borne away by Mallory Shrike through a rip in reality.

PART TWENTY-ONE

WHERE I MAKE A REALLY PAINFUL CHOICE

Someone poured several gallons of freezing water over me.

I shouted—or tried to shout. The water got in my mouth and ears and up my nose, and for a moment I thought I was going to drown. That somehow I'd been thrown in an icy lake and that I was going to sink to the bottom and never be found.

The stream of water ended, and I coughed and retched and spat out water and phlegm, and then I coughed even deeper and brought up acid and bile as my whole body rebelled. Finally, the wave passed, and I was able to suck in a deep, gasping lungful of air, a heavy wheeze that shook my whole frame and flushed blood back through my body.

My eyes were burning—they were open, I realized. I blinked through the water and tried to see. I couldn't move my hands and I didn't know why. My wrists hurt. I couldn't move my feet. There was pain in my ribs and pain along the back of my neck—there was pain everywhere, just in greater or lesser magnitude, radiating out from angry white-hot nodes across my body.

I'd died.

My throat. My throat had been—

I jerked my hands up, but they traveled barely a handful of inches before pain radiated through my wrists again. I cried out and cursed, and realized my throat was clear. I swallowed, and though everything was dry and swollen, it all seemed to be working.

I looked down—my previously white tux shirt was now covered in a horrific spread of red so dark it was almost black.

I was still wearing my tux pants, but they were ripped and frayed. I had no idea what had happened to my coat. My shoes were gone—I was barefoot. And my Instruments had been stripped from my finger and wrists.

It had happened again. I'd come back.

Up until then, there had still been something in the back of my mind that had been skeptical about all of it. A part of me that I had cordoned off and kept in reserve, leery and distant, on the off chance that the first time had been a fluke. That maybe I hadn't died at all, or somehow there had been energy in my Instruments that had kept me alive. Strange things happen to Workers all the time.

But now it had happened twice.

So if I wasn't immortal, I was doing a damn good job faking it.

I shook my head and blinked several more times. There was no more water coming down on me—I could breathe, which I did. And I could *see*—so I looked around.

There was a crumbling concrete wall several feet in front of me. It was grimy and damp in places, and there was graffiti across it—but old and weathered graffiti, with formerly bright blues and shocking pinks that were now faded, dull, and indecipherable. Patches of concrete had broken off and become a scattered spread of rocky debris on the ground. Everything was covered in a layer of dirt and decay that had to have accumulated over years, and in the grime that covered the floor I could make out the imprint of large boots, several different pairs.

I realized that everything was visible, which meant that there was a light, but I couldn't see a light source in front of me. I looked up, careful not to move my head too quickly, and saw a single bare bulb dangling on a chain, with a thin gnarled string tied to a switch on its side.

And beyond that was the ceiling, which was… vibrating.

My hearing crackled back to life like someone had thrown a breaker in my head, and I heard, slowly swelling in my awareness, music. A heavy throbbing beat that was vibrating the solid slab of ceiling, and through it the walls and floor and even the air. It was distant enough that it wasn't *loud*, but it was near enough that I could *feel* it.

Where the hell was I?

"He's awake," someone said.

I tried to turn and look, but I couldn't twist far enough around. The back of my head, right at the base, pounded, and I groaned and had to fight back a wave of nausea.

Just like the last time, it seemed that only the death wound had healed.

Someone walked forward, the soles of their shoes sounding very deliberately on the floor, punching through the layer of debris to strike the concrete beneath.

"Fascinating," a female voice said. "He doesn't heal fully when he comes back."

I managed to focus my eyes. Mallory Shrike stood before me, still wearing her outfit from the auction, minus the blazer. Her dark blouse looked the worse for wear, and I realized I must have done more damage with my final escape attempt than I'd thought. There was a large burned patch on one shoulder, and the hem had a long cut in it, through which I caught a glimpse of pink skin.

She was watching me with a tight, unblinking gaze. Her gaunt face looked particularly skeletal in the harsh overhead lighting.

"Make a note," she said, looking up over my head.

"Done," said a male voice from somewhere behind me.

My mind slowly began to rev up, like a long-unused motor suddenly dusted off, oiled, and gassed. The pistons began to fire, cranking me back fully into consciousness.

With thought came pain, though—with consciousness came a fuller awareness of my tied and bound body. My hands were achingly numb, and so were my feet. I hurt all over. I gritted my teeth against the swelling discomfort and tried to think. Shrike was looking down at me, examining me with a critical, almost scientific, eye. She seemed to be mentally cataloging my appearance, endeavoring to capture every detail.

"What're you looking at?" I mumbled in a way that I wish had been more impressive.

She paused and cocked her head slightly to the side.

"You may speak if you wish," she said.

Oh, really? Giving me *permission*?

My pain became anger, and I acted without really thinking. I hawked some snot into the back of my throat, pulled my head back, and spat.

I've got mad skillz (yo) when it comes to loogies. It flew exactly how I wanted it to and hit her right in the eye. She recoiled and cried out in anger and disgust. I couldn't help myself—I laughed. Partly at her reaction but mostly with a kind of insanity that just took over me. I was laughing as a reaction to where I was, and who was with me, and at the absurdity of it all.

"You—disgusting—*asshole!*" she shrieked, wiping her eye furiously with the sleeve of her blouse. I continued laughing, and she sneered down at me.

"Shut up!"

That just made me laugh harder.

"Stop it—stop it! Be quiet!"

And then she strode forward, put her hand behind her back, and pulled out a black pistol.

I wish I could tell you what kind of gun it was. I wanna say it was a Glock since it looked like all the standard-issue black guns that cops have on TV shows, but I have next to no experience with firearms. Most Workers don't. We can alter the fabric of reality—what need do we have for something that can put messy holes in people?

But it was definitely a gun. And it was such a Blissful thing to do, to pull a gun on someone, and such a Blissful thing to have happen to me, to have a gun pulled on me, that I didn't quite understand at first what was happening. And by the time I did, it was too late.

She pulled the trigger. I never heard anything, I never felt anything. I saw a flash that must have been from the muzzle; my head snapped back; everything went dark.

*   *   *

I came back screaming as someone poured several more gallons of icy water over my head. The screaming turned again to coughing and retching, and I tried to lean forward but couldn't. I was bound at the wrists and feet.

"He's back."

"Gugh," I said, then coughed some more. I didn't know where I was. I looked up—there was a concrete ceiling and walls covered in graffiti. But not new graffiti—it was old and aging, like the concrete it had been sprayed across. The concrete itself was crumbling and there was debris littered across the... floor...

The deep bass thumping from above shook my head, and I realized I'd been here before.

Something red hot speared through my head, and I gasped. The pain disappeared as quickly as it had come, and then I was back in my right mind, and I could remember.

I could remember being shot.

"How long, Shaw?" I heard someone ask—a woman's voice. Mallory Shrike. My mind was reeling again, but somehow I was recovering faster than I had the first time. And this time, just like that first time in the morgue, I felt a wave of euphoria lift me up and buoy me back to full consciousness. It was like an endorphin high after stubbing your toe but times a hundred. I shivered with it and then gasped and clenched my hands.

They killed—they *shot*—

But I was immortal.

I couldn't die. I really *couldn't die*.

"Five minutes," replied another voice.

"Incredible," Shrike said, rounding me to examine my current state. Somewhat more warily now that I'd shown her the range of my loogie abilities, I will say. "Simply incredible. And look—he's healed. Not all of it again, just the bullet wound, but it's gone. I'd never have known he'd been shot if I hadn't done it myself. It's real. I knew it. I *knew* it."

I checked in with myself and realized she was right. My head didn't hurt anymore—which, considering it had just gotten fucking canoed by a *bullet* was really saying something—but everything else, every other scrape and bruise I'd collected that evening, was still present.

The Palace. The fight at the Palace. Kori and Jamal. Had they escaped?

"Where am I?" I managed to ask. My voice was shaky, and it felt like I had to force it out of my throat. Shrike focused more intently on me.

"Do you know who I am?" she asked.

"I know you're a cunt," I croaked. "Does that count?"

Shrike's eyes widened, and she balled a hand into a fist. Then she appeared to have a change of heart and relaxed. She even seemed amused.

"I don't think you understand what's happening here."

She walked somewhere out of sight and grabbed a chair. She pulled it across the floor, producing a nails-on-chalkboard screech and leaving deep tracks in the grime that covered the floor. She sat, then held out her hand. Someone placed in it the wrapped and protected page from Gallimand's *Eternal Cycle*.

I had it with me when she took me.

"You are going to help us counter Gallimand's Working, and then we are going to take the immortality from you. Because it never belonged to you to begin with. It belongs to me, and I will have it if I have to peel the skin off your bones to get it."

I have to admit, I didn't much like the sound of that.

"How about we don't do that?" I croaked.

Shrike smiled, all lips and eyes, no teeth. The humanity she had shown in the hallway when trying to convince me to come with her willingly seemed to have receded. She was staring at me with the intent stare of a big cat playing with its meal.

"Give in, and it will go quickly," she said.

I scoffed a small, pathetic little croak-laugh.

Like a cat seeing a rat twitch, she whipped her hands forward and grabbed my head, faster than I could follow. I grunted in surprise, and then she pulled me toward her, straining my neck until it was noticeably painful. There was hatred in her face, real hatred, and it scared the shit out of me.

I don't think most of you probably know what it is to be hated. Sure, there are probably people who dislike you. Maybe some of you are real assholes and there's a *bunch* of people who dislike you, or avoid you, or just don't particularly think much of you.

But hatred is different.

And Mallory Shrike *hated* me. Or at least the idea of me.

And when someone hates you, there isn't much they won't do to you. You become non-human. You become an other. And if you aren't human, then they don't have to treat you like a human. They can treat you like an animal. Worse—like a bug or a rock, something completely beneath notice. And the best you can hope for is that they don't think it's worth their time to really dig into you.

But right then, Shrike seemed to be gearing up to take all the time she could.

Her fingers dug into my jaw, her long claw-like nails stabbing painfully. The violet talon with its tiny gemstones in particular I could feel: it *burned,* like ice held too long against my skin, just below my eye. I grimaced at the pain and gritted my teeth.

"I didn't recognize you at first," she said. "That was my mistake. You avoided the test we gave you when we had you at the office—a duplicate Gallimand page that should have filled in when you touched it. I don't know how you did it, but you were clever. We've been watching Marlowe, and all this time we thought it would be him who found the way to move forward. I thought he was making a last-ditch effort to steal it from me, Raising you. Using you as a pawn. And it turns out he wasn't involved at all. That it was completely a mistake— an accident."

She must have felt my sudden stillness and realized I was listening more intently. She tilted my head so that I had to roll my eyes painfully to the side to keep them focused on her.

"Yes," she said, "I know Marlowe. I know him very well."

She sneered at me, watching me closely and drinking in my discomfort and confusion. I felt that she was looking past me, too—beyond me. Almost as if she saw me as some extension of Marlowe and not as a separate person.

That was why she hated me. At least partly. She saw me as part of him.

"When we discovered what Gallimand's Works were, I was the one who realized what we could do with them. How far we could go. I was the one who was brave enough to imagine a new world. Marlowe was frightened. Like a little boy. And he ran back to his mansion like a child in superhero pajamas looking for his dinosaur nightlight."

My mind was racing. She was using *we*. Like she and Marlowe had discovered Gallimand and the Works *together*. But Marlowe had said he had no idea who she was.

She released my chin with a violent twist that strained one of the muscles in my neck. I winced and clenched my teeth against the pain. She smirked at me and sat back in her chair. The light of that hatred still shone in her eyes.

"You don't know what the Works are, truly, do you?" she asked.

I made no response. There was no right answer, whether to confirm or deny. And I knew, the way every scrawny kid who's ever been bullied knows, that to speak up in any way would just be to invite further torment.

She smiled at me again, and this time she smiled with her teeth. I preferred it when she didn't. Her mouth was wide, and when she pulled her lips back, I could see almost every tooth, including yellowing molars in the back.

"No, of course you don't know what the Works are." She spoke patronizingly, as if I were Jack Nicholson and she Nurse Ratched. "You think you do, but you don't. You don't understand. He probably never told you all of it because that's the way he is. There's always another door, another lesson, another fucking hoop to jump through. Never the whole truth, out and plain for all to see."

She paused and stared at me for another moment, silently daring me to speak. When I didn't say anything, she seemed to make a decision.

"Well, Mr. James, luckily for you, I'm not Marlowe Frost."

She looked over my head and nodded, then beckoned someone with her hand.

I heard movement behind me, scraping and shuffling, and then three men brought something large and unwieldy into view.

It was a case containing a book. The book was very old and very worn, but it was held together by a thick black cover with gold lettering.

The Collected Works of Gaius Gallimand
Volumes 1-7

I stared at it for a moment, unable to process the sight. Then, slowly, Shrike held up the page she had taken from the auction and pulled it free of the protective covering. She held it up so that I could see it clearly, and I realized she was touching it with her bare fingers.

I don't know what I had expected to happen exactly, but given that everyone had told me that I was the only one who was supposed to be able to touch the Works, I had thought that Shrike would be blasted off her feet or thrown through a wall, or, hell, struck down by a bolt of lightning.

But none of that happened. Instead, she held the page up in front of my face, gripped it tightly in both hands, and slowly tore it down the middle.

Shock is a mild version of what I felt. I was… I dunno, flabbergasted. Bewildered. Dumbfounded, dazed, ACDC Thunderstruck. That page was what everyone wanted. It was what *she* wanted.

It was the goddamn MacGuffin.

She threw the torn page aside, and just watched me, a small lips-only smile (much preferable to the toothy grin) set on her face, her eyes crinkled slightly at the corners. She seemed to be enjoying the external expression of everything that was racing through my mind. She drank it in with the excited anticipation of an alcoholic knocking back the first drink of a bender.

"Open it," she said.

It took me a moment to realize she wasn't speaking to me. The instruction had been for the men behind her. They set the clear case with the book down on the chair she'd just vacated. One of them, in the burgundy shirt of the WA enforcers, held out a Ruiner-clad hand that glowed faintly red. He made a motion like turning a page.

The cover of the book fell back to reveal a single page—the first page of *The Eternal Cycle*, which Shrike had just torn up.

My first thought, still not quite getting it, was that this book was a duplicate. A perfect duplicate. Just how Marlowe had made duplicates of the book and pages he and the others had found, Shrike had made a duplicate of the first page of the Gallimand book that she had somehow managed to obtain.

But then it all clicked together in my head.

Shrike didn't have a duplicate. She had one of the originals.

I breathed in sharply, and my eyes flew back to her. She was watching me triumphantly, as if she had been dying to share this revelation with someone who could fully grasp its import.

"The page was never at the Palace," she said. "I knew the only thing that would draw Marlowe out was rumor of the real thing. He and all those hapless pawns of his have been looking in the wrong places. I found the original through a private collector. It's the genuine thing, one of the second-run copies. It cannot be touched or handled save for the pages already unlocked. Luckily for us, it turns out that it has been open to the first page for quite some time. It can be closed and opened, but no further pages can be read. In fact, no manipulation that we have tried has been able to turn it to a new page, only close it again. The cipher used to conceal the meaning behind the writing, that we were able to work through. It proves the importance of the Immortal, what we have always expected, and the importance of the Immortal as the vessel through which the world can be remade. Not just rebalanced—*remade*. And it was easy enough to create a replica of this one page and then age it convincingly. The hardest part was putting in place a Working strong enough to mirror that which allowed no one to open the book, in order to convince everyone of its authenticity. But I am resourceful. As you have found."

The music above us suddenly increased in volume, and with it came the sound of a crowd cheering. The incongruity of that sound with the situation I found myself in struck me.

But then I felt the power. Chaos, bound within the structure of a building, slowly rising.

It was strong. *Really* strong.

We had to be beneath a concert. Or a… club.

Holy fuck. The club opening.

Was there another one? Were there multiple openings that night?

That seemed very unlikely.

Which meant Roc was up there. Erica was up. Anandini and her friends and probably hundreds of others were up there.

And we were beneath it.

Why were we beneath it?

There was only one reason I could think of, unless it was just a sheer, dumb, completely incomprehensible coincidence. A club opening is a modern bacchanalia. It's an orgy of dancing and music and alcohol and sex and drugs and violence and chaos. And what's more, it's contained within the modern laws of a city, the walls of a club. There's order at the door, people lined up to get in to enjoy the chaos. It's a perfect melding of opposites, which is why so many people seek it out. Structured debauchery, safely losing yourself.

With the right planning, effort, and channel, a strong enough Worker could use it. *All* of it. In one flash of insane power to do something otherwise impossible. Something truly miraculous, like the Workers of old. But it would need something to go through. A channel of some kind.

My eyes slid past Shrike, and I saw again the faded graffiti on the wall.

And then I looked down, past the debris and grime of a dozen years, to the concrete beneath. My vision widened, and marks that I had thought were separate and random suddenly came together in an obvious pattern.

There was a Circle beneath me.

It was unlike any other circle I'd seen. Where Marlowe's was about as traditional as you can get—the three traditional metals, all the primes from two to eleven, traditional gemstones and wood—this one was its polar opposite. It was roughly carved, like it had been dug in the concrete by a jagged metal pole, and the lines weren't straight, but oddly waved and curved like they'd been drawn by a five-year-old still getting used to basic shapes. There were gemstones at the junctions of the lines, but they were all dark—amethyst, onyx, garnet, even what I thought might be black diamonds.

And there were other symbols, symbols I didn't know, in some strange language. But that would make sense. Shrike and I clearly believed in very different things, and whatever language she felt held power was likely dark and ancient.

I still hadn't put together at that point what they were planning to do with it. What can I say, I'd just died twice. I was going a little slow.

I started to panic. Whatever was happening, I had the overwhelming suspicion that I didn't want Shrike to do it.

Could *I* use it? Could I tap into the Circle somehow?

I reached out mentally, and I hit some kind of psychic barrier. It snapped me back inside my own head with an almost concussive violence.

"AH!" I cried out.

Imagine the mental equivalent of punching a brick wall and nearly breaking your hand. Or getting your foot caught in a rat trap.

That level of pain.

I cursed, as, luckily, the pain began to fade. It left me shaking, though.

Shrike seemed to know exactly what I'd done. She held up a finger and wagged it from side to side. "Not for you. So, we return to the purpose of your presence here tonight. A little light reading, and then relief from this burden. If you make it easy, I will make it easy."

Still wincing in pain, I focused back on her.

She seemed serious, and the look of pure hatred had faded. It hadn't disappeared, but it was no longer at the forefront. There seemed almost to be two versions of her: one that was ruthlessly bloodthirsty and full of contempt for me and the world at large; and one that seemed young and uncertain but determined to do what she felt she had to do. It was this second Shrike who had spoken to me in the hallway, and it was she who was speaking to me again now.

She nodded and motioned to the men behind her. They cleared the case with the book off the chair, and then she sat back down, leaning toward me again with her elbows on her knees.

"I don't want to do this," she said. There were no barriers between her and me in that moment. Maybe she's a pure sociopath and can lie like Hitler to Chamberlain, but I swear she seemed to be telling the truth. "I don't want to hurt you. I want the knowledge in that book," she gestured to it, "and I want the gift that is *mine* by right. The gift you got by mistake."

She watched me again for a moment, maintaining eye contact. The club music continued to thump and pound in the background. I don't know if she was waiting for me to say something, but for once in my life, I was speechless.

Because… well, what if I just gave it to her?

I hadn't wanted it anyway.

"I will take it from you either way," she said. "There is enough power here to make it happen. If you resist, I will break you. The only choice you have is how much pain you are going to feel. If you give it to me without resistance, then all of this can be quick. You need not suffer. You may even escape alive, if you survive the transfer."

The overhead light cast dark circles under her eyes, making them look like gems set back in deep caverns. Her lipstick was smeared at the corner of her mouth. She had a small half-moon scar on one striking cheekbone.

"But you need to cooperate," she said. "Will you do that?"

I stared into her eyes, and I couldn't help but believe her. I still do, I think. If I had taken that path, she'd have done what she needed to do, but she'd have done it quickly and efficiently and then she would have taken the immortality out of me. And if I had survived, she might even have let me go, probably with another memory wipe.

Her nail talon caught my eye, though, violet and gleaming with tiny flecks of chipped gemstones, and I paused.

She'd broken the Worker's Code and Worked on Jamal and me. She'd shown that she was ruthless and willing to do whatever it took to achieve her goals. Including, apparently, kidnapping me and tying me up in a nightclub basement like a goddamn serial killer.

And she had pulled from the Space Between Spaces. The men following her had transformed, had melded with a Terror, a Wrathful, and one of the Envious. I'd never even heard of something like that, but she had commanded them to do it and they'd done it with the kind of efficiency that probably meant they'd done it before.

That's the kind of thing Workers like me are meant to prevent. That's the kind of thing I get paid to fix. Rips in reality, tears in the fabric of the world, dangers coming from the Space Between Spaces. I've never wanted to Work in any other way. Ever since I was young, ever since my mother was torn to pieces by a Terror in front of my eyes, I knew that I would stand between the world and all the bad out there. And fuck everyone who won't, you know? Fuck all of the people who stand by and do nothing. Fuck all the people who talk about how awful the bad things are but won't *do* anything about them. I stand up because I *can*. When I was a kid, everyone just stood by and watched it happen to me and my mom. And my dad couldn't handle it and fucked off and left me to pick up the pieces.

I will *never* be like him. I will *never* run when people who depend on me need me to be there for them.

When everyone else is gone, I will still be standing there.

The next moment is long and extended in my memory, though I know in reality it was a handful of seconds at most. Because I knew I was going to refuse. But I also, for the first time, was up against a real test of my idealism. I knew there was going to be pain. I *knew* it. And when you're young and idealistic, you don't think about pain that much. Sure, maybe you break a bone, but you forget about it soon enough. When you live a little longer, though, you start to actually know what pain is. You know how much of it is in the world and how close it is at any given moment. You've tasted it enough to know what a full-course meal would be like.

And I knew just by looking at Shrike that she was willing to feed it all to me. I knew that the hatred she felt would come out again, and she would funnel it into me with no remorse.

"What would you do if you were immortal?" I asked.

She considered me for a moment. I don't know for sure if she was weighing the cost/benefit of lying to me or not, but I suspect she was. I think she saw something in my eyes, though, that told her she wouldn't get away with it.

"I would remake this world," she said. Truthfully, I think. "I would end all of the atrocities committed against innocents. I would wipe out hate and division and oppression. And I would put Workers in their rightful place, atop the governments of the Blissful. To guide the world away from all the horrible things they've put it through. I would take responsibility because no one else seems to want to. I would be what everyone wants. The person who needs to make the hard decisions so that they don't have to."

A tingling sensation ran down my spine. She was like me. More than I wanted to accept. Her motivation almost entirely mirrored my own. And she meant what she said. She meant *all* of it. She really did want to use it for what she thought was good.

What she *thought* was good.

"How?" I asked.

"The Immortal is supposed to go to the Beyond," she said. She gestured to the book, to the first page of *The Eternal Cycle*. "That's what it says. The Space *Beyond* Spaces. Through everything we know. To the heart of everything. And when the Immortal makes it there, that's where they get to make a choice. How the Immortal is supposed to get there, how that choice can be used to rebalance the world, that's what is in the rest of this book. That is what we need to unlock."

I swallowed, hard. A Space *Beyond* Spaces? I couldn't wrap my head around that.

"I meant," I croaked, "what are you going to change?"

Her eyes gleamed, and I heard a few of her men shift. One of them laughed, low and throaty.

"I'm going to rip out the abomination that is this modern world by the root like the weed it is," she said. "I'm going to wipe out this material-obsessed global society and change the fundamental needs of humanity. Unlike every other Immortal who has come along and chosen wrongly. I will make the hard choice, once and for all, so that no one ever has to make a hard choice again. I will unwind the horrible things that people in the shadows have Worked on the world for their own gain. The squalor infecting the world, the disease. You can't pretend you haven't seen it."

She held my gaze, and I was forced to remember walking through the Tenderloin not twenty-four hours earlier. Forced to remember the sense of wrongness that I had felt.

Has someone been… Working? On the Blissful?

New possibilities opened up before me. Working comes from either order or chaos. Long term, order is best. Sustainable, clean, steady. Short-term, though, chaos works just as well. And if you create enough of it, it begins to compound. Was someone building up sources of chaos? How would they ever be able to sustain that, though?

She must have seen something in my eyes because she began to nod.

"You are beginning to understand," she said softly. "You are beginning to see. I am not your enemy, Cicero James. We want the same things, and we have the same enemy, even though you do not know it yet. Marlowe knows them, and I am certain his acolytes do too. He hasn't told you yet. Not everything. But they're gaining power. And they're working against all of us, for their own gain. Demolishing the world so that they can be kings and queens of the rubble. And I am prepared to make the sacrifices necessary to beat them. You don't need to do this."

My head was spinning. There was clearly something here, but there was clearly something missing as well. I was having a hard time telling truth from the partial madness that was also driving Shrike. What was real and what was some strange conspiracy?

"Why doesn't Marlowe want it to be you, then?"

Her expression changed, and she pulled back. Lines of contempt formed around her mouth.

"He can't see it," she said. "He can't see that the rot is all the way through. That it infects every bit of the world, Worker and Blissful alike. He can't make the hard choice, to wipe the slate clean entirely and start over."

"Wipe the slate clean," I said. "You want to…"

"Rid the world of those who are no longer needed," she said. "Cleanse the world."

I closed my eyes and groaned.

Because that's when I realized I really was gonna say no.

Part Twenty-Two

This part is not pleasant

I opened my eyes again and looked at her.

"I was *so* close. Jesus. Why couldn't you just want to give everyone a million dollars and a puppy or something? Fuckin' *cleanse the world*… Jesus Christ, I really wanted an out here!"

She stared at me for a long moment, open-mouthed, and I could feel all of the men in the room doing the same.

"What?" I asked. "You thought I would just be onboard with *wiping out the world?* You're the Howard Hughes peeing in jars, Vincent Van Gogh cutting off his ear kind of crazy, aren't you?"

She stood, pushing the chair back violently enough that it twisted and fell over with a metallic crash that rang inordinately loudly in the small room. The hatred was back. I had pulled it to the forefront with my refusal.

Will Marlowe and the others try to save me?

The question came to me in a small voice that felt pathetic even to me. It was the sound of my fear. And I knew that it was asking questions I couldn't entertain. They didn't even know where I was. How could they? And there was no way to send them a message. Even if I weren't sitting in the middle of some kind of corrupted Circle, it wasn't like I'd be able to just whip out a cell phone and text Marlowe 'ay bro, hit up the club'.

"You're just like him," she sneered.

"If you mean Marlowe," I said softly, "then that's a high compliment."

She snarled something unintelligible at me and whirled away.

"Railsbeck, Shaw—get him ready."

Two of the men came forward, one of them very broad and the other very tall. They untied me and lifted me off the chair. I'd been sitting for long enough, and tied tightly enough, that my hands and feet had lost circulation, and the blood rushing back into them was painful. It made me groan under my breath.

"Jennifer," Shrike said, to someone I couldn't see. "How are we looking?"

"Attendance is even higher than we thought it'd be," someone behind me said, the first other female voice that I'd heard that evening.

Attendance… the club?

"Good. When are they letting the last pre-purchase group in?"

"Half an hour," came the response.

The two burly men were holding me up while someone else cleared the chair away.

Club attendance. They're waiting until it's as full as possible.

"Good," Shrike said. She walked toward me again. Held up as I was by the two men, my knees bent and my lower legs limp, I was basically face-to-face with her.

"Let me be clear about what's going to happen now," she said. "You are going to suffer until you give me what I want. There are two things I need from you. I need you to unlock this book, and I need you to give me the immortality. Both are simple. Take the book and turn the pages. Then just say 'yes', and the burden of fixing the world falls to me. The longer you refuse to do those two things, the more pain you will feel. The more unnecessary parts of your body I will take from you. The deeper I will carve into your mind."

Why doesn't she just take the immortality and turn the pages herself?

I blinked a few times and examined that thought.

She wanted what I had, and she'd gone through the whole process of setting up the Circle, the whole trouble of grabbing me at the Palace and bringing me there. She'd planned all of it, had known the club opening was happening.

But she didn't fully believe. She didn't *believe* that the transfer could happen. In spite of her big talk, she thought that maybe it wouldn't work.

And doubt is the death of any Working.

She needed me to unlock the book *first*. She wanted something in the book that would make her confident, make her believe. And then even if things didn't work, she'd still have the book open and she could use it.

"This is your last chance, James," she said, in that soft and deadly voice.

I wanted to say something. But language at that point was a much higher function than I could manage. I had already retreated inside my mind. I had regressed on the evolutionary ladder to something base and tense and silent.

She clenched her jaw and her nostrils flared. The left side of her mouth jumped and twitched.

"Have it your way."

She stepped back, outside the Circle.

"Suspend him," she said over her shoulder.

The two men lifted their Ruiners. Dull off-white light spooled out and wrapped around my arms at the wrists, elbows, and shoulders. The light spun up to the ceiling where it, like rope, draped over metal hooks. The two men then pulled it tight and anchored it to the walls. I was lifted up and I could stand: my bare feet touched the ground, but if I let my legs go, the light-ropes would keep me suspended.

"You secured his Instruments?" she asked.

"I've got them," the second female voice said from behind me again.

"Shaw—are you ready?" Shrike asked.

"Ready," one of the men who'd hoisted me up said.

"Good."

She locked eyes on me.

"Last chance, James."

I took a deep breath.

"Suck a dick, Mallory."

She sneered. "Burn him," she said.

I can't fully relate what happened next. The memory is… raw. I think it will be for the rest of my life. I'm having trouble even typing this, and I don't really know how to say it.

They did burn me. Shaw did it. He smiled at me the whole time. A kind of wide-eyed smile. Like a toddler knocking a block tower over to see how it all falls down.

The pain was unimaginable. I don't know… I can't say it right.

At a certain temperature, heat isn't really even heat anymore, it's nerve-rending pain. I burned from the inside out, I know that. Shaw started the spark and the second man, Railsbeck, contained it so that it didn't spill out to everyone else in the room.

Looking back, it must have lasted only about a minute. It was hot enough that it couldn't really have been much more than that, otherwise there wouldn't have been much of me left over. As it was, there wasn't a whole lot. They started with my gut, and I remember screaming as the flames burst out of my stomach. And then they moved to my shoulders and arms, and I remember watching my hands curl and blacken, and my fingers crack like twigs in a campfire. I don't remember much else except the pain and the cooked-meat smell. The smell… that part I'll never forget. Like bacon left too long on the stove.

And then they went for my head, and I think… fuck, man. I think my eyes burst. Because I couldn't see anymore. But I could hear, and I could still smell the burning meat smell.

I don't know how long after that it took until I was gone completely. It wasn't literally long, in minutes and seconds, but it felt like a million years.

And that's how I died for the fourth time.

I don't remember anything between the time I died and the time I came back. There's no gap in the experience for me, just lights off and then lights back on.

But the feeling when I do come back is always the same— like a syringe full of adrenaline right to the fucking heart.

I jerked and gasped and strained against the dull-white Working bonds as I broke the surface of consciousness again. The experience for me was pain—horrible fucking agony— and then no pain at all, and suddenly I could stand up again and there wasn't any smoke.

But the smell was still there, hanging in the air.

The euphoria rolled over me again, too, and I shivered as it wrapped around me like a soft, warm blanket. It felt like a morphine hit, just a wave of pure bliss.

And then it passed, and the world was dull and drab again.

I heard someone retching, but I knew it wasn't me. It was someone behind me because I couldn't see them. Shrike and Shaw were the only ones in front of me, and neither of them were doing it, though Shrike had stepped back and looked as if even she were trying to hold onto her composure.

"How long?" she managed to ask. I noticed that she didn't open her mouth very wide. She was clenching her jaw.

Shaw glanced at a simple brown watch he wore. He seemed entirely unaffected. Well, not negatively affected. He seemed… enthralled. Like a zealot who had witnessed a holy rite.

"Thirty seconds," he said in a hushed, awed tone.

I looked down at myself.

I wasn't blackened and burned—my skin was back, whole and unmarred. I was completely naked, though, because I guess there's no Immortal insurance policy for clothing when it gets consumed in a fire. My tattoos were back, ringing my upper thighs, my wrists and arms, my clavicle, and, I assumed, the one on my back, though I couldn't see it.

And what was more—*everything* had been healed. Because, I assume, my whole body had been burned. Every cut and scrape and bruise I had accumulated over the past few days, hell, every *zit*, was simply gone, replaced with new skin.

"Well, James," Shrike said, taking a step forward. She seemed to have regained fuller control over herself. "That was quite illuminating."

I still couldn't quite put thoughts together. The memory of the pain was still there, like a bright and burning brand in my mind. I was swallowing over and over again, and rocking back and forth. I don't know why. I couldn't stop, though.

"The book," Shrike said, holding out her hand.

The second man, Railsbeck, brought it forward, careful not to touch it but holding it on an open tray like some kind of butler with a delicate biscuit offering.

"Open it and turn the pages," she said quietly. "And you'll have relief."

Man, it was a close thing. Some sliver of triumph at having returned back fully to my body, though, had come into my mind and straightened my spine. I was starting to shiver in the cold since I was now very naked, and my words came out shaking slightly.

"I j-just have one thing to s-say."

She watched me.

"It's c-cold in here, so d-don't judge me too harshly."

She frowned, and then her eyes dipped down and back up.

"M-made you look at it," I said.

Fury boiled up and over her face, and her skin flushed an angry puce.

"Drown him," she said.

Turns out drowning is less painful but much more terrifying. Shaw and Railsbeck grabbed me and tied a plastic bag around my head, then did a simple Working to fill it completely with water. I can remember the terror as my breath slowly ran out. I flailed about and struggled, but there was nothing I could do, and that part was horrible. It wasn't as bad as the flames, though. I don't care what people say, physical pain is worse than psychological pain. I don't care for either, but if you have to choose drowning or being burned alive, I swear to you as someone who went through both, choose drowning.

And that's how I died the fifth time.

I came back even faster that time. I *felt* it. Maybe because there was less damage to repair? I don't know. All I know is that I came back dripping and gasping, and I startled the tall man, Railsbeck, who had only just taken the bag off of my head.

"Shit!" he cried, jumping away.

"Was he fully dead?" Shrike immediately demanded.

"Yes," Shaw said. He was still staring at me with a look that… hell, even just remembering it makes me want to take a thousand showers. I'm willing to bet all I have that he tortured animals as a kid. "He was dead. I felt the spark leave him."

I was beyond feeling surprised at that point, but I do remember taking note of him saying that. I don't know how he could know something like that, but some Workers have weird quirks and talents. I'm fairly certain that he could sense life, and the absence of it.

Shrike gave me the chance to read the book again. I refused.

The cycle repeated itself three more times.

They bled me, that was next. Sixth death in total. I thought I'd already proven that I could come back from that kind of death, given the throat-cutting at the Palace, but Shrike decided to have me fully drained, so I could feel the pain and the coldness of life slowly leaving me, drop by drop. Shaw did that one himself. Very efficiently, slitting the major arteries in my arms and thighs. I came back fairly quickly from that one too, though.

The fourth time (seventh overall) they electrocuted me. Lots of pain. Second place after the fire. My body jumped about and shook like a marionette controlled by a toddler in a windstorm. My joints swelled up and even popped before I finally checked out. Took longer to come back from that one. A full minute, for some reason. I still don't know if there's a rhyme or reason to it.

The fifth time (eighth overall), they took me apart, piece by piece. Dismemberment, I guess, technically. They took my feet first, and then my hands, then my legs, then my left arm—and that was all I could take. I didn't die from blood loss, I don't think—I think it was just the pain. I think my mind just gave out and—poof!—lights out. I came back after they'd put all the pieces back together. Something just kicked in and I was reassembled like a doll with magnetic joints.

By then, I wasn't really aware of what was happening anymore. The recurring pain was so much that it had overloaded every circuit in my brain until there was nothing that I could do but exist between bouts of screaming, hanging suspended in a white-hot void.

"Will you read the book?" Shrike said again.

I just groaned. I barely knew who I was.

She drew her hand back. The violet nail gleamed and extended, razor-sharp.

"You're making me do this, Cicero."

Something about her saying my name brought part of me back.

"I... I..."

She jerked forward and grabbed my head and held me. Her nail glowed in my face, casting everything in my sightline in violet shadow.

"Do it," she hissed in my ear. "Do. It."

I leaned against her, all fine motor control gone and only able to make wild, flaily movements with my limbs.

"Marlowe… told me... he told me something," I said.

A flash of victory lit her face, and she clutched me immediately closer to her, holding me like a lover, my lips to her ear.

"Tell me," she said.

Her grip was like iron.

"He told me," I said, slurring the words. "He told me…"

"Say it!" she barked.

"You… stink… like… week-old fish."

She recoiled and stared at me.

"*Down there*," I finished.

There was a long, extended moment where the words seemed to sink in. I knew that more pain was coming, and I began to whimper and convulse in anticipation of it. I couldn't help it. I wish I could say I was holding on out of noble commitment to my ideals, but it was more primal than that. She was hurting me. So *fuck her.* You know?

The music from above us had grown significantly at that point, and I remembered through my haze that the other woman had said the club would be full soon. Was it time yet? I could feel the chaotic potential, and it had built to a fever pitch. The music was louder, and there must have been a DJ or something, because as I listened there was a beat drop, and then a swell of cheering, and the whole room began to vibrate again with a rhythmic thumping that I would have been willing to bet was the crowd jumping up and down.

Shrike motioned to Shaw.

"Decapitation."

This was different from when I'd been dismembered. This time there was no foreplay. Shaw just stepped right up, raised his Ruiner-encased hand, and summoned a dull off-white blade. I heard Railsbeck move up behind me and felt him grab my hair and pull. Shaw swung, and the Worked blade sliced right through everything.

Turns out they're wrong about being able to keep seeing for the first few seconds after death. Or at least, if I was aware of what happened after my head came away from my body, I don't remember any of it.

I want to make a joke here to lighten the mood. I'm really struggling, though. At least we're through the worst of it.

Because that's the last time I died that night.

I guess they put my head back on my body. I don't know for sure, but, hey, my head is on my body *now* and based on everything that happened that night, it seems like the one real hard-and-fast rule is that only once I'm reassembled do I pop back to consciousness.

In any case, when I came back that time—gasping and shaking like a sinner in church—I came to awareness hearing a new voice, one that was familiar.

"This isn't right," it was saying.

"We need him to consent," said a female voice that wasn't Shrike's. What had the name been? Jennifer? "If he doesn't, if he tries to hold onto it… I don't know. It might not work. Or if it does work it might work in some weird way."

"Just take his hand and make him turn the pages."

"That won't work. He needs to consent to both the pages and the transfer."

"Catalin—this isn't what you said."

"It's exactly what I said, McMillin. Just because you weren't listening doesn't mean I'll stop now. Are you dedicated to this cause or aren't you?"

McMillin. John McMillin, the enforcer.

Shaw, apparently oblivious to the conversation or at the very least entirely disinterested, stepped forward and examined my neck as if looking for a seam, like I was Sally from *The Nightmare Before Christmas* or something. He was breathing heavily, excitedly.

Shrike reappeared, and Shaw retreated, taking notes on a pad of paper. I realized then that the notebook was full of pages with narrow, looping handwriting. He'd been taking notes the whole time, probably between deaths.

"So," I managed to croak. My throat and everything were working fine, but I was severely dehydrated, and that didn't seem to be something that coming back to life had an answer for. I'm not sure what would happen if you tried to starve or dehydrate me to death. Shit, I hope I never find out. But at least in that moment, I'd lost a lot of blood and therefore probably—if I had to estimate—a metric fuck ton of electrolytes. So my tongue was swollen in my mouth and I couldn't seem to work enough moisture into it to speak properly.

"So," I said again. "It seems I've been calling you by the wrong name."

Shrike froze, and I could tell even through my daze that I'd hit something.

Shaw and Railsbeck had frozen too, I realized. I wondered if McMillin was still in the room.

"He was supposed to be out for longer," Railsbeck said before Shrike could reply. He seemed confused, maybe even worried. "He was barely gone."

"He seems to be coming back at shorter intervals," Shaw said, flipping through his notes and eyeing them while alternating glances at Shrike. "Jennifer—do you—?"

"I have the same," said the female voice behind me. I heard something thunk and clunk, like some knob or dial being twisted. "We should be ready for the transfer anytime now. We've probably reached the peak."

"I should go," McMillin said. He *was* still there.

"Thanks for visiting, John," I croaked.

I don't know how he reacted, but I hope I made him jump.

"Ignore him," Shrike said over my head. "We're almost done. One way or the other, we'll start the ceremony soon."

"Are you sure it'll work?" McMillin asked.

Shrike paused for half a second longer than she should have, and I knew what that meant.

"Catalin's worried it won't," I croaked. "Why do you think she's taking all this time trying to make me open the book?"

Shrike strode toward me. Her violet nail flashed and became a razor-sharp talon again. I only saw a flash of it before it disappeared into my shoulder.

"ARGH!" I shouted.

She'd hit bone. You'd think after all the pain she'd forced on me up until then, I'd have been somewhat inured to more. Turns out I wasn't.

"Uh oh," I managed to whimper. "Catalin's *big mad!*"

I must have gone crazy. They say torture reveals your true self. Or something like that. Someone on a TV show I saw said it. Whatever—I think it's true. 'Cause if I had to guess, I'd say my true self is a foul-mouthed asshole who doesn't know when to leave well enough alone.

"Be silent," she snarled at me.

She twisted her hand, and with it the talon. I felt something in my shoulder snap—literally *snap* like a rubber band pulled past breaking point—and jump up my arm. At the same time, something like a lightning bolt ricocheted through my body.

"GAAAH!" I screamed.

"End this," she said. She leaned in closer, sneering in my face, her lips inches away from mine and her eyes as big as a harvest moon, drawing me into them. "You have the power to make this stop. Call me whatever you like. But this will all happen whether you give in or not. The only thing you are doing is prolonging your agony. No one is coming for you. You are trapped here, with me. Your whole world is just me. Me, and pain."

I finally wavered.

After everything, I had no reserves of willpower left. She was the only way out. And even if after she had used me up she decided to kill me… well, that was still an absence of pain.

And I think she saw the change in me. I didn't need to *say* anything. We were practically nose to nose; she could see everything I was going through.

"Bring the book," she said, turning her head just enough to look at Railsbeck and Shaw. One of them hurried to grab it and came forward with it again. She backed away far enough that they could present it right to me.

I stared down at it and thought one last time about escape. But there was no way to make that happen. Looking back, I can't think of what else I would have been able to do. I couldn't Work, trapped as I was in the Circle. I couldn't physically resist, held as I was by the light-ropes. There was nothing I could have done.

"Release his right hand," she said. Railsbeck leaned forward. "No—wait."

She leaned forward again and looked me straight in the eye.

"If you try anything, we will start this all over again," she said softly. "I have nothing else to do tonight except kill you over and over and over again until I get what I want. So, when we release your hand, you aren't going to use one of your tattoos. You aren't going to attempt to free yourself or to fight. You are going to reach down and open this book."

She raised her hand and the violet nail glimmered at me. "And if anything—*anything*—else happens, I will sever your spine before you can say 'immortal'. And I won't kill you. I'll leave you alive long enough for whatever it is that resets your body to dissipate. Until you become naturally crippled. And then I'll leave you like that. Do you understand me?"

I wish I could say that I stood up to her somehow and made one last show of defiance, but I didn't. I didn't have anything left in me.

It all comes back to pain. Pain is… a much more powerful motivator than people know. I sincerely hope that none of you have been where I was. But if you have, then you know how hard it is to hold on to any kind of principles when agony is repeatedly pounding you into the ground. How hard it is to willingly be a martyr. How hard it is when someone offers you a way out to turn it down.

So I gave in. I nodded, and I meant it.

"I understand," I croaked through dry, cracked lips. After several seconds, she nodded, looked me up and down, and motioned to Railsbeck and Shaw. Together, they released part of the Working that had generated the dull off-white rope that still held me bound.

Even with the understanding that I wouldn't Work once I was free, I immediately felt the urge to close my fist and summon flame, or Work a tempest that would break open the whole room, and damn the consequences. But all eyes were on me, that violet talon gleaming like a beacon on Shrike's hand. And I knew I wasn't strong enough to break the Circle.

I was kneeling by that point. When the ropes had disappeared, I had been deposited unceremoniously onto the floor. I was left shaking and shivering, naked and cold. I tried to breathe and keep myself upright without the support I hadn't realized I had begun to rely on.

I reached for the book and touched the cover.

I almost flinched back, my body expecting pain. But it didn't come.

It felt like leather—smooth, aged leather.

Everyone waited as if expecting something to happen, but, when nothing did, Shrike/Catalin came and knelt in front of me, the book directly between us. It felt like we were kids on an afternoon TV special opening a forbidden book in a dark basement away from our stern parents.

"Open it," she said.

I did. There was a simple title page inside, then a blank page, and then the first page, which still looked like gibberish to me but which Shrike and co. had apparently already translated. I breathed out and turned that page.

The next two pages were blank, and I felt my heart thud in my chest. But then, as I watched, black lettering in

Gallimand's unmistakable hand began to scrawl across the page, almost as if he were invisible in the room with us and writing it all that very moment.

"Do it now," Shrike said over my shoulder. I heard movement, and then I finally saw the unidentified Jennifer come into view—bespectacled, with long lank hair, dressed in a flowing shawl-type shirt and loose pants, and overweight in all the ways that Shrike was underweight.

She held up a black book identical to the one I was holding. As writing appeared in the book I held, the same writing began to appear in the book she held.

"Turn the page."

I looked up at her and considered again my options. The nail gleamed. The thought of the pain made my body act before my mind could override it.

I turned the page.

She motioned to Railsbeck and Shaw again and pointed to the Circle. "Ready the ritual," she said. "As soon as it's done, begin the transfer."

Everything was going to happen the way she wanted it to. She would become the Immortal after I did what she wanted. Or if it didn't work, she'd at least have the fully translated book.

God, I was a fucking coward.

But you don't know. You *don't*. Pain like that… pain…

Don't think about me that way. *Don't.*

They put everything in place, and the men got around the circle. I flipped through several more pages for Jennifer, moving mechanically. It was happening faster and faster now. Shaw and Railsbeck took out Ruiners, held them up, and began to chant. I heard another two voices join them and recognized one of them as McMillin's raspy baritone.

The energy from the nightclub above flowed down into the circle, and golden light blossomed. Shrike stepped forward and set herself across from me.

Violet light blossomed inside the gold, and I felt something hit me in the gut like a knife. I gasped in pain, but by then I had been in so much pain that I couldn't judge the magnitude.

The energy swelled. The music above increased in volume, and I knew that they were all feeling it too. We were connected to it now, like in a true bacchanalia ceremony of the ancient world. Some of the Blissful above would die, driven past the point of endurance into exhaustion. It would be explained away. Some of them would get into fights, and some of those fights would be deadly. That would be explained away too. There would be sex—some consensual and some not. All of it would be explained away.

Something in me stirred then. I reached up, trying to grab hold of them. Now that the ceremony was in place, I actually felt like I could *feel* them. Like I could feel Roc and Erica and Anandini and all of the faceless people I didn't know.

Run! I tried to tell them. *Run now!*

But I was so weak. Because it was happening. Whatever it was that had made me immortal was flowing out of me and into Shrike. I could *feel* it draining away from me.

The pages of the book were moving on their own. They were blurring, and we were past the first volume and into the second one.

I could feel myself dying. And it was only then that I realized that if the immortality was removed, my body would fall apart. It was the only thing holding me together. I should be dead half a dozen times over, and the only thing that was keeping me alive was some mystical power from the depths of time that no one seemed to understand.

I panicked at that realization, and my willingness wavered. I tried to pull back.

But Shrike continued to stare at me, and she slowly raised her hands. The music above swelled and the ceiling and the floor and the walls all seemed to shake. The beat dropped again, and people began jumping and screaming.

And then I got lucky. We all got lucky.

Because that was when the cavalry arrived.

PART TWENTY-THREE

READY FOR A FIGHT?

I don't know to this day the exact order of everything that happened next. I've put it all together as best I can, but I know some of this is jumbled. I'm going to tell it to you in the order that makes the most sense to me, and hopefully it's close.

The room went dark, and then blindingly bright. I imagine it's what one might experience standing next to a massive bomb right as it goes off—like the second immediately after the explosion but before the world catches on fire.

I remember kneeling in the circle across from Shrike, and then I remember lying on the ground, off to the side of the room, amid the twisted remains of the desk that the other woman—Jennifer—had been sitting at. There were itching, searing patches on my arms that I realized were burns, and there was something long and excruciatingly painful embedded in one of my legs.

I remember too that the ceiling was suddenly just missing. There was a jagged hole open to the sky, and I could see low-hanging clouds.

I don't know who was shouting or what they were saying, but I do remember that shouting was happening. Screaming, too, from all the people above us in the club.

About a dozen Blissful died. I… I don't know what to say about that.

I feel responsible, at least in part. I'm the reason Marlowe and the others forced their way in, breaking Shrike's Circle in the process. And when the Circle broke, it unleashed the energy contained within it the only way it could: up and out through the source of the chaos.

In the moment, I knew none of that. I knew only that I was burned and speared and slammed up against a wall, and that there was cold air coming in through a suddenly ceiling-less room.

I also didn't know if the ceremony had been completed.

I didn't know if I was still immortal.

I could smell the ozone of Working happening around me—and there were beliefs flying through the air, crackling and sizzling like water splashed on a hot pan. Hands grabbed me; I recoiled and tried to force them away.

"It's OK!" someone shouted in my ear. "It's OK! Hold still! Hold—still!"

I didn't listen, and they decided not to wait for me to do so. I think it was Atticus—because whoever it was just held me down and began to Stitch me. The burns on my arms and the wound in my shoulder scabbed and crusted over; my vision returned, along with most of my hearing; and the long piece of wood or metal or whatever it was in my leg fell to the ground as the gash it had made knitted itself back together. The pain receded but did not disappear entirely, and I could still feel something wrong with my left knee.

I grew cold as the energy needed for the healing drained out of me, and then there was a gout of violet light and Atticus was picked up and thrown away, somewhere across the room.

Full consciousness returned to me in increments of segmented time. I remember flashes of the room, ripped and torn apart; there was a body on the ground; there was blood on me and on the walls, and everything was moving and jerking in fits and starts.

I realized next that I could move—that the explosion that had torn open the room and sent me flying had ripped away the last of the Working that had held me bound with the dull white restraints. I was still naked, and freezing, but I thought I could try to stand.

Pain shot up my left leg and my knee buckled. I fell back to the floor.

"Grab him!" someone shouted. I remember it sounding like Jamal, but I couldn't put thoughts together long enough to understand it actually *was* him. The thought that he—that they—that *anyone*—had come for me was so strange, so completely alien to my understanding, that it simply didn't fit into the spectrum of outcomes I would have considered possible.

"I can't—you—get him!"

More shouts and grunts and flashes of Working from all sides. I sat up, but the world spun around me and I was almost sick.

"Go—go!"

Hands grabbed me—strong hands. They picked me up without much trouble and set me on my feet, and as long as I kept my weight off my left leg, I was able to keep the pain away. I forced myself to focus, and finally I was able to actually *see* what was happening.

Paulina and Kori were back-to-back in a corner, Paulina in the remnants of her long dress, Kori in just her torn black jumpsuit, white coat completely gone. They were fighting Shaw and Railsbeck. Atticus was in another corner standing over another man, one I didn't know and hadn't even realized was in the room, crushing him beneath the weight of a ball of shadow that crackled with indigo lightning. Jamal was the one who had pulled me to my feet, but even as I watched he lunged away from me and engaged with another figure in the basement doorway, someone I thought might be McMillin.

But the main fight was in the center of the room, in the middle of a crater that had appeared directly beneath where I had been held.

Marlowe Frost and Mallory Shrike.

Marlowe had his golden glasses on and was holding his Worker cane. His hands and the cane were flying back and forth, countering bright flares and spurts of violet light from Shrike's claw/nail with flashes of gold and silver. Reality itself seemed to be flickering around them, winking in and out with flashes of sunlight, moonlight, water, fire, air as solid as rock, ground as insubstantial as wind. Their competing beliefs were flying so quickly one after the next that it was almost impossible to follow.

Jamal managed to punch through McMillin's defenses and blast him back out of the basement's entrance, straight into a concrete wall at the end of a long hallway littered with boxes and tables and kegs.

"Let's go!" he shouted into the room. "Come on!"

"Wait," I said. "Wait!"

I managed to stumble forward, toward the center of the room.

Toward the Gallimand book, where I had dropped it in the center of the Circle.

"James—leave it!"

I ignored him. My motions were jerky and half-formed, and I mistimed a step and fell. I managed to turn it into a lunge, thrusting out my arm; my hand landed on the book.

"NO!" Shrike screamed. She leaned back and shouted into the air. The walls seemed to writhe in response, and a crack appeared in the center of the basement as reality tore. From that crack came flashes and jagged bolts of shadow. There was more screaming from above, and the music, which continued to blare and bounce, added an unfortunate soundtrack to everything. I could hear Blissful voices above begging for an exit, and I could see flickering, hungry light that had to be from flames.

The basement room flexed, growing smaller, and then expanded. More crackling and sizzling filled the space, and Shrike again opened a hole to the Space Between Spaces, intentionally tearing reality.

What stepped out of the black gash was nearly ten feet tall. It had large scythes of darkness that curved wickedly down from its wrists, and gnashing teeth in the snarling face of a demon.

It was a Terror just like the one I had met in the house in Hayes Valley. Hell, it might have *been* the one I'd met in Hayes Valley. The same thing that had killed me to start everything off.

The hollow shock of recognition reverberated through me. I remembered the feeling of the scythe-like claw spearing me through the chest, the icy cold pain.

Marlowe stepped forward and cried out in response, throwing his arms wide in a gesture that mirrored Shrike's.

I had never seen Marlowe use his full power. I had always known that he was strong and smart and talented, and a dozen other things besides. But I had never seen him use raw power to accomplish a goal, to fight something or someone.

Golden light flared from him, brighter than the sun. It threw me to the floor, though it didn't burn me. I heard shouts and cries all around the room.

The Terror roared and disappeared, consumed by the light.

A single golden beam separated from the rest and speared Shrike/Catalin through the chest, right through the heart.

For a long moment, everything seemed to hold suspended in time. Shrike stared, eyes horribly wide and disbelieving, at Marlowe. She seemed almost to be accusing him of a betrayal, as if, in spite of everything, she would never have expected him to hurt her.

She fell to her knees and Marlowe stepped forward. His face was horrible—full of righteous anger. He blazed with power. But even as I watched, that anger changed to an expression of deepest sadness. I almost thought he might break down in tears.

"I am so sorry, Catalin," he said quietly. "I never should have placed this burden on you."

He knows her. She wasn't lying.

The golden light winked out, and the spear disappeared from her chest. She sagged, sitting on her knees in a full slouch. The light in her eyes went out.

Marlowe turned to the rest of the room, pulling himself back up to his full height. Shrike's men were all suddenly staring at him with fear. Marlowe gestured once more, and a golden shell of light appeared around him and all of us, separating us from Railsbeck, Shaw, Jennifer, the one additional man Atticus had subdued, and McMillin down the long basement hallway.

"Come," he said quickly. "We must leave."

All of us went to him, staggering and running and hobbling depending on how we'd fared.

I remember very distinctly feeling a moment of elation.

We had made it. We had survived. They had come for me. Marlowe had come for me. Before Shrike had been able to finish the Working to take the immortality away. And now we were going to escape. Marlowe had a plan. He was going to get us out.

And then Shrike's body stirred.

I thought for some reason at first that it was the wind, even though there *was* no wind, not down there in the basement.

Still, I thought that it was the wind that was blowing her clothing, shifting her somehow.

And then she lifted her head.

I felt a moment of unreality. It was impossible.

She breathed, and began to stand.

She was alive.

Shrike/Catalin seemed to radiate pure violet light. It grew, swelled, and then, as we all watched, she seemed to turn, somehow—in a way that made no sense. The Terror that she had summoned before reappeared, pulled back from where Marlowe had sent it with his golden light. The black shadow fused with her; its arm became her arm, and together they turned and became the width of a razor blade and sliced forward.

I saw it in my mind's eye before it actually happened. I threw out my hands and tried to stop it—I Worked a raw, unfiltered belief that roared across the space between us, sharp and silvery as a naked blade, a belief that was solid and could not be pierced.

But I wasn't fast enough. The scythe speared Marlowe through the chest, cutting through him as if he were nothing more than a paper doll. It lifted him into the air, and then he fell.

Shrike/Catalin landed, and stood over him, sneering down. Jamal and Kori and Paulina and Atticus were all shouting. The golden shell of protection broke, winking out of existence, and Catalin's men came forward again, attacking.

In my stupor, my brain caught and focused on things that weren't important, or at least didn't seem like they should be important. A broken sliver of metal from one of the chairs. Cracks in the concrete floor. The broken lines of the Circle Shrike/Catalin had used.

Marlowe was still breathing. He had fallen, and blood was pooling beneath him, but I could see him motioning to me, staring at me.

He was holding out his pocket watch. The watch that was gold even though it should have been bronze.

I reached out and took it. A golden light blossomed in my mind, a sense of Marlowe's presence that came from handling one of his Instruments. And then it became something more, something that I couldn't understand. Because it wasn't just an Instrument. It was… so much more.

A power opened up in me that I couldn't understand. Holding the watch, I felt like I could close my eyes and open them somewhere completely new. I could go anywhere I wanted to. I was held down by nothing.

We found one, Marlowe had said. *One of the Prime Gifts.*

"No!" Shrike/Catalin screamed. "*No!*"

She shot forward, turning once more into a shadow and moving in a way that was entirely unreal. I reacted on instinct—I thrust my open palm at her and released energy through the Muse of Fire tattoo. Flame lanced forward, and I felt the Terror shy away from it, unable to handle the light and the heat. It separated from Shrike/Catalin and retreated, still attached to her like a second shadow, and she stumbled as its momentum counteracted her own.

I then touched the black ink along my collarbone.

There are more things in Heaven and Earth,
Horatio, than are dreamt of in your philosophy.

More sizzling and crackling and another hole appeared— another hole ripped in the fabric of reality that looked out onto a yawning black abyss.

I raised my left hand with the tempest Working and unleashed raw wind and lightning at the Terror. Shrike/Catalin was pulled backward, anchored to Terror as she was. A violent wind came from the portal, and a sucking like air rushing out the emergency door of an airborne plane.

She fought against it, fought to keep both herself and the Terror she had bound herself to out of the nothingness that was the Space Between Spaces.

"You thought you were the only one with tricks?!" I shouted at her.

I grabbed a tighter hold of the pocket watch Marlowe had handed me and turned back to him. He was ashen pale, and the pool of blood under him had grown. He looked up at me, with eyes that were starting to glass over. He nodded quickly, seeing the realization in my eyes.

"No," I said. "No! It's tied to you, if I use it—"

Marlowe grabbed me with a supreme effort of will. "I'm already dead," he said with a small, weak voice. "Use it to save the others and you'll claim it. It'll be yours."

He closed his hand around mine, and around the pocket watch. I stared into his eyes for a second longer than I should have, especially considering we did not have seconds to waste.

I bared my teeth, brought my full force of will to bear, and pushed my belief into the watch.

There was a flash of light, a rushing sound, and golden light suffused me. I mentally reached out to Jamal, Paulina, Kori, and Atticus, swept them up in the Working like a mother gathering in rowdy children.

Shrike/Catalin was shouting still, screaming for the others to grab me, to not let me go. I lodged the black book tightly under my arm. I stood and faced her.

I held up my middle finger.

Everything dissolved into golden light.

PART TWENTY-FOUR

PICKING UP THE PIECES

We appeared with a flash in the middle of Marlowe's library.

The Gift's spacial translation may have been perfect, but my use of it apparently hadn't been, because we all arrived several inches off the floor.

Marlowe, who had already been lying down—and me kneeling over him—fell the shortest distance, straight onto the thick carpet laid in the middle of the room.

My left knee, still torn or twisted or who knew what, hit first, and I shouted in pain and rolled onto my back. I heard various other thumps and cries of pain all around me, and I was able to realize that everyone had made it. Jamal had landed on a desk, cracking his hip, and was standing up against a wall cursing under his breath; Paulina and Kori were both in the middle of a now-overturned pile of books and were helping each other to their feet; Atticus was tangled in one of the curtains and trying to extricate himself.

I pushed my pain away—manageable as long as I wasn't putting any weight on my knee—and noticed that there was gray light coming in through the windows. It was almost dawn. I had to have slipped in time as well as space while 'porting. Probably out of habit. I had never 'ported multiple people before—much less multiple people out of a crumbling basement without a park or alleyway to assist me—and never without exchanging time for space. If we'd been lucky enough to only burn a few hours, then the pocket watch Gift was worth a hundred times its weight in gold Guild coins even if I couldn't make it work perfectly.

Almost as I had the thought, I became aware that there was a burning pain in my hand. I winced and opened my fist, dropping the watch to the floor. There was a round burn on my palm, but the watch itself remained whole and was still ticking away. The burn was bad, but, compared to everything else I had gone through that night, the pain almost didn't register.

Marlowe's eyes were closed, and his lips were slightly open. He could have been sleeping. I touched his neck, feeling for a pulse that I knew wasn't there. His skin was still warm. His gold-rimmed glasses were still remarkably in place on the bridge of his nose, but two thin cracks ran through the circular panes of glass. His chest was still.

"No—no!"

Kori had caught sight of Marlowe. She ran forward and pushed me aside. I went easily, rolling onto my good leg. As I did, I realized that I was still naked, something that I'd almost forgotten about down in the basement. I covered myself as best I could.

Atticus, finally extricating himself from the curtains, ran to Marlowe as well, his glasses flaring briefly with light as he examined the body with a Stitcher's eye.

He held his hand over the older man for a long moment, and then pulled back.

"He's dead," Atticus said softly.

"No!" Kori insisted. "Bring him back—shock him, start his heart!"

But Atticus was shaking his head, and I think even Kori knew it wouldn't work.

Someone came up behind me and draped something heavy over my shoulders, startling me. I was jumpy as all hell, my body still expecting pain from every physical interaction, but the big heavy blanket wasn't painful. Jamal came into view, watching me with concern. I swallowed and managed to nod to him, and then I pulled the blanket more fully around my shoulders to cover myself, though my legs below the knee still stuck out, and my bare ass was against the thick patterned rug.

Atticus came to me next, seeing my leg. He knelt down quickly, and this time managed to complete the Stitching job he had started back in the basement. The knee popped and twisted, and I gasped as the pain first flared then faded.

He held a hand out to me, and I took it. He and Jamal helped me stand.

"How did it happen?" Paulina asked, looking stunned. "I didn't see—I was… what did—?"

"Shrike," I said. My voice was still a croaking mess, but I was able to get the word out. "He called her Catalin. But her. She speared him right through the chest. And then he…"

I gestured to the pocket watch on the floor, words failing.

"He gave it to you?" Jamal asked.

I nodded. "He said he was dying. He said if I used it to save you all I would claim it."

"We didn't even know it was working until we were in the basement," Atticus said. "We all met outside the Palace, trying to figure out what to do, and he had it."

"I thought he said it didn't work?" I asked.

"It didn't," Jamal said. "But he pulled it out and had us all concentrate on it, and then he said, 'Help us save the Immortal,' and it started ticking. And then—flash, we're in— wherever that was, and you're there and…"

"He was still connected to it when he gave it to you," Paulina said. "And when you used it—"

"You fucking killed him," Kori snarled, turning on me.

I wouldn't have thought I had the ability to feel any more that night after everything I had gone through, but those words hit something deep. Before I knew what was happening, I had stepped forward to meet her. She reached for her sleeve, going for her wand, and my pain-soaked brain registered her as a threat.

I held up both hands. One of the drawbacks of my tattoos is that they aren't as flexible as more traditional conduits—they just do what they do.

But they are a *lot* faster.

Fire and wind shot from my palms and struck Kori in the chest. Unlike what had happened to Shrike's enforcer in the hallway at the Palace, she didn't explode. Her ring activated, keeping her safe, but the impact threw her across the room straight into one of the bookshelves.

"Stop it!"

"Cicero!"

Kori struggled to rise again, anger now warring with pain on her face.

I threw all the energy I had into my tattoos. The black writing came to life with a crimson flash, and the words thrummed with fierce belief that I was in danger and needed to protect myself. I snarled at Kori and held out both palms straight at her.

"DON'T YOU FUCKING DARE!" I shouted.

I was shaking. I know now that I was in deep shock and minorly hallucinating. In the moment, I was convinced that Kori was just like Shrike, and that she was going to hurt me like Shrike had.

But what pulled me out of it was the look on Kori's face. She was staring at me with real fear. It was only there for a moment, but it was enough. It probably saved her life.

"STOP IT!" Paulina shouted, lunging forward to place herself between us. "Stop, it's not—"

"I didn't ask you to come for me," I said. "I DIDN'T ASK!"

"Of course we came for you," Jamal said, like I was talking nonsense. I rounded on him, snarling like an animal.

"Hey!" he barked, holding up a hand. "Enough!"

I stayed where I was, pulse pounding loudly in my ears.

"I get it," he said. "I get it. You just went through hell. But you're out of it now. You're here. You're back at Marlowe's place. We're safe here. We—"

There was a faint *pop*, and a blue flare of sapphire light entered the room, resolving into the form of Calliope.

"What on earth is going on?" she demanded, her musical voice ringing loudly and out of all proportion to her diminutive size.

Her eyes lighted on Marlowe's body.

I had the irrational urge to jump in front of her and hide him, even though I knew she'd already seen. It felt more real if more people saw, and so I irrationally wanted to keep everyone from seeing—especially her.

"No," she whispered.

That was all. She said it and then she seemed to wilt. She slowly dropped down and came to rest on his shoulder. She held out a thin arm and gently touched his cheek. She sat there, ignoring the rest of us, and began to cry.

My eyes slid from his body to the ancient black leather book lying beside him. Gallimand's Works, where I had dropped it after 'porting.

"Well, let's find out what all of this was for."

I strode forward, grabbed the book, and held it up. Everyone froze, staring at me.

There was a brief sensation of warmth in my fingertips, almost like a welcoming, as if it recognized me—and it was only then that the thought crossed my mind that if Shrike was now immortal, I might not be.

I knew that the plan had been for her to take the immortality from me. I knew that she had done enough of the Working to transfer it at least partially to herself. But did that mean that I was mortal again? Had the arrival of the others broken the Working off soon enough? Was I still…?

The book fell open.

I breathed a shaky sigh of relief.

It wasn't as clear a sign as if I'd died and come back again, but after everything I'd seen that night, I was willing to trust, at least provisionally, the book's judgment.

Shrike and I were *both* immortal now.

Trying not to think about the implications of that, I opened the cover and looked down at the first page. It was still in the coded language that I had seen in the basement, but as I stared at the words, they began to shimmer, and a new page unfurled and appeared from nowhere. Paulina gasped, and Atticus muttered something under his breath. Letters appeared on the page, at first indecipherable. Then they slowly flipped over, writhing, and became English letters.

"How are you doing that?" Atticus asked, looking over my shoulder.

I shook my head. "I don't think I am."

The handwriting was different than I had come to expect. It still seemed to have been written by the same author, but it was strangely… jerky. Almost as if the hand that had so carefully written in the cramped, meticulous style of the other pages was now writing several years later, and much faster.

As the words became legible, I read them aloud.

I hesitate as I write this, and my hand wavers.

This is the second run of this my collected Works, and as such I felt it appropriate to add this short introduction. If you are reading it now, then you have proven yourself to be one of those whom I can trust. You may wonder how I know—and that, too, shall I provide answers to in these Works. I have learned to be cautious. I have learned that lesson to my peril. But this shall I leave you, and shall I leave posterity. For the Cycle shall repeat, over and over, if we are successful in what we do hereafter.

The world was not ready for what I wrote when first I put together these pages. I do not think it is ready yet. In my mind, this only further proves what I already find self-evident—that the Fourth Season is upon us, and that the Cycle of my time is coming to a close.

The Eternal Cycle is not academic, no more than it is academic to state that there is a force that holds us to the earth and a force that holds the stars in the sky. No more than it is academic to insist that there are seasons in nature. There are seasons in us, and there are seasons in history, and there are seasons in the Cycle, though they do not run by a standard set of mortal years.

To you who read this now, please know that I have done what I could to keep this safe, and that the words you read are my best attempt to set down my knowledge. I may be wrong. I have endeavored to make it clear when I know something to be true and when I am working through inference and hypothesis. But I believe. And I hope you do too.

I looked up and saw that everyone was listening to me intently. I turned the page, and there was the first page that we had seen at the Palace, headed with the same title and written in the same handwriting I had come to expect, from the apparently younger Gallimand. It too had translated itself into English.

The Eternal Cycle
Works Volume 1

In these collected Works, I, Gaius Gallimand, shall endeavor to set down what I know of the Eternal Cycle. These words and the studies they reference I consider the crowning achievement of my life, and the most important thing I will ever do.

Let us begin with a definition: The Eternal Cycle is the cycle by which the world has and always will remake itself. It has no beginning and no end. It has repeated since the beginning of the world and shall continue until its end, in one of its many shifting forms.

In an effort at understanding, this author shall employ a metaphor, namely that of the seasons, that has proved to be most helpful.

As every year begins with spring, so too does every Cycle begin with a time of flowering. This is a time of rebirth and regrowth, where the destruction that led to the end of the previous cycle is turned to fertile soil for new life, hope, and optimism. The first season is often a time of birth and reclamation, of art and flourishing.

The second season, the summer, is an expansion of the mind and a sowing of seeds—the flourishing of technology, and the expansion of man's miracles, helped by the silent hand of the Worker that has ever guided it, making sure it flies like an arrow, straight and true.

"The silent hand of the Worker?" Kori interrupted.

The meaning behind that phrase slowly sank in.

"He's talking about Workers manipulating society," Atticus said. "Guiding it. That's… illegal. Not just illegal, it's completely prohibited. The Compendium says it has been prohibited by tradition if not direct law for hundreds of years now. It's one of the foundational principles of the Code."

"The Compendium can be changed," I said slowly. "What if it has been? Can we trust it?"

"Not trusting it fully is different from questioning the founding premise entirely," Atticus said, looking uneasy. "It can't just be edited by anyone. It's not a Worker version of Wikipedia. It requires official approval through trusted Worker sources."

"Like the Workers of America?" I asked darkly.

The realization of what I was saying seemed to fall over the rest of the gathered group like a dark haze. If they could change the Compendium, what else could they do?

Jamal shook his head. "Keep reading."

I did.

> The third season is as autumn. It is the reaping season—the time of great harvest, of the fruit of both good and evil. This is heralded by a time of great sorrow and great happiness. Events of joy and devastation follow in equal measure, and in the reaping is collected the seeds of destruction that will eventually bring the Cycle to a close.
>
> And the fourth season, winter, is the time of change and endings. It is when societies shake and reality begins to crack. War, famine, disease, and death ride forth. The wheel of the seasons itself begins to grind to a halt, and from this season springs the Immortal, he or she who comes to set the wheel turning anew.
>
> Or who may choose to break it.
>
> And against the Immortal shall be arrayed the might of the Beyond, which seeks to break the wheel. Against the Immortal too shall be forces that reach out to corrupt all that they touch in an effort to bend that which cannot be bent. Old beliefs shall manifest—monsters, gods, and devils—and once more touch the Mortal World. Order shall fall away and chaos

shall reign, and only the Immortal and the Gifted shall stand a chance to restore balance.

The Gifted shall open the path, and the Immortal shall tread it. To the Space Beyond Spaces, to the Eternal at the Center of Time.

I reached the end of the page and stopped reading.

"The immortal isn't the beginning of a cycle," Kori said slowly.

"It's the end of one," Jamal finished.

"And when the Cycle ends, there's a chance to remake the world," I said, rereading. "That's what Shrike said. It's what she wants. She knows all of this, she translated this page. She wanted the rest of the book to know for sure, and to find out how to get there. To the… Space *Beyond* Spaces. She kept talking about it. She's obsessed with remaking the world."

"Keep reading," Atticus said. "Let's hear more."

I swallowed and turned to the next page… and saw that it was blank.

I looked up.

"What is it?" Jamal asked.

I turned the book around and showed them the blank pages. I flipped through several more. All blank. I flipped to the end, and there was nothing but a list of Gallimand's other volumes. I flipped back through again and saw chapter titles— the seven Volumes—along with various sub-chapter headings. But all the pages beneath them were blank.

"That doesn't make any sense," I said. "The pages were revealing themselves in the basement. I *saw* them—the whole first chapter filled out, and the second one was filling out too!"

"He built in protections," Atticus said. "He even says it again in that introduction he added. The pages must require a key to unlock them. Something that was present in the basement, maybe. They must be in the book, if you saw them unlock, we just can't see them. Perhaps if we—"

I shut the book with a snap and threw it to the floor. It landed next to Marlowe's body.

Marlowe's *body*. Marlowe was *dead*.

Calliope's blue form was still resting on his shoulder. Silent tears were coming down her translucent cheeks. Where they fell, they created tiny blue ripples in the air that slowly faded away to nothing.

Atticus had his hand reached out for the book, but he did not appear to want to go near Marlowe's body.

"Not now," I told him. "If there's some key, then we'll figure it out later."

"Surely it's important," Atticus said. "We should—"

"NOT FUCKING NOW!" I roared, rounding on him. My words bounced around the room, amplified, and seemed to hang in the air far longer than they should have.

A beat of tense silence.

"We have work to do," Jamal said after a moment. "His death will be noticed. We can't give anyone reason to investigate it."

"What are you saying?"

"Leave it to me," Kori said. "Hobb and I will set it up. It'll look like an accident."

"It has to be soon," Jamal said. "The longer we wait the more suspicious it—"

"You aren't talking about this right now. You aren't seriously talking about this right now."

It was Paulina who had spoken. She stood up from where she had been sitting. The tattered remnants of her dress still clung to her, and she had scrapes and cuts and blossoming bruises all over her. She looked like an Amazonian warrior.

Except for the tears—which were streaming down her face with abandon.

"We *have* to talk about it," Jamal said. "It has to be dealt with now so that the Order stays intact and secret. This was always bigger than any one of us."

"The Order?" I asked.

I caught Atticus motioning to me out of the corner of my eye—shaking his head and his hand to tell me that now wasn't the time.

"He lost his life chasing after that goddamn book, and it was *useless!*" Paulina said, her words ending in a scream on the final word. Her face had crumpled in on itself, and she was shaking. "It was completely fucking *useless!*"

"It is not useless," said a voice. "It is a starting place."

We all whirled around.

Standing in the library doorway was Marlowe Frost.

PART TWENTY-FIVE

MARLOWE 2.0

"Marlowe," Paulina gasped. "I—Marlowe!"

She stepped forward, as if she were about to run to him, but Jamal stepped sharply in front of her.

"Wait," he said. "That's… it's a memograph."

We all looked back at the new Marlowe, and he shimmered as if in response to Jamal's words. He looked entirely real, down to the color of his gold-rimmed glasses and the perfect lines of his pressed slacks.

"You are correct," the memory of Marlowe said. "I… wish I were with you. I do not know what happened in the end, but I know that since I am here, and I see my… body on the floor… it would appear that the worst has come to pass."

"I don't… what is happening?" Kori asked, staring around with wide eyes as if she—quite literally—had seen a ghost.

I had much the same question. The more I looked at the version of Marlowe standing in the doorway, though, the more I realized he was different. He was much closer to who I had known in life, specifically in my youth. He was no longer in his late sixties but back in the prime of his fifties. He was stronger, he stood taller. He still wore his slate gray hair short and combed back, and he still had gold-rimmed spectacles perched on his delicate scholar's nose, but there was a vitality to him that I hadn't realized had waned as much as it had.

I also noticed that he floated slightly—his feet did not touch the floor, but instead rested an inch or two above it, encased in his usual smart shoes with their brogue pattern.

"A memograph is the physical imprint of a memory," Atticus said. "Incredibly difficult to achieve, and it can only be done with a—pardon me—shit load of planning. Any memories he considered important he would have had to implant in this figure one at a time. It is traditionally only activated upon the death of the Worker who sets it."

A memory flashed through my mind—Marlowe coming downstairs earlier that morning. Looking as if he hadn't slept.

"All of that is true," said the memory. It even had Marlowe's mannerisms, holding his hands behind his back as he spoke, dropping his chin so that he could peer over the top of his glasses. "I will be here as long as the Working that created me stays in place, anchored to these walls. As long as this house stands, and as long as it is owned by a member of the Order, I shall be here, unless dismissed."

There was a long pause then, and everyone's wheels started turning.

"Who owns the house now?" Jamal asked. "Did you… is there a will? Is it here?"

The memory Marlowe nodded. "Yes. I know that there is a will, and that once my death is known and officiated, it will be actioned in accordance with my wishes. I do not, however, know the contents of that will. They seem to have been hidden from me by myself."

"What does that mean?"

"It means Real Marlowe didn't put all of his memories into Memory Marlowe," Paulina said. She had stopped crying, but she still looked the most outwardly devastated. Her golden-tan skin had an almost gray tinge to it, almost sickly.

"Why not?" I asked.

"I am not here to be Marlowe," the image said. He had a small, sad smile on his face. "We are not meant to stay behind in this world after death. When our time comes, we must move on. Not just for ourselves, but for those we love."

I thought about what that meant for me, and Memory Marlowe seemed to sense what I was thinking. "You have been given a gift, Cicero," he said. "But it was given to you and not to me. I am certain that the woman known as Mallory Shrike will have told you differently. Yes, I remember the fight. I remember much of this evening, it would appear, save for… how it ended. I must have thought there was a chance this would happen and prepared for the worst. And now that I have seen her… I know who she is. Who she was. But it is important that you understand this—I was not meant to live on. I am not immortal. You are, Cicero. I know not why— perhaps I did in life, I cannot say. But your time will come eventually, too, when your purpose has been lived. It is part of life to die."

"So you're really gone," I said.

The memory nodded sadly. "Yes, my boy. I am so sorry."

I was emotionally spent by then, and there was nothing I could do. I felt like I should be crying like Paulina and Calliope, but I just couldn't.

"The Order," I said. "Tell me about it."

My words sank into the silence with a big metaphorical "plop", like a massive stone thrown into a pond. It rippled through each of them, but no one said anything. Paulina looked at Marlowe's body, then at his memory. Jamal sighed heavily and sat down in a chair. Atticus became suddenly very interested in cleaning his glasses. Kori went stony-faced again.

"Look, you said I'd know about it after all of this was over. Well, the job happened. And I got tortured. And killed. And dragged through space and time. And my oldest friend is *dead* now. So if this group is about fighting Shrike and everything we just saw tonight—then I'm fucking *in*. So *tell* me, goddammit!"

I only realized that I was shouting again after the words were out. I realized that I was shaking, too, my hands balled into fists and quivering. I felt lightheaded, as if I'd taken too many breaths too quickly and there was too much blood rushing through my body.

The others were all looking at me in alarm. Even Kori's hard demeanor had cracked.

"He's right," Jamal said, breaking the silence. "He's right." He turned to look at Paulina, who returned his steady gaze with one of her own.

"With everything we saw tonight," Jamal continued, "we need all the help we can get. And Marlowe trusted him. Hell, he's the only reason we got the book out of there in the end anyway. He grabbed it."

"What did Marlowe think?" I asked the memograph.

"I am sorry," Memory Marlowe said. "I was given no opinion on the matter. I can share that I cared for you deeply—and that I trusted you. As I trusted everyone in this room. I can share as well that I thought you were important."

The others took this in and nodded.

"Are there more out there?" I asked the memory. "More like Shrike. Catalin. The people with her."

"Yes," Memory Marlowe said, his expression darkening. "Catalin is the first among many. She is a powerful foe, but she represents only one of several distinct threats. All are dangerous, and all seek power."

"Power to do what?" I asked.

"In short," Paulina said, gesturing to the book, "to break the world and then remake it. And break you and us and any other Worker that stands in their way."

A memory came to me. "When she was… when she had me. She talked about ruling the Blissful. She talked about remaking the world so that Workers could… take their rightful place."

Paulina nodded. "There is a growing faction of Workers that see the world as Workers vs. Blissful. They see the world as dark and dangerous for Workers, and full of restraints on our power that hold us back. They say we deserve freedom. That the Blissful are too numerous and ruining the world. Starting wars and releasing viruses… it's hard to argue with them sometimes. It's flawed reasoning, but the emotional appeal is strong. We aren't superior just because we're Workers. But… it's seductive."

All the news of the world seemed to filter to the top of our collective consciousness. If you're reading this close to when I'm writing it, which I really hope you are, you have an idea of what was happening in the world that we were thinking about.

"That's what Gallimand is talking about, isn't it?" I asked. "Things are starting to come apart. In the world. For both Workers and Blissful."

"It appears that way," Paulina said.

"Right. So what's the Order? What does it do?"

"It was founded by Marlowe," Paulina said, glancing at the memory. He nodded, encouraging her to continue. "And… me." She looked around at the others, all of whom seemed suddenly surprised. "I haven't been entirely truthful with you all, and I'm sorry. I haven't just known Marlowe for a few months. I've known him for several years."

There was an appropriate moment of reorientation after that announcement.

"Too many secrets," Kori muttered angrily. "Too many fucking secrets."

"This is cards-on-the-table time," Paulina said quickly. "Marlowe's dead. Everything I know and everything I know he knew, I'll share it. If not now, over the next few days."

She took a fortifying breath and waited for any other protestations. When none came, she continued, slightly breathlessly.

"The movement Shrike represents is newer, but it has been growing for several months, capitalizing on the growing anti-Blissful sentiment among Workers. She's been organizing them—well, we didn't know it was Shrike. We knew her from before… as Catalin. We didn't know she'd infiltrated the WA. We didn't know any of that. But Catalin has been organizing, finding people who believe what she does. But they're fighting against a third side, which everyone but Cicero knows about. A side that calls themselves 'Cry Havoc'."

"I—what?" I asked.

"A group of powerful Workers and Blissful working together," Jamal said. "It's only been rumored officially, but I saw it firsthand, too, a few months ago. That's what brought me in."

"Working *together*?"

"Yes," Paulina said.

"On *what*?"

"On bringing chaos to the world," Kori said. "You know—wreaking havoc."

I started to protest, because it sounded like something out of a Dan Brown novel about Illuminati and secret societies, but something stopped me. I blinked, thinking, and a series of what I'd thought to be isolated events suddenly fell together to form a single coherent picture.

The stylized monogram I'd been seeing around SF. The carved and graffitied symbols… with the initials CH at their center. The candle in the Painted Lady that had summoned the Terror. The graffiti in the Tenderloin, next to the tent city. The vandalized seat on the bus on my ride to Marlowe's, where I'd sat bloody and coughing and no one had cared. The card from the Palace stuck in the door that hadn't wanted to open.

"They're here, aren't they?" I asked. "In SF."

Everyone's attention focused on me even more intensely.

"They are," Paulina said. "Why do you ask?"

I slowly reached up and flourished my hand, reaching into my vault. I pulled out the card I'd found at the Palace, the one that had made me feel strangely tired.

Everyone reacted immediately. They recoiled, and I couldn't blame them. I could feel the Working on it, still, and the wrongness of it. It felt the same way it had at the Palace of Fine Arts.

I'd died several times since then, though. That changes a person. And this time I took a good hard look at it.

The card itself was the same as it had been in the Palace—black and silver, with strange patterns on both sides made of sweeping lines. The Working on it wasn't complicated. I'd never seen anything quite like it, but it was simple enough. And it wasn't making me tired, I realized. It was making me feel… sad. Defeated.

The swirling markings began to shift. They coalesced into the same sharp, angular symbol I had been seeing across the city. The stylized 'CH'.

I held it out to Paulina.

"Whoever they are, they were at the Palace tonight," I said. "I've been seeing this symbol all over the city. This symbol was at the house with the Terror that killed me, too. And this card was in a door that wouldn't open. Like they'd put it there intentionally to keep me from getting through."

Paulina swallowed nervously, and then determinedly stepped forward and took the card from me. She shuddered as she touched it, and I couldn't blame her. She looked at it for a long moment, at the stylized monogram that I now knew stood for Cry Havoc. She flourished her hand and it disappeared; I didn't know where she had decided to store it, but I hoped it was somewhere safe.

The pressure in the room dissipated. I felt lighter, and the dark tint my thoughts had taken on slowly faded.

"So that's who we're really fighting," I said quietly.

"Yes," Paulina said.

"Hobb's men," Kori said suddenly. We all looked at her. "I've worked with Hobb for a while now. He's loyal once he's paid. He seemed legitimately surprised—and angry—that those men on his crew turned on us. But they also clearly weren't with Shrike."

"They were surprised to see me," I said suddenly, remembering. "That card—the card reader to get me into the loading bay wouldn't work at first. I had to force it. And then that card was in the doorway when I opened it. And it was keeping me from getting to Hobb and his men. They could have easily set it."

"Do you think…?"

"They were there tonight," Paulina said quietly. "Havoc was at the Palace and we had no idea."

My exhausted mind tried to break down this new revelation but simply couldn't do it. It was too much—one thing too many with which to come to terms.

"They can be anyone," Kori said. "Havoc can be anyone."

"Mass chaos doesn't just help the powerful," Jamal said.

The words rang true. Shrike's rantings in the basement came back to me. She knew about Havoc. She'd known the whole time.

Kings and queens of the rubble…

"What about the Separation?" I asked. "The Blissful aren't supposed to know about Workers."

"Aren't *supposed* to," Jamal said.

"Money and moral relativism get around a lot of 'supposed tos' these days," Kori said.

"Then why don't you bring it to the WOTW?"

"No hard proof," Jamal said grimly. "We've been trying to build a case, but it always ends up like this. We don't even know Havoc is there until it's all over."

"Well, what… what are they doing right now?"

"Sowing seeds of chaos all over the world," Paulina said. "Havoc are in a dozen major cities in America alone. Another dozen across the world."

"And Shrike is one of them?"

"No," Paulina said. "No, she's fighting them."

"*Fighting* them? Aren't *you* all fighting them?"

"I didn't get it at first either," Jamal said. "Think about it like X-men. Marlowe's Professor X and Catalin—Shrike—is Magneto. Cry Havoc are the people who hate all mutants."

"Oh," I said.

"I didn't quite follow that," Paulina said, confused, "but Shrike wants to take *everyone* out and remake the world with the Workers on top. Marlowe always thought there was a better way. That we could do it without killing, that we could fight back on our own terms."

Jamal nodded and gave me a significant look. "X-men," he mouthed silently.

"The Order," Paulina said, "was Marlowe and me trying to organize against Havoc. It was before we knew anything about Gallimand or the book or any of it. We've been… slow. We're behind in the race. We only made things official and started actively recruiting once we knew about the book and read the first few pages we'd found in the Gifts volume. There are only a few dozen of us, including everyone in this room."

"And when you found the pages," I said slowly, "Shrike was still working with you?"

Paulina nodded. "She was. But her name is Catalin. Catalin Moss. She was the one who worked out the criteria for the list of Immortals. Marlowe trusted her with it. And she brought him the list and her name was on it. She was convinced that it had to be her, that she was the best choice. She wanted Marlowe to Raise her to make it happen."

More pieces fell into place.

"But that's not how it works," I said. "She thought he'd finally done it to me, given in. But you can't start the cycle that way, Raising is something else entirely."

"Apparently," Paulina said. "At least that's what Marlowe believed. That we couldn't force the Immortal, the world would generate him or her when the time came."

She glanced at Memory Marlowe.

He nodded. "My memories on this are quite clear," the image said. "We all thought it possible that Raising could start the cycle, but I always had doubts. I thought it too crude, too… inelegant. But Ms. Moss was convinced. She wanted to be Raised, and she was convinced it would make her the Immortal. And she was a strong candidate. Perhaps the strongest, from a certain perspective. Talented, dedicated, intelligent. But her ambition… it always worried me. And made me doubtful."

"How come none of you recognized her?" I asked.

"Marlowe recruited Jamal, Atticus, and Kori after she left," Paulina said. "We told everyone about her, about what she did, but Marlowe and I were the only ones who knew her. And, seeing her tonight… she's changed. She's lost a ton of weight, that haircut and color is completely new… and I have no idea where that talon conduit came from. Even when she was here, though, she was always pushing for us to be more radical, but Marlowe was able to rein her in. When he refused to Raise her, though, it pushed her over the edge. She left. Somehow Jacob Luis knew what it meant before we did. He barred all entries to her, and that was the first clue. We lost track of her, but somehow it seems she's made it into the WA. She's… fanatical. Driven. Extremely capable. She'll stop at nothing to do what she thinks is right, and what she thinks is right is remaking the world into her version of a utopia, and crushing anyone and anything that gets in the way of that."

A moment of silence.

"And now she's immortal too," I said softly.

"Are we sure?" Atticus asked.

"I'm sure," I said. "I felt it. We all saw it."

Silence again.

I found myself staring at Marlowe's body. "Shrike said there was a lot he wasn't telling us." I looked up at the rest of them. "Maybe there was."

I looked past them at Marlowe's ghost, who looked back at me openly and without pretension. If it knew more secrets, it was not sharing them, at least not without being prompted.

"It comes down to if we trust him or not," I said to the others, turning to look at them. "Do we trust that what he did he did for reasons that made sense, to him at least? Do we trust that this path he put us on is the right one?"

They all seemed to take my point seriously and consider it. Lots of furrowed brows and intense staring.

"Because I just died a bunch of times tonight and I'm still here. So the whole immortality part is real, at least. And the crazy bitch who did it to me really was raving about remaking the whole world. Destroying the world, really. Cleansing it.

And now she's immortal too, and she has at least some of the same book that we do since she was making a copy. And we know the Gifts are real because we just used one, so if she collects them and finds out how to get to wherever it is the Immortal is supposed to go, then…"

I stopped and took a deep breath. Even Calliope, who still remained silent, was watching me now. I swallowed again.

"So. Do we trust Marlowe?"

A longer pause. At least a whole two or three minutes.

"I do," Paulina said finally. "Even the things he kept from me, he told me eventually when I needed to know. He always had the right intentions."

That seemed to prompt Atticus.

"I feel the same," he said. "I never expected him to tell us everything. Everyone has secrets. But he always told me what I needed to know when I needed to know it."

Jamal and Kori both seemed to struggle harder against the question, and it was another minute before they responded.

"Fine," Kori said. "Yes."

"I think," Jamal said, "I choose to believe he had good intentions."

"And one of those intentions," Paulina said smoothly, "was for Cicero to officially join us."

I looked over at her, and then around at the rest of them.

"Any objections?" I asked, somewhat wryly and somewhat wearily. Even I have a hard time keeping things jovial when there's a dead body on the floor.

Everyone shook their heads. Special attention landed on Kori, since it was she who had officially rejected me the last time. She stared at me, long and hard.

"Better to have him on our team than not," she said finally.

"A ringing endorsement," I muttered. Atticus gave me a small smile—as much of one as he could muster, at least.

"OK," Paulina said. She turned to me fully and asked in a very official kind of way, "Cicero James, will you join us?"

The answer seemed obvious, all things considered.

"What do I have to do?"

"Just say yes," Paulina said. "And then we'll have you swear an oath in Marlowe's Circle downstairs."

I nodded. "Then 'yes'. But one question—is it just 'the Order'? Or is it the Order of something?"

Paulina blinked.

"Oh. Right. Yeah, it's—"

"It's the Order of the Magi," Kori said.

Part Twenty-Six

We Have a Chance

I'm writing this to you… five days after that scene in Marlowe's library. I think. Yeah, five. I haven't slept much since I started writing, which was… three days ago, I think. Wow. Day two AM—After Marlowe.

I'm back at my place, though I don't know how long I'm going to stay here. With everything that's been happening, the others have all practically been living at Marlowe's. I came back here for silence and concentration, but I'm heading back as soon as I send this out. If nothing else, I'm probably going to need to split my time between here and there now.

That's the story, though. A few loose ends to tie up:

You may have seen the club explosion on the news. It wasn't reported as what it actually was, of course. The official story is that it was a mass shooting and a homemade bomb. Unfortunately, all too believable in the current world climate. There were fifteen Blissful who died, and the city is in an uproar.

Roc, Erica, and Anandini all made it out safely.

Anandini's already invited me to get a drink at Alchemist to tell me about it. We were friends before the benefits, and she's always been a talk-to-process kind of person, like me. I don't think any of her friends died, but… hell, I guess I'll find out.

I reached out to Erica, and she responded a whole day later, which worried the hell out of me. Said she'd see me at the office and that she was fine. The message was short, and I wanted to ask more, but I didn't.

Roc is rebounding in his own way. He texted me a Statue of Liberty emoji the very next night, which is how he brags about getting lucky. He won't want to talk about things, but I can tell by the way he went out hard the next few nights—he posted stories on his social media—that it got to him. He's trying to drown it all in booze and music and… pleasant company.

We haven't buried Marlowe yet—the funeral is set for two days from now. Seven days post death is what was specifically detailed in his will, it turns out. It was good—we needed the time. We had to organize an excuse for his death, with everything that happened. The major hurdle was the very obvious gash in his chest where Shrike had cut into him. Atticus can't Stitch a dead body, but Calliope was able to do something. I don't know how, exactly. She's from the Space Between Spaces, though—and when there's a need, she can just do what no other kind of Working can.

With the wound gone, it looked like he had just passed away peacefully, and that's what we went with. We played it by the book—I cleared out, and so did Kori and Jamal. Paulina and Atticus, who are both known associates/coworkers, 'found' the body and reported it. The Guild sent out a team to preserve it until the funeral, and word got out quickly in the Worker community. Marlowe touched a number of people in his life. Calliope managed a lot of it, as she usually does—she collected the correspondence, sent messages back, and just generally took care of all the little details that would have taken the rest of us ages to sort through.

Speaking of Calliope… she's fading. Now that her bond with Marlowe has been severed, she's slowly returning to the Space Between Spaces. She could stay, if she wanted to, but she would have to create a new bond with a new Worker, which would be… difficult. A bond like that is very intimate. It'd be a little like getting remarried just a few days after your husband dies. Possible, sure, but… you get it. Maybe when we find out who Marlowe left everything to she'll make a final decision.

We haven't officiated Marlowe's will yet. The only detail we know is that the funeral was set for seven days after his death—and that the will will be unsealed on that day. Memory Marlowe was able to help with some details there—he shared that the real Marlowe had always wished he'd had more time when his own father had died. The Workings on the mansion were all tied to him, and Marlowe had had to scramble to keep everything together when his father had passed away. He didn't want that to happen to whomever is inheriting it next.

Until then, things are in a kind of limbo. Calliope is with us until that day, and Jacob Luis is still on a leash but a loose one. He's been chomping at the bit and has turned into something of a poltergeist, basically haunting the mansion. He listens to Paulina, but none of the rest of us. We've had to threaten him a number of times, but he knows he doesn't technically have to listen to anyone until the house's new owner is named, and he's taking full advantage. The other day he turned my shower water into milk, and later that morning Kori came downstairs furious that all of her clothes had been turned inside out and cross-stitched together.

As far as we know, Marlowe doesn't have any living family, and he didn't talk to any of us about the details of the will. Memory Marlowe isn't revealing anything either.

We're hoping he left it to Paulina. He knew her longest—at least as an adult—and she has the strongest tie to the Order of the Magi, since they practically founded it together. She's been reaching out to the dozen or so other members across the country and sharing the news. Everyone is taking it pretty hard. I haven't had a chance to catch up with her since I started writing, but she's trying to get everyone mobilized. We need to know what Shrike is doing, and we need more Gallimand pages.

Luckily, I'm off Shrike's hit list. Unluckily, it's because she has what she needs from me. We'll run into each other again, I'm sure, but for now… she doesn't have all the Gifts or Gallimand pages, and neither do we. And we both have a bigger worry.

Cry Havoc.

The club explosion—and the fight at the Palace—didn't go unnoticed. We're already catching people tailing us, and now that we know what to look for, we're uncovering more signs and ritual symbols. Even more corrupted Circles. The men who infiltrated Hobb's crew all killed themselves before they could be questioned, like something out of a spy movie. They all overloaded their Instruments, the Worker equivalent of enjoying the crisp tang of a cyanide pill. Hobb has made it his personal mission to help us get answers, and he's working with Kori on it. His reputation is on the line, and he cares about that pretty dearly.

We've found a handful of Havoc monograms and broken them, and every time we do it's like the people around them come out of a trance. They actually *see* the world again. They look up from their phones, they talk to each other. It's… I had no idea how bad it was. And we're running blind trying to figure out who's behind it all.

Jamal's cover remains intact, so he's still our inside man with the Workers of the West Enforcers. He was able to find out that Shrike had made it out of the basement, but that she hadn't reported back to the WA, or to the WOTW when they had called her in. Jamal's boss, Smith, who runs the Workers of the West Enforcers, told Jamal and all the others at an official meeting that Shrike had been rebuked by the Workers of the West for conduct unbecoming a Worker. She's since disappeared. The Workers of America haven't issued an official response yet.

We did find out that Mallory Shrike—the real Mallory Shrike—was a Workers of America consultant who disappeared on assignment a little over a year ago, and who then miraculously returned at the same time Catalin Moss left Marlowe. We don't know exactly how Catalin managed it, but she assumed Shrike's identity and *became* her, including taking on her role in the Workers of America. She's believed herself to be Shrike so thoroughly that she's actually partially changed into her—which explains her altered physical appearance. We don't know how long that cover will last, or if she'll try to assume another.

John McMillin is still an enforcer with the WOTW. There was nothing to tie him to the events at the club, and nothing we could provide to Jamal's boss or any other enforcers to pin him as one of Shrike's people. For now he's in there with Jamal, hearing everything we hear about what's happening in the law enforcement arm of Worker society. We're assuming he's passing it all to Shrike the way that Jamal is passing it all to us.

We deciphered more of the book. Some, at least. It's slow going. But it turns out Atticus was right—there was a trick to it. Some of it is legible now, and a lot more of it hopefully will be soon. There's ciphers and keys and shit that's way over my head. Paulina's really leading the charge on that too, in addition to organizing the Order. Atticus has taken time off from Marlowe's practice to help, under the cover of bereavement leave.

One of the things they did discover was how Gallimand had set up the Working that kept the book out of the hands of those who wished him harm. We took a blank page of the book and extracted it, then duplicated it. The protection Working stayed, but it was keyed to us.

Which brings us full circle, and explains how you are able to read this, and how if Shrike or someone from Cry Havoc were to find it, these pages would go blank or become gibberish.

That's right—we literally took a page out of Gallimand's book.

Full circle pun. Boom.

Cry Havoc… could be anyone. We've confirmed that it's not just people in positions of traditional power. It's people in positions of cultural power, too. Influencers, social change leaders… some of them are Blissful who have no idea about any of this, and some of them are Workers who are up to their necks in it. And some of them—a lot more than I'd hoped— are just regular people like you who have given in.

The hardest part is that there's no obvious way to tell who's who. Who's working with Havoc and who's with us in the Order. I wish it were as easy as saying it's all one group or another, but it's absolutely not. It's completely mixed across every class, gender, race, political party, and religion.

And what's worse—none of those divisions matter. They're all distractions. All of it is what Havoc is using against us, using to divide up the world to make it easy to dismantle, piece by piece. What matters is what you actually *believe* in, not what team you play for or were born into.

If you believe that tomorrow can be better than today, then you're one of us.

If you believe that there's nothing worth fighting for…

Well, I'm really hoping to change your mind.

We're up against some pretty tall odds. We've got people after us who are powerful, ruthless, and willing to go through us and you to get what they want. People who want to end the world as we know it.

But we have a chance to stop it. And we need you to believe we have that chance. Because belief is power. If you can find it in yourself to believe we can do this, then you give us strength. And you take it away from the people who want you to believe that there is nothing but darkness ahead.

We need you to not give up.

We need you to believe that things *can get better again.*

There's more of us every day. We're recruiting. We may even reach out to you, who knows—Havoc is breaking down the Separation, and we're following suit.

Until then, I'll be writing again soon, or one of the others will.

We believe. I hope you do too.

– CICERO JAMES

About the Author

Hal Emerson is the author of ten books, including the award-winning Exile Trilogy, beginning with *The Prince of Ravens*. He is a graduate of UCLA with a BA in theatre, where he studied Shakespeare, Chekhov, and the Greek and Roman Classics. He also has an MBA from UC Berkeley.

Some of his favorite books and series include *East of Eden*, *The Brothers Karamazov*, *The Lord of the Rings*, and *The Wheel of Time*. As a young reader he was particularly inspired by *The Chronicles of Prydain*, and he is an avid Harry Potter fan.

He still believes in the Oxford comma, and he has seen every Robin Williams movie.